VERA BRITTAIN

(1893–1970) grew up in provincial comfort in the north of England. In 1914 she won an exhibition to Somerville College, Oxford, but a year later abandoned her studies to enlist as a VAD nurse. She served throughout the war, working in London, Malta and the Front in France.

At the end of the war, with all those closest to her dead, Vera Brittain returned to Oxford. There she met Winifred Holtby – author of *South Riding* – and this friendship, which was to last until Winifred Holtby's untimely death in 1935, sustained her in those difficult post-war years. In 1933 Vera Brittain published *Testament of Youth*. This haunting autobiography, a vivid and passionate record of the years 1900–1925, conveyed to an entire generation the essence of their common experience of war. It was a bestseller in both Britain and America on its first publication and again in 1978 when it was reissued by Virago and became an acclaimed BBC Television serial. In 1940 Vera Brittain published *Testament of Friendship*, in which she commemorated the life of Winifred Holtby. This was followed in 1957 by *Testament of Experience* which continued her story, covering the years 1925–1950. These Testaments are also published by Virago.

A convinced pacifist, a prolific speaker, lecturer, journalist and writer, Vera Brittain devoted much of her energies to the causes of peace and feminism. She travelled widely in Europe and lectured extensively in the USA and Canada. twenty-nine books in all: novels, poetry, biography biography and other non-fiction. Of her fiction *Account Rendered* (1945) and *Born 1925* (1948).

In 1925 Vera Brittain married the politica Catlin and had two children, one of whom

Vera Brittain

BORN 1925

A NOVEL OF YOUTH

Thou turnest man to destruction;
again thou sayest,
Come again, ye children of men.
PSALM XC, VERSE 3

Virago

Published by VIRAGO PRESS Limited 1982
41 William IV Street, London WC2N 4DB

Reprinted 1983

First published in Great Britain by Macmillan & Co. Ltd 1948

British Library Cataloguing in Publication Data

Brittain, Vera
  Born 1925.
  I. Title
  823'.912 [F]   PR6003.R385
  ISBN 0-86068-270-6

Printed in Finland by Werner Söderström Oy
a member of Finnprint

CONTENTS

Prologue

On a Saturday morning in May, 1929, Adrian Carbury, aged three-and-a-half, stood at the window of his third-floor nursery in St. Saviour's Vicarage looking down over Armada Square.

Long, long ago, just after breakfast, Nannie had told him that his mother and father were going to give him a big surprise that day. When he asked excitedly whether it would be a Dismal Desmond, or a Hornby train, or the red motor-bus which he had seen yesterday at the Eureka Toy Fair in Queen Elizabeth Street and coveted immediately, she had only smiled, shaken her head, and refused to answer. Then, unaccountably, she had disappeared, and he had not seen her since. She did not even come to take him for his morning walk in the Green Park or along the Embankment, which throughout his short life he could never remember having missed.

Like all only children, Adrian had grown accustomed to playing alone. After looking regretfully through the open barred window at the pleasant spring sunshine, which gave the old Square a rejuvenated appearance like that of a newly-cleaned carpet, he pulled a box of coloured bricks from the bottom of his toy cupboard, and decided to build castles until someone came in to tell him what to do next. But on this strange day nobody did come — neither Mummy nor Daddy nor Nannie nor Maria. Feeling lost and forgotten, he sampled one after another the entire contents of the cupboard until motor-cars, monkeys, jigsaw puzzles, picture-books, and Lu-Lu, his favourite golliwog, lay piled on the floor beside the unfinished castle. He had reached the end of his resources and was feeling inclined to cry from hunger and loneliness, when Maria, the cook-general, came to take him down to lunch in the kitchen.

That was a treat, of course. But Maria assured him it was not the surprise.

" You won't have to wait much longer, love. Just go on playing in the nursery like a good little boy, and Nannie'll soon come to fetch you. I'd let you stay here, but I've got the kitchen to scrub and you'd get your feet wet. Everything's got to be like a new pin this afternoon ! "

As Adrian climbed dejectedly back to his nursery, there seemed to be a funny smell in the house. It reminded him of the smell that sometimes came out of the kitchen when the taps on the gas-cooker were not quite turned off. Forgetting it, he was aimlessly thumbing the familiar pages of his picture-books when a new idea occurred to him. Pulling off one of his over-large brown shoes without undoing the button, he placed it carefully in a corner of the nursery. Then, extracting one or two pages from the largest of the books, he tore them into shreds, rolled the shreds into pellets, and from the hearth-rug in front of the fireless grate tried to throw the pellets into the empty shoe. He had just scored one hit and nine misses when his attention was distracted by the sound, louder than usual, of voices in the Square. Thrusting his foot into his shoe and hurrying back to the window-seat, the small red-haired boy eagerly looked out again.

The London scene before him was typical enough. His day nursery, like the front of the Vicarage itself, faced west across the wide Square, and his night nursery, with its side windows at the south-east corner, looked towards the near but invisible Thames. Sometimes, when the wind blew in the right direction across the city roofs, he could hear the sirens on the tugs and barges passing under Waterloo Bridge towards the Pool of London and the distant sea.

On the north, Armada Square was bounded by Queen Elizabeth Street, the broad thoroughfare which ended at Piccadilly Circus and thus linked the Square with Piccadilly itself. In the south-west corner stood Queen Elizabeth's Hospital, with its famous accident-ward where London's casualties received swift and efficient attention. The south side itself was occupied by a large cinema and several fashionable restaurants. On the west a row of expensive shops ended with the big store of the Armada Book Company. Next door stood the Drake Hotel, where a crowded and popular grill room, much patronised by journalists, authors, actors, actresses, and occasional film stars, stayed open until 1 A.M.

Between the hospital and the cinema a narrow road-way, known as Sir Francis Avenue though it was little more than an alley, ran in the direction of the river. In spite of its narrowness and the Square's reputation, inherited from Regency days, as a haunt of prostitutes, Sir Francis Avenue had become the respected location of several well-known publishing houses. On week-days their wares, a Beggar's Opera assortment of orange, scarlet, jade, amethyst, and royal-blue dust-covers, challenged the passer-by from the Armada Book Company's double-fronted window.

St. Saviour's Church and Vicarage, divided from each other by an ancient graveyard where the identity of the dead beneath their moss-grown tombs had long been forgotten, filled the eastern side of the Square. Today the weather-vane on the Church's substantial grey tower oscillated gently in the warm breeze, and in the church-yard a budding laburnum, brilliant with young leaves, threw a delicate shadow across the anonymous flagstones. But Adrian would not have been interested in the familiar

3

Church and graveyard even if he could have seen them from his observation post at the nursery window. His attention was absorbed by the middle of the Square, where something really wonderful was happening. . . .

The middle of Armada Square consisted of a large unrailed space, thinly surrounded by plane trees and divided from Queen Elizabeth Street by a row of taxi-cabs. In the centre stood a lofty pedestal surmounted by a belligerent-looking statue of Sir Francis Drake, holding a large ball in his left hand and a drawn sword in his right. Each corner of the open space was adorned by a stone-carved replica of the Tudor vessels which defeated the Spanish Armada. Before each galleon spread a small flower-garden, and a clipped screen of privet grew behind. Because of its size and traditional freedom from restrictive police regulations, the Square had long been a favourite place for public meetings. On these occasions members of the audience were accustomed to perch comfortably on the stone cross-benches of the model sailing-ships, but, with a characteristic British respect for flowers, they never trampled on the miniature gardens or destroyed the privet hedges.

As Adrian, entranced, watched from his window, a short procession of men and women carrying scarlet and yellow banners paraded into the Square. Close behind them followed some half-curious, half-amused members of the good-natured crowd which frequents Piccadilly and Regent Street on Saturday afternoons. One man had brought with him a peculiar object resembling a pair of steps, which he unfolded and placed at the side of the open space nearest to the Vicarage. Another, who wore a scarlet and yellow rosette in his button-hole, carried two large posters. In full view of Adrian's enraptured gaze, he placed these on the plinth of the statue.

4

" Oo-er ! " breathed Adrian, clutching the bars of the window in his excitement. At three-and-a-half he could hardly have been expected to read the black hieroglyphics on the red poster, which made up the ironical caption : " Safety Last ! " But on the orange one he could see the large portrait of a man with a pipe, though oddly enough he was standing on his head. Adrian would have been even more mystified by the slogan on the back, which read : " A Vote for Stanley Turns Tranquillity Upside Down ! "

Suddenly a man from the poster-parade climbed the pair of steps and began to shout. After a few minutes of strenuous oratory, inaudible to Adrian, he jumped down, and another — a very tall man with a large black moustache — took his place on the top of the steps. This individual was greeted with a volley of applause from the crowd, and very soon clapping and cheers punctuated every sentence of his speech. Each time his hearers applauded, Adrian stamped noisily on the floor. He was engaged in thus registering his approval, when the door opened and Nannie came in.

" Well, I never did ! " she exclaimed. " Making all that noise, and your poor Mother hardly awake ! "

But Adrian, not listening, pointed out of the window. " Nook, Nannie ! Nook at all those people in the Square ! "

Nannie sniffed indignantly.

" I've seen them all right," she affirmed. " They just would go and hold their blessed meeting there, today of all days ! It's a good job your Mother's at the back ! "

" What are they doing, Nannie ? Why have they got those big pictures ? Who's the man talking ? "

" It's all to do with the General Election," said Nannie. " You'll understand when you're older."

" What's a 'lection ? " inquired Adrian, undeterred by the implication of excessive juvenility.

" Oh, just a lot of people all over the country talking nonsense about politics! " To forestall the inevitable " What's pol'tics ? " she added hastily : " It's something you don't need to trouble your head about for many a long day ! Now just you hurry downstairs with me, or your Mother'll think we're never coming to see the surprise ! "

In the large second-floor bedroom with its windows looking east towards the City, Sylvia Carbury lay with her newly-born daughter asleep in her arms. Still drowsy from the after-effects of ether and oxygen, she had not yet faced the now certain complication of a second child added to the demands of an exacting career.

Beside her sat her husband, the Vicar of St. Saviour's, his face as pale as hers from the strain of his night-long vigil and his abnormal capacity for entering imaginatively into the sufferings of others. Even the tenderly absorbed love with which he watched the sleeping baby did not extinguish the habitual expression of self-depreciating anxiety that lay like a shadow across his face. In the eyes of his innumerable friends and admirers, Robert Carbury, with a beautiful actress wife and a lively little son added to his astonishing popularity and remarkable success as a preacher, was one of the most fortunate of men. Few of them suspected that in his own heart the Vicar remained convinced of his innate unworthiness, and certain that, in spite of all apparent evidence to the contrary, life's loveliest gifts of responsive affection and confidence-inspiring respect from those whom he cherished would for ever pass him by.

Like conscientious modern parents aware that a child who has been the sole occupant of a nursery may suffer from paroxysms of jealousy after the advent of a newcomer, Robert and Sylvia had done their best to prepare Adrian for Josephine's arrival.

"Would you like a little brother or a little sister?"
Robert patiently questioned him. But Adrian remained
stoutly indifferent to this fascinating alternative.

"Want a golly!" he persisted. But even when
Lu-Lu, the super-golliwog with black curls and a scarlet
petticoat, had been presented to him as a special gift
since his birthday was not till November, Adrian continued to regard the prospective new-comer as an acad-
emic question of no interest to himself. So it was with
some apprehension that his parents awaited his first
reaction to the sight of the baby.

"Now don't forget," admonished Nannie outside the
door, "your Mummy's a bit poorly, and you mustn't
make a noise!"

Almost as eagerly as Sylvia and Robert, the elderly
nurse watched the handsome little boy, his auburn curls
clinging silkily to his neck above the turned-down collar
of his brown buster suit, creep anxiously on tiptoe from
the doorway to the bed. With his shining hair almost on
a level with his mother's, he peered over the edge of the
shawl at a small wrinkled reddish face like the skin of
an aged apple.

"This is Josephine," Sylvia explained. "She's your
little sister."

But Adrian still looked worried.

"Is it alive?" he inquired sceptically.

"I should just think so!" responded his father.
"You wait till you hear her cry! She's quiet now because
she's asleep." And very gently he pulled aside the folds
of the shawl, showing Adrian a tiny pear-shaped head
covered with upstanding wisps of fine dark hair.

An expression of pure joy wiped the anxious uncertainty from Adrian's face.

"Oo-er!" he exclaimed delightedly. "It's got hair
just like Lu-Lu!"

7

Sylvia smiled, a little wearily, and closed her eyes. Robert lifted the baby from her arms, and turned to Adrian.

" Now you've had the surprise, you must run back to the nursery, old man! You'll see Josephine again to-morrow."

Hand-in-hand with Nannie, Adrian went meditatively upstairs, where tea was now ready.

" When will it be able to play with me ? " he demanded. " Does it talk ? Can it make castles ? "

" You must say ' she ', not ' it ', when you're speaking about a little girl," corrected Nannie. " She won't be able to play with you just yet ; she's too small. But she'll soon be big enough to come to the nursery and lie on the hearth-rug and kick, like you did when you were a baby. Now bring up your chair and we'll have our tea."

As Adrian obeyed, pushing his high wheel-chair from the wall to the table, Nannie noticed that he walked unevenly.

" Why are you limping ? " she inquired at once. " Is there anything wrong with your foot — or your shoe ? "

Adrian took a long drink of milk before he replied.

" I fink," he said apologetically, " it must be a bit of *Jesus Nuves Me*."

Casting her eyes over the chaos on the floor, Nannie picked up the religious picture-book, its cover showing five cherubs' heads against a cerulean background, which Robert Carbury had passed on to his son.

" A bit of *Jesus Loves Me* ! . . . You don't mean to say you've been pulling pages out of your Daddy's book ! "

" It was only one or two," explained Adrian. " I was only frowing paper bullets into my shoe."

" That was *very* naughty, Adrian ! You know I've always told you not to tear things ! It's only destructive little boys that pull their lovely picture-books to pieces."

" Well, you see, I had nuffin' to do while I was waiting for the s'prise."

Nanny relented, remembering the hours in which she had been obliged to leave Adrian to play alone.

" You did have a long time to wait, I know. I'd have taken you up earlier, but your Mother was asleep nearly all afternoon."

For a few moments Adrian ate his bread and jam in silence. Nannie's last words had reawakened a vaguely disturbing trouble in his mind. Finally he inquired: " Nannie, why was Mummy in bed? It isn't bedtime."

" Well . . . you see, she's very tired."

" Why? "

" Because she had to fetch the little baby."

" Where did she fetch it from? "

" Why, Adrian, I thought you knew! Josephine came from God, of course."

" Where's Dod live? "

" You know that too. God lives in Heaven."

" And is that a long way from 'Mada Square? "

But Nannie's resourcefulness had reached its limits.

" Look here," she said, " I've got something else to do but sit here all day answering questions. If you want to know any more, you must ask your Daddy. It's his job to tell people about God, not mine! "

She put down her cup and pushed back her chair.

" Now you just stay here quietly and finish your tea like a good boy. I must go downstairs and take Baby for Nurse."

Tiptoeing past the door of the bedroom where the midwife lay sleeping after her wakeful night, Nannie carried Josephine in her basket cot to the night nursery. At last thankfully alone, since Robert had gone to the vestry to take a five o'clock committee meeting of St. Saviour's Youth Club, Sylvia rested against the pillows with closed eyes. She thought, with unexcited pleasure, of the small daughter who would some day, she hoped, follow her on the stage; and then let her mind wander drowsily over the nine years of her marriage with the most popular Vicar ever appointed to the living of St. Saviour's, Armada Square.

*

PART I

CHAPTER I

Conversion of a Hero

NEITHER the Reverend Robert Carbury, V.C., nor his actress wife, Sylvia Salvesen, was very young when their son Adrian was born on November 15th, 1925. Robert, then Curate at All Souls, Battersea, in South-west London, was thirty-four, and Sylvia nearly thirty-one. He was not her first husband though she was his first wife, and the only woman he had loved or ever would love.

Robert had not originally intended to become a priest. His position was still that of a curate because he had been ordained only seven years earlier. An accident had made his decision for him — the enormous accident of the 1914 War, and the part that it had demanded from his unprepared youth.

Before 1914, Robert's most serious problem had been his strange inability to decide what to do with his life. In spite of every reason for hopeful confidence, he had a peculiar tendency to find himself a square peg in a round hole. This disturbing indecisiveness, so uncharacteristic of the vigorous and gifted Carburys, caused perpetual anxiety to Robert's father, then Liberal Member of Parliament for the Hoddershall Division of North Staffordshire. James Carbury had no one to share his perturbation, for owing to the death of his wife after Robert's birth in 1891, his son was an only child. Robert's much-travelled and distinguished father, who for a short period filled the post of Lord Privy Seal in the Liberal Government of 1906, never married again. He cherished the same obstinate loyalty to one woman — in the jargon of a later generation, the same " fixation " — that Robert was subsequently to display.

Concentrating all his hopes and affections on this only son, James Carbury planned Robert's future in accordance with the intellectual and social traditions of the well-born, well-endowed Whig family to which he belonged. Robert would of course go to Eton like his father before him, and then to Christ Church, Oxford, where he would read " Greats " and play a conspicuous part in the debates at the Union with the idea of taking up his father's political career almost where James had left it off. There was really no reason, thought the elder Carbury, why with these advantages Robert should not ultimately become Prime Minister — or at any rate Foreign Secretary. For that glorious end, James was ready to spare neither trouble nor expense.

But Robert had not reacted in the orthodox and expected fashion. He was affectionate and responsive, conscientious and intelligent, and as he grew up it became clear that he had inherited his mother's tall slender figure and wistful, attractive good looks. Yet always there seemed to be in him some quality which defeated James and left him guessing; a negative factor — was it excessive humility or a genuine lack of confidence ? — that his father instinctively compared with the " fault " sometimes found in a stratum of hard rock which may cause earthquakes and tidal waves.

At thirteen, Robert duly went to Eton — and disliked it. There was no reason for this reaction that James could perceive, for everyone assured him that his son was extremely popular both with his contemporaries and with the masters. And though Robert's skill at cricket and

football was not sufficient to carry him into the First
Eleven, he more than atoned for this deficiency by his
prowess in field sports and especially in running.

By his own wish, Robert left Eton early — a sad disappointment to a parent in whose catalogue of allegiances
the Eton Boating Song came second only to the National
Anthem. When barely eighteen, he went to Oxford to
be coached for a year in the classical studies for which
his school reports had shown him to possess no special
aptitude.

" I do wish," he once said wistfully to his father, " I
could go to Cambridge and do science — or mathematics."

But James was so obviously distressed by this unconventional proposal — which would provide, he expostulated, " quite the wrong sort of background for a
political career " — that Robert, always reluctant to
cause pain to anyone who loved him, withdrew the
suggestion at once and explained that he had not meant
it to be taken seriously.

He was happier at Oxford than he had been at Eton,
and, with his tutor's painstaking help, managed to pass
not too discreditably the entrance examination into
Christ Church. But even in that first year of preliminary
study he had begun in spite of himself to spend most
of his spare time, not at the Union but in the Science
Laboratory, and to read philosophy in books which,
like the works of Bertrand Russell, approached the subject from a mathematical standpoint. When he only
achieved a Third in Honour Moderations, his disappointed
father resignedly agreed to let him change to Mathematics — a subject in which Robert triumphantly captured First Class Honours in the same term as he won
his Blue for running.

But that year of success was 1914. During the Summer
Term and in the period between his Finals and the

Viva-Voce, Robert had been so deeply immersed in his own uncertainties that he disregarded the growing national fear of Civil War in Ireland, and even the assassination of the Archduke Franz Ferdinand which occurred while his mind was still absorbed by his recent examination. Sensitive, introspective, secretly unsure of himself and his aspirations, Robert so anxiously weighed the claims of a political career against the possibility of becoming a Mathematics tutor at Cambridge, that August 4th broke into his consciousness with the shock of the lightning flash that strikes down its victim from an apparently cloudless sky.

Afterwards he always associated that calamitous late summer with the terraced garden of the family home at Hoddershall Ash, named for the ash-grove which concealed the manor-house from the small market town at the foot of the hill. There, gazing day after day upon the exuberant gold and scarlet of dahlias cultivated by his ancestors for three generations, he read the newspapers which gave steadily worsening reports of the Retreat from Mons, and discussed with James the merits of the invitation to a mathematical tutorship at Emmanuel College, Cambridge, which he now held in his hand, against the disconcerting claims of military service.

His dejected father, striving not to influence him, saw in imagination those memories and hopes which had been the mainspring of his busy life buried under a cross in Flanders. To a politician with his background and traditions, there seemed to be only one choice.

" ' Who dies if England live ? ' ," he would ask himself, gazing mournfully at his reflection in the shaving-glass, and knowing that, morning after morning, Robert was asking himself the same question, and would give the same answer. But those autumn weeks, and his subsequent months as a subaltern in the Staffordshire

Light Infantry, taught Robert some new and disquieting facts about himself which his life had not hitherto compelled him to face.

In 1915, the few months that he spent in France clarified and underlined this uncomfortable knowledge. Robert became aware that, in the sense in which the newspaper-reading public understood courage, he was not a brave man. He learnt that physical danger, and even the threat of it, caused him a perpetual nagging anxiety like a neuralgic headache : that the employment of mechanical science for destructive purposes filled him with a horror which he could not subdue. His secret realisation of his physical cowardice led him to underrate his exceptional moral courage, which in later life was to nerve him unflinchingly to face misrepresentation and calumny, and would have enabled him, if ever his convictions had demanded such a sacrifice, to accept a martyr's death without hesitation.

For Robert, as for most human beings, the quality that he did not possess bulked larger in his imagination than his genuine and outstanding virtues. Characteristically he won his Victoria Cross by an act of desperation which his inward censor recognised as such, though it appeared to the admiring world as a deed of superb heroism. From the first moment that he found himself under fire, he had known that his only choice lay between ignominious flight and the blind valour of despair. His strong moral control of his perpetual anxiety impelled him, in the teeth of every normal instinct, to choose the second alternative.

*

On September 25th, 1915, the Staffordshire Light Infantry took part in the Battle of Loos, and thereby experienced the first of those costly infantry massacres which were to decimate a generation of men.

A fortnight before the battle, Robert came home on ninety-six hours' leave. When he bade a resolutely cheerful farewell to his father outside the barrier at Charing Cross Station, they both knew that his return to his regiment waiting amid slag-heaps and chimney-stacks for the coming offensive might mean death for the one and perpetual loneliness for the other. Robert spent the night before the attack watching the tall white searchlights stabbing the sky above Lens, and arguing with the persistent inner voice which uncompromisingly warned him that, as soon as he went over the top, he was liable to desert his men and run away.

When the preliminary bombardment began, the thunder of heavy missiles from caterpillar howitzers and the sharp scream of high-velocity shells produced a violent pandemonium of battle orchestration. By the time that Robert started to climb the ladder to lead his platoon over the parapet in the second wave of the attack, his senses as well as his hearing were dulled. He was nearly half-way up, when the body of the soldier preceding him fell on the top of him and bore him down into the trench. Without consciously realising it, he observed that the dead man had been killed by a machine-gun bullet clean through the head. Back up the ladder in a second, he stooped low as he led his men into a diabolic hail of machine-gun fire. Although he shouted to them also to duck as they ran, in a few seconds half the platoon seemed to be lying dead and wounded around him. The rest, hearing their comrades scream and seeing them bleed, began to hesitate, to waver, to look back.

Sick with terror, yet conscious that at all costs he must avert a panic, Robert had perceived, between wavering wraiths of dawn fog just above the soggy earth, a fallen chimney-stack in front of the enemy's trenches which evidently concealed the machine-gun. Reacting violently against his frenzied desire to flee, he clutched the two hand-grenades in his pockets, and heard himself crying, in a raucous, hysterical voice quite unrecognisable as his own : " Who's coming with me to wipe out that gun ? " Again bending as low as he could he raced in the direction of the gunfire, followed by half-a-dozen men and the Hanley sergeant who had been his benevolent guide from the moment that he joined the battalion.

His desperation was so extreme that he hardly noticed one burning stab in his left shoulder and another through the flesh of his right thigh. He found himself on the top of the Germans almost before he knew it, clambering over shattered masonry, flinging his grenades, and plunging in with his bayonet amid the still resounding explosions. The next few moments were a red confusion of noise, pain, and blood, in which he afterwards remembered seeing two of his companions drop like weighted sacks, and a wounded German gunner, stripped naked by blast, running round in circles, laughing shrilly.

His bayonet stuck fast in the ribs of another. Unable to withdraw it he let go, and began madly to pelt his opponents with bricks from the fallen stack. The noise of the gun suddenly ceased as he lost consciousness. He came round to find himself lying beside the wreckage of the post, spitting out the blood that poured into his mouth from a bullet wound through his cheek, and listening, as though from a great distance, to the anxious voice of his sergeant.

" Sir ! Sir ! Where be you hit ? Where've they got you, Sir ? "

He opened his eyes and, hardly audible, whispered, " God knows ! You all right, sergeant ? "

" I think so, Sir. Nothing serious, any road."

" Did we silence the gun ? "

"We did that! Sir, you was grand! . . . I'll get you in when I can . . ."

The sergeant had stayed with him, protected by the wreckage of the chimney-stack, until the late evening. He examined Robert and gave First Aid to his multiple wounds, of which, by an unlikely miracle, not one seemed to have involved a vital spot. But by the time that the stretcher-bearers found them and he was back at the dressing-station, he had fainted again from pain and loss of blood. In days before blood-transfusion had become a regular surgical resource, it was that loss of blood which threatened his life. He realised his peril when he found his father beside him at the Base Hospital in Rouen, summoned to France with other near relatives of dangerously wounded men.

James remained there for several days, until Robert was well enough to be moved to the 4th London General Hospital on Denmark Hill. After many weeks of operations and painful dressings, he was sent for his long convalescence to a country manor, run by its owners as a hospital for wounded officers, at Evansford in the Forest of Dean. The only wound likely to have permanent effects involved an injury to his left knee, which was to leave him with a slight limp and end his achievements as a runner for ever. But the shock to his whole system was abnormally deep, and long before his convalescence ended he learnt that he was to be discharged as unfit for further military service.

He was at Evansford when he received, from his now proud and happy father, the news that he had been awarded the Victoria Cross. But, after the first incredulous rush of bewildered excitement, he could find no satisfaction in his astonishing elevation to the status of a hero, nor enjoy the congratulations which tumbled in upon him from his father's constituents and his own

Eton and Christ Church contemporaries. The contrast
between the stalwart imperviousness which, he felt, should
be typical of a V.C., and the potential cowardice of
which he knew himself more likely to be guilty, intensified
his profound conviction of inferiority, and condemned
him to a perennial lack of confidence in himself and
his attainments.

Haunted by the fear that sooner or later someone
would find him out, he was to confess five years afterwards to Sylvia : " I'm not really at all brave, my darling!
I'm just a charlatan — a fake who sports false colours.
But with your help, please God, I may learn some
courage . . ."

*

His secret awareness of his unworthiness was by no means
the only psychological complication which delayed
Robert's recovery. From the time that his name was
taken off the danger list he had begun to think, first
with compunction and finally in an anguish of remorse,
about the Germans whom he had killed in that desperate
action which won him the V.C.

Lying on his lounge chair in the garden, where
golden-crested yews bowed gravely to each other across
a sunken lawn, he remained unaware of the fugitive scent
carried on the warm breeze from the purple buddleia.
Beneath its boughs, sunflowers, poppies, and late del-
phiniums displayed their yellow, scarlet, and blue in
vain ; nor did he notice the pink ramblers surrounding
the daisy-sprinkled lawn with untidy grace. Though
he usually loved to watch birds and butterflies, he did
not even see the brown water-hens which chugged like
miniature motor-boats across the pool at the bottom of
the garden, jerking their white-rimmed tail feathers up
and down as they swam.

Only the sentinel firs impinged upon his consciousness, so that for the rest of his life the dry intoxicating smell of fir-cones in hot sunshine was to bring back the memory of his spiritual conflict. Apparently gazing at the violet peaks of the Welsh mountains rising above the Forest of Dean, he saw instead the smitten upturned faces of the German gunners, and the look of shocked astonishment in the eyes of the man whose body had received the full force of his bayonet.

Two years afterwards, in the chapel of the East End Settlement where he acted as Warden during the closing months of the War, Robert was to pray perpetually for those slaughtered gunners, for their wives whom he had widowed, and their children left orphans by his act of violence. When the hurt, bewildered expressions of young British soldiers prematurely in contact with life at its worst brought back the recollection of the men whom he had killed, he was to agonise over them as he knelt alone in the autumn darkness; and then to plead for all the German people, and to intercede for the enemy being pushed back to humiliation and defeat. The unity of their essential humanity with his own was to become so clear, that he would never again be able to recall the mood in which he had seen them as opponents. . . .

Directly he was strong enough to leave the garden of Evansford Manor, Robert sought diversion in solitary expeditions to Chepstow, to Monmouth, to Tintern Abbey, serene as a carven flower against its background of wooded hills. But he could not escape his relentless memories, which accompanied him everywhere. At Symond's Yat, sitting on the giant rock which overlooks five counties above the circular curve of the Wye, he struggled with his newly-awakened conscience until the urgency of his thoughts obliterated all sights and sounds.

The War from which he had escaped, though it still engulfed millions of men and women, appeared to him now as a gigantic Calvary : the Calvary on which man, caught in the logical conclusion of his own sins, crucified Christ anew. Words came into his mind from the general Confession once repeated so mechanically among his school-fellows at the Communion Service in Eton College Chapel :

We do earnestly repent, And are heartily sorry for these our misdoings ; The remembrance of them is grievous unto us ; The burden of them is intolerable. . . .

That was the word : intolerable. The writer of that plea for forgiveness had understood what was meant by the price of sin. Perhaps he had once reflected, like Robert, on the splendour of human courage, and its wastage for ends which could never advance the spiritual welfare of the race of men. Wars, thought Robert, came as a consequence of man's disobedience to God's Will. Surely, then, the only work for a man who was free, and qualified to do it, was to try to teach God's Will, and persuade his fellow men to accept it ?

Before the War, the idea of entering the priesthood had never occurred to Robert, but now there seemed to be no alternative that he could honestly choose. He realised that it would mean a hard life, and probably little happiness. He faced the fact that he would almost certainly fail to achieve that which he now saw as man's vital necessity. If Christ Himself could not induce more than a handful of men and women to acknowledge and practise the Will of God, what could be done by him, a coward and a sinner ? Yet he knew that there would never again be peace of mind and conscience for him if he did not try.

He had spent some weeks in this turmoil of specula-tion, when he was sought out by the most appropriate visitor whom he could have received. It was almost as though, he thought afterwards, God Himself had taken a direct hand in his conversion. . . .

In France Robert had passed many hours with the Chaplain of his battalion, Captain Anselm Ensor, formerly Vicar of St. Mary Magdalene, Stoke-on-Trent, and a third-generation member of a famous clerical family. Captain Ensor, a Londoner by birth and a Scholar of Robert's own college, had long desired a post amid the poor of South London. Now, recalled from France to be Suffragan Bishop of Battersea, he came to congratulate Robert and tell him this news.

The congratulations were hardly spoken when Robert, to Captain Ensor's surprise, disclaimed his title to any award, and bitterly confessed his own sense of unworthiness.

" I'm not a bit what I seem — or, rather, what people think me ! In peace I was no good to anyone — not even to my long-suffering father. I did nothing but disappoint him."

" But you took a First in Maths, didn't you ? "

" Yes. But I only got it because the subject came easily to me, and Classics didn't. Science always fascinated me, and yet not enough to give me a driving aspiration for any special career. Then in war I was a coward. I suspected it in England, but I knew it for certain when I got to the front."

" My dear Robert, cowards don't win V.C.s ! "

" That's where you're wrong, Anselm. I wouldn't mind betting that half the V.C.s in the Army get their decorations for the same reason that I did. They're so frantic with fear that nothing but an act of extreme violence prevents them from running away."

" But surely," expostulated the Chaplain, " it's the overcoming of fear that constitutes courage, not the mere freedom from it ! "

" Have it your own way, my friend. The point is that I no more wanted to be a good officer than a good M.P. I never knew what I *was* after till my life threatened to leave me. And then, quite suddenly, I realised I wanted to live. I can't remember the exact day, but it it was during my time at Denmark Hill. I began to feel sure that as soon as I was fit enough to think things out, I should know what I ought to do."

" And do you know ? "

" That's exactly what I'm going to tell you. I did most of the thinking down here, and as a result of it, I want to enter the Ministry. When you wrote you were coming to see me today, it was just as if God had sent you. You're the one person who can give me the advice I need."

For a moment Anselm Ensor was silent. Then he said : " You couldn't have given me better news, Robert. Your award electrified the regiment — it's never had a V.C. before, you know — and I'd looked forward to seeing you more than I can say. But I never dreamed you'd have these good tidings for me. Of course I'll help you, with all my heart ! "

The young man and the ex-Chaplain, fifteen years older than himself, talked in the garden all afternoon. Captain Ensor explained to Robert that an ordinary University Degree Course was not normally considered an adequate training for Holy Orders, especially when the candidate had not mentally and spiritually prepared himself for the Ministry while at college. Robert, he thought, should accept the necessity of a year at a theological seminary, however irksome its discipline might prove after several months as a subaltern at the front. He promised to make inquiries about some of the colleges, but he thought that Bellsley would probably turn out to be the most suitable.

*

As soon as Robert was sufficiently recovered to leave
Evansford Manor, he received his discharge from the
Army and went to Hoddershall to spend some weeks
with his father. There he told the elder Carbury of his
decision.

James, shaken out of his noble rut by the War, took
the news quietly. He was so thankful to have his only
son back from death and reprieved from the necessity
of further military service, that he would hardly have
protested if Robert had announced a determination to
become custodian of the Reptile House at the Zoo.
Anselm Ensor made the promised inquiries; and in the
autumn of 1916, a year after the revolution created in
his life by the Battle of Loos, Robert went to Bellsley
College in Berkshire to enter upon the first stage of his
ministry as a Christian priest.

At twenty-five, Robert was older in both years and
experience than his fellow candidates, most of whom had
come direct to Bellsley from a University. At first, after
his months of close acquaintance with death, he found
the utter remoteness of the College from the fierce living
of the past two years almost more than he could bear.
Soon he was complaining ruefully to the Bishop of
Battersea of its formality and pomposity. He longed,
he wrote, for men who were less " stuffy " than his
Bellsley associates; he missed the friendly unpretentious
companionship of the non-commissioned officers and
privates in his platoon; he wanted to work among the
poor, the unprivileged, the dispossessed.

" Will you help me," he implored, " to get into a
working-class London parish when I'm out of here ? "

Anselm Ensor replied sympathetically, approving of
Robert's aspirations, but telling him that, accident apart,
he saw no immediate likelihood of an opening either in
South London or the East End. It was probable, how-

ever, that the Wardenship of Alton Hall, an Anglican
Settlement near the London docks, would shortly be available, as the elderly deaconess who had taken the place of
a Chaplain now dead from his wounds in France had
mentioned to him her wish to retire. He suggested that
Robert might usefully put in a year or two at Alton
Hall until some appropriate position in a poor parish
became vacant.

Robert's wish was soon gratified. The Vicar of the
parish, who was also interested in Alton Hall, offered
him a Title, and at the Trinity Ordination he was admitted to the Diaconate. His appointment as Warden
followed almost immediately, and he began his work
conscious that he had reached a moment in his life which
deeply renewed and yet strangely comforted his gnawing
sense of unworthiness. Content at last with his labours
amongst the obscure and humble, he learnt to appreciate
the sharp-witted kindness of London's Cockneys, and
made friends with the Elder Statesman of Bow, George
Lansbury, while he waited for the clerical post which
Anselm Ensor had promised.

Eighteen months afterwards, when the Armistice had
been signed and thankful idealists throughout England
were rededicating themselves to social service in the illusory
hope of a lasting peace, the opportunity came in Battersea
itself. The Curate at the old riverside Church of All
Souls had asked to be translated to a country parish
owing to a threat of tuberculosis: would Robert care
to take his place? So, shortly after his Ordination to
the priesthood, Robert moved to lodgings in Battersea.
Within three months, his unexpected gifts as a preacher
had begun to fill the echoing emptiness of the massive
pews at All Souls with a growing congregation, which
appeared to be as much surprised to find itself there as
he was to see it.

Through his father, and his school and college, Robert had many contacts with well-to-do young men from political and legal families. Many of these had been killed in Flanders or the Dardanelles, but now that the War was over he persuaded several of the survivors to undertake social work in Battersea. Very soon the increasing size of his local congregation, and the accounts of his sermons which spread to Mayfair through the wealthier social workers, began to attract visitors from the West End.

It was probably Robert's Victoria Cross that first aroused their curiosity; they wanted to see what kind of job this distinguished young warrior made of a parson's career. But it was his unashamed sincerity, his passionate faith in his work, and the strange sense that he conveyed of being " chosen ", which retained and increased their interest. He possessed no superficial charm of manner; the secret of his attractiveness lay in his capacity for becoming absorbed by the problems of each human being with whom his life brought him into contact, and perhaps in his very failure to develop that façade of clerical bonhomie which is sometimes worn like a suit of armour-plating to deflect the barbs of mortal distress. His " fan-mail " soon became extensive, and he was obliged to engage a secretary whose files ultimately contained one of the largest collections of authentic life-stories in London.

He had been at All Souls, Battersea, for nearly six months, when in the late spring of 1920 he met Sylvia Salvesen.

CHAPTER II

Tragedy of a Heroine

Long before the run of *Romeo and Juliet* had ended at the Temple Theatre in November, 1917, Lawrence Mayfield and Sylvia Salvesen knew that they were in love.

Perceptive members of the audience realised it too. Other Romeos and Juliets had moved them with their histrionic ecstasies, but this was the real thing. Hardened elderly playgoers felt tears pricking their eyeballs as they watched the rapturous love-making between the dark, handsome, twenty-five-year-old boy, and the graceful girl of twenty-two with her sensitive face and copper-red hair. When the play's run was finally ended by Lawrence's long-deferred call-up, the immediate announcement of their engagement was no less of a sensation because so many people had expected it.

When Lawrence joined his unit of the Royal South Hampshire Regiment, he found himself incongruously in camp near Sunderland. But after a month the battalion, to Sylvia's joy, was brought south to Richmond Park. They arranged to get married on her twenty-third birthday, March 21st, 1918, and Lawrence was promised special leave for the occasion.

Unlike some of their stage contemporaries, neither of them even contemplated anticipating the ceremony. Lawrence was the youngest son of a Colonial Bishop, and Sylvia came from a highly-respected shipping family of Norwegian origin living in Newcastle-on-Tyne. As he watched the performances of a North-country amateur dramatic society, a theatrical manager scouting for talent had discovered her remarkable gifts.

On the morning of the wedding disturbing rumours,

later confirmed by the early editions of the evening papers, spread through London of a huge German assault on the British lines now too thinly extended along the Western front. But Sylvia, engrossed in last-moment preparations for her wedding at St. Clement Danes and the reception afterwards at the Savoy Hotel, remained unaware of the news. She anticipated no harsh incursion of national tragedy when, amid an effervescence of hand-shaking with every conspicuous personality on the stage, Lawrence was suddenly called to the telephone.

" What was it ? " she asked as he returned, and he answered casually : " Oh, just another message ! " But when she had changed into her travelling-dress and their taxi was on its way to Waterloo for the first stage of their honeymoon in Cornwall, he stopped it abruptly and spoke to the driver.

" Don't go to Waterloo, please. Just drive round for half-an-hour, and then go back to the Savoy."

" Why, darling ? " exclaimed Sylvia, mystified and perturbed, " Aren't we catching this train after all ? "

Lawrence put his arm round her, and drew her close to him. " My sweet wife . . . I'm afraid I've got some rotten news."

The telephone call, he told her, had been from an apologetic Adjutant, recalling him to his unit, which had received orders to entrain for France at six o'clock next morning.

" It's this damned German push, I suppose — it just *would* come now ! Charlesworth said he didn't know how to give me such a message on my wedding-day. . . . He said he really ought to recall me at once, but it'll be all right if I'm back by midnight."

Sylvia did not speak. Her face had turned white, and her fingers in their pale suède gloves were locked together in her lap. Lawrence took her left hand in his, removed the glove, and pressed his lips against the thin bright circle of the wedding-ring that he had put there two hours before.

" My darling," he said miserably, " we've got exactly seven hours together. . . . I thought we'd wait till all the guests are out of the way, and then go back to the Savoy and ask them to give you your room again for the night. You can stay there and rest after I've gone. And you could come and see me off tomorrow morning if you'd like to. . . ."

Half-an-hour later, locking the bedroom door against the eloquent commiseration of a too-sympathetic chambermaid, he knelt before her in unconscious imitation of a gesture by Romeo, and cried from the passionate bitterness of his frustration : " Sylvia ! . . . my own Juliet . . . you'll let me make you really my wife before I go ? "

" Oh, my love, of course ! " They were the first articulate words that she had spoken since he told her of the telephone message. Seeing her own desire burning in his eyes, she forgot every Victorian restraint imposed upon her by the middle-class provincial family which had brought her up. Tightly locked in his urgent arms, she pressed her impatient young body against his in the abandonment of despair.

" Now, Lawrence — now ! Don't let's wait . . . something else may happen ! "

For two hours they clung desperately together, love and anguish so closely intermingled that neither would have known whether to describe their experience as joy or sorrow. At eight o'clock, when they still lay exhausted and half-asleep in each other's arms, Lawrence regretfully roused her. He telephoned for supper to be sent to their room, and they tried to eat it almost in silence. When a taxi took him to Waterloo for the last train to

Richmond, she remained standing outside the hotel door long after he had vanished into the traffic of the Strand.

Early next day, in the grey bleakness of a spring morning after a sleepless night, she went to Charing Cross to say goodbye. Then the Great Retreat engulfed him, heart-broken, half-trained, keenly imaginative, and ill-adapted to war. Three weeks after their wedding, when the Channel Ports were threatened and Sir Douglas Haig was urging his exhausted armies to fight on with their backs to the wall, a telegram came to say that Lawrence had been killed.

At first, overwrought to the point of abnormal exalta-tion, Sylvia concentrated her pent-up emotions upon the hope of bearing Lawrence's child. Surely that perfect and prolonged act of union could not be fruit-less; surely life must come from so conscious and fervent an affirmation of life! But as the desolate weeks went by and no promise of motherhood rewarded her anxious vigilance, she was forced to realise that with Lawrence had perished that immortality of which she had prayed to become the instrument. The frightened little maid-servant, terrorised into acquiescence by a lustful master, could conceive in a moment; the unions of the syphi-litic might be cursed instantly with unwanted children; but she, Sylvia Salvesen, the beautiful idolised actress, could not re-create the life of her lover fallen in battle.

Then indeed despair, reaching exhaustion in apathy, descended blackly upon her. For months she moved like a sleep-walker about the London that she could not bring herself to leave, yet to which she seemed to have nothing more to give. On Armistice Day she fled from the cheering West End crowds to Richmond Park, where she had so often gone to meet Lawrence before their marriage, and spent the intolerable hours wandering like a homeless spirit over the wet heath amid the dripping trees. Throughout 1919, solicitous friends entreated her to attempt one new part after another. But she successively refused them all, and at length announced her intention of leaving the stage.

Early in 1920, a middle-aged actress who specialised in character parts and had played the Nurse in *Romeo and Juliet*, prevailed on Sylvia to leave the two-roomed flat where she was living alone in Bloomsbury, and share her studio in Glebe Place, Chelsea. Caroline Attenborough was as motherly by nature as the Nurse whom she had represented. By one thoughtful expedient after another, she now tried to rouse Sylvia from the spiritual catalepsy which imprisoned her. A Sunday evening visit to Battersea to hear the young Curate whose sermons everyone seemed suddenly to be discussing, came after a long and unsuccessful series of these experiments.

To Sylvia's protests of scepticism and indifference, the persistent Caroline only replied : " He's no armchair parson, dear. I wouldn't want to listen to him myself if he were ! He got the V.C. in one of those early battles — Neuve Chapelle or Ypres or Loos — and there's no harm in hearing what he has to say. It's only across the Bridge, after all. If we don't like him, we needn't go again ! "

*

At a Holy Communion service in May, when even the littered Battersea streets seemed to be washed clean by the mild morning sunshine, Robert Carbury first noticed an unfamiliar face in his congregation. Unfamiliar faces were no longer exceptional at All Souls, but they usually appeared at Evensong, and had never worn such a wistful, haunting beauty as the face of this young woman. To his suddenly smitten senses, it seemed as though one of the pale copper-haired angels in the stained-glass windows had stepped down into the Church.

Jerking himself back into the service, he went on.

" ' Hear what comfortable words our Saviour Christ saith unto all that truly turn to him. Come unto me all that travail and are heavy laden, and I will refresh you. . . .' "

As he uttered the familiar phrases he thought he saw the young woman's lips quiver, as though someone had struck her a sudden blow and she was trying to check her tears. When she knelt before the Altar rails, the sorrowful loveliness of her face uplifted to receive the Sacrament made his breath come sharply and his fingers tremble.

Throughout that week his preoccupation with the possibility of seeing her again disturbed his concentration on his daily duties. The chance that she might be present made him decide to prepare for next Sunday's Evensong the vigorous sermon that he had long contemplated on the obligations arising from the War. He would speak, he resolved, of the responsibility that lay upon his generation to redeem the un-Christian terms of the Versailles Treaty, and build a new international society in which all men would live together as brothers. Almost as though this decision had become intuitively known, his congregation that evening appeared to be larger than ever before. Even the ageing philosophical Vicar looked mildly astonished by its size.

Robert was engaged in vehemently defining contemporary Christian purposes, when he saw the young woman again. She was sitting just below the pulpit, and this time she wore discreetly modified but unmistakable widow's weeds. His realisation of her grief, and his correct supposition regarding its cause, lent a passion to his concluding exhortations which surprised even himself, and caused many members of his congregation to kneel for the final Benediction with their handkerchiefs pressed against their eyes.

When the Church had emptied, Robert felt exhausted yet strangely exultant. He interrupted the Verger's flow of congratulations to put, as casually as he could, the question that had been troubling him all the week.

" Matthew . . . have you any idea who that young widow is who was sitting just under the pulpit this evening ? "

Conscious of his ability to impart interesting information, Matthew Peckworthy answered with restrained eagerness.

" Surely you noticed her last Sunday, Sir, when she came to Communion ? "

" Yes . . . I did. But who *is* she, Matthew ? "

" Do you really mean to say you don't know, Sir? Well, that's the worst of working so hard and taking no relaxation ! I don't suppose you even know the names of the leading film stars ! "

Robert struggled to conceal his impatience.

" You still haven't told me who she is. Is she a film star ? " She's certainly lovely enough, pronounced his emotional judgment, but he locked his lips against a too-revealing expression of opinion.

" No, Sir. She's Sylvia Salvesen, the actress. Specialises in Shakespeare and suchlike highbrow parts. They say she made her name several seasons ago, playing Juliet to Lawrence Mayfield's Romeo. That would about be when you were at Bellsley, Sir. Anyway, she married her Romeo soon after; it was a big romance among stage people. But the poor young chap went to the front right away and never came back. She was terribly cut up and still is. They do say nobody can persuade her to act any more."

" Poor girl! She's very beautiful, Matthew," said Robert in spite of himself.

" Yes, Sir. She has that reputation. But you ought to have seen her when she was first on the stage. The wife and I saw her once in a matinée of *Midsummer Night's Dream*; the fairy queen, she was. It isn't that she's got any older or plainer since young Mayfield was killed. After all, it was only two years or thereabouts ago. But she just looks as if some kind of light in her had gone out."

On Tuesday morning at breakfast, Robert opened one of the many letters in unfamiliar handwritings which now filled his post-bag. But at the sight of the signature, " Sylvia Mayfield ", he caught his breath in a tension that was physical pain.

DEAR MR. CARBURY [he read],

I want to thank you for your wonderful sermon last night. For me it was an awakening, a kind of resurrection from the dead. My husband was killed in April, 1918, soon after our marriage. You made me see that after all he may not have died in vain. I began to understand something of what he and others were fighting for.

I also realised that it was selfish of me to have given way to grief for so long. I want to make the right use of my life, but I don't quite know how. Can you help me? May I call on you some time, and ask for your advice?

Yours sincerely,

SYLVIA MAYFIELD

When Robert had replied, asking her to wait for him in the vestry after Evensong next Sunday, the remainder of the laggard week seemed to prolong itself to a year. He felt thankful that it was the Vicar's turn to preach that night; such a conflict of thoughts and emotions possessed him that he knew he could not this time have risen to the occasion. The Vicar, as usual, left soon

34

after the service. A distinguished Hebrew scholar, he had always handed over most of the parish responsibilities to his Curate, and amid the little crowd of parishioners whom he was now accustomed to see waiting for Robert every Sunday evening, he did not notice the pale young woman in black sitting quietly behind the vestry door.

Keeping a resolute grip on himself, Robert disposed more rapidly than usual of the routine problems assembled for his attention. Then, the last questioning parishioner gone, he found himself alone with Sylvia.

He realised at once that his own turbulent emotions were not present in her; or, if they were, it was not with him that they were concerned. In spite of the deep human compassion that she had sensed in him, he understood that in her eyes he was an institution rather than a man; an institution through which, perhaps, the spirit of consolation might speak. Within a moment of his first shy greeting, she had released, as she was never to release for him again, the pent-up torrent of the lonely grief against which the barrier of her negative reticence had so long been imposed. She spoke of Lawrence, telling Robert how he had become the mainspring of all her life and actions during the nine months' run of *Romeo and Juliet*; of their marriage and his immediate departure; of her frustrated hope for his child; and then of the long winter night of desolation.

" You've made me see it's wrong to let one's self be broken, even by losing someone who meant more than life," she said in the musical voice which would have unbearably assailed his vulnerable senses if it had not first been eclipsed by her face. " I want to do something, to help make that better world you spoke of. But how? Oh, Mr. Carbury, tell me what to do ! "

Robert had listened without speaking, his expression of grave solicitude acting as an effective screen for the conflict of pity, sorrow, compunction, and hope (for what?) that her story had aroused in him. It was his duty, he knew, to subdue his inconvenient and hitherto dormant manhood ; to be the impersonal Father Confessor through whom the Holy Spirit might speak and guide her. And, in the moment of silence that followed her appeal, it seemed to him that a spirit of positive wisdom did indeed respond to his will.

" You must go back to the stage," he told her without hesitation. " I don't know much about the technical side of your work, but can you get into contact again with the people who used to give you your parts ? "

" Yes," she said, " quite easily. Managers sometimes write and suggest jobs to me, even now. And if they didn't, the friend I live with is an actress. I could get in touch with people again through her. . . . But why must I go back ? "

In his reply, Robert struggled to convey the profound sense of vocation which had sent him from the battlefield through physical suffering and mental conflict into the Anglican ministry.

" Mrs. Mayfield, your art is your method of seeking truth and interpreting it to others. It means — or could mean — the same thing to you as my halting attempts to practise and preach God's Will mean to me. I came to my ministry through penitence for taking the lives of the men I killed. Just in the same way, you could reach the highest levels of interpretation by conveying to others that suffering can be sublimated through service."

He continued with a greater effort.

" I'm sure that's what — your husband — would have wanted you to do. Aren't you really sure of it yourself? Your art, your playing which I know is exquisite, were part of what he loved in you. Wasn't it through your gifts that he first gave you his love? Can you believe for a moment that if he could speak to you from one of those many mansions which our Master prepares for His servants, he would want you to give up the very thing for which he admired you? And least of all would he want you to give it up out of grief for him. He would say, ' Go back, my beloved wife, and take on the hard job of giving the world the inspiration we once gave it together! ' "

" I believe you're right," she said slowly. " Lawrence was a real idealist. He might have said that very thing."

" I'm sure of it, Mrs. Mayfield. No man who loved you could say otherwise. Humanity needs you. It's for you to give it hope and faith in your own way."

*

Robert Carbury, servant of Christ, had never realised what a painful experience love at first sight could be. And it was not only painful; it was deeply disturbing to his meditative powers and the consecrated practice of his vocation. When he knelt down to pray, he found himself murmuring " Sylvia! " When he lifted his eyes to the Mother of God enthroned in the red and gold of the East window, he saw only a delicately-moulded face crowned with copper-coloured hair.

A week after their conversation, Sylvia wrote to tell him that she had already taken his advice. Melisande Allen, the leading lady of the Pall Mall Repertory Company, had recently collapsed from overwork, and had been ordered a long rest. The management had asked Sylvia to take her place, and her time was now filled with emergency rehearsals for the part of Clare in Galsworthy's play *The Fugitive*, which was to open next week. Although nothing could ever be the same as playing opposite Lawrence, something of the old pleasure in creating a part had come back to her, and she wanted to thank Mr. Carbury again, most sincerely, for his kind advice. . . .

As soon as he had read her letter, Robert telephoned the Pall Mall Theatre. Although he had never seen a play since his embarkation leave in 1915, he booked a seat at the back of the stalls for the first night of *The Fugitive*.

After the mingled pain and intoxication of that experience, Robert went to the Pall Mall Theatre whenever he could spare an evening from the parish. Each time he saw Sylvia she seemed to add something new to her part, and he realised that for a gifted actress every performance of the same play meant a fresh effort of creation. By her invitation he went at discreet intervals behind the scenes, and was initiated into back-stage mysteries. Sometimes rehearsals now occupied her Sunday evenings, but whenever she was free she still came to his Church in Battersea. A violent thumping of his heart coincided with his realisation of her presence, and he hardly knew how to finish the remainder of the service which divided him from the now more than formal hand-clasp and the few moments of conversation before she went home.

In mid-July he spent another evening at the Pall Mall Theatre, watching her take the part of Andromache in Gilbert Murray's rendering of Euripides' great drama, *The Trojan Women*. As she stood before the battlements of desolate Troy holding the child Astyanax in her arms, the realisation that he was capable of becoming a father as well as a husband came upon him with the force of an apocalyptic discovery. The play, with its deep human compassion for the victims of war and its ageless appeal to men to fulfil their noblest rather than their cruellest instincts, moved him to a point at which his passionate idealism and turbulent masculine emotions merged into one and became all but uncontrollable. This performance, he felt, challenged him to make some kind of decision. Just what decision was required he did not yet know; but it certainly involved a long talk with Sylvia about those fundamentals which were, it seemed to him, the mainspring alike of her art and his ministry. Obeying an impulse too urgent to be resisted, he went round to her dressing-room and asked if he might take her out to supper.

" If you're not too tired, that is," he added, still half apologetic.

" I'm not tired at all," she said. And certainly, as she removed her make-up and turned to him smiling, she did not look it. In the two months that had passed since their first conversation, the change in her was astonishing. She seemed fully alive now, vital and eager; her oval face appeared rounder, and the nightly application of cosmetics left the delicate bloom of her skin unimpaired. He felt overwhelmed by an emotion which resembled remorse but did not stop there as he realised that here, restored to life almost completely, was the beautiful girl whom Lawrence Mayfield had loved.

" Is there anywhere special you'd like to go? " he inquired.

" No," she replied. " I'd love to go wherever you choose, except " — a barely perceptible shiver passed over her — " except the Savoy."

" I wasn't thinking of the Savoy. It isn't exactly in my line. I wondered if you'd care to come to the Green Parrakeet on Chelsea Embankment. It stays open till 1 A.M. and I can easily take you home afterwards. Would that bore you? "

" No," she answered truthfully. " I should love a quiet place for a change. I've been there once or twice with Caroline. It's got something none of the West End restaurants have — a kind of atmosphere."

So they took a taxi to the Green Parrakeet, and for an hour and a half, till the little restaurant closed, sat talking over the polished wooden tables illuminated only by candlelight. They spoke of war and death, peace and the fugitive hopes of mankind. He told her of the experience that had gained him his V.C. and the unexpected conversion to which it led, and she disclosed the aspirations which had driven her from her Newcastle home to the London stage. Finally she talked a little of Lawrence Mayfield and the unbearable love which had left her utterly shipwrecked, lampless and rudderless, after his death.

Robert now understood, all too poignantly, what such a passion had meant. He lost all sense of his surroundings, living only in her and the intensity of his emotions. Afterwards he supposed that they must have ordered food and eaten it, but he could never remember what it was. At one o'clock the elderly waitress's gentle reminder that the restaurant was closing struck him like an intolerable blow.

As he rose reluctantly she asked him a question, using his Christian name for the first time.

" Are *you* tired . . . Robert ? Your life's so much harder than mine."

" Tired ! " The very word seemed fantastic. " Tired ! " he exclaimed. " Why, I could sit here and talk to you for ever . . . Sylvia."

" Then don't let's go home yet," she said. " We're so close to your parish here. I'd like to see Battersea at night. Won't you show me the Church, and the streets, and the warehouses by the river, as they look when everyone's asleep ? "

Robert was far beyond the stage of asking himself

what the Vicar and the parish would think if someone reported that he had been seen wandering about Battersea with a strange young woman long after midnight. Taking Sylvia's arm, he led her across the bridge over the river which nowhere divides two such sharply contrasting districts as Battersea and Chelsea. Almost without speaking, they walked for nearly an hour through the mean streets dignified by night.

In daylight the houses on either side of the road were revealed as old-fashioned two-storied workers' homes, built of dingy grey brick. Only their little front plots, surrounded by dirty palings of decaying wood and sometimes planted with shrubs or sooty flowers, distinguished them from their counterparts in the East End. But now the warm darkness made silent shadows of these unlovely dwellings, disguising their details as completely as it concealed the Italian names above the many small hairdressers' shops and the historic signs motionless in the summer air above ancient public houses.

It was after two o'clock when Robert suggested that, before going home, Sylvia might like to rest for a while in his Church. Turning towards the river, they went through the small churchyard between old grass-grown tombstones, leaning towards one another as though the dead were exchanging salutes. Quietly he unfastened the heavy door that now, by his request, was never locked.

The wide Hanoverian church with its heavy wooden pews was very dark; a gallery on either side eclipsed the pale light that pushed its way through the low stained-glass windows. Only the East window, coloured chrome and vermilion, faintly suggested a fading sunset, and showed the vague outlines of the small high pulpit and elaborate Georgian sarcophagi on the walls. From the gallery opposite the pulpit a large clock, vehement in the stillness, steadily recorded the minutes of the night.

For a short time they talked intermittently in under-
tones. Then both became silent, dominated by the
insistent symbolism of the ticking clock. In the chill
hour which comes before dawn she shivered a little, and
when, tentatively, he put his arm round her, she did
not resist. Gradually light began to emphasise the
colours of the windows, and to filter, blue-grey, through
the plain glass panes above the gallery.

" Let's walk again," said Sylvia. " I want to see the
river at dawn."

" Certainly, if you wish," he answered, " but the sun
won't be up just yet. Come into the vestry, and I'll
make you a cup of tea before we go out."

Leaving their pew, they went into the room where
they had first spoken together. Robert put the kettle
on the gas ring ; Sylvia tidied her hair in the little cloak-
room half filled with cheap glass vases, and then helped
him to prepare the tea. When they went out into the
churchyard, the dawn light washing the grey-brown brick
of the Church with its short copper spire still left the scene
almost colourless. From across the river, where the day's
work had already begun amid warehouses and small
factories, came the sound of Lot's Road Power Station like
the beating of a great tin heart. To the east of its four
lofty chimneys ran the line of eighteenth-century houses,
in many shapes and colours, which composed Cheyne
Walk. It was broken only by the high red-brown tower
of Chelsea Old Church, its gilt weather-vane alert to
catch the first beams of the rising sun. Opposite All
Souls churchyard a huddle of wharfs and boats flanked
the wide Chelsea reach of the river known as the Bay,
where sea-birds cried plaintively from the mast-heads of
ancient barges.

Standing with Sylvia beside the small tangled garden

which surrounded a forgotten tombstone, Robert waited
for the sun to rise. The beating of his heart seemed
louder to him than the noise of Lot's Road Power Station,
for he knew now to what decision the night had brought
him. As the sun came up exuberantly behind the Church
and drenched the warehouses across the river with yellow
light, his emotions became so overwhelming that he could
trust himself only with the simplest words. Resisting
the intolerable impulse to put his arm round her again,
he asked very gently : " Will you marry me, Sylvia ? "

He added nothing to the direct request. For a long
moment there was silence between them, broken only by
the shrill crying of the sea-birds rising to meet the sun.
Then she spoke, as quietly as he.

" I believe I do care for you, Robert, but I'm not sure
I ought to marry you. Something died in me when
Lawrence was killed. . . . You wouldn't be marrying
a whole person. I couldn't give you what you'd give me.
It wouldn't be fair."

Robert clasped her hands in his, the passion of his
desire now almost choking him.

" Whatever Lawrence left is enough for me ! " he
cried, firmly believing that he meant what he said.
" Sylvia, my beloved, give me only that ! Let me help
you, comfort you, bring you back fully to life if I can ! "

" Very well, Robert," she said, almost inaudibly.
The words were a half-sigh rather than a murmur of
responsive ecstasy. But there in the dawn silence of the
churchyard, as he kissed for the first time her beautiful
mouth lifted submissively to his, he hardly noticed the
deep sadness of her quiet capitulation.

*

" I always knew it, Mr. Carbury," said Matthew Peckworthy decisively. He recognised with pride that he

was the first recipient of the news which Robert could no longer withhold when he had returned to the Church after escorting Sylvia home across Battersea Bridge. " I guessed," he went on, " how things would go the first time you spotted her in the congregation. And when you took to going to the theatre — you, of all people! — well, then I was sure."

" How did you know I went to the theatre? " inquired Robert, a little startled, but too deeply enchanted by his new happiness to care how much the parish had known of his less orthodox occupations.

" That would be telling. . . . But I do congratulate you, Sir! You've picked a real beauty, and no mistake. They take some keeping in order, though, them stage people do."

Robert smiled gaily.

" And do you think I shall be able to keep her in order, Matthew? "

The Verger meditated, seeing as an interested on-looker the possible future pitfalls of the young preacher's family life more clearly than Robert himself. Then he replied with affectionate frankness: " I shouldn't wonder, Sir! Anyways, you're liable to have a better shot at it than most. As I've always said to the Vicar, you're more than half an actor yourself! "

Robert often speculated on the truth of Peckworthy's comment as he went ever more frequently to the West End, and began to identify himself with the various actors who played opposite Sylvia. On the night after they had decided to get married in two months' time and go away for a short October honeymoon, he watched her play the part of Nina in Chekhov's play, *The Seagull*. Newly impressed by her physical beauty, he realised that its quality lay even more in the immaculate elegance of her pose than in the subtle charm of her face. Thinking of their coming marriage, he suddenly pictured her as pregnant, and a wave of compunction swept upon him.

Afterwards, sitting over the candles at the Green Parrakeet, he interrupted their conversation to say hesitantly : " There's something that disturbs me a good deal, my darling. . . . It came over me specially to-night, seeing you in that lovely part."

" What is it, Robert ? What troubles you ? "

" It's just this," he said, after a brief pause. " I've always imagined myself, when I married, as leading a more or less normal family life. . . . I mean, having children . . . playing with them in the nursery . . . going away with them on school holidays . . . enjoying their companionship when they're older. . . . At least, I knew I had when I saw you in *The Trojan Women* with the baby in your arms. But . . ."

" But what ? "

" You're so beautiful," he explained apologetically. " You're so exquisite in your form and all your movements. . . . If asking you to have children isn't fair to you . . . why, then, of course . . ."

She put her hand lightly over his.

" It's just like you, Robert, to think of me before your own hopes — and desires. But it's all right about children. I always meant to have them when I married. I don't mean " — and she laughed with the occasional laughter that twisted his heart because it came so seldom — " that I'm contemplating a family of ten ! But I think I'd like two children, at any rate. Without them, there's a whole world of tenderness and understanding that one never knows."

" I agree," he said gravely. " And I expect it's as important for an actress to understand the springs of ordinary human emotions as it is for a priest."

" I'm sure it is. And, after all, two children aren't

really a great handicap. It isn't as if women nowadays went in for the enormous infants of Victorian days, or lay about on sofas for months letting all their muscles go flabby."

She crumbled the roll beside her plate, and went on reflectively.

" But even if it did spoil my figure a bit, I wouldn't care. One's art isn't worth much if it depends purely on external things. Elegance and poise don't last unless they come from within."

Eight weeks afterwards, Robert and Sylvia were married quietly at All Souls Church by Anselm Ensor. As the Bishop enumerated the familiar causes " for which matrimony is ordained ", the words " procreation of children " brought back to Robert's mind the conversation at the Green Parrakeet. Deeply stirred by the tide of reverent gratitude which mingled with his love, he took Sylvia's hand tenderly in his and touched it with his lips.

CHAPTER III

A Child is Born

BUT the years went by, and the children did not come.

It was not that Sylvia had no time for them. When Robert moved, before their marriage, from his lodgings into an old-fashioned but relatively convenient small house looking east over Battersea Park, the devoted Cockney widow who " did " for him as a bachelor curate volunteered to act as their housekeeper with the help of a married daughter who came in part-time. Mrs. Moneypenny's admiration for Sylvia lost nothing from the envy which she knew that she and her daughter would arouse in their neighbours if they became part of so glamorous a household.

" Your lovely lady's got summat else to do but shoppin' and cleanin'," she announced decisively. " It'd be a real shame if she 'ad to leave the stage. Let me take on, Sir, and I reckon you won't regret it ! "

Robert accepted the offer with gratitude, and Sylvia with profound relief. There was nothing now to handicap her re-established career, for her husband, who had been responsible for her return to the stage, was the last person to resent the preoccupation which each new part involved. With no domestic routine to trouble her she calculated that, with the help of a trained nursemaid when the time came, she could manage the two children whom she had promised to Robert, and suffer no loss of opportunity or skill. But in spite of the plans so efficiently laid for their coming, the children did not appear.

" I wonder," Sylvia sometimes meditated, " if there really is something wrong with me ? I wonder if I ought to do anything about it — see a doctor, perhaps ? "

But her speculations, less absorbing than the successive plays which dominated her imagination, never led her to positive action. If Robert was disappointed by fate's apparent denial of the fatherhood that he desired, he gave no hint to Sylvia; the ever-new wonder of her presence in his life seemed to fulfil even his exceptional capacity for devotion. When their busy, absorbing days added up to twelve months, then twenty-four, then thirty-six, she remained undisturbed by her childlessness. The frustration of her passionate desire for a child by Lawrence had left her with no yearning enthusiasm to bear children to Robert.

As the months marched on, she gradually perceived how ill-founded had been her evanescent hope that Robert, since he had brought her back to life, could rekindle her power to love. She realised that, among the many definite emotions which he aroused in her, love as she had known it was not one. Love, it seemed, was a too-subtle essence, neither to be commanded by kindness, nor distilled from admiration, gratitude, and affection. Occasionally she found herself wishing that there was more unrestrained lust and less tender reverence in Robert's caresses; she longed for him just sometimes to take her inconsiderately, without asking first.

After four years of marriage in which she had striven to be adequately responsive to his undiminished adoration, she found herself thinking of Lawrence with a persistence that she had not known since the period following his death. Perhaps, she thought, she was tired by the long and all too successful run of Stafford Vaughan's *The Triangle*, in which she who preferred the variations of repertory had played the exacting rôle of Judith for eighteen months. No doubt, lacking the ever-fresh excitement of creating new parts, her mind, in need of both rest and stimulus, had turned in upon itself and its memories.

When at last the run of *The Triangle* ended, an invitation came to Sylvia from Caroline Attenborough to join her Christmas Riviera party, and spend six weeks in the South of France.

Immediately Robert read Caroline's letter, he urged Sylvia to go. A break was just what she needed after that harassing part, and their household had maintained its simple, unconventional time-table for so long that there was no chance of any domestic disturbance. As for the parish, if he wasn't used to its Christmas routine of services and " socials " by now, he never would be.

" All the same, I don't like leaving you just at Christ-mas-time," she said, conscientiously trying to banish the mental picture of palms and pines against a blue Mediterranean sky which had made suddenly intolerable the grey dreariness of Battersea streets in December.

But Robert, seeing with love's clairvoyance the same vision of sunshine and the South, became more insistent than ever.

" It'll do me good to be alone for a bit. Sometimes I think you mean almost too much to me. . . . I'm sure it's God's Will that I should relearn how to stand on my own feet."

" But not at Christmas ? "

" That's where you're wrong, my darling. Christmas and the New Year are typical stock-taking periods. And, believe me, for a so-called popular parson stock-taking's an unpleasant process that's best undergone alone ! So write at once and say you'll go. And don't dare to indulge in the luxury of remorse ! "

*

When Robert expressed a desire to be alone, he was not entirely self-sacrificing; there were some personal pro-blems to be faced which he was reluctant to discuss with Sylvia. They could best be considered while her still emotionally disturbing presence was temporarily else-where.

Superficially, in relation to his parish activities, Sylvia's companionship had meant rest and refreshment. When he returned from visiting a querulous invalid or presiding at an argumentative meeting of the Parochial Church Council, the fact that she belonged to another environment and talked a different " shop " was an agree-able relief. Her theatrical friends often came to their house, where he welcomed them as a safeguard against loneliness. For, reluctant though he was to admit it, he became conscious of loneliness only when he and Sylvia were alone together, and he was forced to acknowledge her remoteness and his inability to capture the essential Sylvia for himself. He had never known her irritable or peevish; she was consistently gentle and affectionately responsive. Yet he realised that he, who loved her so deeply, stood perpetually on the hither side of the gulf created by her self-contained detachment.

Perhaps, he thought, determined to find some compensation which was creditable to her, she really served him best by the sense of isolation that she unintentionally imposed. It had compelled him to seek the friendship of Christ; to turn to Jesus as an Elder Brother who had passed on before him, but whose words and ideas were still of recent memory and whose very voice could almost be heard.

He knew that this cultivation of spiritual unity with the living Christ had made their once remote Master more real to his parishioners. He now brought the name of Jesus into ordinary conversation as casually as he introduced the name of the Bishop, and the normal embarrassment felt by worldly church-goers at a sudden reference to Christ had disappeared so completely that he and they might have been discussing the local doctor or a visiting priest. The personality of the Son of God seemed to have become part of the fabric of the old Hanoverian church. Now, alone for a time, Robert could intensify and extend that enriching communion.

But some of the problems which he had to consider were more concrete than his mystical fellowship with Jesus and the psychological subtleties of his relationship to Sylvia. They were not involved by his own profession, for though, at thirty-three, he was still only a curate, he had been privately assured by Anselm Ensor that preferment, satisfying and even sensational, was impending. It was best, said the Bishop of Battersea, that he should retain his present large and established following until a living became available which would really test his powers.

The dilemma that troubled him arose from the childlessness which, he now reluctantly admitted, seemed likely to be permanent. Six months after their marriage his father, though barely sixty, had died from a sudden heart attack at the close of a late session in the House of Commons. Always a supersensitive son, Robert grieved greatly for his devoted parent; but the merciful swiftness of his end brought some consolation, and a profounder kind was provided by Sylvia's restrained but unfailing sympathy.

After James's death the family home at Hoddershall was taken over by his younger bachelor brother, a sporting squire who found his *raison d'être* in the hunting and fishing of rural Staffordshire. But three years later he too succumbed to the after-effects of a riding accident, and Robert found himself not only wealthy, but a man of property. Hoddershall Ash, that beautiful and beloved white elephant of an estate which he was never likely to occupy, was now on his hands, and he could not make up his mind what to do with it.

He loved his old home and the surrounding countryside so deeply that the remotest prospect of a son or daughter would have induced him, without hesitation, to shoulder the heavy cost of the manor's upkeep as a future home for his children and grandchildren. But now, with no heir or the hope of one, was a sentimental attachment rooted in memory worth its price in rates and taxes? Was he even justified in retaining possession of land which would provide the perfect site for a school or sanatorium?

By the time that Robert had decided to keep Hoddershall Ash for one more year and then sell it if his hope of
a family remained unfulfilled, Sylvia had become comfortably intimate with Caroline's exotic little company
of writers and players at her villa near Agay. With one
of them, Damon Sullivan, the forty-two-year-old Irish-
American playwright who had come to London for the
production of his political drama, *Dublin Sunday*, that
intimacy threatened after three weeks to reach a point
beyond comfort.

Ten years ago, Sylvia had met him during a season
of Irish plays which coincided with her first few months
on the London stage. Now she sat beside him on a dry
carpet of pine-needles in a wood overlooking the fashionable but still secluded coast between Saint-Raphaël and
Cannes. The too-intoxicating winter sunshine of the
Riviera cast lacy shadows over his dark, dissipated, good-
humoured face as he sprawled beneath the pines, looking
up at her from lazily ironic blue eyes veiled by long
feminine lashes, silkily black. There was an abnormal
exuberance about those lashes, and she wasn't sure
whether they fascinated or disgusted her.

" I'm telling you," he said. " The boys on Broadway
thought someone was kidding them when they heard
you'd turned pious and married a parson ! "

" My husband's a remarkable man," said Sylvia with
determined loyalty. " He won the V.C. at the Battle
of Loos. That's why he decided to go into the Church
— as a sort of answer to war. He's one of the best
preachers in London."

" I daresay. But does your saintly V.C. come up to
scratch ? "

" I don't know what you mean."

" I guess you do, honey. Shall I tell you what's the
matter with you ? "

" I'm not aware that anything's the matter."

A small sardonic smile displayed the soft fullness of his lips.

" You can't deceive Damon," he said smoothly. " I'm too much of an old roué not to know all the symptoms. What you're suffering from is sex-starvation."

Sylvia, startled out of her habitual equanimity, resisted a violent impulse to fling a pine-cone into Damon's taunting, complacent face. Why do I let him talk to me in this insufferable way? she asked herself. Aloud she said stiffly :

" That's nonsense. There's no reason for any such thing."

" Isn't there? Are you sure you know what love can be? "

" Yes," she answered quietly. " I do know that."

" And you ask me to believe the parson taught you? "

" I'm not asking you to believe anything. But you seem to have overlooked the fact that I've been married twice."

" Sorry, darling, I did. I'd forgotten poor Mayfield."

" I shall never forget him," she said, looking beyond the pines to the red rocks and serene indifferent sea.

" Why should you? He evidently knew how to love."

" I don't want to talk about him."

" All right. We won't. But there's no reason why we shouldn't talk about love."

" I don't think I want to discuss that either."

He moved still closer to her, and spoke in a whisper.

" Why not, sweetheart? I'm something of an expert, you know. I've had lots of experience."

" I'm sure you have."

" The women I make love to always stay friends with me."

" How interesting ! " she said coldly.

" Well, it's something of an achievement ! "

" No doubt. I congratulate you."

He seized the hand that lay passive beside her on the pine-needles.

" Look here, honey, I don't want to annoy you. But I hate to see a lovely woman not getting her due. . . . If only you'd let me call on you tonight, I'd show you what you're missing."

" Thanks very much," she said. " But I don't want to know." She thought of Robert in their Battersea sitting-room, urging her to go away. (" *I think you mean almost too much to me. . . . I'm sure it's God's Will that I should relearn how to stand on my own feet.*") God's Will ! She continued sharply : " I suppose you realise you're inciting me to be unfaithful to my husband ? "

" Well, you wouldn't be the first, would you, my sweet Victorian ? "

" I don't care what you call me," she said, caring just the same. " I'm not that sort."

" Aren't you ? O.K. The offer stands open if you change your mind."

The next day, and the next, he returned to the attack, and she realised with incredulous horror that her resistance was beginning to weaken. How was it possible that these crude advances, these unsubtle innuendoes, could stir her to physical reactions of a kind that she had not experienced since the day of her marriage to Lawrence, with its virginal instinctive passion ? Damon's love-making, she knew, would be as easy, sophisticated, and vigorous as its preliminaries. It would be hallowed by no glow of tenderness, no counterpart of the mental and spiritual affinity which had glorified her first incomparable union. And yet . . .

After another evening of the prolonged and insistent siege which exhausted her physically without leaving any hope that Damon could bring life to the arid desert of her unfulfilled emotional desire, she decided in panic that she must go away. Just because the passions of real life now seemed less authentic than the histrionic ardours of the stage, she feared that she might surrender to Damon out of the same profound indifference that had been responsible for her consent to marry Robert.

The next day, while Damon was lunching with friends in Cannes, she told Caroline that Robert needed her urgently, packed a suitcase, and fled to Marseilles. There she took the night train to Paris, and the following afternoon stepped out of her Pullman coach at Victoria Station into Robert's arms.

Her telegram from Paris, announcing her return ten days before he expected her, had surprised and perturbed him. But her brief explanation that she wanted him and could no longer do without him moved him too deeply to arouse any wish to investigate her motives.

" You really *needed* me, darling! Enough to come back to Battersea at the beginning of February? " he asked again, hardly able to believe his all-too-receptive ears.

" Yes, Robert," she said, leaning wearily against him as they drove along the Embankment. " Battersea doesn't matter after all. Home is where you are. It always has been — ever since I first came to you to be comforted. You haven't forgotten? "

" Forgotten! " he exclaimed. " Heaven help me, Sylvia, I believe I could forget the Divine Love itself before I forgot that! "

In the nights that followed, his tender caresses, their ardour intensified by her absence and the joy of her unexpected return, were consoling and reassuring to that awakened sense of physical frustration which she secretly acknowledged with resentment and shame. She gave herself up to them with unwonted gratitude for the imaginative quality of their loving restraint.

*

Six weeks later, the virtual certainty that she was pregnant drove her to seek confirmation from a West End gynaecologist who had once attended Caroline. A young medical woman, Dr. Erica Varley, had recently come to Battersea with high qualifications from Cambridge, but an uncharacteristic perturbation which defied analysis made Sylvia reluctant to consult even the most reliable of Robert's parishioners.

From Dr. Sybil Winchester, she learnt that her belief was correct. The baby, said the gynaecologist, would arrive in mid-November or perhaps a day or two later. At last she could give Robert the news for which she realised that he would gladly have sacrificed all his earthly possessions, though for the last two years he had never mentioned his passionate longing for a family which they had once discussed at the Green Parrakeet.

As she came out of the consulting-room, the narrow length of Wimpole Street swept by the March wind seemed to be outlined with peculiar intensity, like a street in a powerfully executed engraving. She had often heard that a sentence of death could suddenly transform the external world for those about to leave it. Did the annunciation of impending birth have the same effect?

Still feeling overwrought and, oddly enough, guilty, she called a passing taxi and drove back to Battersea. There could surely be no possible connection between the invasion of her mind by Damon's lustful, dominating personality which had left her so nervously tired, and this long-delayed fulfilment of her powers as a woman and a wife. Yet it did seem as though that ruthless psychological technique had roused her reluctant physical

self to a pitch of vitality which was able at last to respond
to Robert's urge for mortal continuation. He trusted
her utterly, and she felt as if she had betrayed him.
Yet the ephemeral would-be lover whose persistence
threatened her control had perhaps, through the incalculable mysteries of biology, done him a service after all.

She arrived home just as Robert was returning from
his mid-week Matins. From the taxi window she watched
him, unconscious of her observation, go up the short
paved path and enter the house. Seeing, as though
for the first time, the lean hurrying figure, slightly limping,
the thin face with its anxious but wholly benevolent
expression, the ascetic yet kindly lips with the bullet
scar still faintly visible above one corner, the dreamy
hazel eyes perpetually seeking some unattainable but
never relinquished purpose, she was content that he
should be the father of her child. At the same time,
she felt glad that she did not love him deeply enough to
suffer from any inconvenient impulse to tell him about
Damon's disconcerting campaign. She would never be
compelled, emotionally and foolishly, to undermine his
confidence by superfluous information.

Hearing her come in at a time when she was normally
rehearsing, Robert appeared instantly in the passage.

" Sylvia! You're back already? What is it? Is
anything wrong? "

" Yes! . . . No . . ." She opened the door of his
small ground-floor study, threw her hat on the desk, and,
still feeling for once moved and tense, turned to him
breathlessly.

" Robert," she said, " we're going to have a baby. I
had to know for certain, so they let me off the rehearsal."

He did not speak. But with a feeling of envy she
watched the dawn of incredulous joy, like light breaking
over his face — a joy that could never be hers because,

however lovely her offspring might be, no child she bore
would be Lawrence's son or daughter. Then, suddenly,
she swayed as she stood ; that morning's turmoil of strange
agitation had pierced her habitual armour of self-restraint
and brought her to the verge of collapse. But Robert's
arms were round her before she could fall. Holding
her as though he could never let her go again, he carried
her up the shallow staircase and laid her down on their
bed.

" Forgive me, my darling," he whispered, incoherent
with happiness and anxiety as he knelt beside her. " It
was inconsiderate of me to keep you standing there . . .
I ought to have realised . . ."

" You didn't keep me standing," she said, pushing
back the rich coils of her loosened hair as the colour
returned to her face. " I chose to stand. It wasn't
exactly the kind of announcement one makes sitting
down."

With a sudden surge of the remorseful compunction
which she could never explain or even acknowledge to
him, she took his hand between both of hers.

" I knew how pleased you'd be, my dear. I'm very
glad."

" Pleased ! " Her quiet understatement of his almost
unbearable exultation seemed fantastic ; yet, master of
words though he was, he could find nothing better. " I
should just think I was ! I'm as pleased as if I were the
first man on earth to be given the hope of a child by the
wife he adores ! "

★

Robert had never known a period like the months that
followed. His elusive happiness seemed, for once, captured and tangible ; it was a crystal goblet, full to the
brim. Even the post-war international scene, of which
tumultuous echoes occasionally found their way into his

sermons or the speeches that he made as Chairman of
the North Battersea League of Nations Union, seemed
painfully to be reaching relative normality in time to give
the new generation a more stable background than that
of his own.

If he had previously doubted that prayers were
answered, he would have believed it now. It was not
that he had actually prayed for the gift of a child, for he
never used that type of prayer which treats the Deity as
a kind of celestial Woolworth's. Praying, for him, was a
habit, a discipline, the lifting up of his whole being to
God until his own desires became one with God's Will.
But God, whatever else the mystery of His Being might
contain, was an affirmation of life : had He not sent His
Son into the World in order that men might not only
have life, but have it more abundantly? Perhaps out of
the very act of communion with the Source of all Creation
had come the vitalising power from which new life was
born.

Because he and Sylvia would not much longer now
be alone together, he accepted more realistically the
fact that there were depths, or heights, in her that he
would never touch. For all her charming day-by-day
companionship and gentle responsiveness to his desires,
he knew now that her quiet reticence concealed a hard
core of indifference which remained unaffected by his
solicitous tenderness and unmoved by his pride in her
coming motherhood. But to this new life he might one
day come really close, and find in his son or daughter
someone who loved him as he had never been loved
since his father's death.

About the sex of his child he was genuinely uncon-
cerned ; he saw in it only the pride of his maturity, the
strong yet benevolent companion of his declining years.
On Sunday evenings, when he permitted himself an hour's

relaxation after his sermon, he would lie back with closed eyes in his study chair, and picture the time when he would take his firstborn to see Hoddershall Ash. Sometimes, in happy imagination, he walked up and down the beloved terraces beside a stalwart son who cooperatively suggested intelligent measures for improving the old place. Sometimes he showed the rose-garden or the dahlias to a lovely daughter with Sylvia's russet hair, whose eager appreciativeness reinforced his deep sense of family piety. Only the thought of danger and anguish for Sylvia had power to check his palpable rejoicing, and the fact that his own mother had died after his birth intensified his fear. Ceaselessly he prayed that somehow, in his own flesh, he might confront Sylvia's peril and endure her pain.

But throughout the months of waiting, Sylvia's health remained vigorous and unimpaired. Once the first shock of surprise had worn off, her prospective motherhood presented merely an extra challenge which demanded new skill and discretion on the stage. Robert became anxious, and even protested vigorously, when as late as September she accepted the part of Queen Katharine in Thrale Duncan's production of *Henry the Eighth*. But Sylvia only laughed at his perturbation, and Dr. Erica Varley, who was now in charge, supported her determination to go on working. She continued to interpret the rôle of Katharine of Aragon until a fortnight before the baby's birth. Her supple, well-trained body seemed instinctively to understand its powers; the necessary self-discipline of her profession had kept her physically much younger than most women of her age. Punctual to the predicted moment of his arrival, her son was born without difficulty at midday on November 15th.

They called him Adrian, and adapted their lives to his assertive but seldom exacting presence. In Newcastle Sylvia's mother, whose ideas of child-rearing belonged to the nineteenth century, found an old-fashioned nannie well-supplied with exemplary references, and Sylvia, in spite of some mild misgivings about the elderly woman's seniority to herself, thankfully accepted the convenient arrangement. Three weeks after Adrian's birth, Nannie Higginbotham was established at the small house in Battersea. There she and Mrs. Moneypenny took entire physical charge of the child, with occasional help from Robert. Though he knew that his impending prefer-ment would not now be long delayed, and was working harder than ever in order to leave no loose ends for his successor to tie, he spent every moment that he could spare in his son's company.

" 'E's got the patience of an angel with that there baby," Mrs. Moneypenny declared to her friend Mrs. Slaughter of the Golden Dragon. " There's nothin' 'e won't do for the little chap, from changin' 'is nappies to pushin' 'im round the Park of a Saturday."

But Sylvia, who played with Adrian every evening before going to the theatre, saw only the more aesthetic aspects of infancy. As the boy left babyhood and became a lively but self-contained toddler, she realised that he was her own son, made in her physical image. She could imagine him Lawrence's child, or Robert's, just as her fancy chose.

He was nearly eighteen months old when, in April, 1927, Robert was appointed to the important living of St. Saviour's, Armada Square.

CHAPTER IV

Servant of Christ

THE living of St. Saviour's was important because
Robert's appointment represented a minor revolution in
the ecclesiastical administration of London.

Situated in the middle of the West End theatre district,
the large draughty Church with its heterogeneous and
transitory congregations would not have represented an
easy proposition if it had been administered by a succession of archangels. But this had not been its good fortune.
Because of its position in London's pleasure centre and its
difficulty in attracting worshippers against such formidable competition, it had been treated as a City living, and
run by a non-resident Vicar assisted by a curate. Now
the Bishop of London had decided to transform it into
a parish church, in the hope of creating a permanent
religious influence to check the traffic in human flesh
and blood which nightly eddied round the popular
theatres and fashionable restaurants in the neighbourhood.

For some time he had been looking for a man with a
sense of vocation strong enough to overcome the obstacles
which kept St. Saviour's half empty, and preaching gifts
sufficiently outstanding to compete with the surrounding theatres and cinemas. The choice of incumbent
could not be made in a hurry, for nothing less than an
ideal selection would transform the negative character
of the place into a source of spiritual life. More than a
year before the birth of Adrian, the Bishop of Battersea
had first put forward Robert's claims to the appointment.
His senior already knew of Robert's gifts as a preacher,
and admitted that his Victoria Cross, though it no longer
possessed the publicity-value of the immediate post-war

period, would be an asset in attracting a congregation. But he watched Robert's work at All Souls for two and a half years before finally deciding to offer him the living.

The choice was even more inspired than it appeared at the time of its making. St. Saviour's was to prove Robert Carbury not only an exceptional priest in the unconventional tradition of Conrad Noel and Studdert Kennedy, but an outstanding administrator whose ideas and resourcefulness never failed. The greater the difficulties which faced him, the more rapidly his mind was to work on schemes for overcoming them. Suggestions, plans, solutions of other men's problems, flooded through his brain like a perpetual spring tide.

It was only for his own problems, as life emphasised or created them, that he was sometimes to seem incapable of finding any solution. But the less he solved them, the more resolutely he was to forget them in the service of men whose humble exterior represented for him an image of God. The lack of confidence in his heart, the perpetual sense of unworthiness for his responsible position, caused him to strive only the more assiduously to make that divine image real to the imagination of his parishioners.

When Robert first visited St. Saviour's he reflected, half rueful and half amused, on the incongruity between his ideals for human brotherhood and the name of the Square, commemorating one of England's most famous victories, with which his new labours were to be identified. No premonition that his own name would one day be as closely associated with Armada Square as that of his lofty naval competitor, Sir Francis Drake, came to mitigate the apprehension which filled him when he pushed open the dark heavy door of the Church and began his investigations.

A lover of flowers, he noticed at once that there were none on the Altar, and determined to have a supply sent

63

regularly from Hoddershall Ash. Apart from a strong smell of beeswax round the pulpit, the Church lacked atmosphere and felt chilly. Its relatively small frontage on the Square gave no idea of the long narrow interior, flanked by the disused churchyard and tall department stores with windows facing Queen Elizabeth Street, which extended behind it. Its shape was uncomfortable, and its acoustics, he felt certain, were poor; to preach there would be like preaching in a corridor. The place seemed to have been built in the worst period of nineteenth-century architecture to fulfil some function which was no longer clear, but must in any case be superseded. It possessed no distinguishing feature except for the great bell in the tower, which was rung twice every twenty-four hours to proclaim midday and midnight to West End London.

When Robert mounted the steps of the pulpit, he discovered that it was even loftier than the pulpit at All Souls, and exceptionally shallow. Unlike his present church, the elongated building on which he looked down possessed no gallery, and he felt himself already sighing with nostalgia for the galleries crowded with enthusiastic parishioners which so cosily surrounded him when he preached in Battersea.

" One would need to be a very High Churchman to get used to this ! " he reflected lugubriously. " I shall be almost as isolated from the congregation as Drake on his pedestal. And a too-enthusiastic gesticulation might easily topple me over that narrow ledge on to the heads of the people below — assuming there *are* any people. . . ."

Yet it was when he looked desolately from this elevated perch through the open door into Armada Square that St. Saviour's first seemed to him to have some possibility of a message and a mission. He had come there on a

Saturday afternoon, and in the Square a small crow was gathering round the organisers of an open-air meeting who were setting up their portable rostrums between two of the carved stone galleons. Surely, thought Robert, a church standing right beside that metropolitan forum should be able to exercise some influence, whatever its practical infelicities.

At the doorway he picked up a copy of *St. Saviour's Quarterly Magazine*, and sat down on a seat in the farthest corner of the Square to read it. Quarterly! he pondered. How can one keep in touch with one's congregation by writing to it once a quarter? And if the magazine comes out so seldom, surely they might have produced something better than this uninviting little rag! He glanced through the flimsy pages, to find only the conventional material circulated by the normal agencies, which touched bottom in the short story of the church-resistant stenographer who Made Good.

"No wonder all the typists avoid this place!" he concluded. "At least, I assume they do. They wouldn't be girls if they didn't. . . . We'll turn the rag into *St. Saviour's Monthly*, and make it a real magazine! That, at least, gives me a job to start on!"

The following week-end, he persuaded Sylvia to come out with him after the theatre and explore his prospective parish at night.

"Remember the time we walked round Battersea?" he said, shyly uncertain, as he took her arm, how far she would welcome an emotional memory. "Somehow, one gets the *feel* of a place better after dark — though in this part of the town it's apt to become a bit too tangible!"

After an hour's intermittent exploration they spent the small hours, not in the Church, but in the casualty ward of Queen Elizabeth's Hospital, where a case of attempted suicide and two " drunks " were brought in as they waited. Then followed an early breakfast at an all-night shelter, the Wayfarer's Club, run by an unattached group of socially-minded young men for the derelicts of London's hidden life. When they came out of the basement canteen, the spring dawn was creeping over the Square. Long before the sun rose above the tall roofs of the City offices, a shaft of hidden light smote the silver weather-vane on the top of the tower. Looking at the Church in that uncertain hour between night and day, Sylvia felt that St. Saviour's, in spite of its unpropitious qualities, had an aweful and mysterious life of its own which compelled her, quite apart from Robert, to accept its challenge. To this ugly, neglected church, the spiritual implications of her own art — however apparently remote from the more normal duties of a parson's wife — had something special to contribute.

She realised that those normal duties could not be avoided with the comfortable detachment of the past seven years when they entered the Vicarage, where the resident curate, now departing to a country parish, had camped in two rooms. The big inconvenient house appeared to have been designed by a Victorian architect with an overmastering passion for carved wooden screens, and its dark, oak-panelled walls looked ominously resistant to any attempt at home-making. Like the Church the Vicarage was narrow, but it was also tall; two rooms on each of the five floors stretched backwards from the Square, divided by a polished wooden staircase with heavily carved oak balustrades.

" This is the first thing I've seen here that really frightens me," commented Sylvia, gazing from the un-carpeted hall to the upper gloom of the attics.

Robert agreed. " It is rather a sarcophagus, isn't it?

I don't wonder it scares you!"

"I shall never manage to run it, Robert. I wasn't cut out for a parson's wife, and it's rather late to begin. Now that Adrian's really walking, it'll be a full-time job to stop him falling down those stairs."

"Never mind, darling! You can just pretend to run it for a few weeks, as a gesture to the parish. After that — well," he laughed reassuringly, "there are already some dear, good, conscientious, fearfully domesticated women in the offing, and I suggest we just give them their head!"

One such woman, he surmised, would be Augusta Martelhammer, wife of the Bellsley contemporary to whom he had offered the senior curacy at St. Saviour's. Theodore Martelhammer, a small stocky man with more imagination than his appearance suggested and an unlimited capacity for hard work, had spent the past five years as assistant priest at St. Michael's, Melbourne. Recently returning to England, he had brought with him a robust Australian wife whose physical vigour and domestic capabilities intimidated both Robert and Sylvia. Now, as Robert locked the Vicarage door and for the first time carried away the duplicate key, they tacitly agreed that the militant domesticity of Mrs. Martelhammer might here find unexpected scope.

*

In June, 1927, when Robert Carbury, three months before his thirty-sixth birthday, was instituted by the Bishop of London into the living of St. Saviour's, Armada Square, exactly thirteen people attended the ceremony. He often wondered afterwards whether this inauspicious number was unlucky or otherwise. But his Battersea reputation had gone before him into the more permanent working sections of his future parish, and at his first

Sunday morning service he had a fair congregation.

Preaching from the high, shallow pulpit, he forgot his initial sense of being St. Simeon Stylites ascending his pillar as soon as he began to tell them that they were only the vanguard of the multitude he meant to bring there. St. Saviour's, he said, must become the home of all kinds of men and women who were prepared to try a church as their stand-by in the pains and problems of mortal life even if the idea had never occurred to them before. He hoped that those who had joined the flotsam and jetsam of humanity, often through no fault of their own, would regard St. Saviour's as especially theirs. Its name was symbolic; like Christ Himself the Church was ready to become their saviour if they would only trust in it. It would be their refuge from the buffetings of fate, never closed and always lighted. But he couldn't do this job alone. If it was to succeed, it must also be the combined effort of all his parishioners.

" Won't you help me," he pleaded, " to set up a new Temple of Jesus in the centre of London, which for so many millions is the centre of the universe? There is not one of you, however obscure — or however rich and busy, or careful and troubled about many things — who cannot contribute something to the life of this Church. Your Saviour and mine will not refuse the humblest gift of service from those that love Him!"

There was a palpable silence when he had finished. Not one member of his congregation could doubt that a new spirit had come to St. Saviour's. It was a spirit that, during an important period of London's history, was to endow the dry bones of Anglicanism with colourful life.

Robert understood the wisdom of gradual innovation, and was surprised, at the end of his first year in Armada Square, to find how much he had actually accomplished.

Immediately after his institution he established a daily Eucharist, at which the first half-dozen shy communicants grew in a few months to scores who filled the body of the Church. He persuaded the group of unattached young men who ran their shelter for the down-and-outs to organise a second canteen in the ever-open Crypt, which soon became the scene of committee-meetings, whist-drives, and informal dances. Within a fortnight he had turned the uninviting magazine into *St. Saviour's Monthly*, with an etching of the Church on its gay vermilion cover, and had invited an Oxford contemporary, Morgan Penrose, who was now a leader-writer on the *Evening Globe*, to become its editor.

The Youth Club that he started soon led to the revival of his own half-forgotten qualifications. He discovered that one of the members, a sixteen-year-old assistant in a publisher's packing-room who was trying to matriculate during his evening hours and become a clerk in the firm, had been forlornly seeking for someone to give him extra coaching in his weak subject, mathematics. Robert's offer to teach him twice a week inspired further requests, and soon he had a permanent mathematics class of twenty or thirty boys and girls in the Crypt. Once a week Sylvia herself appeared there, to coach the members of the newly-formed St. Saviour's Dramatic Society in stagecraft and elocution. In 1928 the Society put on a midsummer pageant in the ancient churchyard, and the following Christmas played A. M. Buckton's mystery play, *Eager Heart*. The performance, which ran for a week, drew crowds to the Church from all over London, though Sylvia's vivid interpretation of the voluptuous rôle of Eager Sense caused some talk among those parishioners who knew that she was expecting her second child.

Robert's most difficult achievement, and one that took him much more than a year, was the gradual replacement of ageing churchwardens who perceived in their office only its socially respectable status, and of church officials who resented this incursion of popular and youthful vitality into their once comfortable, unexacting vegetation. But Robert's Youth Club turned into a kind of spiritual bodyguard, cheerfully and perpetually in league against his elderly foes. When St. Saviour's evening service was broadcast for the first time in January, 1929, an impudent member christened him " Broadcasting Bob ", and for the next decade he was " Bob Carbury " to the ever-growing national congregation which switched over its wireless sets to St. Saviour's every third Sunday in the month. His Church with its great summoning bell, of which the sound was always relayed before the radio service, became internationally known as an ever-open sanctuary, welcoming casual passers-by into the presence of the Master after whom it was named. From the standpoint of endowments the living was poor, but the vitality of its spirit, and the size and quality of its membership, gave a permanent impression of gaiety and splendour.

Robert had his critics, of course. No parish, least of all in the West End of London, is without its envious practitioners of calumny. There were some who said that he was nothing more than a first-class actor manager, a superb impresario who used for his ministry the gifts which his wife employed more candidly on the stage. One change in Robert certainly did occur, as it occurs to all who graduate from encouraging but uncertain progress to triumphant authority. His early success in the new parish so richly nourished his external confidence that the expedients which he devised for " advertising " his Master and his Church became rapidly more imaginative and efficient.

Inwardly, his sense of unworthiness remained unaltered; no armour developed to shield that vulnerable Achilles heel of his spirit. But if he had brought with him from Battersea any surviving awkwardness of manner, it disappeared after a few months at St. Saviour's. He had emerged from the inexperienced curate, shyly astonished by his unsuspected gift for preaching and a little bewildered by his personal popularity, into the full adult stature of priest and prophet. His capacity for recalling the details of individual problems, for recollecting faces seen only once but made memorable to him by their stark lines of suffering or perplexity, was a form of spiritual genius which caused many men and women whom he hardly knew to regard him as their intimate friend.

Even the Vicarage, that large inconvenient dwelling in which the supply of hot bath-water was never adequate and the task of finding a competent domestic staff seemed almost insuperable, gradually came to be assimilated by the Carburys in the fashion that Robert had predicted. After a few weeks of absent-minded endeavour to be a conscientious clergyman's wife, Sylvia was appropriately offered the title-rôle in a special performance of Barrie's *Mary Rose* to raise funds for Queen Elizabeth's Hospital. With Robert's enthusiastic cooperation she returned thankfully to the stage, leaving Theodore Martelhammer's domestically-minded helpmeet to organise both the Vicarage and the " women's side " of the parish.

Augusta Martelhammer, who was jealous of Sylvia's reputation and elegance to a degree which sometimes shocked her own well-regulated conscience, assumed the responsibility with an air of martyrdom and a secret sense of deep satisfaction. The conspicuous Mrs. Carbury might be a popular actress and a distinguished interpreter of Shakespeare and Shelley, but she had no more idea of looking after the Vicarage than a fly. Playing Portia or Beatrice Cenci to crowded houses was not, it appeared, a qualification for appeasing the cook and reprimanding the butcher. Augusta's discovery of the devoted cook-general Maria Pickering, and her young half-sister Ethel, gave her a masochistic enjoyment which she would never have experienced had she been engaging a staff for herself.

But the parishioners, with a few disgruntled exceptions, preferred their Vicar's ministry to be adorned by his marriage to a celebrated actress, rather than reinforced by the unobtrusive cooperation of a conscientious but glamourless housewife. Sylvia was now appearing as Mrs. George in a revival of Bernard Shaw's *Getting Married*, and the makers of gleeful underground comparisons between her and the virtuous Augusta ruthlessly applied to the curate's wife the words used in the play of his absent spouse by Mr. Collins, the philosophical greengrocer : " You see, she's such an out-and-out wife and mother that she's hardly a responsible human being out of her house, except when she's marketing."

By the time that Josephine was born, giving an eagerly accepted opportunity to Mrs. George's understudy, Sylvia had shaken off the Vicarage with the same unobtrusive, graceful determination as she had displayed in passing over to others the care of her small house in Battersea.

*

At Matins on the Sunday which followed Josephine's birth, Robert Carbury added a new clause to St. Saviour's Litany. He had written this Litany himself, and sometimes, by special request, it was used at his broadcast services. Now, standing before the Altar with its two silver vases which Mrs. Elias, the Verger's wife, had filled with white rosebuds in honour of the newly-born child, he prayed on behalf of the disappointed and despondent millions of mankind.

" For all who are lonely and sick at heart; for the frustrated who desired experience and have been deprived of it; for the desolate who long to give and receive love, but are repudiated by their fellows; for the childless who hoped to share in the pain and dignity of birth, but are denied the fulfilment of parenthood; for all who suffer from a sense of inferiority, and believe themselves despised and rejected of men—"

" We beseech Thee to hear us, Good Lord," murmured the congregation, even more moved than usual to responsive participation in their Vicar's mystical relationship with the Giver of all life.

As he uttered his prayer, Robert had felt deeply stirred by compassion for the unsatisfied men and women whose dearest human wishes had not been granted. Again and again, especially at the sun's going down and its uprising, he counted the gifts that the years had brought him, and strove to enter with full awareness into the good fortune for which others envied him. To his initial advantages of relative wealth, a good appearance, sound health, and a fine intelligence, had been added several conspicuous achievements such as many men dreamed of romantically, but only the few attained. There was his First in Mathematics, his Running Blue, his incongruous but indubitable Victoria Cross, his incredible popularity as priest and preacher. And, as if this were not enough, life had given him in Sylvia the dearest mortal object of his worship; and now, in answer to that uplifting of body and spirit which for him was prayer, the son and daughter for whom he had longed ever since he became aware of his first adult impulses towards love and fatherhood.

It could only be some weakness, some flaw in himself, which left him without fundamental confidence, and gave him the sense that he had somehow missed his apparent rewards. Bitterly he chided himself for that basic ingratitude towards the generous Providence which had bestowed so much upon him. How could he have imagined that, in the concluding words of his new inter-cession, he had really been pleading for himself?

As the swift, over-burdened months hurried by, he had further reason for thankfulness in the beauty, health, and intelligence of his children. Before Josephine was three years old, her irrepressible gay vitality had brought into the dark Vicarage the liveliness of a perpetually chirruping canary. She danced, singing, up and down the steep staircases, pirouetting across the landings on strong, shapely little feet which already promised that Sylvia's hope for a successor in drama or ballet was likely to be fulfilled.

Adrian, as soon as he had passed through the ques-tioning period of babyhood, grew into a quieter, more self-contained child, always absorbed in fairy-tales, or gazing, entranced, at the night patterns of the sky. The attractive and remarkable appearance conferred upon him by his red-gold hair, fine delicate features and reticent blue-grey eyes, brought him a degree of attention from Robert's parishioners which he did not seem to appreciate, and avoided whenever he could.

Occasionally he revealed, to a degree which Robert found disquieting, that capacity for suffering, inherited from both his parents, of which his father was still all too conscious. An episode that centred round a broken tea-pot was to haunt Robert's memory for several years.

One late winter evening he came home from a Con-firmation Class to find the two children, on Nannie's half day, playing alone in the nursery. Adrian, then aged six, resembled an idealised advertisement of a perfectly reared child as he lay on the hearth-rug draw-ing moons, stars, and long-tailed comets. Three-year-old Josephine, in a pink Viyella frock, was building bricks beside him. Her hazel eyes and dark-brown curls might have been deliberately designed as a foil to his colouring.

Robert, looking round, saw the black-and-white Wedgwood tea-pot given to him as a wedding present by his old Vicar at Battersea standing dangerously near the edge of the toy-cupboard; Ethel had left it behind when she removed the nursery tea. Why, he wondered, was Ethel, and for that matter Maria too, completely unable to discriminate between one tea-pot and another? She was just as likely to put the old brown nursery pot with the cracked spout on the tray the next time he entertained the Bishop.

" What are you looking at, Daddy? " queried Adrian.

" Only at the Wedgwood tea-pot. Ethel seems to have forgotten to take it away."

Adrian sprang to his feet and ran to the cupboard.

" I'll take it down to the kitchen, Daddy! Do let me! "

" Sure you can manage it, old man? "

" Yes, of course. I often carry things down for M'ria."

Robert took the tea-pot from the top of the cupboard and put it firmly into Adrian's hands.

" Be careful how you hold it, son. It's rather valuable."

Five minutes later he was building castles on the floor with Josephine when the door opened slowly and a small woebegone figure came in. There were streaky traces of tears on Adrian's face, and he looked terrified.

" Why, laddie! " exclaimed Robert, standing up. " Whatever's the matter? "

Conquering his fear with an obvious effort, Adrian limped across the nursery to his father. His right knee was cut and bruised, but that was not the source of his trouble. Without a word he put his hand in his pocket, and pulled out the spout of the Wedgwood tea-pot. Then

75

he stood rigid, wincing visibly in anticipation of the expected blow.

Robert looked at him in distressed astonishment.

" He actually thinks I'm going to hit him ! " he thought. " He's thoroughly scared, but he means to stick it if he can. . . ." The pathetic helplessness of childhood became suddenly real to him. A mist dimmed his eyes, and he found his voice difficult to control.

" Look here, old man . . . there's nothing to be frightened of ! I don't suppose you meant to break it, did you ? How did it happen ? "

Incredulous relief broke like daylight over Adrian's face, though his lip still quivered. Swallowing his tears, he found his voice.

" I don't know zackly what happened, but I fell down the bottom of the kitchen stairs. . . . It dropped out of my hand, and I found it all b-b-broken on the floor." His voice trembled again as he inquired anxiously : " Daddy, was it *very* vallable . . . ? Was it worth hundreds and hundreds of pounds ? "

Robert laughed, thankful to be able to reassure him.

" No, lad, of course not ! It was a good tea-pot, but it wasn't worth all that much. A matter of a fiver, perhaps."

Adrian's face had cleared now. It was even a little reproachful.

" Why, Daddy, when you said it was vallable, I thought. . . . You see, M'ria said I'd have to pay for it, and I didn't see how I could. . . . I've only got two sixpences and a freppenny bit in my money-box, what I saved from my Saturday penny. . . . I was saving it for Mummy's Christmas present. . . ."

" My darling boy," said Robert decisively, " I wouldn't take your money if the tea-pot was worth ten times as much. You ought to have been more careful going

76

down the kitchen stairs, but you didn't mean to break it
— or hurt your knee — did you ? "

" No-o. I didn't *mean* to . . ."

" Well, that's the only thing that matters. Give me
the spout, and don't think any more about it."

But as he was undressing that night, when Adrian
was asleep in the day nursery and Josephine had been
tucked up in the night nursery with two Dismal Desmonds
and a fluffy rabbit, Robert meditated remorsefully over
the broken tea-pot and Adrian's agitation.

" He thought I was going to beat him . . . my little
son whom I waited so long for . . . and wouldn't lift a
finger against, whatever he did ! Why did he think that ?
No one's ever whipped him, so far as I know. Have I
passed on to him my own cursed streak of apprehension ?
Or is this fear of grown-up authority a heritage of the
human race . . . some kind of father-phobia, too deep
for rational analysis ? Poor little lad — how pathetic
he looked, standing there with the broken spout in his
hand, waiting for me to do my worst ! And what a
damned fool I was to give him the idea the tea-pot was
so valuable ! If I hadn't made him nervous, he'd
probably never have slipped on the stairs."

To Sylvia, who had heard the incident from him at
supper, he said aloud : " I wonder why Adrian expected
me to punish him this afternoon. I'm not in the habit
of punishing adults, let alone small children. I've never
smacked him. Why did he think I would, this time ? "

Sylvia sat down on the bed in her pale-blue wadded
dressing-gown, and began to brush her hair. Although
she was now thirty-seven, it still looked as bright to
Robert as it had been in her twenties.

" He feels things too much," she said. " He always
has. He never takes life easily like Jo does."

Robert looked at her ruefully.

77

" I'm afraid he's got that from both sides, hasn't he ? "

" Perhaps." He could not understand the sad little
smile that twisted her lips, nor infer the thought that
caused it : " From you, certainly — but did he really
get it from me ? Why do I never feel that anything
matters, even the children ? Oh God, if only I were
still alive, instead of half dead ! "

She plaited her hair and coiled it round her head
before she spoke again.

" Sometimes I think Nannie's getting too old for such
young children. She leaves Adrian alone too much."

" He seems to prefer playing by himself. Perhaps
it's time he saw more boys of his own age. Don't you
think he ought to start going to school ? "

" I daresay he ought. The years go so fast when you're
as busy as we are, you forget the children are growing
older all the time. I'll ask Augusta to find out whether
there's a good school anywhere near for boys of his age."

So in January, 1932, thanks to a tea-pot, Adrian
Carbury graduated from the nursery, and became a
pupil at Mrs. Prendergast's Kindergarten for Boys and
Girls in Dover Street, off Piccadilly. At that time the
Disarmament Conference was about to begin its abortive
labours, and a National Government, swept into power
by a panic-stricken public afraid for its savings, had
replaced the Labour Government which Adrian had seen
in process of election in 1929.

But even to a politically and socially conscious West
End clergyman, there still seemed to be no reason why
his son's career, less buffeted by fate than his own,
should not follow its predestined course through school
and college to some chosen vocation in which he would
dedicate his life and possessions to the redemption of
England and the service of God.

CHAPTER V

The B.O.J.

As the nineteen-thirties plunged fatally onwards through national complacency towards international chaos, the redemption of England, and of Europe, came to appear to Robert as the most urgent and practical aspect of the service of Christ. Yet the more heavily this major obligation weighed upon his conscience, the less time to think about it he seemed able to command.

" My mission here at St. Saviour's is a contribution, but it isn't enough," he would meditate in his troubled questioning. " It may be a national leaven, but it has no international authority. . . . I ought to *do* something, start something new."

But what ? The opportunity for the quiet concentrated thought from which inspiration emerges seemed always to be lacking. As his life became ever more crowded by people and activities, he found himself longing, not for loneliness of which he was still always conscious, but for the prolonged solitude in which alone the richest fruits of the spirit can be gathered. Often he envied Sylvia her privacy off the stage, and the regularity with which the times when she belonged to the public fell neatly within the confines of three acts and two and a half hours. His own work, like a housewife's, was never finished ; the life at St. Saviour's might be a Christian turmoil, but it was a turmoil none the less. Yet, with his belief in the individual human soul and its needs as the first priority, what else could he expect ?

" Why is it," he inquired wearily of Anselm Ensor, now promoted from Battersea to be Bishop of Southwest London, " that the more desperately one's spirit

needs refreshment, the less accessible the Fountain of
Life seems to become? I don't even get time nowadays
to prepare my sermons properly, let alone read the books
and newspapers I ought to be reading."

Anselm felt more concerned by Robert's appearance
than he allowed himself to express. The Vicar of St.
Saviour's looked unusually pale and tired, he thought;
the old limp was more pronounced, and his perpetual
crescendo of popularity seemed to be a burden rather
than a stimulus in his search after some new cure for
society's now evident sickness.

" I always told you," he said, " that when preferment
did come, it would be a challenge to all your powers.
You don't regret that challenge, do you, Robert ? "

" Of course not. One doesn't regret the superb
opportunities that all men long for. What I lack is the
serenity which will show me how I can best take advantage of them."

" Seek enlightenment in prayer," advised the Bishop.
" You always had a gift for praying, my friend. I have
honestly never met any man who was able to get more
quickly into communication with the Source of our being.
Try to spend more time with Him, Robert, even if it
means cutting down your sleep."

In after years, when Adrian looked back upon his
childhood at the Vicarage, he associated his first realisation of Europe's bogey-man, Adolf Hitler, with the
morning that he and Josephine found their father praying
alone, long before breakfast, in front of St. Saviour's
altar. They were up very early because it was Saturday,
and Nannie had promised to take them to Wimbledon
Common. Believing the church to be empty, they had
slipped in to look for a penny which Josephine thought
she had dropped there last Sunday.

Hearing the children scuffling uncertainly behind

him, Robert rose from his knees, helped them to retrieve the lost penny, and, hand in hand with each, took them back to the Vicarage. But his expression of anxiety was so deep that even seven-year-old Adrian noticed it.

" What's the matter, Daddy ? " he inquired, feeling puzzled and a little frightened. " Why were you in church so early, all by yourself ? "

" I was praying to God for a miracle, my son."

" What sort of miracle ? "

" I asked Him to change Herr Hitler's heart."

" And will He ? "

" Perhaps. We must watch and wait." He sighed. " God doesn't always work through miracles. More often His plan is based on the law of cause and effect."

" What's that, Daddy ? "

" Something we all learn about, sooner or later. It means that everything we do has its consequences, whether we like them or not."

Though his turmoil might be exhausting, Robert never wearied of the children. He always found time to answer their questions, tell them stories, take them out for special treats whenever he could arrange to escape for a few hours from the parish. Another of Adrian's early memories was a visit to Oxford, where his father had taken him and Josephine to see their mother play the part of Etain in an open-air performance of Rutland Boughton's fantasy, *The Immortal Hour*, at an Oxford Festival. Long afterwards he still connected his first sight of the grey spires and green quadrangles with the haunting lilt of Etain's song, sung in Sylvia's light, sweet voice :

" How beautiful they are, the lordly nes,
Who dwell in the hills, in the hollow hills . . ."

It was that play, thought Adrian, which first caused

him to look upon his mother as a person, instead of a
convenient human institution. He was not aware that,
in the eyes of the dramatic critics, her rôle in *The Immortal
Hour* was better suited to Sylvia Salvesen's indefinable
genius than any part she had played in recent years.
He only knew that her interpretation of the ageless
elusive sprite in the filmy blue-green robe made him
suddenly conscious of the absent-minded reserve which
was his mother's predominating quality, as though half
her life were lived in some other-worldly atmosphere
which was more real to her than the intrusive present.
When he was old enough to estimate Sylvia from the
standpoint of adulthood, he still vaguely remembered his
conversation with Josephine going home in the train.

" I liked that play," he said, looking ruminatively out
of the carriage window at Berkshire's summer fields.

" So did I. 'Specially the music."

" Didn't Mummy look lovely in that green dress ? "

" Mummy always looks lovely."

" I know. But that dress was just sort of right for her.
It was right with her hair. You know, Jo, she's sort of
queer. Rather like a fairy — one of the lordly ones. . . ."

" Don't be silly. Ladies can't be lordly."

" Yes, they can, in a way. You can be lordly if you're
a king or a queen. Mummy's like the queen of a kingdom
that isn't quite here."

" ' My Kingdom is not of this world '," meditated
Robert, silently listening. Was that why, for all the
years of unfailing love that he had given her, Sylvia
remained permanently uncaptured, never quite his in
body, mind or spirit ? Was her Immortal Hour awaiting
her elsewhere, to be shared throughout eternity with
someone he had never known ?

*

By the parish, Robert's children were regarded as a credit to him. They were very popular, though before they reached the age when they could be trusted to behave appropriately in all circumstances, they had been guilty of one or two awful lapses. There was, for instance, the autumn Saturday afternoon when, after helping all morning with pious enthusiasm to put up the harvest thanksgiving decorations, they were discovered at tea-time in one of the two largest family pews playing football with the big vegetable marrow from the base of the font. But worse still was the occasion when, shortly before Adrian's ninth birthday, elderly Mrs. Collingham, the old-fashioned mother of the People's Warden, invited them both to tea.

Robert had been too busy that Saturday with the first rehearsal of St. Saviour's Christmas Mystery Play to notice the children intermittently whispering together, or to observe that Adrian was teaching Josephine to repeat a rhyme. As soon as she knew the words she bounced up and down the nursery, singing them to a tune of her own invention. Nobody watched or listened to her, for the children, theoretically shared between Sylvia, Maria, and Augusta Martelhammer, were enjoying an interval of unaccustomed freedom from supervision. Their parents, having at last persuaded Nannie Higginbotham to retire, were awaiting the arrival from Lausanne of the Swiss governess who was to teach Josephine French and German. The two children wept copious tears when Nannie sadly departed for Newcastle. An hour later, they had forgotten her as completely as though she had never existed.

Old Mrs. Collingham's values, like her drawing-room, were rigid and Victorian. Her mind, crowded with prejudices and traditions, held as little room for challenging surprises as her over-filled china cabinet for a modern

Toby-jug. When tea could be no further prolonged because Adrian and Josephine had avidly consumed everything that she had provided, an awkward interval stretched before six o'clock, the hour at which the rehearsal ended and Robert had promised to fetch them. For ten minutes they looked unenthusiastically at ancient photograph albums while Mrs. Collingham thought censoriously of their mother, who was playing Hilda Wangel in an Old Vic matinée of *The Master Builder* instead of being present to lighten her obligations. Then Josephine began to fidget, and Adrian, peering at the bored old lady through his long golden-brown lashes, divined her reflections with cynical perspicacity. " Oh, Mr. Carbury," he murmured under his breath, " why don't you come and take these children away ? I'm so tired of them ! "

Aloud he remarked cheerfully : " I expect Daddy'll be a bit late. He's usually late when he's got a rehearsal. I daresay he won't be here till half-past six."

" Well," said Mrs. Collingham resignedly, " is there any game you'd like to play till he comes ? "

Adrian looked round the room. Crowded with bric-à-brac and heavy furniture, it resembled the show-room of a provincial antiques-shop. He continued helpfully : " I don't think we can play any of our games in here. . . . But Jo can dance. She's going on the stage when she grows up, like Mummy."

Mrs. Collingham refrained, with difficulty, from giving them her opinion of this intention.

" Can she recite any nursery rhymes ? " she inquired.

" No," Adrian responded mildly. " She never remembers nursery rhymes. But she can sing. She sings beautifully."

" Yes, I can ! " piped Josephine, eagerly jumping out of her chair. " I know a lovely song about monkeys."

Mrs. Collingham glanced at the clock. To her relief, it said five minutes to six. She hoped Mr. Carbury would be punctual.

"Very well, my dear. You've just got time to sing it to me before your father comes."

Josephine tripped into the middle of the over-furnished room. In her scarlet plaid frock she looked like a spring anemone blooming amid the dusty shadows of a junk store. Unconsciously striking an attitude as though some invisible future audience were watching her, she began to sing in her innocent childish treble:

> "In eighteen-eighty-four
> The monkeys went to war.
> They had no drums,
> So they beat their bums,
> In eighteen-eighty-four . . ."

But the sudden awful silence which smote the room penetrated even her histrionic absorption. The frozen countenance of Mrs. Collingham seemed to loom larger and larger, like the nightmare face of an angry giantess, when to her bewildered but intense relief the door opened and her father came in.

"I hope I'm not late," he began, but Mrs. Collingham silenced him with an affronted gesture.

"It's a pity you weren't here five minutes ago, Mr. Carbury. Josephine has just *entertained* me by a most disgusting song which no little girl ought to know — let alone sing in a drawing-room!"

Robert, as much puzzled as Josephine, looked from one child to the other. Adrian, with an air of complete detachment, was gazing at the ceiling. Josephine, crimson and crestfallen, appeared to be on the verge of tears.

"I'm sorry, Mrs. Collingham," he said. "I must find

out what they've been up to."

" I should hope so, Mr. Carbury. Such behaviour would be reprehensible in a common little street urchin. In the Vicar's children, who ought to set an example, it's absolutely unpardonable."

Robert spoke with determined equanimity.

" I'm afraid Adrian and Josephine are still too young to be examples to anyone. . . . What you mean, of course, is that *I* ought to set an example. That's a proposition I fully agree with. I must try to be a better one."

" It isn't your fault, Mr. Carbury. I blame their mother. They ought to see more of her — and so ought the parish."

Robert's voice became still quieter.

" The parish isn't my wife's job," he said. " She has a job of her own. I wouldn't want to interfere with hers, and I should just hate her to get mixed up in mine." He turned to the children. " Now, you two, where are your coats? Hurry up and find Jo's for her, Adrian; it's past her bedtime."

When he had said goodbye to Mrs. Collingham after briefly apologising for Josephine's mysterious behaviour, the three of them walked silently homewards along the broad length of Queen Elizabeth Street, its road-surface reflecting the neon lights which eclipsed the November stars. Robert, who was holding Josephine's hand, felt it suddenly quiver, and realised that she was sobbing quietly in the darkness.

" Cheer up, Jo," he said gently. " I don't suppose you were as bad as all that, were you? "

" I d-don't understand, Daddy. I wasn't naughty! Why was she so cross about my song? "

" What was your song about, my dear? "

" It was a lovely song about n₁·monkeys."

" And where did you learn it ? "

Josephine was silent for a moment, vaguely conscious that more trouble was waiting to jump from the next corner. At last she confessed reluctantly: "Ady taught it to me."

" Oh, he did, did he? Where did *you* come across it, my son? "

" At school, Daddy," said Adrian with engaging candour. " Barker Major told it to me and Gregory."

" All right. When we get home, I want you to repeat it."

At the Vicarage Josephine, now tired and sleepy, was carried off to bed by Maria while Adrian went with Robert into the dining-room and unwillingly recited the offending lines. As Robert listened, the picture of Mrs. Collingham's affronted face rose disconcertingly before him. Suppressing by sheer self-discipline all evidences of unseemly mirth, he gazed at Adrian with exaggerated solemnity, not trusting himself to speak. Defiantly Adrian returned the gaze, ill at ease but unintimidated. He's not frightened of me any more, thought Robert, remembering the tea-pot. In three years he has grown from a baby into a boy.

" Look here," he said at last, " you're going to be nine the week after next. Isn't it time you cultivated a little discretion? "

" What's that? "

" It's knowing when to do things, and when not to.

" I think I do know that, really," admitted Adrian with reluctant honesty.

" I think you do, too. You certainly knew that wasn't a drawing-room song, didn't you? "

" Yes, Daddy."

" And don't you think it was a bit mean of you to teach Jo something that would get her into trouble? "

" I suppose it was."

" All right. I'm not going to punish you. But to-morrow morning, first thing, you can take on the job of explaining to Jo just why she mustn't sing that song again."

*

Five days after Mrs. Collingham's tea-party, Robert went over to Battersea to conduct the funeral of Dr. Erica Varley, who had superintended the birth of his son. From the tragedy of her early death came the inspiration which he had been seeking for some new initiative in the life of England, some move to check the downward spiral of international amity.

First as an assistant, and later in her own surgery, young Dr. Varley had become one of the best-loved medical practitioners that South-west London had known. Her refusal to spare herself was partly responsible for her death. Returning at midnight on her bicycle from a difficult maternity case, she had collided with a lorry in the dark high road and never recovered consciousness.

At the inquest the lorry driver, a local man named Ted Rogers, had been exonerated. The husband of Dr. Varley's patient testified that the birth of his daughter was prolonged and exhausting. The doctor had been tired out when she left his house, and the spot where the accident occurred indicated that, probably half asleep, she was riding on the wrong side of the road.

Robert remembered Ted Rogers as a decent lad who had belonged to the Battersea Boys' Brigade, which he used to accompany for summer picnics on the Surrey Downs. As he conducted the Burial Service in the familiar church before the crowded mourners, he noticed Rogers, pale and distressed, sitting alone in a side aisle beneath the gallery. The lorry driver carried a huge

wreath of scarlet hothouse carnations which must, thought
Robert, have absorbed his savings for half a year.
Throughout the singing of *Jerusalem*, with which Dr.
Varley's relatives had asked Robert to conclude the
service, he noticed that Rogers remained on his knees
with his face hidden.

The following night, when Robert was composing his
Sunday morning sermon, the Verger, Alfred Elias, came
to his top-floor study. He had converted one of the
attics for this purpose in order to do his more concentrated
work as far as possible from the hubbub of activities
below, and though he was officially always accessible,
Elias refrained from disturbing him on sermon nights
unless the business was genuinely urgent. So when
Robert looked up from his desk and inquired, " Well,
Alfred, what's the trouble ? " it was because he knew
that some problem had arisen with which the Verger
felt unable to contend.

Elias explained that a man who had been in the
Church all afternoon and evening was asking to see the
Vicar.

" Sometimes he was sitting, Sir, and sometimes
kneeling, but he never went away. He hasn't had a bite
for hours. . . . Now he says he's killed somebody, and
he wants to see you before he goes."

" You'd better send him up, Alfred," said Robert
gravely. But his fear that he was about to receive an
embarrassing confession of homicide vanished when he
saw Ted Rogers. He made the white-faced lorry-driver
sit down and drink a cup of the strong coffee which he
always kept beside him on sermon nights, before asking
him to unburden his trouble.

" It's about Dr. Varley, isn't it, Ted ? "

" Yes, Sir. She were that good to me poor mother.
. . . Mr. Carbury, Sir, I feel like a murderer ! What

can I ever do, to make amends, like? "

Robert knelt down on the hearth-rug and added some coal to the fire. Still kneeling, he spoke very quietly.

" We never can make amends to the dead. That's one of life's great tragedies . . . because so often we don't realise what they meant to us till they're gone beyond recall. The only thing we can do then is to carry on the work they were doing as best we can — to live as they wished to live in their inspired moments."

He rose from his knees, and crossed the room. " I'm going to show you something, Ted — something I've never shown to a soul but my wife and one or two intimate friends." He opened the cupboard, and came back with a German steel helmet. Handing it to the lorry-driver, he sat down and said : " I killed the man who wore that tin hat."

Ted Rogers' pale face brightened a little as he took the helmet.

" Would that be when you won the V.C., Sir? "

" Yes, Ted. I knocked out some Germans who manned a machine-gun, at the Battle of Loos. When the battle was over my sergeant went back to the wreckage of the gun, and found this helmet. I was in hospital, wounded, and he brought it to me as a souvenir when he came home on leave. . . . If ever I'm tempted to feel pride or complacency, I just take a look at it."

" But it was a grand job you did, Sir, for certain sure ! "

" Was it? They saw fit to give me the Victoria Cross, but I'm not proud of my decoration. I never was. It doesn't make me less of a murderer."

" A *murderer* — you, Sir! " Ted Rogers looked startled.

Robert took the helmet from him, and examined it for a moment in silence. Then he said : " Yes, a murderer.

I know exactly how you feel, because I'm more of a murderer than you are. You didn't mean to kill Dr. Varley, but I did mean to kill the man who wore that helmet.''

" But, Sir . . . I just don't get you. Killin' a Boche in fair fight — *that* ain't murder ! "

" Isn't it? That Boche was a human being, Ted — a man, with a mother like yours and perhaps a wife like mine. He was my brother . . . just another young man caught in a political quarrel which neither he nor I was responsible for. And I killed him. . . . Because I killed him I decided to become a priest, and work for a really Christian world where there wouldn't be any more killing or getting killed. Not in war, anyway.''

Ted Rogers meditated for a long time on this surprising information. Then he said slowly : " That was a way out for you, Sir. I'd give all I've got if there was a way out for me. But the likes of me ain't eddicated for the Church . . . and yet I've got to make amends, some'ow. You know . . . ' build Jerusalem ' — like the song said, yesterday afternoon. He knew summat about England, did the chap who wrote that song.''

" He did indeed ! He was a poet called William Blake, who lived at the beginning of the Industrial Revolution. He saw the ' satanic mills ' being put up all round him, without anyone to protect the people who worked in them. We've got a better England than his, thank God, but there's still plenty of room for improvement.''

He rose, and opened the door.

" I'm going to ask Maria to give you some supper, Ted, while I finish my sermon. I can't answer your question tonight, but I'll think about it, and pray. I'm sure there's some way that an accidental murderer like you can help an intentional murderer like me."

But when he had taken Ted Rogers downstairs to
the dining-room and returned to his study, he did not
continue his sermon. Instead he sat down in front of
the fire, with the thunderous chords of *Jerusalem* ringing
through his head. The eye of his imagination saw again
the pews of All Souls, crowded with humble burdened
women weeping for the comforting young life that they
had lost. In his ears still echoed Ted Rogers' pitiful
plea for guidance: " What can I ever do, to make
amends, like ? "

Suddenly he thought: " Why don't we start a campaign of some kind — something that the Ted Rogers
can join, in memory of the Erica Varleys? Couldn't
I invite the help of everyone in the parish who is ready
to ' build Jerusalem ' by joining a crusade against the
enemies of man — poverty, disease, injustice, oppression,
war ? It would be a stupendous programme — but each
member could be asked to contribute in whatever way
he felt most fitted for, and to concentrate on the cause
he preferred."

Robert abandoned the sermon that he had intended
to write. On Sunday morning he told his congregation
instead about the life and death of Erica Varley, and
his idea of an organisation in her memory for those who
were prepared to help him work in various practical
ways for the realisation of Blake's mystical "Jerusalem".
If anyone present felt called to this form of self-dedica-
tion, would he or she write to Robert and indicate what
kind of cooperation was possible ?

By the end of that day, Robert knew that he had the
loyal support of Theodore Martelhammer, his two Church-
wardens, and the Verger, Alfred Elias. On the telephone
he spoke to Jonathan Wiltshire, the new Vicar of All
Souls, Battersea, who had asked him to conduct Dr.

Varley's funeral, and learnt that this contemporary, an ex-chaplain, was also ready to cooperate. During the next few days his bulky post-bag doubled and trebled in size, and he was obliged to engage two extra secretaries to deal with it. The letter that impressed him most was a short manuscript note from Beatrice Trevelyan, the woman preacher who had taken his place as Warden of Alton Hall fifteen years ago.

"This, dear Robert, is a victory idea," she wrote. "But surely it's too big an idea to be confined to St. Saviour's, even with Battersea added on? In spite of its warlike reputation, you can't fight all Four Horsemen of the Apocalypse in Armada Square! Start the movement in Erica Varley's memory by all means; I'm sure she deserved a fine memorial. But it is much bigger even than she. This should be a national crusade on the largest scale you can manage. Get some of us in to help you with it! In England things are in a reactionary backwater, while on the Continent the situation is drifting from worse to worst. We haven't much time, so Go Ahead!"

After a long conversation with his editor, Morgan Penrose, Robert issued a special number of *St. Saviour's Monthly*. In it he published a leading article entitled "Build Jerusalem", inviting his readers to join him in a great campaign against poverty, privilege, and war. Thousands of copies went out to key people all over the country, and in his next broadcast sermon he repeated his invitation. The response was enormous. In a month he had the names of 100,000 people who wanted to be enrolled in his crusade.

Robert took offices for the campaign in Plymouth Hoe Avenue, a byway of once fashionable houses leading from Queen Elizabeth Street to Summerfield Market It was officially launched by the distribution, to loca

93

organisers throughout the country, of enormous posters bearing the words :

A CALL TO CHRISTIAN PEOPLE EVERYWHERE!

ALL WHO CARE FOR THE SPIRITUAL FUTURE OF THEIR COUNTRY ARE INVITED TO JOIN ROBERT CARBURY, CHRIST'S HUMBLE SERVANT, IN A NEW ENDEAVOUR TO 'BUILD JERUSALEM' AND ESTABLISH THE KINGDOM OF GOD ON EARTH

Robert called his organisation " The Builders of Jerusalem ". Before joining, each member was asked to sign, and send to the office in Plymouth Hoe Avenue, a blue card on which was printed a brief declaration :

> I repudiate hatred.
> I repudiate injustice.
> I repudiate cruelty.
> I repudiate war.

> " I will not cease from mental fight,
> Nor shall my sword sleep in my hand,
> Till we have built Jerusalem
> In England's green and pleasant land."

Before the signature-cards began to descend like a tidal wave on the B.O.J. offices, Robert appointed Cyril Benjafield, Morgan Penrose's assistant, to be Secretary of the movement. At the first informal Committee, composed of Theodore Martelhammer, Jonathan Wiltshire, Beatrice Trevelyan, Alfred Elias, the two Churchwardens, and, by special invitation, Ted Rogers from Battersea, Robert was unanimously elected Chairman. Not wishing to dominate the organisation, which was already known unofficially as " Bob Carbury's Builders ", he looked round for a President and, obeying his first impulse, wrote to Anselm Ensor.

But this time his old friend and benefactor sent a cautious reply.

"One plank in your platform", ran his letter, "is the repudiation of war. And war, you must know as clearly as I do, is no longer a sinister but improbable chimera; it is a rapidly growing and actual threat. As one who is not only a Bishop but a political realist, I have always been a believer in collective security. The fact that the League of Nations has repeatedly failed because collective security has never really been tried, strengthens rather than weakens my faith in the collective method as the only hope of peace in our time. If there were ever to be the remotest chance of the nations employing it to withstand the armed doctrine of Fascism, I could not sincerely repudiate war. My Christ is not only the high priest of love who called on His followers to pray for their enemies; He is also the uncompromising Master who threw the money-changers out of the Temple. So although I wish your organisation well, dear friend, I regret that I cannot accept your invitation."

Reminded by Beatrice Trevelyan that the B.O.J. must inevitably become not only a religious but a political movement, Robert turned from the Church to politics for his President. The position of conspicuous figure-head was eventually filled by Lord Westerly, ex-diplomat and a political rebel of the Great War, who occupied a flat overlooking the Thames in Westminster Embankment Court, on the fringe of Robert's parish. A suave and courteous bachelor, Frederick Westerly had become the urbane exponent of unpopular views in the House of Lords, where he was regarded as a Liberal Independent with a leaning towards Socialism. His spectacled brown eyes and tonsure-fringe of curly grey hair round a bald head gave him the appearance of a benevolent priest, though he was a professed agnostic who, like many other professed agnostics, had formed the habit of attending Robert's church. He was well known as the author of several scholarly works on political philosophy and even more celebrated for the now historic aphorism : " God is the first suspect in war-time ".

At the end of his or her initial month in the movement, each member was issued a royal-blue badge, bearing the initials "B.O.J." in silver letters. Quite a number formed the habit of signing themselves "John Brown, B.O.J.", or "Mary Smith, B.O.J.", thus rashly proclaiming their political and religious affiliations to cautious professional colleagues or reactionary government servants to whom all " progress " was a form of Bolshevism. Only a realistic few amongst Robert's eager and aspiring followers thought of their country as actually threatened with perils even more imminent than those suggested by the published warnings of the B.O.J. Still fewer suspected that, in the green and pleasant England which they had sworn to regenerate, they would ever be subject to the hostile vigilance of bureaucratic officials made Gestapo-minded by fear.

*

On an April afternoon in 1935, a few weeks before King George the Fifth's Silver Jubilee, Robert and his Committee organised the first big " Social " for the B.O.J. in St. Saviour's Parish Room.

Augusta Martelhammer made the arrangements with her customary combination of complacency and resentment. She could not resist a keen delight in her own efficiency, but neither could she forgive her husband for refusing preferment in order to remain in the consecrated whirlpool that eddied round Robert Carbury and St. Saviour's. With jealous disapproval she contemplated Sylvia, who had been persuaded to pour out the tea in order to make the occasion decorative as well as inspiring.

Sylvia stood gracefully behind the urn in a long jade-green dress of its own fashion, her russet hair brushed smoothly back and coiled in the nape of her neck. Wearing the usual remote little smile, she greeted each stranger with impersonal cordiality as she looked from her detached position at the heterogeneous, enthusiastic crowd, their faces shining damply in the warmth of the mild afternoon. The young girls, hatless, in their newly-pressed silks and cottons, looked fresh and attractive as they came up to her with their little albums, asking shyly : " May I have your autograph, Miss Salvesen ? " But she felt more critical about some of the others.

Beside her, equally detached, stood Lord Westerly. Wearing an elegantly-cut lounge suit and immaculate blue shirt, he was waiting to make a short speech when tea was over. Amid the noisy, talkative throng, he resembled an elderly eagle which had inadvertently strayed into a barnyard full of cocks and hens. Glancing over the large room his eye lighted with approval on Josephine, now nearly six, threading her way in and out of the guests with a plateful of cakes. Her dark curls, tied with blue ribbon, already reached her shoulders, and her strong, shapely legs were growing long and thin.

Lord Westerly was impressed by her indubitable resemblance to Robert. Beckoning her to come to him, he took a cake and remarked amiably : " I like your face better than any face here ! "

" You ought to like Ady's too," said Josephine, as Adrian, carrying sandwiches, came up behind her. She added, with explanatory pride : " He's my brother. When he's grown up he's going to be a 'stronomer."

" Indeed ? Well, in that case his face isn't so important, is it ? And are you going to help him ? "

97

" No. At least, not always. I want to act, like Mummy."

" She sings very well," said Adrian, not to be outdone in family advertisement.

" I'm sure she does." Lord Westerly turned to Sylvia. " It must be satisfactory to have such a determined successor. But it's the boy who favours you, Mrs. Carbury. He's yours to the last eyelash."

When tea and speeches were over and the guests had gone, Robert sat down for a few moments' rest in the drawing-room. Tired, as he always was, by the prolonged exercise of cordiality which seemed so spontaneous to those who encountered it, he picked up the evening paper but did not read it. He was glad to be interrupted by Sylvia, who came in before going to the theatre to play Jennifer Dubedat in *The Doctor's Dilemma*.

" Some of your followers do wear peculiar costumes," she remarked mildly.

" Do they, darling? I hadn't noticed."

" One or two hats I saw looked as if they'd been packed in suitcases for weeks and then sat on for hours. And I never saw such a collection of green trousers! They were all shades from olive to peacock."

" What's wrong with green trousers? "

" Oh, nothing, I suppose, if you see them individually. But they're a bit overwhelming *en masse*."

Robert laughed.

" You always get some oddities joining a crusade for a cause. But they're all good, sincere people, and I'm glad to have them with us."

" I'm sure they are," she said. " From a moral standpoint I know I can't hold a candle to them. But they wouldn't be any worse if their taste in hats was better."

" You're rather a specialist, aren't you, darling? You shouldn't judge other people's hats by your own.

Besides, I don't suppose most of them are too well off."

" But it isn't really an economic matter, Robert. Look how smart Ethel looks on her Saturdays off. It's a question of the clothes you choose at the price you can afford."

" And the person who puts them on." He smiled at her proudly. " We're not all as beautiful as you, my beloved. Anyhow, does it matter what they wear ? "

Folding her grey squirrel cloak around her, Sylvia considered the problem quite seriously.

" Not very much, perhaps. But it does matter a bit. I never can understand why social workers wear the clothes they usually do. And so many people who take up good causes look as if they did it because they hadn't a chance to do anything else."

" Well," he admitted, " I must say that thought has occurred to me once or twice when I've seen the Temperance Sub-committee going home."

She bent over and kissed him.

" Thank Heaven," she said, " I don't want to crusade for anything — except a National Theatre. But if I did, I should try to look as if I could do anything on earth I wanted, and had chosen that particular thing because it was the most worth-while."

A few minutes earlier, Josephine had come into the room in her dressing-gown to say good-night. She now climbed on to her father's knee and surveyed Sylvia appreciatively.

" That's what you do look like, Mummy ! You always look lovely. People shouldn't ought to wear funny hats, should they, Daddy ? " She patted his head affectionately and clambered down. " Got to go now. Mam'selle says I'm tired. I'm not, but she says I am 'cause she wants to go out. Good-night, Daddy ! "

" Good-night, Jo," he responded. That's a comforting

child, he reflected when he was alone again. She never seems to get under my skin, as Adrian sometimes does. Is it the effect of his new prep. school, I wonder? Or has he inherited much more of Sylvia than her face and hair . . . that strange faculty she's always had of making one feel alone, for instance, even when she's kindest. . . . Will that develop as he grows older? . . . Will he grow towards me . . . or away from me? Adrian . . . my son. . . . What does the future hold for him? . . . for both the children? . . . I wonder? . . .

His head fell forward on his chest and, exhausted by the afternoon of convivial idealism, he slept.

CHAPTER VI

Prelude to Adolescence

As long as Adrian could remember he had been fascinated by the stars, though fear rather than pleasure was his first incentive. By the time that Josephine, his sole confidante, announced to Lord Westerly that he intended to be an astronomer, the fear had long vanished. But the effort to overcome it had been so great, and was to remain so memorable, that its conquest represented an important moment in his development.

His anxious interest in the solar system began one Sunday in early childhood, when he heard his father read a passage from the fifth chapter of the Book of Judges. He was never afterwards able to recall the exact year or the precise occasion, but he could not, he thought, have been more than five or six, for Josephine was still too young to listen to his perplexities with the intelligent interest that she began to display from four years old onwards. That Sunday he paid no more attention than usual to the Bible reading until a mysterious sentence, which became more frightening the more he reflected on it, leapt out from the narrative of remote events and penetrated his consciousness with a stab of disquiet :

" The stars in their courses fought against Sisera."

Who Sisera had been, and the reason for this unfriendly attitude on the part of the stars, remained matters of indifference to Adrian. It was the fact of their hostility which obsessed him. This indication that the bright celestial bodies which he had hitherto accepted as part of his environment took sides for or against human beings and influenced their destiny was a new and alarming idea. Obviously it was a good thing to make friends with the stars — but how ? They were so far away that you couldn't even talk to them.

Adrian usually slept immediately and soundly when he was put to bed, but that night he lay awake, huddled under the bedclothes, sweating with fear. He had never been afraid of death, which was still unreal to him, but he dreaded the end of the world. Where this particular terror originated he never knew. In after years he thought that it might have come from hearing his father or Theodore Martelhammer read the eschatological prophecies in Luke 21 before he could assess their allegorical significance. He then resolved that if ever he had children, they should not go to church before the age of twelve.

Lying in the dark in his nursery, he remembered without recalling the exact words one terrifying prophecy : " Fearful sights and great sounds shall there be from heaven." From heaven! That meant that the end of the world would come through the stars in their courses which fought against Sisera, and presumably against other unlucky individuals as well. Why, if somebody annoyed them enough, the end of the world might come tonight!

As the awful thought turned him cold with terror, three clearly recollected words — " the last trump " — flashed into his mind. He had no idea what a " trump " was, but it presented itself to him now as an appalling sound, beginning far away amid the angry stars, and gradually nearing until it blasted the whole earth with its insistent summons. Years later, when in early manhood he listened to a beautiful rendering of Brahms's *Requiem* in Southwark Cathedral, the triumphant crescendo of music which accompanied the words, " The trumpet shall sound and the dead shall be raised ", caused a reminiscent shiver to chill his blood.

For hours, during that long-remembered night, he seemed to lie half paralysed beneath the bedclothes waiting for the trump. He tried to picture what was happening in the sky. The fact that he could find out immediately by getting up and going to the window, he rejected at first as demanding an impossible measure of courage. Then, gradually, his shuddering resolution mounted. To see what the sky looked like would be terrible, but not to know had become intolerable.

Slowly, shivering, he drew the bedclothes away from his face. Robert and Sylvia were up-to-date parents in their insistence, despite Nannie's complaints, on open windows and undrawn curtains, so as soon as he permitted himself to observe what was happening, Adrian became conscious of vivid moonlight striking the floor like a glancing spear. After what appeared to be hours of indecision he struggled out of bed, and crept like a thief afraid of detection across the shaft of light to the barred window. Recalling this memory in later boyhood, he could never decide what the time of year had been. But as he remembered staying a long time out of bed while barefoot in his pyjamas, he concluded that his experience must have occurred on one of those early autumn nights when the air stays warm after dark, and even in brilliant moonlight the stars remain clear.

His terror had not been of the moon so much as the stars, but now, as he stood petrified before the window, the moon above the chimney pots appeared the most frightening phenomenon in the whole shining heavens. It was nearly full, and for the first time the strange marks which he was later to recognise as vast dusky plains covered with ring-craters took on the semblance of a leering face. It was not the eyes but the huge mouth which held his gaze with its sinister fascination; at any moment he expected it to open and emit that dreadful trump which would be the signal for inconceivable horror and appalling chaos.

He was about to rush blindly back to the shelter of the bedclothes, when the first dawning rudiments of conscious moral control caused him instead to clench his fists round the cold iron bars. At that moment, too, he heard the sound of a hymn coming from the Church, where Robert held community singing every Sunday evening from nine till ten o'clock. The words which drifted clearly up to him above the muffled sounds of traffic not only showed that his period of wakefulness had been less prolonged than he imagined, but were vaguely reassuring in themselves.

" Holy, holy, holy ! though the darkness hide Thee,
Though the eye of sinful man Thy glory may not see,
Only Thou art holy, there is none beside Thee
Perfect in power, in love, and purity."

" I *won't* be a funk," he said to himself, though his body still shook with terror and his teeth were chattering. Resolutely he forced himself to look away from the threatening moon to the hostile stars.

But the stars, after all, did not seem hostile. In comparison with the leering moon, the twinkling remoteness of their silver tranquillity appeared reassuring and even friendly. They did not look as though they were planning sinister outrages or contemplating a trump. He found himself winking at them, and they, from their immeasurable distances, seemed to wink back. Gradually the process made him feel sleepy. Soothed by starlight, he tiptoed back to his cot and immediately fell asleep.

From that time onwards, whatever might have been the misfortunes of Sisera, he regarded the stars as his friends and allies. Probably, he thought, Sisera was a naughty man who deserved to be punished. He, Adrian, would be good, and keep on the right side of these mysterious but obviously powerful influences.

Night after night, whenever there were stars to be seen, he would get out of his cot and gaze at the sparkling pin-points of light. Their reassurance never seemed to fail him ; he always returned to bed to drift contentedly into sleep. As he grew older, he began to realise the variations in the position of the stars and the relationship between one star and another ; they seemed to him to move all together in an ordered pattern, like a column of well-disciplined soldiers perpetually on the march.

One summer night he compelled himself to remain awake, watching them, until nearly dawn. For the first time, during those exhausting but wonderful hours, he received the impression that the whole heavens were slowly turning on an invisible pivot high up in the northern sky. Without realising it he was reaching, by these independent elementary observations, the intellectual position of the early astronomers who believed that the sun and stars moved round the Earth — an illusion soon corrected by the young science master at Wilton House, Knightsbridge, the London boys' preparatory school into which he passed from Mrs. Prendergast's Kindergarten at the age of nine. His questing, unformed mind was already an infinitesimal impulse in man's restless passion for knowledge. Unconsciously he had accepted the challenge of the unknown, and his pathway through life was to be determined by the compelling influence of its power.

Gradually the ever-unfolding panorama of the infinite heavens came to offer a permanent escape from the finite humans who moved, in their formless exasperating confusion, perpetually in and out of the Vicarage. A natural lover of solitude as a refuge from the inward tumults which he desired the more earnestly to hide from others the more clearly he realised them, Adrian was subconsciously oppressed even as a baby by the crowded background of his everyday life. When he reached boyhood he began to feel resentment, definite though not yet violent, against the throng of strangers, suppliants, down-and-outs and their earnest benefactors, who surrounded his father. The less he felt that he fitted into this turbulent pattern, the more unfailingly the tranquil, imperturbable stars became his friends.

*

It was in 1934, just before his ninth birthday, that Adrian first began to realise the fact of death and to connect it with war. Somewhere in those same depths which impelled him to seek knowledge from the stars, the consciousness developed that war was not just an occurrence in history books, but a threatening monster close at hand, waiting unseen to spring on him when its time was come.

The fact that thoughts of war, however unrealistic, should often have entered his mind was not surprising. He seemed always to have known that his father's Victoria Cross was a decoration for valour in battle, though it had never occurred to him to inquire why or how this superlative award had been obtained. Robert himself never spoke of it. It was important to Adrian only because it inspired envy in his classmates at Wilton House, eliminating the contempt that they would otherwise have felt for him as the son of a parson.

Then, too, the grown-ups around him continually referred to a mysterious period which they spoke of as " before the War " — a time apparently as different from the present as B.C. from A.D. When Adrian first began to learn history, he had imagined that at the end of B.C. the whole human race died out, and after an interval began again with A.D. Although he now knew that the history of humanity, despite some serious ups and downs, had so far maintained an inexorable continuity, the same kind of Rubicon seemed to him to divide " before " the War from " after ".

" My Mummy's very old ; she was alive in the War," he once announced informatively to a parish tea-party, and felt hurt and bewildered by the gust of laughter which came from the numerous guests who had seen Sylvia, lovely and elegant, play the part of Kate Hard-castle the previous week in an all-star matinée of *She Stoops to Conquer*.

" Before the War " had no reality for Adrian whatsoever. He was incapable of imagining a period in which every family amongst his parents' acquaintances had not, as a matter of course, gaps in its circle which would otherwise have been filled by fathers, brothers, or sons. Those gaps did not signify tragedy to him ; they were simply part of an incompleteness that seemed normal everywhere.

On the day that the connection between war and death first became real to him, he went up to the attic before breakfast to find an old football which Robert, whose Rugby-playing days were ended by the machine-gun bullet that smashed his knee, had preserved for precisely the purpose to which his son intended to put it. Because it was Saturday Adrian was not going to school, and had promised to practise kicking with Harbottle Minor in the Green Park that morning.

As he came out of the attic with the football, Adrian passed the half-open door of his father's study. Automatically glancing in, he noticed an unfamiliar object on the roll-top desk. It seemed to be a kind of hat, but it was made of metal and shaped like a coal-scuttle turned upside down. Without consciously knowing, he sensed that this vaguely sinister headgear was a military helmet. Just why it preyed on his mind all day, giving him the impression that the period known as " the Great War " was not so utterly remote as it had hitherto appeared, he could not have explained. But that evening, finding his father alone in the dining-room eating a late tea after a Youth Club expedition to the Natural History Museum, he felt impelled to make a few inquiries.

" Daddy, what was that funny metal hat I saw in your study this morning? "

" It was a steel helmet," said Robert. " What time did you see it? " he added, remembering that, though he had left the helmet on his desk after talking to Ted Rogers, he had put it back in the cupboard before starting his day's work.

" It was before breakfast, coming out of the attic. . . . What was it doing there, Daddy? Is it yours? "

" It wasn't always, but it is now. I was showing it

to a man who came to see me last night."

" Who did it belong to before you ? "

" A German soldier."

" What happened to him ? Was he killed in the War ? "

" Yes," answered Robert. Adrian isn't a baby any more, he reflected. He might as well know now, before someone puts the idea into his head that mass-murder is glorious. Slowly he added : " I killed him myself."

Adrian looked startled and a little alarmed. The man whom he had regarded, V.C., popular preacher and all, as his safe, unadventurous, middle-aged father, suddenly appeared strange and unfamiliar.

" *You* did, Daddy ! You killed a German ! "

" I killed a man. Perhaps several men," said Robert gravely. " I thought it was right at the time, because England and Germany were at war. But now I know it's always wicked to kill people. War is wrong because killing is wrong and God forbids it. It doesn't become right even if your government tells you to do it."

" I see," said Adrian, though Robert's simple presentation of the case against war had touched only the surface of his understanding. What he did perceive for the first time was his father as a soldier — a soldier who killed people, and might have been killed himself. From that evening onwards the German steel helmet became, in his mind, a symbol of death. It never reappeared in his father's study, though often when the door was open he looked for it surreptitiously. But it lived in his thoughts and even more in his dreams, assuming with increasing vividness the semblance of a scalp.

With that grim identification, death and war also became one in his mind, and neither seemed any longer to be far away. In the next few years they came quickly closer, for when he first saw the helmet the world was on the threshold of events which were to hedge him and his contemporaries with disasters more insistently threatening to childhood than any young generation had previously known.

He had been at the Wilton House Preparatory School for about a year when the Italian invasion of Ethiopia began. Throughout the spring and summer of 1935, when Mussolini was pouring troops and supplies into Eritrea and Somaliland, the name Abyssinia began to appear increasingly on posters and in newspaper headlines. Adrian first noticed it after Mr. Humpherson, the history master at Wilton House, had given a lecture to the School's Junior Branch of the League of Nations Union on Italy's challenge to the League and the importance of collective security.

Adrian had been too young to apprehend those earlier indications of a downward spiral in international affairs which had been largely responsible for the foundation of the B.O.J. by his father. His mind had not registered as disturbing events Hitler's accession to power, the failure of the Disarmament Conference, and the first breach of the Versailles Treaty by the reintroduction of conscription in Germany. Even Mr. Humpherson's lecture, passionately straightforward though it was, did not convey much to him.

But it conveyed enough to make him dimly conscious that the personal security which he had so long taken for granted was not unassailable and perhaps never had been ; that it did not depend wholly on his parents, nor on the busy absorbing life of the Vicarage which had seemed to him as inevitable as the movements of the planets ; nor even, perhaps, on England herself. His fear that violent inroads of disturbance might enter the great city which included his father's parish, and upset his own normal routine, was increased by the rapid growth of Robert's preoccupation with the B.O.J. after the " Social " which preceded the King's Silver Jubilee.

From the beginning of the Abyssinian crisis the B.O.J. had begun to hold meetings all over Britain, pointing out that Italy was a " Have-Not " power with few sources of raw materials, inadequate markets for her products, and insufficient outlets for her growing population. The best way of preventing the invasion of Abyssinia, said the B.O.J. speakers, was an offer by the " Have " countries of some constructive alternative. They urged the summoning of a Conference, under the auspices of the League of Nations, to discuss the formation of a permanent body which would ensure the fair allocation of the earth's resources.

Enormous posters, displaying the words " Call a Conference ! " and " Wars Will Cease When Men Share Their Privileges ", began to appear in every large city. In between his sermons, broadcasts, committees, youth conferences, and parish councils, Robert seemed perpetually to be catching trains to take the chair at B.O.J. meetings in Liverpool, Manchester, Leeds, Glasgow, Plymouth, Cardiff, and a dozen other widely separated centres. Lord Westerly, similarly engaged, now appeared in the House of Lords only when an important debate on international relations was scheduled.

But in spite of these devoted activities no Conference was called, and no sharing of privileges ever officially suggested. British and French statesmen, apparently hypnotised into their policy of weak provocation by threats of disasters too huge to be apprehended by mediocre mentalities, gave the League enough support to anger Mussolini but too little to make its authority effective. To the end of his life Adrian remembered a large newsplacard in Armada Square on May 1st, 1936, bearing the words ITALIANS ENTER ADDIS ABABA. For it was after that date, which almost coincided with the panic following Hitler's reoccupation of the Rhineland a few weeks earlier, that Adrian began consciously to acknowledge the different character of human society from his original supposition.

Though he was not yet eleven he now saw the Earth as a place without security, a nightmare planet dominated by the fear of death. It had little or nothing in common with the orderly existences of Mercury, Venus, Mars, and Jupiter, which he could now locate through his toy telescope as easily as he could pick out the buildings along the Embankment with his naked eye. Even his own life seemed to be threatened by gigantic catastrophes, sometimes near, sometimes distant, but always impending. Though he still felt vague about their actual character, he knew that they were more imminent than the end of the world which had once so profoundly alarmed him.

He accepted this new certainty with the silent stoicism of childhood, which cannot express its deepest fears because it has not yet learned the appropriate words for conveying them to others. But he was impelled towards the conclusion that he had reached when terrified by the moon ; he believed the only sure defence against disaster to lie in the capacity of the individual for unlimited endurance. Too young by many years for the constructive conception of courage that begins with adolescence, he interpreted his semi-formed philosophy in terms of the small daily challenges which confronted him at school.

He must stop himself from crying when the older boys kicked him. He must pretend he did not mind when they pulled his thick auburn hair and called him " Carrots " or " Ginger ". He must be stoically indifferent when the masters punished him.

He must learn to be tough.

*

The catastrophes that Adrian had begun to anticipate piled up with a rapidity which horrified his elders. On the top of the Abyssinian crisis came the Civil War in Spain, and Mr. Humpherson left Wilton House to join the International Brigade. He never returned to teach Adrian history, for he was killed a year later in the defence of Madrid.

Throughout the spring and summer of 1937 Robert Carbury seemed to spend all his week-day evenings away from the Vicarage, for during that year which saw Japan's second invasion of China and the formation of the Rome–Berlin Axis, the B.O.J. redoubled its efforts. He found himself booked for public appearances almost as often as Sylvia, who characteristically sought refuge from international tension in a Galsworthy season at the Connoisseurs' Theatre. The B.O.J. was undoubtedly making progress. Apart from its obvious appeal to the intelligent who realised that Hitler and Mussolini were not the cause but the consequence of political insanity, Robert's crusade was receiving the less reliable support of thousands who hated war as a major interruption in a comfortable routine and viewed the prospect of another with extreme reluctance. Much evidence, highly disturbing to bureaucratic minds, of its increasing hold upon the popular imagination began to accumulate in official dossiers.

In the autumn of that year Robert sailed to New York for a few weeks in the United States, leaving Theodore Martelhammer and his junior curate, Archibald Hynd, in charge of St. Saviour's. Although the advertised purpose of his visit was a preaching tour organised by the Federal Council of the Churches, his underlying motive was the raising of funds for the B.O.J. During his absence, dollar cheques flowed steadily across the Atlantic into the ever-extending offices in Plymouth Hoe Avenue, where Cyril Benjafield had now a staff of assistants and Ted

Rogers was installed as permanent caretaker. At the end of his tour Robert rested for a week at the home of an old acquaintance, Richmond B. Downing, who had been with him at Christ Church as a Rhodes Scholar, and was now Dean of the Faculty of Arts at Cayuga University in New York State.

Amongst the other passengers who sailed to Southampton with Robert in the *Aquitania* early in December was one who became keenly aware of his presence as soon as he read the passenger list. Robert himself had long forgotten that in her letters from the South of France during the winter before Adrian was born, Sylvia had mentioned Damon Sullivan as being among Caroline Attenborough's guests at Agay.

Damon had planned to spend a few months in England, and to inaugurate a series of Irish plays at the Orpheum Theatre with his own new comedy, *Bantry Bay*. His return after thirteen years to Europe revived a long-suppressed desire to question Sylvia about her flight from Caroline's house-party. He remembered, too, the sense of defeat and exasperation that he had felt when he learned, a few months after Adrian's birth, that Sylvia had a son.

" So that damned war hero of a parson got the better of me after all ! " he reflected ruefully, knowing well from his own studies of human nature that the deeper the remorse his uninvited love-making had inspired in Sylvia, the more gratefully she would turn to her husband for kindness and reassurance.

Early in 1925, when he went back to the United States, he had found his thoughts inconveniently obsessed by her. His dreams were haunted by her graceful body, which he had longed to possess with a passion that surprised himself. Among the many women who had stirred his blood she was the only Englishwoman, and he wondered

whether her quietly determined resistance to the shock
tactics which had never failed before was a national or
personal characteristic. If only he'd had her, even for
a night, her memory would not dominate his imagination
in this troublesome fashion. Suddenly alarmed lest he
had run the risk of forming a permanent attachment inconsistent with his carefree existence, he had avoided
writing to her and had even stayed away from England
until his work compelled a visit.

Being uncertain how much or how little might be
known in the Carbury household of his brief incursion
into Sylvia's life, he began the voyage by carefully avoiding Robert. But long before it ended he decided that
he might as well have saved himself the trouble.

The tall spare clergyman with the slight limp, and the
anxious sensitive face which he had hitherto seen only in
photographs, showed to him when they encountered each
other on gusty walks round the First Class deck exactly
the same pleasant, practised courtesy as he displayed to
everyone else. For Damon Sullivan, as for the others, the
sudden charm of his smile chased away the shadow of
anxiety, leaving his expression a momentary model of
benevolent attention.

At Southampton, from a carefully selected distance,
Damon watched him disembark. He felt an inconvenient
twinge of reviving emotion when Robert was met, and
embraced with every symptom of enduring affection, by
a woman, still russet-haired and beautiful, who was
undoubtedly Sylvia. Beside her were two children, a
boy of about twelve and a younger girl. The child's
dark curls were tied with scarlet ribbon, and her shapely
legs appeared to resist with difficulty the impulse to dance.

" That's a cute little kid ! " thought Damon, but it
was the boy who interested him most. Unobserved by
the family party on the dock below, he leaned over and

examined him. He was handsome and well-made, and his abundant wavy hair beneath his dark-blue school cap was auburn like Sylvia's. At least he didn't resemble the parson, thought Damon with satisfaction. Somehow Robert's failure to perpetuate his image in his son took part of the sting from his own long past but unforgotten defeat.

The following day he booked a seat for the evening performance at the Connoisseurs' Theatre, where Sylvia was playing Chloe in *The Skin Game*. At the end of the Second Act, he sent a note round to her dressing-room inviting her to supper when the play was over. She replied by a message asking him to wait for her at the stage entrance.

After she had joined him there, Damon took a taxi to the Berkeley Restaurant. There he ordered cocktails which they drank almost without speaking, silenced by the reminiscent emotions that possessed them both. Was she not perhaps taking too great a risk, Sylvia wondered, in satisfying the curiosity that his note had aroused, even after all these years? At fifty-five Damon was still swarthy and handsome, though his black hair had begun to turn white at the temples and the tendency towards an easy-going corpulence which had been a mere hint at forty-two was now pronounced. Stirred, to her surprise, by long-forgotten feelings of remorseful compunction towards Robert, Sylvia avoided his eyes and kept her own fixed on the fine dark hairs covering the back of the powerful hand that held his glass.

He studied her with close attention as they moved to their table and began supper, still mutually embarrassed by recollections that seemed to grow clearer as the evening wore on.

" She's changed, and yet she isn't," he reflected. " She looks different . . . still more detached, less in the midst of things somehow . . . but she doesn't look much older."

He finished his soup and scrutinised her again, thinking how absurd it was that one woman among so many should cause his experienced heart to beat even a few seconds faster. " Well, I certainly hand it to her for that ! If I'm right in my calculations she'll be forty-three next spring ; but no one would take her for more than thirty — or thirty-five at most. She doesn't look middle-aged. She looks like a girl who has been over-working and is rather tired."

Throughout dinner they discussed the shows running on Broadway, spoke of the forthcoming Irish plays and his own comedy which he was to begin rehearsing next day, reviewed the Galsworthy season at the Connoisseurs' Theatre and Sylvia's parts in *The Silver Box*, *The Mob*, and *The Skin Game*. It was not until he had ordered coffee and Chartreuse that he firmly put aside their conversational small-talk.

" Look here, Sylvia, I didn't bring you to this place to talk about the theatre. There's a question on my mind, and I've wanted an answer for a dozen years."

" Not so badly that you had to write and ask me," she countered, smiling ruefully to herself rather than at him as she played with her liqueur glass.

" Well," he said, " I've never been a letter-writer. Too much like work. But now I'm over here there's something I've got to know. Sylvia . . . why did you run away from Agay like that, without saying goodbye ? Was it " — he moved closer to her — " was it because you'd have come to me if you'd stayed ? "

" I don't know," she answered after a pause. " It's difficult to remember details when it's all so long ago."

" I guess you do remember, just the same. Don't you, honey ? "

" Perhaps I do. Perhaps I should have given in to
you. And if I had," she added with sudden emphasis,
" I should never have respected myself again ! "

His laugh only half concealed an unwonted feeling of
acute humiliation.

" Indeed ! Am I such a monster ? "

Seized with compunction for her candour, Sylvia laid
her hand on his arm.

" Forgive me, Damon. I didn't mean to imply that.
But Robert's different from any man I've known. He's
a real Christian — a saint. If I were disloyal to him, I
should be letting down something that matters more than
either of us."

" Just what exactly do you mean by that ? "

" It's difficult to explain. But I should have been
false to a faith, a standard — part of what he tries to
teach."

She stood up, ready to end their conversation and
fetch her fur coat before going out into the winter night.

" There's one thing I'd like to ask of you, Damon.
Robert never knew why I came back from Agay before I
meant to. Except that he admires your plays your name
means nothing to him, and I don't want it to mean anything. It isn't that I make a habit of deceiving him.
But he trusts me, and he's never had any reason not to."

" Indeed ! I'm sorry to hear you've been that virtuous."

" It's true, however improbable you think it. Robert
carries a stupendous load, and I don't want to add to
it by even the suspicion that I encourage other men to
make love to me."

" Encourage ! " This time the bitterness of his laugh
was unmitigated. " O.K., honey," he said, signalling to
the waiter for his bill. " I quite realise your household
paragon's got a vested interest in morality. You can
trust your old admirer to keep his indiscretions to himself."

At intervals throughout that winter, Damon took Sylvia out to lunch or supper. Although he told himself that he ought to resist the revived desire which was equally inconvenient to them both, he begged her several times to become his mistress — just once. But she was still keeping their relationship resolutely platonic when in February, 1938, a new outbreak of sabre-rattling speeches began in Germany. The anxious British public, their eyes now on Austria, lost the impulse to go to the theatre. At night, instead, they apprehensively watched displays of practising searchlights and listened to sinister rehearsals of air-raid warnings, while by day every conversation seemed to find its way back to conscription, evacuation, and air-raid precautions.

When *Bantry Bay*, playing to half-empty houses, was finally withdrawn, Damon Sullivan booked his return passage to the United States.

"A little of modern Europe goes a long way!" he remarked to Sylvia, coming round to her dressing-room at the Connoisseurs' Theatre to say goodbye. "Look here, honey, why don't you come across with those two fine kids of yours, and take a part in a Broadway show till this international ballyhoo blows over? I'll soon get you fixed up in a job you'll enjoy."

"What, and leave Robert to face the music, alone here in London?" She pushed back her chair and confronted him, her blue-grey eyes opaque with memory. "You forget — I've lost one husband in one war. I'd rather share the fate of another in a second, if it has to come."

He gripped her hand, more moved than he had ever thought possible for himself by the threat to her safety of prospective events, of which the character was becoming obvious even to a playwright who specialised in the self-centred politics of small turbulent nations.

" And are you prepared for your children to share it too ? "

A momentary shiver passed over her as she reluctantly foresaw the impact of unwelcome decisions on the world of mime and make-believe which she had so long preferred to reality.

" Ah, no ! That's another matter. The important part of my life is over for me, but theirs is all in the future. I'm not entitled to be indifferent about them."

" And supposing you had to part with them ? Could you bear it ? "

" Oh, yes," she replied, a little surprised by the question. " I shouldn't worry about them once I knew they were safe."

" Wouldn't you really ? But what about the kids themselves ? "

" They wouldn't worry either," she asserted, with an instinctive knowledge that Robert's passionate love for his son and daughter prevented him from possessing. " I'm not the kind of devoted mother that children miss."

" Well, honey," he said, " if trouble blows up over here and for any reason you need my help, I'm prepared to behave like the devoted father I shall never be. There's hardly a thing I wouldn't do for that red-headed lad of yours."

" I'm glad you approve of him."

" I certainly do. He's you all over again."

" Thank you, Damon," she said gently. " I'll remember that."

" And you promise you'll let me know if I can help you or the kids ? "

" Yes. I promise."

Suddenly giving vent to the desire which he had so uncharacteristically restrained, he took her in his arms and kissed her lips, smoothing back her bronze hair again and again with his hand. Then he opened the door abruptly, and went out through the stage entrance into the cold March night.

A week later Hitler invaded Austria, and the season of Irish plays, another victim of international aggression, abortively petered out.

CHAPTER VII

History Takes a Hand

MANY of Robert's parishioners were surprised when, two months before Adrian's thirteenth birthday in 1938, he sent his son to Eton.

If Adrian had gone to a modern school like Bryanston, or a coeducational school like Bedales, or even to a large London day school such as St. Paul's or Westminster, there would have been no comment. But Eton seemed to be a choice inconsistent with Robert's habitual championship of the under-privileged and his unconventionality as preacher and political leader, which his followers expected to see repeated in every department of his life.

Only one or two close friends — such as Frederick Westerly, who had now entered Robert's inner circle owing to their constant association in the B.O.J. — understood the profound influence of family tradition, which became deeper as Robert grew older. They perceived it to be a significant part of the spiritual refuge that he sought periodically from habitual devotees with their wearisome adoration which gave them, in their own eyes, some kind of claim upon him. Into his family, past and present, he escaped from the pathetic but tedious elderly spinsters, always finding some excuse to telephone or call at the Vicarage, who tried to push themselves into his small group of intimates; and above all from the brash young men who called him " Bob ", constantly sought his advice about their wives, jobs, or recreations, and inflicted upon his non-existent leisure the reading of immature manuscripts which they hoped would find a comfortable home in *St. Saviour's Monthly Magazine*.

A wholly consistent Christian Socialist would undoubtedly have sold Hoddershall Ash, and sent Adrian and Josephine to the nearest elementary school. But for Robert, Adrian was heir not only to himself, but to his father and grandfather and their distinguished ancestors. Though he gave away most of his private income and lived on the stipend attached to the living of St. Saviour's, he retained possession of the Staffordshire manor house with the same family motives that had inspired him, two days after Adrian's birth, to enter his son for Mr. Kidderminster's house at Eton.

His own dislike of the school as a boy had been due, he thought, to his reluctant acceptance of it as the first step towards an orthodox political career for which he had no taste. He hoped that Adrian would eventually follow him into the Ministry by way of Christ Church, Oxford, and some modern variant of Bellsley. He did not, however, intend to coerce his son in any way. He had learned, he felt, too much from his own early frustrations for that.

But he had not reckoned that Adrian's first real break with home would have to be made amid the tensions which accompanied the Munich crisis, that penultimate Nemesis of the policy of weak provocation. When he took Adrian to Eton between Neville Chamberlain's visits to Berchtesgaden and Godesberg, Robert was already beginning to calculate how much longer the green and pleasant land which the B.O.J. had tried to rescue would remain immune from hostile assault.

Adrian had adapted himself with resolute equanimity to the routine of existence at Mrs. Prendergast's Kindergarten and at Wilton House, but he could not conceal his reluctance to go away to school. Though he was still too young to understand the sequence of international events which caused the strained faces around him and the whispered adult conversations that ceased when he appeared, he fully realised that the twin threatening spectres of War and Death had come appreciably closer. And just at this tense, miserable moment, beneath the huge shadow of their menace, he had to leave everything that meant security and begin a harsh, unfamiliar life.

For once his private philosophy of " toughness " let him down. With occasional tears splashing inconveniently on to the paper, he spent his last morning at home filling in the stars on a skeleton sky-atlas that he had saved three months' pocket-money to buy. When they parted at Eton, he clung to Robert's hand with unwonted, shame-making dependence. Two more conspicuous tears, meanly escaping from his eyes and trickling down his cheeks in spite of his tight lips and stony expression, made Robert question for the first time the wisdom of his choice of school.

In later years Adrian could never dissociate his first fortnight as a new boy from the international crisis, which pervaded it just as the inevitability of coming doom pervades the struggling hapless mortals in a Greek tragedy. Having no standards of comparison, he accepted as a matter of course his small sunless study looking out on a row of dust-bins in an anonymous back yard; and in normal times his determined philosophic resistance might have carried him unscathed through his initial rôle of

insignificant fag. But the accompaniment of p litical
tension, and the growing fear that war, with its unima-
ginable consequences, might suddenly materialise and
imprison him in these alien surroundings for ever, made
the cuffs and curses a nightmare memory from which his
fully developed mind was always to turn instinctively away.

When Neville Chamberlain returned from Munich, to
be tumultuously received by politicians who twenty
months later were to repudiate him for the arrangements
that they now applauded, Adrian shared in the sudden
relief brought to the school and the country by the
temporary illusion of " peace in our time ". But the
nation-wide madness of hysterical rejoicing came too late
to modify the silent endurance of secret misery which
Eton meant for him, and was always to mean.

Long afterwards, when he tried to recall that misery,
it invariably took the pictorial shape of boats on the
autumn Thames at Windsor, and ampelopsis turning
scarlet on grey college walls. For him the vivid colours
of the beautiful creeper were to remain a symbol of heartbreak and loneliness, keenly realised beneath the shadow
of death. But as his eyes rested absently on the glowing
walls and glittering water, his mind was formulating the
first decisions of an adult quality that it had yet made.

His present wretchedness, he reflected, was the consequence of pious reverence for family custom; it was
his father's respect for his own forebears and their way
of life which had dictated his choice of Adrian's school.
Very well, then; he, Adrian, would break with that
tradition. No son of his, if he ever had one, should suffer
through parental desire for a link with the past.

That characteristic decision represented his first conscious breach with the now nationally popular father
whose values, despite periodic rebellion, he had hitherto
taken for granted. In the process of making it he com-

mittcd a typical error of juvenility, which on one instance
of mistaken judgment condemns outright an adult's total
framework of personal standards. Because Robert,
moved by filial piety, had sent him to a school which
meant purgatory for an introspective boy with a natural
love of solitude, Adrian began secretly to criticise adversely
all that he understood of his father's religious teaching
and political opinions.

If, in the blotted paragraphs of his semi-articulate
letters or later in conversation during the holidays,
Adrian had given the smallest hint of the mental and
physical distresses which had replaced the home that
now seemed a paradise, Robert would have removed
him instantly from Eton, and whatever his own disappointment have sent him to a school where his peculiarities
would have been more tolerantly treated and better
understood.

But by the time that the Christmas holidays came,
Adrian's carefully-cultivated habit of concealing his true
feelings and opinions was already based upon the notion
of his father as chief antagonist. So when Robert asked
him in the taxi going home from the station, " Well,
son — was it really so bad being away at school after
all ? " Adrian said nothing about the misery that he had
suffered from the operations of an anachronistic machine.

He only replied, resolutely unemotional, " Oh, I get
along all right, Daddy," and stared mutely out of the
taxi window at the December cheerlessness of Hyde Park
while Robert wished, as he was beginning to wish so
often, that his adored only son could show even a frac-
tion of Josephine's puppy-like responsiveness to parental
affection.

At this stage of his development Adrian would have
felt less reluctance to confess his sorrows to Sylvia, for
he sensed rather than positively suspected that Eton, like

so many other aspects of their family life, meant nothing to her. But during the past year or so he had come to think of his mother as a person in whom one did not confide — not because she would not understand, but because she would not be interested. Grateful as he was for her gentle detachment which made no demands on his attention or affection, he perceived intuitively that her real life was reserved for the stage, and his own capacity, inherited from her, for exclusive absorption in one pursuit made him instinctively reluctant to disturb others who were similarly preoccupied.

*

So Josephine, still too young to understand more than the external aspects of his misery or do otherwise than listen sympathetically while he described the manifold humiliations of a junior fag, remained his sole confidante. But in the spring of 1939 he nearly lost even her. Just before mid-March, after a night of sickness too gallantly endured without complaint, she was found to be suffering from acute appendicitis and hurried into Queen Elizabeth's Hospital. Weak but cheerful, she appeared for some hours to be making satisfactory progress after the operation when a sudden relapse occurred, and she began to cry pitifully for Adrian. Robert telephoned Eton, and met his son, stony-eyed and silent, at Paddington just before midnight.

It was certainly remarkable how Josephine began to rally as soon as she saw him. But the next day, when she was still in danger, Hitler's troops invaded Prague. To the nightmare of her illness was added the national fear of immediate war, of sudden bombs dropping upon Queen Elizabeth's Hospital before she was well enough to be moved from London. On the morning of March 15th, after reading newspapers shrill with journalistic

recriminations and resonant with rumours of further sensational " swoops " in the Balkans, Robert, now as silent
as Adrian, stood at the dining-room window after breakfast and looked into the abnormally deserted Square.
Once again, in spite of the devoted labours of concerned
minorities such as the B.O.J., war was hammering at the
gates of Europe. It had crept over the world as a rising
wind creeps over a meadow, slowly at first, in short gusts
almost unperceived, but gradually increasing and at last
reaching the hurricane strength which whips and flattens
the long grass, and scourges the trees into tortured shapes
like the agonised figures of baroque sculpture.

" I bloody well can't stand this," thought Adrian, his
father's double anxiety communicating itself to him.
Unobserved by Robert he slipped out of the room and
through the back door of the Vicarage. Thankful to
have achieved solitude without interrogation, he walked
hurriedly through Sir Francis Avenue and down the series
of sloping streets which led to the Embankment.

There the trams and speeding automobiles seemed to
be clattering and screeching on their usual errands, unmoved by the inconvenient enterprises of Germany's
restless dictator. The Thames barges, too, chugged
serenely on towards the Pool of London, laden with heaps
of coal or sacks of flour or bales of paper. Reassured,
Adrian was walking along towards the City when a newspaper poster outside the Temple Underground Station
smote his attention : WAR IMMINENT.

His heart-beats seemed suddenly to choke him, and
his hands and feet turned cold. As he glanced from the
frightening placard to the crowded thoroughfare beside
the river, he saw in imagination that event which was
discussed in anticipation by the grown-ups who stopped
talking when he approached. The Embankment appeared
to be filled with a fleeing population, mothers and fathers

with their children frantically speeding in every variety of vehicle towards Westminster and Chelsea, and then through Putney, Richmond, and Kingston into the open country. It wouldn't take them long to reach it, he reflected — and then became aware that, if Hitler's forces were invading London as they had invaded Prague, they would get there quickly too. For the first time he realised how circumscribed was his native island in terms of modern war. But the problem of his own fate inevitably became paramount.

" I suppose I'd have to stick at Eton," he thought glumly, recapitulating the secret miseries of the Munich crisis. " However would I stand being cut off from home for good ? " But, as usual, this thought was accompanied by the inward determination to endure whatever came to him without word or sign. He walked back to the Vicarage expecting to be reprimanded with that restrained Christian tolerance which he had begun half-consciously to dread more than school scoldings and canings. The measure of Robert's preoccupation was revealed to him by the fact that his absence had not even been noticed.

But next day the imminent war had still not begun, and Josephine was pronounced out of danger. Adrian returned to Eton, to find as before that national calamity was perpetually minimised by the compulsion to accept routine afflictions without conspicuous emotion. A fortnight later he received without surprise the news that his parents had decided to send Josephine, like himself, out of London the following term. She was to go to a coeducational school in Somerset for " under-fourteens " after they had both spent the Easter holidays at Bexhill-on-Sea.

A few months afterwards Adrian could hardly remember those holidays or the summer that followed them, so completely were they overshadowed by September and war. He only recalled how slowly the weeks, laden with approaching events, appeared to move, and how deeply the anticipation of coming disaster seemed to carve the lines on his father's face.

Josephine, endowed with natural gregariousness, enjoyed her new school and promptly forgot the intimations of war. Sylvia, with her customary detachment, escaped from political turmoil into a short run of Lancelot Wynforth's *The Chasm* at the Albany Theatre, where the play, chosen for its emphasis on the greatness of England, drew small but consistently appreciative audiences. But Robert, like his son, found almost unbearable the leaden-footed onset of international doom. Never had the devotion of his parishioners seemed more wearisome or his own capacity for consoling the apprehensive members of his congregation less capable of standing the test of upheaval. His perpetual popularity had become an Old Man of the Sea, never to be lifted from his shoulders until the merciful hand of Death should remove the burden and cast it before the judgment-seat of posterity.

*

Three weeks before the outbreak of the Second World War, the Bishop of South-west London called unexpectedly on the Vicar of St. Saviour's. That evening Robert was alone, for Sylvia, after the withdrawal of *The Chasm*, had taken both children away for a visit to a cousin's family in South Wales. He had begun ostensibly to prepare his Sunday sermon but was actually preoccupied with plans for evacuating the children of his parish to a safe area, when the Verger, a little breathlessly, announced Anselm Ensor's unheralded arrival.

" You must pardon me for not telling you I was coming," began the Bishop when Robert had joined him in the drawing-room. " I've long wanted a word with

you, and an unexpected summons to a Conference at
St. Paul's gives me the opportunity. I'm glad to find
you alone."

" There's nothing unusual about that at the moment.
It makes me specially pleased to see an old friend."

" I'm afraid you mayn't be so pleased when I've said
my say."

Robert smiled, the sudden erasing of the lines on his
face giving him, as always, the relaxed appearance of a
mature but benevolent schoolboy.

" So I'm on the mat, am I ? What have I done now ? "

But the Bishop's gravity remained for once impervious
to the disarming informality of this beloved disciple.

" I want to make sure, Robert, that you do understand
what may happen to you and your work here if war comes.
And I confess I see no way of avoiding it."

" I assume you're not just warning me about bombs.
What else do you think will happen ? "

" Nothing much, probably, if this country never has
to face defeat or direct attack — as, please God, it never
will. But if once things began to look ugly . . ."

" What precisely do you mean, Anselm ? "

" It's your Builders of Jerusalem I'm thinking of. It
might make you suspect. Some of the members are not
exactly sound."

Suspect ? Sound ? The words that were to become
so familiar to Robert during the next five years had an
alien ring in his ears.

" What aren't they sound about ? " he inquired.

" Well . . . they won't be a hundred per cent behind
the War, will they ? "

" No. Will you ? "

The Bishop meditated. " Perhaps not a hundred per
cent. Wars always lead to moral laxity among the weaker
sections of the population. But what I want to see is

world peace, and as a realist I know there's no hope of
seeing it with Fascism rampant."

" I don't accept that. If the Church chose to *lead*,
neither death nor hell nor Fascism could stand up against
it. That's why the elimination of war has always been
a main plank in the B.O.J. platform. Are you suggesting
that this makes its members traitors to their country ? "

" Of course not. I know as well as you do that they're
solid British citizens, and probably better Christians than
most. Undoubtedly the Government knows it too. But
you can't expect politicians engaged in a life-and-death
struggle with a powerful enemy to look with favour on
London's most popular church becoming a centre of
pacifism."

Robert made a movement of impatience.

" Pacifism ! I've no use for those meaningless labels !
We've never called ourselves pacifists. We try to live by
the principles embodied in the teaching of our Master,
Jesus Christ. You can't expect me to compromise on
that."

" But compromise is the essence of statesmanship.
Christ Himself recognised it. What else is the meaning
of ' Render unto Caesar the things which are Caesar's ' ? "

" Yes, but He didn't tell us to render unto Caesar the
things which are God's. You're an historian, Anselm. Can
you deny that the liberties of this country have been won
by the men and women who refused to compromise ? "

" I don't deny that, up to a point. But most of them
died for their refusal, Robert."

Robert looked at an ebony crucifix that hung on the
wall beside the mantelpiece. Taking it in his hands, he
spoke very quietly.

" Just after I was awarded the V.C., Anselm, I told
you I was a coward. That was true. It's always been
true. But do you think I'm such a coward that I wouldn't

pay the cost of my deepest convictions?"

"No, Robert. You'd be more likely to pay it twice over. That's why I want you to understand exactly what it may be . . . Disgrace, humiliation, prison, even death. Once war begins, none of these things are excluded — not even for the most idolised leader if he sets his face against the will of the people."

"You mean the will of the majority. But it's the will of the minority that changes history."

"In the end, perhaps. But in no end that you or I can hope to see."

"What does that matter? The love of Jesus makes such ends visible to the eye of faith." Laying down the crucifix, Robert went up to the Bishop and grasped both his hands. "My old friend, you didn't really think you were going to frighten me by this talk of disgrace and prison and death?"

"No, my son. I knew I should not. I don't share your views; but you wouldn't be the man I have loved and admired all these years if I had persuaded you to change them."

"Then why——"

"I had a duty to perform. I was the person most responsible for putting you into this great key position. It's true that when I did it I hardly visualised history repeating itself again in my time, or even in yours. But now that war is almost here, I had to make an attempt to mitigate the consequences of my handiwork — for England and for you."

He rose to leave, and Robert accompanied him downstairs to the door.

"And you expect me to apologise because you haven't succeeded?"

"No, Robert. I never thought I should succeed. God be with you, my son, in the perils before you — both

those that come from our enemies, and those you invite
from our friends."

★

On the day that the Nazis invaded Poland, Sylvia returned
to London to face the immediate future with Robert. It
did not frighten her. No national calamity could frighten
her any more. Because, as she told Damon Sullivan, she
had lost one husband in a First World War, she was ready
to share the fate of another in a Second — not through
love, but through indifference to death.

That indifference did not extend to her children, and
she meant to leave them both in Wales. But she was not
altogether surprised when Adrian, using his three-and-a-
half years' seniority to make Josephine remain behind,
insisted upon coming with her to London. True to her
early resolve that cooperation with her son and daughter
should atone for the passionate devotion which she had
never given them, she made no attempt to persuade him
to stay. Robert, she perceived, was divided between fear
for Adrian's safety and pride in his readiness to encounter
danger. If he thought her acquiescence irresponsible, he
made no sign of disapproval.

At ten o'clock on Sunday morning, September 3rd, a
group of left-wing political organisations held a mass
meeting in Armada Square. The organisers introduced
a series of speakers to a rapidly gathering crowd which
before 10.30 extended into Sir Francis Avenue and half-
way down Queen Elizabeth Street towards Piccadilly.
At 10.45, speakers and organisers, followed by part of
the huge audience, marched in a procession round the
Square carrying banners inscribed HANDS OFF PO-
LAND and FIGHT FASCISM NOW. Just before eleven
o'clock, they erected a microphone through which the
expected declaration of war was relayed to the assembled
throng. An uneasy hush descended upon the waiting

hundreds of men and women as they listened to the Prime Minister's reluctant words :

" This morning the British Ambassador in Berlin handed the German Government a final note, stating that, unless we heard from them by eleven o'clock that they were prepared at once to withdraw their troops from Poland, a state of war would exist between us.

" I have to tell you now that no such undertaking has been received, and that consequently this country is at war with Germany. You can imagine what a bitter blow it is to me that all my long struggle to win peace has failed. . . ."

When the brief statement concluded, Robert, who had postponed Matins, held a short unorthodox service. Standing on the steps of his Church above the Square, he summoned the heterogeneous crowd to pray for their enemies, and for the preservation of those human decencies which made man at his best only a little lower than the angels. He asked them to plead daily with God to give their leaders the moral strength to refrain from carrying war to the limits of violence, and the spiritual courage to negotiate an early and merciful peace. Then, asking the organist to play Hymn No. 214 from *Hymns Ancient and Modern*, he remained kneeling on the top of the steps with his head bowed in prayer as his own congregation in the Church sang the significant verses :

" Lord, Thou canst help when earthly armour faileth,
Lord, Thou canst save when deadly sin assaileth,
Lord, o'er Thy Church nor death nor hell prevaileth ;
    Grant us Thy peace, Lord.

" Grant us Thy help till foes are backward driven,
Grant them Thy truth, that they may be forgiven,
Grant peace on earth, and, after we have striven,
    Peace in Thy Heaven."

As the crowd in the Square joined in the " Amen "
he rose to his feet and addressed them, with the congregation of St. Saviour's standing behind him.

" My friends, I have only a few words to say, for most
of you will have plans to consider and decisions to make.
I want you, after you go home, always to remember the
lines you have just sung here. ' Lord, o'er Thy Church
nor death nor hell prevaileth ! ' It is for you to make
this true.

" I want you also to remember that the foes of whom
our hymn speaks are the permanent spiritual enemies of
Jesus, and not the nation upon whom our Government
has seen fit to declare war. Political tyrannies come and
go, but the perpetual enemies of our Lord are hatred,
cruelty, falsehood, injustice, envy, oppression, fear, and
war. The duty of a Christian is to help his Church to
prevail over death and hell by conquering these foes.
Unless you achieve this, the only true victory, your military
victory will be an illusion. It will become, like the last,
a mere incentive to further war."

Half turning towards his own congregation and the
Church with its grey tower incongruously bathed in the
mild September sunshine, he made a gesture which seemed
to present them to the throng of strangers before him.

" Whatever the future may bring," he said, " I promise
you that this Church will continue its endeavours to
' build Jerusalem ', and to stand for those values which
all who have prayed and worshipped here during the past
twelve years have come to associate with it. If the love
of God cannot conquer and change even the Nazis, then
there is no God and no love. But since God lives and
His love is unfailing, the task of overcoming them is His,
not ours. If His Vengeance comes to them it will come in
the consequences of their own acts, through His law o.
cause and effect. It is not for us to take that Vengeance

upon ourselves. He can carry Vengeance without sin, because His Vengeance is also His Forgiveness. But we, being imperfect, become greater sinners than the men on whom we revenge ourselves if we seek to usurp His task."

He stood erect, facing them, and his voice rang clearly across the Square.

" Lift up your hearts, my friends and fellow-countrymen! Even a second Great War cannot last for ever. But whether it continues for months or for years, we at St. Saviour's shall never abandon our quest for that peace in which alone the Will of God is made known to men. We ask you to help us in this endeavour, believing that He who told us to forgive our enemies will be with us always.

" The God of Love be with you, and grant you His courage to fight and conquer the real foes of His Heavenly Kingdom."

Robert had just raised his hand to bless the crowd, now standing silent with bowed heads, when the air-raid siren wailed over London. At first, as though their conscious minds refused to accept this ugly challenge from the kingdom of death and hell, the men and women in the Square seemed petrified. Then a shudder passed over them, and they scattered in all directions. Some sought shelter in the Crypt of St. Saviour's; others ran to the Underground stations or jumped on to passing buses. In two minutes Robert was left standing on the steps with only Sylvia and Adrian beside him to face the empty Square.

Somehow, now that war was actually here, it seemed more bearable to Adrian than he had anticipated when he saw the poster on the Embankment and pictured the evacuation of London. Yet, excited and vaguely frightened, he realised that history, which had been pursuing him for the past six years, had at last caught up with him, and was likely in the immediate future to play the chief part in his education.

For his father " the dark night of the soul ", foreseen by Anselm Ensor, had already begun.

*

PART II

CHAPTER VIII

Spring at Cayuga

On May 9th, 1941, Adrian and Josephine Carbury, evacuees since June, 1940, at the small American city of Acropolis, New York, raced to the middle of the suspension bridge above Dagger Creek Gorge, the deep ravine which bisected the campus of Cayuga University. Aspens, shaking their brown catkins, grew close to its edge, and the trunks of the cottonwoods glistened greenish-white. Two hundred feet below, a narrow galloping rivulet, reflecting the young leaves of the sheltered bushes growing at its margin, appeared through their branches as a frothy turbulence in pale shades of green and gold.

Beyond the gorge spread the dramatic Iroquois country, like a wild and vivid landscape by van Gogh. Once the home of the Five Nations of Indians who caught their fish in its Finger Lakes and hunted their prey through its dark forests of fir and spruce, it was now the challenging site of a great experiment in New World education. The University spread itself lavishly over the heights above the miniature township, which tailed off, with the unfinished slovenliness habitual to the outskirts of American cities, on the nearer shore of a narrow, wind-ruffled lake forty miles long.

In the middle of the bridge, Josephine stopped. Clinging to the rail, and jerking her long twelve-year-old body violently from side to side, she caused the delicately balanced structure to swing with her weight. Then, run-

ning along the swaying planks, she sprang on to a high
ledge of rock overhanging the hither side of the ravine.

" I wish you wouldn't do that ! " admonished Adrian,
pursuing her. " I always tell you not to, and you always
do it ! "

" Why shouldn't I ? " demanded Josephine, climbing
the rock and looking down unmoved at the barely visible
stream in the depths below. " It's such fun ! "

" It's dangerous, Earwig. You could easily slip and
fall into the gorge."

" You are silly, Wasp ! I believe you're frightened of
crossing the bridge yourself ! "

" Of course I'm not frightened. But Mummy and
Daddy told me to look after you, and if you kill yourself
they'll blame me."

Josephine regarded him sceptically.

" Mummy wouldn't blame you. She never blames
anybody."

" Well, Daddy would blame me then ! I expect you're
right about Mummy. I don't ever remember her getting
mad with anyone — not even with him."

" Why should she get mad with Daddy ? "

Adrian ruminated, gazing fixedly at the trunk of a
young hemlock which perched so close to the rim of the
chasm that it seemed to be keeping watch over its neighbours growing from lower clefts in the rock wall.

" It's hard to explain exactly," he said. " But I know
I should often feel all worked up if I was his wife."

" How could *you* be anybody's wife, you coon ! "

" I can use my imagination, can't I, stinker ? "

As he spoke he looked down, though heights intimidated him, and became immediately fascinated by the
symmetrical lacework of budding leaves on the tree-tops
below. Somehow it reminded him of the design made
by the myriad stars on a chart of the Milky Way in his

sky-atlas. Not for the first time, he was struck by the frequency with which Nature repeats her patterns — in the calyx of a flower, in the network of veins beneath the human skin, in the delicate intricacies of an animal's carcass.

Just visible from the summit of the plunging rocks, he could see the edge of the town stretching, as though drawn by a magnet, towards the desolate lake which remained the colour of steel throughout the summer. Broken up into sections by hills and ravines, this small city in the western half of the Empire State defied arrangement into the customary geometrical plan. Its Main Street and State Street, typical enough in their names, neon signs, and sardine-like assemblage of closely parked cars, were tilted at one end as though somebody had tried the experiment of imposing the pattern on the inside of a basin.

From the steep pavements of these angular streets, oaks, maples, and sycamores of giant stature cast their shadows over little frame-houses with sun-porches painted green, yellow, or brown. Soon after the children had arrived at Acropolis the maples began to turn scarlet, and the oaks mellowed to gold of a depth and warmth unknown in an English autumn. Beyond the town the main road skirting the campus came to an amiable end in rural lanes and woodlands, where tiny streams ran, and the winds of that sunny, cold, beautiful region found temporary quiet.

These woods offered a constant refuge to Adrian, who explored them for signs of North America's belated spring, and took pleasure in each budding windflower and the brightening of the grey-white lichen at the base of the trees. But Josephine, being still too young to appreciate natural beauty and in any case more instinctively sociable, preferred to examine the small haphazard houses whose architects had seemed determined to thwart the mathematical planners of the intersecting streets. At night no discouraging black-out eclipsed their friendly unshaded windows, and no privacy-securing hedges divided their little grass-plots, now carpeted by fallen yellow petals of forsythia, from the benevolent curiosity of next-door neighbours.

The children themselves lived on the campus in a large frame-house with planks grown grey from the rigours o. successive American winters. Raised by the height of three wooden steps from the ground, it had a sheltered sun-porch in front and was surrounded by its own plot of untended grass. A stone-flagged pavement divided this private patch from the huge green sward which enclosed the University's mammoth buildings. Every evening at sunset a carillon of bells in the Library tower opposite the house played the pleasant, sentimental tunes of hymns familiar at St. Saviour's, a daily reminder to Adrian and Josephine of their distant imperilled home. As the gentle melodies echoed across the grass, the children listening on the porch of the grey-boarded house watched the smoke from wood-fires in the town rise skywards in a soft blue haze, which vanished into the clear sky left ᶦade and vermilion by the after-rays of the setting sun.

The big frame-house belonged to Dean Richmond B. Downing, one of the best administrators that the University had ever appointed to its Faculty. A quiet, laconic, kindly man with horn-rimmed spectacles and greying hair, he regarded the children of his old friend Robert Carbury as minor though colourful additions to the large student body which constantly sought his advice. His wife Kathleen, dark and lively, revealed her Irish origin in her sparkling deep-blue eyes and the relative indifference that she displayed towards the small-town sartorial competitiveness of the other Faculty wives. She adored both children, but especially Josephine, with uncritical fervour, finding compensation in their animated presence for the childless home which was a source of melancholy rather than bitterness to a mutually devoted husband and wife.

As the young Carburys continued to explore the evergreen topic of their parents' personalities, Josephine sat down on the hard rock with her legs dangling over the edge, and Adrian, more prudently, perched on a pine stump close by. In the grass at his feet, wild geranium and starry white hepatica were already in flower.

" You know," he ruminated, " I'm sure Mummy's got a temper even if she never does get cross. Bud Libby says all red-haired people have tempers, like me. . . . Do you know what I think, Jo ? "

" No. What do you ? "

" I think Mummy never gets mad with Daddy because she just doesn't care about him enough."

Josephine looked startled and perturbed.

" Oh, Ady, you are awful ! What a thing to say about your own parents ! "

" Why shouldn't I say it if it's true ? After all, Dad's nothing to get crazy about."

" A good many people do seem to get crazy about him, just the same."

" People ! " exclaimed Adrian scornfully. " You mean googly-eyed women, and peace goofers, and men in corduroy trousers ! I can't think why Mummy ever married him. I'm sure she doesn't like having cranks in and out of our house all day long. You could never get away from them and be by yourself, like you sometimes can here."

Though only sometimes, he mentally added, thus registering his instinctive disapproval of American gregariousness. He realised that it had developed as a form of national compensation for the vast inhuman emptiness which once quenched the spirits of the New World pioneers; but it had too much in common with the gregariousness of St. Saviour's to attract his natural reticence. Not yet old enough to perceive that the loneliness from which his father's parishioners fled was purely spiritual, he had still to recognise their wilderness as the lost deserts encountered by the isolated soul in its search for God.

From the first moment of the children's arrival the Faculty at Cayuga and the sociable residents of Acropolis had lavished upon them a spontaneous wealth of hospitality and kindness, combined with an unlimited commiseration which Adrian secretly resented, feeling that neither of them deserved it. This, he thought objectively, was particularly true of Josephine, who being the younger had more of it, and indiscriminately enjoyed it all. At the small private school to which she was sent, unlike Adrian who was judged old and tough enough to go to the local high school, a sympathetic psychologist had examined her and pronounced her to be suffering from " shock ". Though Josephine's greatest regret up to date was that she had never heard an air-raid siren, her classmates were forbidden to mention raids, bombs, or torpedoes in her presence. Their function, said the kindly headmistress, was to help Josephine to forget the War. But when, in a Composition hour one morning, she described her voyage from England, including its submarine risks, with every symptom of manifest enjoyment, the school's conception of appropriate social behaviour was severely shaken.

" I didn't mind the people at the Vicarage," she now remarked truthfully. " But Daddy sometimes used to say they made him feel tired."

" That's what he *said*. I believe he really liked them all the time. But Mummy ought to have married someone more exciting than a parson. I'm sure she could have."

" I guess she could. She's beautiful in a queer kind of way, isn't she? And she doesn't look old or young or middle-aged like most people. She doesn't seem to be any age at all."

" No. And she's somehow . . . remote, as if half the time she wasn't quite here. . . . Jo, do you remember when she was Etain in *The Immortal Hour*, at Oxford — in a green dress, with her hair down her back ? "

" How funny ! That's the way I always think of her."

Adrian meditated. Then he said pensively : " I bet lots of people loved her when she was young. Wouldn't it be queer if I wasn't Daddy's son after all ! I'm not a bit like him."

" Oh, *Ady* ! " exclaimed Josephine, really shocked. " How can you call your own mother a fallen woman ! "

Adrian regarded her with profound contempt. "Fallen woman, indeed ! You're just a dumb-bell ! You talk like a Victorian novel ! "

" Well, an immoral woman, then."

" You don't become an immoral woman just because you have one or two love affairs with people who aren't your husband," said Adrian sententiously. " Anyway, I think it's just as immoral to marry someone you don't love."

" Perhaps Mummy did love Daddy when she married him. After all, people do change."

" It might be falling in love with someone else that changed her. . . . I wonder whose son I could be if I wasn't Daddy's ? Wouldn't it be grand suddenly to find out you were the son of the Prime Minister ! "

" *I* wouldn't want to have the Prime Minister for a father — a fat old man who's always smoking cigars and drinking champagne."

" Well, the Foreign Secretary, then. He isn't fat."

" No. He isn't fat. But he looks very moral."

The clock on the Library tower struck eleven. A group of boy students, not yet departed for the long summer vacation, came whistling over the bridge, disturbing the children's reflections on the blameless private life of Mr. Anthony Eden. Adrian stood up, stretching himself.

" Let's go down into the gorge, Earwig. I'm getting stiff, and there are too many people around this bridge. They bore me."

★

When the long downward climb had been safely accomplished, Adrian and Josephine seated themselves on a large boulder beside the rapidly flowing stream. Their feet rested on a carpet formed by millions of ancient pine-needles beneath the brown surface of last year's leaves, oak, ironwood, and beech. The tree-tops were now far above their heads, and the narrow arch of sky, its clear blue swept by cirrus clouds driven before a light wind, seemed incredibly far away.

" Wasp," Josephine inquired suddenly, " have you got those letters from Mummy and Daddy that came this morning ? "

Reluctantly Adrian pulled an air-mail envelope out of his pocket, addressed in his father's small scholarly handwriting. He could not have put into words the fathomless aversion that he always felt against opening those frequent, regular, and affectionate letters. He only knew that they inspired in him a deep-rooted apprehension, a fear of being harrowed and disturbed that amounted almost to panic.

" I'd forgotten all about them," he said. " I haven't even opened them."

" Oughtn't we to find out if everything's all right ? "

" I suppose we ought," agreed Adrian. He took a pen-knife from his pocket, and with characteristic neatness slit open his father's letter.

" Read it to me, Ady — if it isn't private."

" I wouldn't mind reading it to you if it was," he said.

Spreading the closely-written sheets on his knee, he began to read aloud.

"'My own dear son,' . . . Why does he have to begin like that! I wish he'd just call me 'Adrian,' like Mummy."

"Well, he isn't like Mummy. Anyway, never mind what he calls you. Go on."

Adrian started again.

" MY OWN DEAR SON,

"I am glad to tell you that, in spite of some rather rough times lately in battered old London, your Mother and I are still here up to date. I do hope you and Jo were not worried by what you read in the American newspapers about our big raid on April 16th-17th."

Adrian looked up. "Worried?" he remarked. "Why, I never even heard about it, did you?"

"No. When was April 16th? What were we doing?"

"It's nearly a month ago. It was about when Kay took us to see *Dumbo*."

"I remember that O.K."

"Of course you do, idiot! . . . Poor old Dad, I suppose he thinks we spend our time reading about what's going on at home!"

He turned to the letter and continued :

"Neither of us got damaged at all, and once again the Church and Vicarage were lucky. But it was one of those occasions when I had to be on my toes all night, helping to look after the poor souls who were less fortunate than ourselves. The B.B.C. gave a very full broadcast about the raid as soon as it was over, so I am going to risk the Censor letting through just a brief account.

"The siren went at nine o'clock, and the All Clear did not sound till 5 A.M. — eight solid hours of it, with hundreds of planes overhead, and bombs dropping every few seconds. According to one of the newspapers, 450 German bombers took part in the attack. The Nazis say it was retaliation for our raid last week on Unter den Linden and the centre of Berlin, and all of us at St. Saviour's had been expecting it for days.

" Right at the start the incendiaries began to crackle down, and there seemed to be thousands of flares in the sky. Then, at midnight, came the ' heavies '. Some were so large that one big building I had to go to (name and place unspecified for obvious reasons) rocked like a ship at sea. Much as one dreads these raids (for I don't pretend to be braver than most) it is extraordinary how detached one feels once they begin — like a person looking on at a show that concerns other people but not himself. I have often felt like that when I have been helping some of the unfortunate victims to salvage their belongings, with plaster and bits of wood falling on my head !

" Just after the All Clear I heard Big Ben strike five, and was thankful to learn from this that it was still there. By that time the broken water-mains in several streets sounded like heavy rain, and the sky was a scarlet glare from numerous fires. I need hardly say that the mains were soon mended and the fires put out ; we've learned now how to do these things quickly ! But plenty of minor damage gets done in addition to *some* major damage (it is extraordinary how much of what you think is major begins to look minor after an hour or two's work). At dawn the streets were ankle-deep in glass, bricks, and charred fragments of wood, yet it was nearly all gone when the shops opened at nine o'clock. I was glad, though, that I had my old shoes on, because clothes are getting pretty scarce and rumour says they'll soon be rationed. We're no longer like the fortunate people in America, who can still walk into a shop and buy as many pairs of shoes as they want.

" I must have walked miles and miles amid the debris, and long before I got back to the Vicarage from a final tour of the parish the sun was rising. In a strange way it was a wonderful sight, for the waning moon was still in the sky when the rosy clouds of dawn met and mingled with the red-tinted smoke from the various fires."

" Oh, Ady ! " exclaimed Josephine. " Doesn't it sound exciting ! I *do* wish I'd been there, don't you ? "

" I don't know," said Adrian cautiously. " Reading about things isn't quite the same as being in them. . . . After all, you didn't even hear the siren that started the War ! "

" Were you frightened, Ady ? "

" I was, a bit," he admitted. " But so was everyone else. All the people in Armada Square scuttled like rabbits."

He went on reading.

" I saw plenty of damage during the night — to flesh and blood as well as buildings — but I came across one of the most grotesque sights when I was going home for a late breakfast. A shop window was smashed to atoms in a street you know very well, and in front of it a glove stretched on a wooden hand was lying on the pavement, looking so dreadfully real that for a moment I felt quite startled. And next to it, on a drunken-looking stand, was a bowler hat smashed in at one side, as if its owner had indulged in a night out ! I was thankful to find your mother all right, as she had to come back from a rehearsal at the Albany Theatre after the raid began. She actually managed to snatch a few hours' sleep in the basement, though how she did it I really don't know.

" Later in the day came the tragic news that a beautiful church once dear to us both had been totally destroyed. I do not mean my own former church ; for a change that unfortunate parish came through pretty well. But the one that is lost was a beloved landmark for many years. I feel as if part of my life had gone with it."

Robert's guarded phrases conveyed only remotely to Adrian the incommunicable grief he had felt in the afternoon of the day that he was describing. Driven by sinister rumours to make a hurried visit to Chelsea, he had stood on the Embankment smitten into silence by the fantastic heap of anonymous rubble which had been Chelsea Old Church. Fallen in upon itself and the five fire-watchers who had sought refuge beneath the tower when they saw the parachute-mine coming down, the macabre ruin symbolised the fate of the serene civilisation to which the Church had belonged.

Buried somewhere amid those fallen stones and crumpled rafters was the gilded weather-vane which had caught the rays of the rising sun on the morning that Robert asked Sylvia to be his wife. Part of his past, he felt, had been bombed away with that reassuring red-brown tower. Only the ornate tombstone of Sir Hans Sloane, the speculative builder of the 1720's who exploited the beauties of the river and put up the first houses in Cheyne Walk, remained ironically undamaged to show where once a church had been.

Prevented by the Censor from drawing morals and adorning tales, Robert had concluded his letter :

" But at least there is much valuable service to be done in these terrible days. Even if salvage work is now practically all that remains of my Ministry which once extended so widely, at least it is work which is vital and necessary, and in which the love of God can still find expression. There is a spiritual fellowship in suffering which unites men and women as nothing else can. Perhaps it will be by the world-wide members of this fellowship, in which those whom we call our enemies share, that the temple of civilisation will be rebuilt when peace returns.

" God bless you and be with you, my dear son. Do not think that I ever forget you for one moment. The days when a letter comes from you are now the happiest days of my life. My thoughts are with you and Josephine every hour, and I pray without ceasing that the time may soon come when we shall be reunited.

" With love to you both from your devoted and affectionate
FATHER."

For a short time the children were silent. Then Josephine said: " You haven't read Mummy's letter. Does it say anything about the raid? "

Adrian picked up the envelope addressed in Sylvia's picturesque calligraphy, strangely eloquent, with its large generous capitals, for a personality so restrained.

" It's written on the same day," he said, " and it begins in the usual way:

" MY DEAR ADRIAN,

" I am very sorry that I have not written to you for nearly a fortnight, but I have been extremely busy with rehearsals for a new play which goes on at the Albany Theatre next month. Not a classical play this time, but a new drama by Stafford Vaughan, who has just been in London on his way to America. He is getting an old man now, but when we met to discuss my part he seemed just as keen and alive as he was when I acted in his play *The Triangle*, the year before you were born. In this new drama I have to be a regular vampire of a mother ; it is a most interesting part to interpret, but I am quite glad that neither of you will see me in it, or you might begin to think I was really like that. The title he has chosen is rather unusual ; it is *But for the Family*."

" That's certainly a queer title," commented Josephine. " But what does she say about the raid? "

Adrian glanced quickly down the front and half-covered back of the single sheet.

" Nothing at all," he said. " It's all about her play and the people in it. Here, finish it yourself, lazybones. I'm tired of reading aloud."

Josephine took the letter, but gave it only a cursory glance.

" You know, Ady," she said slowly, " those raids on London don't seem *real* to me somehow. I can't think of them as happening to real people like Mummy and Daddy."

" Jo," inquired Adrian suddenly, " would you mind if we heard they'd both been killed ? "

Josephine's open, friendly face looked troubled. But, because she was an unusually honest child, she answered candidly.

" It seems an awful thing to say about one's parents, but I don't believe I should, right now. If we'd never gone I would have, and I might if we ever went back. But right now it's somehow different. They seem so far away, like people in a book."

" *I* shouldn't care at all," said Adrian decisively. " After all, we've been here a long time. In another month it'll be a whole year. Perhaps it isn't so much for me now I'm fifteen. But it's a whale of a time for you. I don't suppose you even remember much about coming here."

" But I *do* ! " exclaimed Josephine indignantly. " I'm twelve next week — I'm not just a kid ! I remember the docks, and those two rough days, and that iceberg. . . . Ady, did you *mind* coming away ? "

" I did rather," Adrian admitted reluctantly. " I never wanted to come."

" Then would you like to go back ? "

Adrian meditated. " I don't rightly know," he said at last. " Now I'm actually here, it's different." Suddenly confidential, he acknowledged to her what he would have told no one else. " I just hated the chaps at Eton calling me yellow, though they were all stinkers. It wasn't fair. It was Daddy who was yellow, not me. I might feel yellow, though, if we never got back till the War was quite over. But I don't want to go for a long time. I'm tired of always being moved about ; I want to stay put somewhere. And here one's so much freer, somehow. Dean D. doesn't worry about us like Daddy did. Nor does Kay, though she does have more time to be with us than Mummy."

"No. She and Mummy are alike for not worrying. But she isn't beautiful like Mummy. And in spite of being American, she's not nearly so smart."

"I'd like to be quite old before I go back — old enough to stand up to Dad," continued Adrian, ignoring Josephine's comparisons.

"*I* wouldn't mind going back," she announced. "But then I didn't mind our coming. Nor did Mummy. I don't believe she minded at all. The person who got upset was Daddy."

"Yes, didn't he! Do you remember his face when we went up the gangway, and that tarpaulin thing came down? I can see it now. He looked as if he was going to cry."

"Perhaps he did. . . . Oh, Ady, wouldn't that have been awful? What a good thing we got away first!"

"Yes," said Adrian. "We got away all right. We got away. . . ."

And he relapsed into silence as his mind, in a lightning series of scenes, re-pictured the events which had carried him and Josephine from the outbreak of war to the unknown shores of the New World.

CHAPTER IX

"*The Dark Night of the Soul*"

FIVE days after his brief Sunday morning sermon on September 3rd, 1939, Robert Carbury had received a letter from the Home Office. Though discreetly and courteously worded, its significance was clear.

A report, it said, had been sent in to the Department which concerned Mr. Carbury's address in Armada Square just after the declaration of war. While respecting in every way his personal opinions, and without wishing unduly to limit his freedom of utterance, it was the duty of the Home Department to make clear that any attempt, direct or indirect, to incite opposition to the war effort among those eligible to serve in His Majesty's Forces now came within a category which rendered the offender liable to prosecution if the Government saw fit. It was, of course, hoped that no such necessity would arise. The Department felt sure that such an outstanding Christian leader as Mr. Carbury would wish to cooperate with them in their difficult task of defending the national security during a period of grave emergency.

Robert's reply was also polite, and equally firm.

" I am greatly obliged for your communication ", he wrote from his desk which still stood in the window of his top-floor study, where he felt very close to the barrage balloons floating like prehistoric fish with opalescent bodies in the sky above his head. " I am sure it was sent with the most courteous intention, and I am grateful to you for notifying me of the effect which the outbreak of war has already had upon traditional British freedoms.

" But my view of Christian ideals and obligations remains the same as it has been during the twelve years of my ministry at St. Saviour's. It has not undergone modification because the Government of this country has seen fit to declare war against a foreign power. The present situation, I feel, makes more demands rather than less upon the integrity of Christian leadership.

" I acknowledge my obligation to the State, and the debt I owe to it for services and protection. But the authority of my Master, Jesus Christ, comes before that of the Government. I have always put it first, and I shall continue to do so. I can recognise no limits to the range of the Gospel which I am pledged to teach."

The Home Office made no further attempt to restrain Robert's utterances, but the hidden hand of a State making incompatible and embarrassing endeavours to wage total war and at the same time maintain its democratic principles, soon revealed its grasp in other ways.

Police officers, usually in plain clothes though occasionally they wore uniform, seemed suddenly to develop an increased enthusiasm for the services at St. Saviour's. The warm welcome that they received from the friendly, well-lighted Church and its Vicar as they came in from the smothering gloom of the black-out sent some of them back to Scotland Yard with a guilty sense of being ill-adapted to the rôle of Judas before the Crucifixion.

One Sunday evening, coming in through the back of the Church for Evensong, Robert immediately recognised the face of the uniformed young policeman sitting awkwardly at the far end of the last row of pews. It belonged, he recalled, to a recent member of St. Saviour's Youth Club.

" Hallo, Joe ! " he exclaimed, going up to the young man with extended hand. " I'm glad to see you back here ! " One of his most disarming smiles broke over his face as he added : " You've come to keep an eye on me, I suppose ! "

The former Youth Club member looked humiliated and miserable. " I'm that sorry, Mr. Carbury. I wouldn't have had this job for toffee. But it's orders. I've got no choice."

" Of course you haven't ! " said Robert. " Don't worry, Joe. If you ever have to arrest me, I promise I'll go quietly ! "

Other policemen, less sympathetic to Robert's now " suspect " opinions, began also to attend B.O.J. meetings in different parts of the country. Shortly after the outbreak of war, Robert had sent an emergency summons to the B.O.J. Executive. This was attended by several eminent Vice-Presidents and also by Ted Rogers, now a married man with two children, but still caretaker at the national headquarters and a part-time open-air speaker on Tower Hill.

It soon became clear that the appetite for martyrdom of the B.O.J. representatives had increased with their opportunities. Without exception they affirmed their willingness, and that of all the members whom they had been able to contact, to follow their beloved leader, Bob Carbury, through imprisonment and death to the realisation of " Jerusalem " here or hereafter. Their eagerness to bear witness to their ideals in law-court and prison became, indeed, so manifest that a private official instruction went out to the police urging them to refrain from arresting B.O.J. speakers except in cases of extreme provocation. Those members who were of military age and became conscientious objectors would be dealt with by normal legislation under the provisions laid down in the National Service Acts. In the case of the others, it was pointed out, a large number of willing martyrs would merely extend the undesirable influence of the organisation. These instructions applied particularly to the Reverend Robert Carbury himself. Any action which made him still more conspicuous would only serve to increase the unfortunate size of his extensive following.

Without doubt, the popular Vicar of St. Saviour's had become one of their worst headaches to conscientious, bewildered officials nervously searching for scalps. The prestige which he had, unhappily, so strongly consolidated during the twelve years of his ministry could not be dis-

credited by the customary allegation of " Fascism ". His
unquestioned practice of democratic Christian Socialism
in his parish throughout his tenure of the living of St.
Saviour's made the accusation ridiculous, while his Victoria Cross won in the 1914 War rendered equally absurd
any attempt to depict him as moved by cowardice or
"armchair convictions". There was nothing to be done
but restrict his opportunities, in so far as they could be
restricted at all, to the indeterminate bounds of his
London parish.

One of the first concrete symptoms of official disapproval was the cancellation, after only three weeks of
war, of the regular monthly service broadcast on Sunday
evenings from St. Saviour's. This service, usually conducted by Robert himself, had been a feature of English
religious life ever since its institution in 1929. Now, after
nearly eleven years, it was brought to an end by an
embarrassed and apologetic letter from Broadcasting
House.

They were sure, said the writer, that Mr. Carbury
would realise, in view of the national emergency, how
important it was to give the maximum time in B.B.C.
programmes to those types of religious celebration which
were designed to encourage the war effort. The letter
concluded with a politely expressed if somewhat vague
hope that the broadcast services would be resumed after
the celebration of Britain's victory — " a happy outcome
of the present crisis which we feel certain will not be
unduly delayed ".

During October and November, 1939, the number of
people who wrote to the B.B.C. to express their sorrow
at losing the sound of St. Saviour's great bell and the
friendly voice of " Broadcasting Bob " — which had already comforted them at sea, on remote air-fields, and
in the loneliness of foreign service stations — must have

run into thousands. Robert could guess their total from his own correspondents, who deplored the lost consolation, and asked why, just when war made their need so much greater, the Vicar of St. Saviour's should choose to end it. Not to one such letter-writer did it apparently occur that the Vicar of St. Saviour's had now passed under Government control, or that the man who seemed to them a simple lover of God and the most genuine Christian whom they knew had become, from the standpoint of war-organising authorities, " unsound ".

" I wouldn't mind their stopping my broadcast services if they'd found someone to do them better," said Robert to Lord Westerly just before his now truncated Christmas festival. " But in the midst of world-wide tragedy, with people daily saying goodbye to their nearest and dearest, why deny them the help that only the love of Jesus can give ? "

" My dear Bob," answered Frederick Westerly, whose Presidency of the B.O.J. had brought him into still more frequent contact with Robert since the outbreak of war, " don't you realise that for war-making Governments your beloved Jesus is the arch-Fifth Columnist ? He's a suspect not only in one country but in all — the super-nationalist who stands for humanity against a narrow belligerent patriotism, the inconvenient symbol of the very values which must be destroyed before ' victory ' can be won."

" Oh, I realise that all right ! I feel as if I'm standing on an island, and all round the totalitarian tide is encroaching. Every day it steals a bit more of the area in which I can function effectively. Well, I take off my hat to the Government for the skill of its methods ! It's so much more stultifying to be quietly frustrated than directly attacked ! "

I suppose, he thought, struggling for reconciliation

with his official critics after Lord Westerly had gone, I shall ultimately find my understanding deepened by these successive humiliations. I shan't just feel sympathy *for* my down-and-outs, but *with* them. All that well-concealed sense of superiority will go, just because I'm now one of them.

But to the soldiers in uniform who still crowded his Church and often spent nights in the Crypt air-raid shelter when beds were not available elsewhere, the Vicar of St. Saviour's did not appear to be an object of humiliation. He was their friend who faced with them the bleak realities of war, the teacher who had no sentimental illusions about its glories though he had won a decoration which each one coveted. Nor did he seem ineffective to the civilians who were cared for, as black-out casualties, at the First-Aid Post in the Crypt where he was officially in charge, and the youngest curate, helped by a volunteer district nurse from the parish, bandaged cut foreheads, sprained wrists, and twisted ankles.

With Robert himself those threatened civilians, through the dark, cold, and all too quiet winter of the " phony war ", waited apprehensively for spring.

*

When Adrian came home for the first Christmas holidays of war-time, he noticed a change in his father. It was unmistakable, though difficult to define. In spite of the fact that in his son's eyes Robert had always been "fussy", he could never have appeared even to his children as a strident personality, so that it was incorrect to describe him as quieter. But he was, in some subtle way, more reserved and less spontaneous in his approach to the routine problems of daily life. Since this made his demands upon his son's responsiveness less frequent, Adrian might have been expected to welcome the change.

And yet, somehow, it disquieted him.

The stir of strangers and suppliants at the Vicarage had not diminished, yet if he could have found the appropriate words, Adrian would have described its atmosphere as less positive and hopeful. A never-expressed but palpable dread seemed to darken it, and to wear a shape that he could almost touch. It was like a black bat with overhanging wings, hovering in the air, waiting to pounce. He only escaped from its shadow at night, and then the barrage balloons, glistening in the moonlight above Armada Square, seemed to exercise a conscious supervision over his most secret thoughts. The pig-like heads emerging from the swaying fish-shaped bodies appeared to be endowed with critical eyes; they reminded him of a text — " Thou, God, seest me " — which had always alarmed him in his nursery days.

Beyond them the distant stars, now clearly visible in the unilluminated night, looked so intimate and comforting that he could not imagine how he had ever thought them hostile. They made even the waiting unoccupied trenches and sand-bagged shelters in the dark city appear less sinister.

After Easter, when the German invasion of Scandinavia had begun, the change in his father seemed still more marked. It oppressed him so much that he even brought himself to ask his mother for an explanation.

" What's up with Daddy? He seems somehow queer these hols."

Sylvia could have given him at least a partial answer, for that very morning Robert had shown her one of the anonymous letters which had now begun to arrive in growing numbers at the Vicarage. (" To Robert Carbury : How glad you must feel that your friends the Nazis are only just across the North Sea ! If you can't keep your mouth shut, why don't you go over and join them ?

And don't come back ; stay where you belong. We shan't miss you.")

Since Robert had long realised that anonymous letters were invariably the products of abnormal and unbalanced mentalities, Sylvia did not understand why they so much distressed him. Perhaps she could hardly have been expected to perceive that the self-confidence which Robert, in spite and not because of her, had spent thirty years in building up could be destroyed in an hour. But she knew that he would not want his reactions disclosed to his children, so she answered Adrian evasively.

" Oh, he's only worried about the way the War's going. Everybody is. After all, the Nazis are rather near now they're in Denmark and Norway. I'm glad you and Jo are out of London in term-time."

Adrian was hardly back at Eton before the breath-taking rush of events began which shook Europe to its old foundations, and carried the tide of warfare right to the coasts of Britain for the first time in nine centuries. In common with the rest of the school Adrian listened to histrionic though realistic broadcasts by the Prime Minister demanding blood, toil, sweat, and tears, and committing the British Empire to fight on " if necessary for years, if necessary alone ". But amid the usual burdensome routine of prayers, lessons, gym, cricket, and preparation, which was harder than ever to endure with equanimity, the evacuation of Dunkirk seemed a far-off melodrama taking place on another planet. More significant, as the rolling German legions occupied the Channel ports, were visits to some of the younger boys by agitated parents, who according to current school rumour removed them from Eton for journeys to America or the Dominions. The picturesque and merciless comments made on the manners, morals, and ancestry of the departed by the scornful majority which remained caused Adrian uneasily to hope that the shame-making notion of sending him abroad would not occur to his own father and mother.

★

The day before the fall of Paris, Lord Westerly called on Robert Carbury with an early edition of the *Evening Crier* in his hand.

" I thought you ought to see this," he said, handing the newspaper to Robert.

" Thank you for coming so promptly, Fred. It's another attack, I suppose."

" Yes — and even more scurrilous than the last."

Robert opened the paper and began to read, under a black-lettered headline, "The Quislings in Our Midst", a conspicuous leading article.

Why, at a time when we are facing the greatest national emergency since the Battle of Hastings, do our weak-kneed bureaucrats continue to tolerate the presence amongst us of men and women who are no friends to this country ? Why, for example, is the *Reverend* Robert Carbury permitted to take refuge behind a mere clerical label and continue to occupy the influential pulpit of St. Saviour's, Armada Square ? Are our myopic officials even aware that young men and women in the Forces, innocent but misguided, still flock to this church to hear the high purpose for which they wear His Majesty's uniform disparaged and misrepresented ?

Sunday by Sunday, this self-styled " Christian leader " is allowed to make his treasonable utterances to these impressionable boys and girls, thereby undoubtedly giving great comfort to England's enemies. The *Evening Crier* believes that those who thus blasphemously use the sacred name of Christ for the purpose of traducing our nation's great sacrifices in the cause of righteousness should have their mouths shut for them, and be kept in a place where they can do no harm during the present critical period.

But this ranting cleric, though the worst because the most

dangerously popular of our conspicuous quislings, is not the only one. . . .

Robert methodically folded the paper and handed it back to Lord Westerly.

" Before the War began," he said, " Anselm warned me that this kind of thing would happen, I suppose it would have come earlier if the first months hadn't been so quiet. There's nothing to be done but endure it."

" I'm not sure. You can't altogether ignore persistent attacks of this kind."

" What do you mean, Fred? Surely you're not suggesting I should take legal action? "

" Certainly not. No action against a newspaper for such an article would have an earthly chance in the present state of opinion. You'd only damage your real claim to be called a Christian. No, it's others I was thinking of. You have a duty to those who are dear to you."

" A duty? Because of this article! What kind of duty could that involve? "

Lord Westerly put the newspaper in his pocket, and spoke with quiet deliberation.

" If I were you, Bob, I'd take advantage of the present overseas evacuation scheme to send your children out of the country."

Knowing Robert's devotion to his family, he had not expected this advice to be favourably received, but he was hardly prepared for the stricken pallor that spread over Robert's face. For a moment there was silence. Then Robert spoke, almost inaudibly.

" Oh, I couldn't — consider that. It would be a terrible thing to do! " Regaining control of himself, he added : " Just think of the effect on the parish! All the children in London can't go! "

" Which matters to you most," asked Lord Westerly gravely, " your popularity, or the fate of your children? "

" Good heavens, Fred, it wasn't my popularity I was thinking of! That's about gone anyway. What matters is the example I set. How can I take a step that isn't open to everyone else? "

" Because you're not in the same position as everyone else. There's no one in England who *is* in the same position." Lord Westerly laid his gloves and stick on the table and spoke emphatically.

" I want you to listen carefully, Bob, to what I'm going to say. You're regarded, not without reason, as the leading Christian in this country. No, don't protest. I said the leading *Christian*, not the leading cleric. . . . Now, do you suppose the Gestapo doesn't know that? A Christian resistance will be as inconvenient to Hitler as the other kind — more so, because it's less calculable, and its leaders would be inspired by the spirit of martyrdom which is ready to sacrifice everything but the soul. If invasion comes, you'll be about the first person the Nazis will arrest. On the other hand, you'll be equally unpopular with our own officials. They're centuries away from understanding what is meant by mental or spiritual fight. For them the men and women who resist war are simply the first people to put down on the Home Office black list."

" But — do you seriously think invasion will come? "

" Nobody knows. Neither the Lords nor the Commons could tell you if they wanted to. Even Churchill can't guess the workings of Hitler's mind. But everyone behind the scenes thinks there's a ninety per cent probability. The Nazis would have to pay heavily for it, of course, but we can't challenge their air superiority. You'll soon see that when the raids on London start — as they will any day now. If they choose to pay the price, they'll come here. God knows we're not in a position to stop them."

Robert meditated on this first-hand political information.

" I realised last year that Adrian and Josephine ought
to stay out of London," he said. " But that's something
anyone's children can do. If the South becomes dangerous, Sylvia can take them to her people in Newcastle.
Or I could open up Hoddershall Ash."

" I should hardly choose Newcastle-on-Tyne as a
refuge," commented Lord Westerly. " The enemy aren't
likely to confine their attack to a stupid bee-line across
the Channel. Anyhow, in the kind of invasion that's
probably coming the relative security of different parts
of a small island is neither here nor there. And even if it
were, you can't be certain of Sylvia's safety."

Robert started.

" *Sylvia!* But, good heavens, Fred, she's never taken
any part in politics! Except for an occasional stage performance to raise funds, she's had nothing to do with the
B.O.J. I've sometimes wished she'd cared more. But if
what you're saying is true, it's probably a good thing
she hasn't."

" I'm afraid you still can't be sure nothing would
happen to her. I wish one could be — but people mad-
dened by war and fear don't make subtle distinctions,
and the authorities won't take chances when the country's
in peril. If the position were reversed and we were
invading Germany, do you suppose our military pundits
would feel any tenderness for Göring's wife ? "

The ghost of a rueful smile flickered over Robert's
pale face.

" Are *you* suggesting I resemble Göring ? "

" Only because you both married actresses. I don't
suppose Fräulein Emmy Sonnemann was any more interested in politics than Sylvia when she was on the stage.
But that doesn't mean we should let Frau Göring go

where she wanted and do what she liked if we ever became conquering heroes."

For a moment they both remained silent. Then Lord Westerly continued.

" I was an organised minoritarian in the last war, Bob — yes, when you were in France winning your V.C. . . . I remember being thrown out of the Queen's Hall in March, 1918, when our armies were retreating in France. I came round in Marlborough Street Police Station after being knocked silly for half an hour. But the peril we faced then is nothing to the one that threatens us today. Once let the Nazis touch our shores, and the public won't stop at throwing speakers out of meetings. Would it be fair, in those circumstances, to put all the responsibility for the children on your wife — even if she were free ? "

Robert turned and looked out of the window. It was the early afternoon of a beautiful June day. In the Square an intrepid municipal band was playing selections from Gilbert and Sullivan. He felt overwhelmed by the incongruity of their conversation and its fantastic assumptions of invasion and arrest, torture and death, with this tranquil familiar scene hardly changed by its inconspicuous trenches and little piles of sandbags from the Armada Square of his first June at St. Saviour's in 1927. To assimilate the fact that the fantasy was the reality and the tranquillity the illusion required an imaginative effort of which even Robert was hardly capable.

Lord Westerly walked over and joined him at the window.

" I'm warning you, Bob, as seriously as I know how to do it. Once the Germans land, there'll be a race between the Home Office and the Gestapo to arrest you first. I wouldn't guarantee your liberty for half an hour. . . . My dear friend, I know something of the concentra-

tion camps in Germany. I wrote a pamphlet about them
for Gollancz seven years ago, when half the Tories were
saying what fine fellows the Nazis were——"

" I know you did, Fred. It was a courageous job."

" Well, invasion will mean a concentration camp for
you, either British or German — and almost as certainly
for Mrs. Carbury too. We shall doubtless all be in it
together. What about your son and daughter then? The
life of children whose parents are in prison is sheer unmitigated hell, even if they're not taken themselves and
shut up somewhere at the back of beyond. Adrian anyhow is old enough to be shot by the enemy as a possible
spy. The chances are you'd never see either of them
again. So why not take a political veteran's advice, and
send them to some other country where at least you know
they'll be safe? "

Looking at his watch he rose to leave, and Robert
accompanied him downstairs.

" You've given me a good deal to think about," he
said. " I'll talk it over with Sylvia."

" That's the best thing you can do," agreed Lord
Westerly, putting on his pale yellow suède gloves with
meticulous care. " If I'm not mistaken, Bob, your wife's
a thoroughly well-balanced woman. She's less emotional
than so many stage people. I'm sure she'll give you some
wise counsel."

Closing the front door, Robert went slowly upstairs to
their bedroom. Sylvia, he knew, was there, studying her
part for a revival of *Lady Windermere's Fan*, which was to
open, if the Nazis permitted, at the Connoisseurs' Theatre
the following week. From her chair beside the open
window she looked up as he came in, and perceived immediately from his haggard face and troubled eyes that
one of the profound conflicts with which she was familiar
was tormenting his mind.

" You look tired, dear," she said. " Has something gone wrong in the parish ? "

" Not exactly in the parish," he replied, sitting down beside her. " Frederick Westerly has just been here. He brought an article to show me, in the *Evening Crier*."

" What was it ? Another attack ? "

" Yes. Even more bitter than usual. . . . Darling, Fred Westerly thinks that if the Germans land I might be arrested. He thinks we ought to send the children out of the country."

For a few moments Sylvia sat silent, meditating. Then she said : " I believe it's a good idea, Robert. You're entitled to your opinions, of course. Everybody is, especially those who feel as strongly about things as you do. But we oughtn't to expect Adrian and Jo to pay for them."

" In effect that's what Westerly said. And he also said," continued Robert, feeling as though he were signing his own death-warrant, " that you, God forgive me, might be involved too. My darling, if we have to send them away, you ought to go with them."

She stood up, closing her copy of Oscar Wilde's play.

" Thank you for thinking of that, my dear. I know what it means to you. But it's something no one but myself can decide."

Almost unconsciously taking her hand and holding it tightly in his, Robert went on.

" Westerly may be an alarmist, of course. But he isn't usually. He seemed to think invasion might mean imprisonment and even death — for us both."

" I daresay it would," she said, as calmly as though he were announcing the probability of a slight cold in the head. (" Fear death — when Lawrence died ! " whispered the voice of her secret obsession.) She added quietly : " I don't intend to go abroad with the children.

I shan't even leave London unless my work takes me away. I'm staying here with you."

"Oh, my love! God knows I want you!" he cried in his anguished dilemma. "But that means they'd go alone — face the journey by themselves — live with strangers in a country they've never seen. . . ."

"I know. It can't be helped."

"But, Sylvia," he protested, shocked and incredulous, "wouldn't you *mind*? Think of someone else bringing them up, for months or years . . . perhaps even taking our place in their lives. . . ."

"I shouldn't care so long as they were well and happy," she said. "It's the fact of their happiness that matters to me — not whether I'm responsible for it. . . . But if they're going I suppose it ought to be soon. Delay won't make the journey any safer."

"My God, no! I'll think about it, darling. I'll pray about it. . . ."

"Yes, do, dear," she said, pitying his mental agony, but feeling it, as she always did, to be incredibly remote and unreal. "It'll help you to make up your mind."

He crossed the old graveyard and knelt down in the chancel of his Church, bowing his head on his arms in the blue and violet light of the deep-hued east window. That chancel had been the scene of so many wrestlings with his soul, so many searchings after union with Jesus, so many recent prayers for charity towards those who insulted his name, frustrated his work, and thwarted his mission. But now it became the scene of a darker, more primitive conflict — a struggle which involved his love, his fatherhood, his family life, all the precious heritage of the departed years. A rising nausea seemed to choke him; his head swam, and great drops of sweat started out on his forehead as once they had appeared on the forehead of his Master at Gethsemane.

" O God," cried his heart in its half-articulate torment, " if it were only my life that must be given ! . . . Such a little thing, to die ; to sleep in peace. But to give up Adrian and Josephine, my darlings, my life's joy and blessing — that's more than I can bear. . . . Don't ask that of me, Lord Jesus ! Beloved Friend, let this cup pass ! This one, just this, I cannot drink. Let it pass, my Father ! To lose them now is too much. Even though Sylvia, my beloved, stays with me, I cannot bear it ! "

Hardly realising that he was now murmuring his prayers aloud, he went on.

" O my God, change history for one week — one day — one hour ! Just to give me the right to keep them with me. . . . No, I can't ask that for myself alone ! Even though I strove with heart and mind and soul, I failed to prevent the international consequences of human sin — the sin of us all. For that failure I must pay with the rest. How then can I sacrifice the children's lives to my love for them ? . . . Adrian, Josephine, my dear ones — must I let you go ? Jesus, not my will but Thine. Show me the way ! "

Intolerable hours seemed to pass before he rose from his knees, still undecided, and stumbled back to the Vicarage. On the silver tray in the hall lay a cable addressed to himself. He opened and read it :

Please send your boy and girl to us till things improve.
KATHLEEN AND RICHMOND DOWNING

It was a timely, if unwelcome, answer to prayer.

CHAPTER X

Nine Days in June

OVER the docks at Liverpool drifted a film of smoke, blown from chimneys and funnels by a light, intermittent wind. Uttering their hoarse squawking cries, scores of sea-birds circled the grey-painted ships and flapped above the cranes in the harbour.

A week after Robert's conversation with Lord Westerly, Adrian and Josephine stood in a large covered shed waiting for the immigration officials who would confirm their right, as evacuated children, to seek refuge in a far-off continent from Nazi invasion. Hating everybody and everything, Adrian edged further and further from his parents. As he perceived with dismay, they were recognised by nearly all the other families present. The fundamental disturbance so long dreaded had come at last in this utter uprooting of his short, unsettled life. Its lack of stability seemed to be symbolised by the small heap of battered school luggage over which he was keeping guard.

When the summons to leave Eton came to him, he knew from the previous experience of equally rebellious contemporaries that it would be useless to resist. Quietly and lugubriously, he packed his suitcases with the urgency demanded. He told the undesired news to none of his schoolmates, sought nobody out to say goodbye. Even so, he had not altogether escaped some opprobrious comments from boys encountered by chance in the corridor as he hurried with his baggage to the waiting taxi.

On the docks he looked round with shame at the collection of tired, grimy toddlers who were to be his fellow-passengers. Fatigued by the journey from London, they now raised their exasperated voices in protest at the long delay, yet further wringing the conflict-ridden hearts of their dejected parents. Boys and girls of his own advanced age seemed to be disconcertingly few. Even Josephine emphasized her lack of equivalent years by obstinately clasping a dilapidated toy monkey. When a queue of older girls from a school which was evacuating all its pupils marched placidly on to the dock, his heavy heart lifted with relief. Still, they *were* only girls! He felt thankful that his *bête noire*, that big bully Hammersley Major, could not see him in this humiliating situation. How awful it would be if private television sets were ever invented!

A middle-aged woman in the dark-green uniform of the Women's Voluntary Services entered the shed, pushing a wheeled trolley loaded with packets of biscuits and cartons of milk. At the sight of it the lamentations of the wailing juveniles ceased as abruptly as though a tap had been turned off, and were instantly replaced by a loud jubilant clamour. When the younger children had been served and were temporarily preoccupied, the Good Samaritan with the trolley came to Adrian and Josephine.

" Have some biscuits, sonny? I'm sure you're ready for your tea."

Adrian winced a little at the mode of address, and accepted only one biscuit.

" Thank you," he said, with what he hoped was adult dignity, " I'm not very hungry."

But Josephine, undeterred by his restraint, grabbed three biscuits apiece in each grubby hand.

" You silly, Ady!" she exclaimed. " They're Digestives!"

As she consumed them ravenously, even Robert's tired face relaxed into a rueful smile.

" How can she!" he whispered enviously to Sylvia.

She too smiled, pushing back the long blue veil blown over her face from the back of her pre-war Paris hat by the restless sea-wind.

" Surely it's comforting, isn't it ? " she said. " At least the children aren't worrying. What does it matter about us, when it's just a fine adventure for them ! "

She realised, as she spoke, that she was not describing Adrian's state of mind with precision. Rebellious and incommunicative, he looked almost as pale and weary as his father. But there was no purpose in emphasizing to Robert his son's obvious reluctance to face the long perilous voyage and the unknown farther shore.

To Robert and other apprehensive parents, dreading the moment of departure yet longing for an end to the protracted anguish of farewell, the immigration officials seemed to delay their arrival for an incalculable age. But they appeared at last, and began to examine currency and documents with the detached equanimity of State servants to whom tragedies of separation are part of an habitual daily routine. Waiting for the slow fulfilment of the long formalities, Robert suddenly perceived, be- yond the tarpaulin-shrouded enclosure, the grey-painted, anonymous little Cunarder which was waiting to carry his children to Canada for the first stage of their journey to Acropolis, New York. At Montreal an unconventional temporary guardian was to meet them in the distinguished person of Damon Sullivan. Partly to test his sincerity, and partly to spare the Downings unnecessary travelling, Sylvia had cabled reminding him of his promise made to her in 1938. Adrian and Josephine, she told him, would soon be on their way to a destination which he could ascertain from the New York offices of Thomas Cook & Son.

With a promptitude which she had not expected, Damon cabled replying that he would meet the children and see them on their journey as far as New York.

"It's not the shortest way from Montreal to Acropolis," he had written in a letter which Sylvia was still to receive, "but they'll get more kick out of New York than Toronto. Your Mrs. Downing and I have figured out the trains between us over the telephone. I am going to see the kids off on the night train, and she will meet them at her end in the morning. I'm sorry that the expected had to happen, but we will take good care of your boy and girl over here till the storm dies down and you can have them back. God bless you, honey; and don't let the Nazis catch you before the guns of old England blow them all into the sea!"

A stir like a light wind set the families on the dock in motion. The time for embarkation had come. Hardly waiting to say goodbye to their desolate and still doubting relatives, some of the younger children ran excitedly to the gangway. A few babies, solemn and bewildered, clutched the hands of their mothers who were taking them to Canada. Josephine, now thoroughly dishevelled, flung her arms round her father in an enthusiastic bear-like hug.

"Look, Daddy, we're going! Isn't it exciting! But I do wish you and Mummy were coming too!"

"Oh, Jo! So do I!" he murmured, his lips pressed against her tangled dark curls. Unconscious of his pain, she cried "Goodbye, Mummy!" hugged her mother with similar energy, and sped towards the gangway.

Awkwardly Adrian put out his hand, and his father gripped it.

"Goodbye, and God keep you always, my beloved son!"

Oh, Lord, thought Adrian, this makes me sick! But at least he isn't going to kiss me, thank Heaven! He turned abruptly from his father. "Goodbye, Mummy. I'll keep an eye on Jo."

" Thank you, Adrian," she said quietly. " I know you will."

With his head and back erect, Adrian followed Josephine to the gangway. At the bottom of the steps she spun round, and waved both hands gaily.

" Goodbye, goodbye ! Mummy, Daddy ! Bye-bye ! "

But Adrian did not wave to his parents. Glancing half round as he walked towards the ship, he saw through the crowd the pale ovals of their faces, his last link with the secure familiar things which had signified home. Then, turning his back, he followed Josephine up the steps without a word or sign of farewell.

For a long moment Robert stood as though fixed to the ground, gazing at the flapping tarpaulin which half-hid the gangway where the children had disappeared. Gently Sylvia touched his arm.

" We might as well go now, my dear. There's no point in waiting. The ship isn't likely to sail for hours."

Without speaking he signalled a taxi, which took them, now both silent, to the train that carried them back to London. The following evening the revival of *Lady Windermere's Fan* opened at the Connoisseurs' Theatre, and before the play was half-way through, Sylvia had forgotten the children. But Robert sat in his study till long after midnight, remembering his ache of longing in the years before their birth, and wondering whether he would ever see them again.

*

After twenty-four hours of despondent homesickness on the *Lavinia*, Adrian decided that it would be sensible to lose his nostalgia in a book. But all the sunny parts of the deck seemed to be alive with small, shrill, indefatigable children, skipping and perilously playing " tig ". Still smaller children, of whom some were always crying, came out for periodic airings in their mothers' arms.

Already the ship suffered conspicuously from the austerities of war-time. Though the deck was now warm and cheerful in the afternoon sunshine, there were no deck-chairs; the passengers sat on coats, rugs, or their life-jackets, though this was officially forbidden. Even in nine months an indefinable shabbiness had crept over everything. Whether he was behind the blackened port-holes or out in the air, Adrian felt oppressed by the characteristic smell of the ship, compounded of paint, rubber, oil, and tar. On the boat deck above him he could see the small slung lifeboats with their coils of rope and chains attached, and wondered with a sinking of the stomach whether he would ever have to escape in one from the hovering, unseen peril that was never absent from his thoughts.

Somewhere among those boats Josephine, whom he had already abandoned any attempt to control, was zestfully playing hide-and-seek with a group of younger children. Adrian felt lonely and ill at ease. He was too old to be interested in the games of the juveniles, but too young to be invited to join the small groups of adults — mostly mothers or grandmothers of evacuee children — who congregated in the corners of the lounge, endlessly recapitulating the circumstances in which they left home and the reasons that had led to their departure.

With an air of indifference to them all Adrian slouched across to the deck rail, and immediately forgot his loneliness in the sheer beauty of the day. The sea was smooth and pale, like skim milk, with sparklers at the edges of the waves. On the horizon the sky appeared a gentle azure, deepening to cobalt in the huge pavilion overhead. He walked across to the starboard side and saw the faint outline of the Irish coast. Because it was his last contact with the country of his birth, it reminded him of their journey to Liverpool the previous day.

They had travelled in a long littered compartment, stacked high with baggage discreetly and uninformatively labelled. In the next coach a young baby wailed incessantly. Outside the windows lay the green, mildly rolling countryside which divides London from Cheshire, so completely devoid in its tame urbanity of any feature that reflected the heartbreak and sick uncertainty gripping most of the passengers. The fields covered with half-grown wheat and the railway banks in their June dress of wild roses suggested a pretty pink, white, and green carnival, where no one wept, swore, or got wildly drunk.

As they reached the Midlands the elms spread fanwise, their freshness gone after two months of uninterrupted warm weather. Electric pylons rose incongruously from sloping meadows. Towns with familiar names — Rugby, Stafford, Crewe — seemed to flash past the non-stop train; their stations and railside houses had lost such trimness as they ever possessed after nearly a year of war. Beyond them narrow canals, spanned by little bridges of red or grey stone, flowed sluggishly between hawthorn hedges; cows fed placidly in buttercup fields; from the grass several plover, disturbed by the train, rose crying plaintively into the air.

" Will the children remember this if they never see it again ? " Adrian's father had asked himself from his laden heart. " Will they ever realise how typically, profoundly English it all is ? "

Already the details were a blur in Adrian's mind, but the impression remained.

Next day the ship crossed that point beyond Ireland, familiar to all travellers to Canada, which is known as the Devil's Hole. Here the ocean lies deep, and fierce cross-currents meet in a swirl of tempestuous waters. The sun never seems to shine at this spot, and even the sea-birds shun it. Feeling seasick and miserable, Adrian retired to the small cabin which, despite his age, the crowded passenger list compelled him to share with Josephine. Unmoved by the weather she waited on him with inexpert good nature and superior commiseration, to which he was indifferent since it came only from her.

At first he almost welcomed his prostration, which quenched apprehensive speculations in discomfort and gave him an excuse to avoid the crowded lounge where Josephine was blithely at home. But two nights later, when sea and sky were calming down again, he had grown weary of lying solitary in his upper berth. Just before midnight, unable to sleep, he put one eye close to the top section of their port-hole, and through a crack in the black paint saw one vivid star. Obeying a sudden impulse he threw his coat over his pyjamas, crept down the corridor, and climbed the steep staircase to the empty boat deck where he could be quite alone.

" I *won't* mind ! " he said to himself. " It's silly to mind things. After all, I'm not a baby. I'm fourteen and a half. If it wasn't for Jo, they wouldn't have made me come ! "

He rubbed his eyes fiercely, hating himself for the unmanly moisture which had gathered there. " The chaps said I was yellow. I'm not ! It's Daddy who is — V.C. and all."

He pushed open the heavy door, and went out on to the deck. Looking up at the sky, he caught his breath at the sudden glory, like an apocalypse, of the bright northern stars as he stared at the now familiar constellations divided by the enormous arch of the Milky Way. Divinely impersonal and so far removed from the heated emotions of agitated adults, they soothed and comforted him as they always had. There, like a bright fixed lantern, was the Pole Star in the constellation of the Bear. Still farther to the north he perceived the constellation of

Perseus and identified Algol, the Demon Star. Glancing first east and then west, he murmured the familiar names.

" There's Pegasus, and Pisces — and that must be Aquarius. And there are Virgo and Leo, just where the sun sets." Turning towards the south, he recognised Sagittarius and Scorpio. Above them, he knew, was the track of the planets.

Long ago Adrian had realised that he could not see, at any given moment, the total population of the heavens. This fact had gradually given him a dim idea of the vastness of the universe ; a conception of measurements and dimensions beyond the range not only of his eye but of his thought. Standing alone on the deck, with the sea swishing gently against the grey sides of the hull far below, he let his imagination roam over the movements of those stars which were lost to sight beneath the horizon.

Where, for instance, was Alpha Centauri, the brightest star in the now invisible constellation of the Centaur, and the nearest to the earth though it was 280,000 times as far away as the sun ? He wondered which of the prehistoric astronomers, Chinese, Babylonian, Egyptian, or Jewish, discovered that stars shone in the sky by day as well as by night. Mr. Halliburton, the science master at Eton, had told him that this was one of the most important advances in knowledge ever made, because it involved the discovery of unseen phenomena. Did they, those early astronomers, also keep track of the mysterious travellers of the sky, which made their strange journeyings to the confines of the solar system and back ? One of his own minor ambitions was to live to the age of sixty-one and see Halley's Comet, that visitor which came at intervals of seventy-six years, and had last appeared in 1910 when his father, who had described it to him, was at Oxford.

Suddenly, as Adrian stood looking at the sea and sky, a vivid green light leapt from the northern clouds. It spread, candelabra-like, over the water, and flickered spasmodically across the star-studded arch above him. For a moment he felt vaguely alarmed. Was this a searchlight from some hidden and perhaps hostile ship, or a mysterious effect of the secret wonders of radio? Then another fountain of light sprang up, away to the northeast, and Adrian felt warm with a surge of delight as he realised that he was in the presence of one more phenomenon, which was putting on a performance especially, it seemed, for his benefit.

" It's the Aurora Borealis! " he whispered to himself, entranced. Though he could hardly bear to leave the celestial exhibition for a moment, he ran down to his cabin and shook the sleeping Josephine awake.

" Quick, Jo — the Northern Lights! Come up and see them! "

Half protesting yet excited, she dragged on her coat and followed him. But the boat deck was no longer empty; twenty or thirty adult passengers were now up there, watching the storm of green light which flashed and flickered over their heads. The brilliant springing fountains stretched above the ship right across the sky; as far as the horizon the sea was illuminated as though by electric light. To vigilant hostile eyes the grey vessel beneath the incandescent radiance would have been fatally clear, but the two children, ecstatically craning their necks as they leaned against a lifeboat, had completely forgotten the lurking submarines.

Fortunately the submarines seemed to be equally neglectful of them, though to the dismay of Robert in London they were active in other parts of the Atlantic. As the *Lavinia* moved through the Strait of Belle Isle on the sixth day of its voyage, the chief threat to its safety was not submarines but icebergs. Early in the morning Adrian, who was already up, saw a small one floating close to the ship, white, jagged, and translucent. Since he now altogether avoided the lounge, crowded with weary harassed mothers and tired children crying amid a debris of chocolate wrappings and orange peel, he was still on deck when a great berg, almost the size of a cathedral, appeared against the horizon. Three miles from the ship in midday sunshine, it first suggested a Spanish galleon in full sail, and stirred in Adrian a sudden nostalgic memory of Armada Square. Then it gradually changed to the semblance of a snow-white pterodactyl floating on the waves, its nine-tenths of submerged bulk invisible.

Next day the children found themselves moving up the St. Lawrence River towards Farther Point, where the pilot was to board the ship. On its port side stretched the Gaspé Peninsula, slate blue and tawny green, covered with spruce and scrub; it was the largest fragment of virgin geography that they had ever seen or imagined. Towards evening the huge estuary began to narrow, and on the starboard horizon appeared the faint blue outline of its opposite bank. Sea-birds of many varieties unknown to Adrian's nature books began to fly round the ship, lighting on the mast, dipping into the water. Occasionally they turned upside down and disappeared, leaving faint ephemeral marks of their progress on the surface. As the sunset deepened the sky changed to indigo, and the red embers glowed serenely beneath purple evening clouds.

Ever since his first sight of the Aurora Borealis, Adrian's attitude towards their voyage had gradually changed. The days of resentment and regret which culminated in that superb celestial exhibition had formed yet another layer of defensive crust over the raw surface of his solitary pain. Thrust inward, the grief of his uprooting was temporarily forgotten. By the time that the ship moved up the river towards Quebec on the final stage of its journey, he was almost ready to join Josephine in regarding their

migration as an adventure which need involve no misgivings.

The air, on that last morning of their long voyage,
possessed a clear, stimulating quality which raised his
spirits in spite of himself. Not having experienced the
after-effects of champagne he had no basis of comparison ;
he only knew that he had never breathed an atmosphere
so light and rare. Now only a short distance from the
ship, the steep fir-covered banks of the St. Lawrence rose
sharply, the young trees shining pale green against the
older foliage and tawny earth. Tiny scarlet buoys floated
in the water in front of small fishing or lumber villages,
each having its lighthouse and miniature church with
white puritan spire and sloping silvery roof to let the
winter snows slide to the ground. Far in the distance the
children could now see the shadow of a city, like a mirage
in the sky, dominated by the roof of a huge building which
resembled the wing of some mythical monster.

To their right flashed the white spray of the Mont-
morency Falls as they passed the Isle of Orleans with its
brightly-painted frame-houses, red, white, orange, and
green. Then, as the ship swept round the huge leftward
curve of the river, Quebec suddenly loomed above the
crowd of children now pressing excitedly on to the boat
deck, its Château de Frontenac like a fantastic terra-cotta
cathedral with a jade-green copper roof.

" O-oo ! " breathed Josephine, dancing up and down.
" It's like a picture in my *Arabian Nights* ! "

She was disappointed when they did not stop to explore
this fairy-tale city of grey buildings with green roofs and
white-painted windows. But shortly afterwards Quebec
Bridge, famous for the optical illusion which suggests that
it is too low to allow the masts of ships to pass beneath,
consoled her for their inexorable progress, and by supper-
time she had forgotten Quebec in the fascinated contem-

plation of a thunderstorm which broke over the water-
side city of Three Rivers with its long frontage of paper
factories.

Adrian and Josephine woke early next day to realise
that the ship had stopped. Scrambling into their clothes,
they rushed on deck to see the dawn sun glowing red on
the grey skyscrapers of Montreal. Their hurried early
breakfast was followed immediately by a noisy confusion
of baggage, docks, officials, and customs-sheds, which suddenly became the mere kaleidoscopic background for a
big, heavy, swarthy man with blue eyes and black and
white hair, who appeared like a good-natured genie before
them.

*

When a taxi had taken them to the Windsor Station for
their journey to New York and they were settled beside
their baggage on Pullman chairs in the large comfortable
train, Damon Sullivan surveyed his incongruous companions with amused though sympathetic interest.

By this final stage of their journey, Josephine had
become the embodiment of amiable disorder. Despite
Adrian's efforts she had lost all her hair-ribbons and
mislaid her brush, while the succession of garments which
she had pulled out of her suitcase and put on one after
another had left her without any clean clothes to wear
ashore.

" Well," Damon privately reflected with the good-
humoured indifference of a bachelor uncle, " what else
could one expect of a kid only ten or eleven? It's a good
job Sylvia can't see her, though! "

But Adrian, now conscious of moral support, determined to make Josephine's appearance more worthy of
their distinguished escort.

" Don't you think she ought to wash her face, Mr.
Sullivan? " he suggested. " When she's finished, I know

how to do her hair. I've got her last hair-ribbon in my pocket. It fell out of her suitcase when the Customs were going through it."

" Sure," agreed Damon, " it would be a good idea. She can get clean while I order breakfast. I guess you're both ready for another ! "

" We wouldn't mind," said Adrian cheerfully, his apprehensions vanishing in the pleasant warmth of this uncritical companionship. " Get along, Earwig ! " he commanded severely, and Josephine, after pulling a hideous grimace, vanished without further resistance.

Shy and apologetic, he turned to Damon.

" I'm awfully sorry she's in such a mess. But we hardly saw our stewardess from start to finish. She had about a hundred children to look after, mostly younger than us."

" You've certainly had a tough time," said Damon with a man-to-man intimacy which made Adrian feel flattered and reassured. He went on : " You've grown like fun since I last set eyes on you. Here was I expecting a kid, or at most a big boy, and I find a young man ! "

" Well," responded Adrian, immensely pleased, " I *am* growing up. I'm nearly fifteen. I don't suppose my father and mother would have sent me across if it hadn't been for Jo."

" Of course they wouldn't ! " agreed Damon, instantly perceiving the depth of Adrian's resentments. " But you couldn't expect them to send a cute kid like that over here without a big brother to take care of her ! "

Scrutinizing the boy as they talked, Damon again perceived how closely he resembled Sylvia. He was more like her now than he had been at the still indeterminate age of twelve ; like not only in his dark-lashed, blue-grey eyes and the red-brown hair a few shades deeper than hers, but in the graceful movements of his hands and the

well-balanced proportions of his slender body, already
on the tall side of middle height.   With that shining
sculptured hair and face tanned by a week at sea, he
suggested the bronze statue of a Greek boy in motion — a
runner, perhaps, or a discus-thrower.

" And how did you leave your mother ? " Damon
inquired, putting the one question to which he really
wanted an answer.

" She was quite all right," Adrian replied.   " Daddy
was rather upset about the War, but Mummy didn't
worry.   She never worries about things like that."

" No.   She doesn't believe in crossing her bridges
before she gets to them," said Damon.

I hope she comes through all right, he thought.   It's
queer how badly I want to see her again. . . . Was it
really because he'd never had her that he could not put
her out of his mind ?   Not one of the many other women
with whom he had been intimate could have compelled
him, of his own volition, to undertake this absurd ten-hour
journey in the company of two travel-soiled juveniles
under fifteen.

Just before the train reached the American frontier,
Josephine returned.   The visible portions of her had now
been restored to relative cleanliness, and with clumsy but
practised fingers Adrian tied the crumpled scarlet ribbon
on her tousled hair.   When the formalities at Rouses
Point had been completed, they settled down to the lavish
breakfast of iced grapefruit, cereal, fried bacon, eggs, toast,
coffee and cream that Damon had ordered.   Josephine
regarded the feast with unconcealed jubilation.

" Can I eat *all* those things ? " she demanded eagerly.
" Really all of them ? "

" Sure, sister," he responded good-humouredly.   " One
after another, or all together, just as you like ! "

By the time that the prolonged meal had ended, the

heavy train was running southward through Vermont, skirting the shores of Lake Champlain between the Green Mountains and the Adirondacks. With its trout-streams, clumps of fir, and forest-covered hills, the country resembled Scotland which was still unknown to the children. The vividness of the sunlit sky and shimmering blue water seemed brighter than any picture they had ever seen.

" Well," inquired Damon after a long silence, " and what was the War doing when you left home ? "

" It hadn't quite got to us yet," answered Adrian. " I mean not into England. But we've been expecting to be invaded ever since Dunkirk. Daddy even thought it might come before we started for America. That's why he got us on to a ship so quickly."

" He was right to do that. If you *were* coming it was better to come at once."

" Yes . . . I suppose so." Adrian surveyed the wild, vast, empty country, seeming so far removed in time and space from the threat which pressed against his own crowded island.

" Mr. Sullivan," he asked, " do you think America will ever come in ? "

" To be frank, I don't," replied Damon, his wish the father to his convictions. " The President talks a lot, like all Democrats — from which you'll rightly figure I'm a Republican. But I doubt whether he'll act. If England goes down, it'll be a question of saving what we must as quickly as we can. That'll be the moment for a judicious peace."

" But — do you really think England will go down ? "

" I wouldn't want to say, son. I certainly hope not. She'll throw every darn Nazi into the sea before she does. But even if a miracle happens and she stands up to Hitler, I don't see this country letting Roosevelt drag us in. In fact I've got such a hunch he won't be able to, I'm fixing my own plans on the assumption of our continued neutrality."

" What plans, Mr. Sullivan? What are you going to do? "

" Well, maybe you know I'm a writer of plays? "

Adrian nodded. Judging correctly that he was really interested and not just being polite, Damon explained that since the outbreak of war he had felt that the Irish themes of his plays were no longer topical or relevant. So he had been looking for a new background, preferably that of some other small, politically-conscious country.

" I've got about six months' work to put in on the play I'm doing now," he explained. " Then I want to see it produced in Boston. After that I'm going to the Pacific to collect material for a political drama on Philippine independence."

" How marvellous! " exclaimed Adrian with genuine enthusiasm. " It must be wonderful to go to places like that! I want to travel a lot when I'm older."

" Well, you're putting in a pretty good instalment now, aren't you? "

" Oh, but I mean *really* travel." He tried to explain the distinction without a difference which was in his mind. " When I'm grown-up I'm going to be an astronomer. I want to see what the stars look like from various places all over the world."

" It sounds a good idea. So you're a mathematician, are you? " said Damon, somewhat surprised by Adrian's choice of profession.

" Yes, I suppose so. I've always found Maths quite easy. I didn't realise it till I went to school and discovered how most of the chaps got tied up in them."

" Then you've never thought of following in Father's footsteps? "

It was Adrian's turn to look surprised.

" God, no ! Catch me being a parson ! Why should
I ? "

" I'm with you there, brother. Still, you must admit
your Dad's made a pretty good job of it."

" So's Mummy ! " Josephine now chimed in loyally.
" I'm going to be like her ! I want to go on the stage and
be an actress."

Damon smiled appreciatively, with expert judgment
sizing up the long lithe body and shapely legs. Physically
she resembled her father, but evidently she too owed
something to Sylvia.

" I'm with you too, sister ! You couldn't do better.
And if you're only half as successful as your mother, you'll
have every reason for being a proud girl."

Rightly judging that the children, in spite of their late
breakfast, would be equally ready for an enormous lunch,
he ordered fruit cocktail, soup, chicken à la King, tomato
salad, and chocolate ice-cream when the waiter came
round with the luncheon menu. After they had done
full justice to this second meal, he was hardly surprised
to see them both sink into replete and contented slumber.
But though they remained silent and motionless until the
train reached Poughkeepsie, he did not open the book or
newspapers that he had brought with him. Instead he
leaned back in his chair and gazed out of the window,
thinking how odd it was that this day, which he had expected to be so full of tedious if willingly-shouldered
obligations, should have proved so highly entertaining
after all.

He really would have liked, he thought, to have had
a son ; a son whom he could claim and befriend — if
only the hampering obligations of matrimony had not
been involved. Still, Adrian was a pretty good substitute.
At least his mother was the one woman who had dominated Damon's mind against his will.

When the train slid into Grand Central Station and the children, now fully awake again, stared enraptured and overwhelmed at the great Concourse, Damon determined that they should have one more memorable experience to fix New York firmly in their minds.

" It's seven o'clock," he said. " Just about dinner-time. There's quite a good eating-place at the top of Radio City. It isn't far and it's got a band. You can sit there and look at skyscrapers till you really believe in them ! "

On the sixty-fifth floor of the huge rock-like building, Damon demanded and obtained a window table. From the vantage point of an aeroplane and with as much excitement as flying would have given them, Adrian and Josephine looked out upon the skyscrapers of Manhattan, still washed gold by the evening sunshine of the long June day. A short distance to the south the Empire State Building, the chief pinnacle higher than their own, challenged the light summer clouds above the city. Beyond Battery in the smooth blue sweep of the Upper Bay, the vessels on the water looked like ants crawling over the surface of a painted floor.

When they had almost finished their dinner the orchestra struck up " There'll always be an England ", and the children, moved in spite of themselves, became silent, listening. It no longer seemed strange to Damon that he, the famed bachelor playwright, should be sitting in a crowded restaurant high above New York in the grimy company of a boy and girl whom until that morning he had hardly known. In some indefinable fashion they had become his ; his because their mother was really his too, whether she knew it or not. Though he might never again kiss her lovely mouth which still curved like a young woman's, or repeat the poignant moment of farewell at the Connoisseurs' Theatre when at last he had held her exquisite body in his arms, she belonged to him, and he never would, or could, put her out of his mind.

He would write to her, he thought, and tell her so. The children gave him a good excuse; she would want to know how they had come through their journey, talked, behaved. He would tell her that he was not just the would-be paramour, importunate but inconstant, that she had quite warrantably thought him; that he knew now he had always loved her, and would love her till he died. At the hour of his death it was her face he would see, her eyes that would look into his. . . . Somehow, he decided, he must make her the heroine of his Philippine play. Thus she would always be his, captured by him in time, whatever damnable competition for her might go on in eternity.

A woman at the next table leaned across, breaking into his meditations.

" Pardon me, but can you tell me if it's nine o'clock yet ? "

He looked at his wrist watch. " It's a quarter after nine. . . . Heavens, you two, we've got to get a move on ! We must make that train at Penn Station before ten o'clock ! "

The children rose obediently. They had finished eating, and through the deepening twilight were watching an American liner, brightly lit among the dark ships of the belligerent nations, move slowly out to sea. Though they did not want the evening to end, sleep, impossible to fight much longer, was creeping over them again.

At Pennsylvania Station Damon completed his official obligations by finding the sleeping-car for Acropolis, and installing Adrian and Josephine in their reserved section. But he had one final voluntary duty to perform.

" Stay put, both of you," he enjoined. " I'll be back in five minutes. I'm going to buy you some candy."

Hardly more than that time had passed when he returned, his arms piled high with shiny illustrated magazines and, on the top of them, two outsize boxes of chocolates and a heap of hard candy in coloured paper wrappers.

" Here's something to read if you can't sleep," he announced, " and something to eat if you wake up hungry ! "

" Oh, Mr. Sullivan ! " exclaimed Josephine. " Are you really giving us all these things ? At your own expense ! "

Damon laughed. " Don't worry about the expense, sister ! They only cost a few bucks."

" It's awfully decent of you," said Adrian. Remembering his responsibility for the family manners, he added politely : " I'll write and tell Mummy how kind you've been to us."

Good lad, thought Damon, feeling fully rewarded for his strenuous hours. He patted their shoulders protectively, oddly stirred by this unusual parting.

" Well — so long, kids ! Get to bed quickly, both of you ; you've had a pretty tough day. And don't forget your Uncle Damon ! "

" Goodbye, Mr. Sullivan ! Of course we won't ! " cried the two young voices in chorus. Too tired to undress or wash, they handed their baggage to the negro porter whom Damon had instructed to put them off at Acropolis in the morning, and lay down on their berths behind the heavy green curtain.

" He's a top-hole chap," thought Adrian. " Absolutely top-hole ! How wonderful it would be to have someone like that for a father. . . ."

Then his fatigue overcame him and, abandoning the realms of speculation, he fell asleep without pursuing his thoughts to their logical conclusion.

CHAPTER XI

Stars above the Catskills

THROUGHOUT 1940 and for most of 1941, Adrian received communications at intervals from Damon Sullivan. As Damon had once told Sylvia, he was no letter-writer; but for some reason which he did not try to explain to himself he went on sending occasional picture postcards to the children. At Christmas, 1940, another extravagant box of candies came for Josephine, but to Adrian he sent a complete set of his plays, each volume autographed in his surprisingly small, decorative handwriting.

" I don't flatter myself that you will want to read these now, if ever ", ran the short note which accompanied the gift. " But when I have departed altogether from this scene of experiments and indulgences, the autographs may be valuable. Then you can sell them."

Half-way through 1941, the stamps and pictures on the postcards changed. Now they showed tropical landscapes in lurid colours, for Damon had allowed himself to be guided by his " hunch " and had gone to the Philippines. Even at Christmas, 1941, when America had turned crazy with belligerent excitement after Pearl Harbour, more chocolates arrived for Josephine, and for Adrian came a large, expensively illustrated sky-atlas. But these gifts had been ordered from two New York shops, Schrafft's and Brentano's, before Damon went away, and they contained no message apart from his card.

After that both postcards and presents ceased, for the Japanese had occupied Manila, and when General MacArthur had escaped to Australia the American forces in the Philippines were obliged to surrender at Bataan. Just before the summer vacation of 1942, Damon's name was published on a list of distinguished Americans who were " missing " after the Japanese victory.

When Kathleen Downing told Adrian this news one evening and showed him the paragraph in the *New York Times*, he shook off Josephine with unusual determination and went for a walk by himself along the heights above Dagger Creek Gorge where the two of them had discussed their parents the year before. He wanted to be alone and think, for the news about Damon, and the various gruesome possibilities that might have been his fate even if he was not dead, had brought back the feelings of guilt and shame which had made him so miserable nearly two years ago on Liverpool Docks.

Adrian was sixteen-and-a-half now, and better able to analyse those feelings which, for two years filled with new experiences, values, sights, colours, and sounds, he had almost forgotten. He knew now that they meant he had never wanted to escape what others were obliged to endure ; that the wish to " stay put " and be unmolested which he had once expressed to Josephine represented only one mood among many and no longer held sway. It seemed unbearable to be safe, comfortable, expensively clothed and lavishly fed, when men like Damon, who was a famous writer and had been so kind to him, were inappropriately obliged to suffer or die. The sense of war's atmosphere and the challenge it made, which his parents' constant perils in London had failed to convey, came to him through the fate of a man whom he had known only for a few hectic but unforgettable hours.

By one of those coincidences which occur so frequently in life, a much-delayed letter from his father arrived the next morning. It told Adrian, as a similar letter also informed the Downings, that now the threat of invasion had receded from England and the Nazi armies were deeply involved in Russia, Robert saw no reason why the children should remain in America. Raids, of course, still sometimes occurred, but they were avoidable for the young who need not live permanently in London.

To Adrian he added a paragraph which did not appear in the letter to Dean Downing. Even from his brief knowledge of the United States he feared, Robert wrote, that now America was herself involved in war, the emotions of her people would grow more tense, more belligerent, than they were likely henceforth to become in England. At home the 1940 panic had been replaced by a mood which was stable, dogged, resigned, and even, so far as Robert could judge, largely resistant to the war propaganda that still poured from the Sunday newspapers and the B.B.C. He was therefore making inquiries about all possible methods of bringing Adrian and Josephine home, perhaps by a neutral ship going to Portugal whence they could come by air. Meanwhile he expressed, in both letters, the hope that the children would help their foster-parents to get their passports and all other necessary papers in order ready for departure.

" Oh, Kay ! " cried Josephine in mingled excitement and disappointment. " I *would* love to fly ! But does it mean I shan't be able to go camping ? "

The previous year both she and Adrian had been sent to one of those open-air vacation boarding-schools which are known as " camp " to American juveniles. Josephine had adapted herself immediately to the gregarious, informal outdoor life, and was eager to go again. For Adrian the arrangement seemed to the Downings to have been less happy, and they had made different plans for him this year. At the suggestion of Dean Downing, who thought that Adrian's interest in astronomy ought to have more encouragement than it had apparently ever received, he had been invited to spend six weeks at the summer home of Clarence Brinton, formerly one of the Dean's

students.   Professor Brinton had recently been made head
of the Geography Department at the nearby University
of Eleusis, forty miles north-east of Cayuga.   He was not
only a relatively young man ; he had long been an ardent
amateur astronomer who owned a private observatory
attached to his " shack " in the Catskills.

" I don't think either of you need worry," said Kathleen
Downing smiling, though the letter from Robert Carbury
was a blow which she had dreaded ever since the children's
arrival had transformed her quiet orderly house into the
lively home that she had always desired.   " It'll probably
be months before your father gets a passage for you, and
I'm sure I shall be weeks putting your papers in order."

" Then I shan't have to miss going to Waterford ? "

" You certainly won't, Jo.   And I hope you'll be here
a long time after you get back.   Richmond and I don't
want to lose you."

Reassured, Josephine departed to her camp on the
New England coast at the beginning of June.   The following day Clarence Brinton picked Adrian up at the Downings' house.   He drove him not only to the Catskills, but
into a new chapter of the personal history which was
already so crowded with changes and events.

*

At thirty-seven Clarence Brinton was a boyish, attractive,
young-looking man, with a story as romantic as his appearance.   He had always been proud of the Red Indian strain
which three generations ago had entered his family on
the female side, permanently transforming its Anglo-Saxon
qualities.   He himself was exceptionally tall, with thick
black hair as smooth and glossy as embroidery silk, a
brown skin, and reddish-brown eyes, where unplumbed
depths seemed to hide beneath the sparkle of surface
vitality.   But he had better reasons for pride than these.

As a Cayuga student aged nineteen, he had spent a long vacation in New Orleans. There he met Juanita Ramados, the eighteen-year-old offspring of an American family of Spanish origin. As the orphan granddaughter of a wealthy shipowner who had taken his share in developing the carrying trade of the Gulf of Mexico, she was then enduring an austere education by an uncle and aunt who had been appointed her guardians until she came of age. Long before he learned of the half-million dollars which she was to inherit at twenty-one, Clarence had fallen as deeply in love with Juanita as she with him. Before his vacation ended, they were secretly married early one morning at a Catholic church on the outskirts of the city. When he returned to Cayuga, Juanita left her severe guardians for ever and went with him.

But in spite of their enchanted happiness, her southern blood never became acclimatised to the bitter winds and long winters of the Iroquois country. Before Clarence was twenty-one she died of pneumonia, leaving their baby daughter, six months old, in his care. On her last day of life, she scribbled on a half-sheet of paper her only Will, bequeathing to him the fortune which had been settled on her.

" It's all yours," she had whispered, fighting for breath. " But you must marry again, just the same. I'd hate you to be lonely. Take care of Carol, and don't forget me. That's all I ask."

But Clarence Brinton had neither forgotten nor replaced her. When he emerged at last from the sunless wreckage which her death seemed to have made of his life, he returned doggedly to his study of physical and political geography. Being too naturally well-endowed to work badly whatever his other distractions, he managed to take a good degree. But those other distractions had been considerable, for he had determined that, with the devoted help of a coloured nurse, he would give to Carol as much attention as she would have received from her mother. Richmond Downing, whose lectures he had attended for the political and historical side of his work, still clearly remembered his junior colleague from Eleusis as the tall black-haired boy, his keen vitality quenched in sorrow, who wheeled his baby daughter round the campus for two hours every afternoon.

As Clarence grew older and became first an instructor at Cayuga and then Assistant Professor of Geography at Eleusis, it was evident to his friends that Juanita's place in his life had gradually been filled by two other loves. One was the passion for astronomy which had developed out of his geographical studies. The other was his daughter, Carol Juanita, whose beautiful name was obstinately abbreviated by her class-mates at Eleusis High School to Carol Jane.

The tastes of Carol's father were simple, and his dead wife's bequest never tempted him to consort with the wealthy or change his standard of life. He used a quarter of Juanita's money to establish a private observatory in the Catskills, and built beside it the plain but capacious summer residence which he had modestly described to Adrian as " my shack ". The rest he put aside for Carol, mentally resolving that it should never handicap her or tempt him to possessiveness. Achievement meant more to him than money, and he was deeply ambitious for this only child. When her school work revealed that she possessed abilities which were far in excess of mere intelligence, he renewed his determination to leave her future choices in life unhampered by affection or gratitude.

Knowing nothing of the Professor's history, Adrian paid little attention when Dean Downing told him that his future host had a daughter. Without giving the subject much thought, he assumed from Clarence Brinton's youthful appearance that this girl was a child, and vaguely hoped he would not have to spend too much time in playing with her. He felt too shy to ask questions when his host, conversationally indicating notable landmarks, drove him the hundred and forty miles from Acropolis to Neontora, the scattered village three thousand feet above sea level which climbed the peak where he had built his summer home. In any case, the prospect of a juvenile companion was less interesting to Adrian than their swift ascent from the valley and the domed roof of the little observatory on the mountain top.

The " shack ", he noticed with surprise, was a considerable dwelling erected on the hillside just below the summit, its roof adjoining the stone floor of the observatory. Round the big comfortable living-room of the house ran a wooden gallery with a doorway, which gave direct access to the observatory on stormy days.

Clarence Brinton jumped out of his car and opened the front door, which faced down the steep road that they had just ascended.

" Come in and meet Carol," he said. " I'm sure she's kept some tea for us."

Adrian followed, expecting to see an American variant of Josephine. What he did see dumbfounded him.

Carol Juanita was then only a month past her seventeenth birthday, but the elegant loveliness of her poise, instinctive rather than sophisticated, was as ageless and immaculate as his mother's. All the grace, freshness, and intensity of her young parents' unspoiled passion seemed to have gone to her making. It was strange, Adrian thought afterwards, that she should have reminded him immediately of his mother, for Sylvia's beauty was essentially northern, cool and detached, whereas Carol belonged to a southern type — if the word could be applied to anyone so unique — which gave an impression of restrained passion beneath the quiet external control.

Like her father she was black-haired and dark-eyed; but her clear warm skin was olive rather than brown, and though she looked tall, her diminutive mother had modified, in her, Clarence's unusual height. Probably, thought Adrian, trying hard not to stare impolitely but quite unable to restrain himself, she was really no taller than lanky, leggy Josephine. But in her simple faultlessly-cut summer frock of light orange wool, with her lacquered finger-nails, tiny crystal ear-clips, and short necklace of red-brown garnets, she looked completely adult. Clarence appeared to be her elder brother rather than her father. With the help of the negro housekeeper who had once been her nurse, she ran his home, whether at Eleusis or Neontora, with the same effortless competence as she wore her clothes.

" Do sit down and have some tea," she said to Adrian, in kindly, almost maternal tones in which only the most sensitive listener would have detected a note of patronage. Handing him his cup, she added : " We've always had tea since my father and I were in England two years ago. I expect you're ready for it. You must be tired after that long drive."

" It wasn't so very long," he protested, " and I'm not a bit tired."

" Still, people don't usually drive a hundred and forty miles in an afternoon in England, do they? "

" No, not usually. But I haven't seen England for some time. It's two years this month since I came over."

" I didn't realise you'd been here as long as that," said Carol. " Where do you go to school? "

" Nowhere special," he answered, wondering how he could steer the conversation on to more adult levels. " I only go to the high school in Acropolis. But I like it much better than Eton, my English school."

" Goodness ! " ejaculated Clarence Brinton. " I didn'
realise we had an Etonian in our midst ! " He added
proudly : " My grown-up daughter finished with school
this term — after walking off with more prizes than any
girl there ever took before."

"Don't be ridiculous, Daddy ! " She turned to Adrian.
" I was like you — I only went to the high school at
Eleusis. Anybody could get prizes there. When I go to Bryn
Mawr in October, he'll learn what a moron I really am ! "

" So she's just going to college," thought Adrian,
swallowing his tea. He could have kicked himself for
his juvenility. I wonder, raced the thought through his
brain, if I couldn't get Dean D. to let me leave school
next term, and go to Cayuga as a student? And then,
as though his mind had been riding in an aeroplane and
suddenly crashed, he remembered that his schooldays in
America might already be over. Recalling all that he
knew of his father, he realised that Robert would never
rest until he had brought him and Josephine home. The
school in which he was reluctantly chained to childhood
might be an English school. Not Eton. Neither Robert
nor anyone else would make him go back there. But still
an English school, where he'd have to start, like a junior
kid, all over again. . . .

At that moment he realised that the compulsion to
return to England and the War had gone. Not even the
thought of Damon Sullivan could smite him into remorse.
For some reason that he couldn't have explained, he
wanted to stay on with the Brintons — for ever and
ever. . . .

*

To Adrian's mortification it soon became clear that, in
spite of his deep voice and now considerable height, Carol
regarded him as a child. Her close companionship with
her father had made her completely at home in adult

society. Apart from Clarence, her favourite companion at Neontora seemed to be Warren Converse, the thirty-year-old instructor in Government at Eleusis, who owned a log-cabin in the woods where he stayed every summer with his sister.

One evening some days after his arrival Adrian sat alone on the living-room verandah, telling himself how unreasonable it was to feel sore and exasperated because Carol had just gone off with Warren to an impromptu dance at the small Country Club. From the feathery green tops of a young planting of trees immediately below the house a delicious scent of warm fir-cones drifted up to the verandah. Though the days at Neontora were very warm the nights were cold, and Adrian never felt tired. The vigorous, rarefied mountain air reminded him of the champagne-like atmosphere of the St. Lawrence.

Beyond the little wood he looked from his hillside upon a dramatic panorama of mountains and forest-clad valleys. Spreading steeply downwards from Clarence Brinton's house, oaks, beeches, maples, birches, sumac, mountain-laurel and many trees whose names Adrian did not know filled the great bowl of the valley with every shade of green from pale emerald to deep olive. On its hither side, range upon range of peaks still higher than the one where he sat climbed the pale-blue horizon like the celestial back-cloth of a natural amphitheatre made for the gods.

When he first saw this incredible display of virgin loveliness, it had recalled to him a poem which he must, he thought, have heard his father quote or his mother recite, for he could not remember who wrote it:

> The blessèd Damozel lean'd out
> From the gold bar of Heaven. . . .

Well, perhaps the Professor's home — called " Alcyone " after the consoling legend of the halcyon which became

one of the largest stars in the Pleiades — might not exactly
be Heaven, though it seemed very near it.   But it certainly
contained a blessèd Damozel, and if you did lean out from
Heaven you could hardly hope to see a more exciting view.
Though he did not yet realise it, the primeval beauty
before him symbolised the prodigality with which America
squandered, as superfluous riches, treasures that less well-
endowed nations struggled to preserve as rarities.   He
only guessed that it would be possible to cut down those
forests for years without anybody noticing that the trees
had gone — except, perhaps, the austere dwellers of the
mountain villages.   Almost English in their clothes and
demeanour, they looked as though they had disappeared
with Rip Van Winkle soon after they landed in America,
and had only just re-emerged.

But this evening, though the sun had begun to set
superbly, Adrian was not thinking about the Catskills and
their summer grandeur.   He was too deeply preoccupied
by his endeavours to recapitulate the conversation that he
had just shared with Carol and establish it in his memory.
In spite of his moody resentment against Warren Converse which could, he thought with shame, justly be
called jealousy, he felt encouraged and stimulated by
the consciousness that this long talk had given him of
being in close touch with events and ideas of great importance.

" Daddy was telling me last night you want to be an
astronomer," Carol had said, coming out with him on to
the verandah after supper and sitting down in a large
old-fashioned wicker rocking-chair.

" Yes.   That's why Dean Downing arranged for me
to come here."   He watched her, fascinated, as she swayed
lazily backwards and forwards.   In her low-necked, short-
sleeved scarlet shirt and long grey slacks, she seemed to
him the loveliest thing that he had ever seen.   He added

shyly : " It was awfully decent of your father to have me
— and of you, too."

" Oh," she said, ignoring his reference to herself,
" Daddy likes having people here who really care about
his work at the observatory. He isn't a professional, of
course, but he's done some quite good things. He discovered a new comet the year before last."

" I know — he was telling me. You'd think all sorts
of people would be interested to come here and study
with him, and look at the stars through that marvellous
telescope."

" They do like looking once or twice, and then they
get bored. There aren't many specialists round here and
Eleusis has no Astronomy department, so he doesn't even
find them among his students."

" What about you, though ? "

" Oh, I do well enough when he wants to check things
over. But I'm not the same as someone like you, who
really means to take it up seriously." She added thoughtfully : " For some reason there don't seem to be many
women astronomers. I might have had a shot at being a
Mary Somerville if I weren't so keen on the job I'm going
to do."

" What's that ? Do tell me ! "

" Why should I bore you with my ambitions ? "

" Oh, but Carol — they don't bore me ! I mean . . ."
He struggled after words which would convey what he
wanted to say without any hint of the sentimentality that
he knew she would detest. " I can't think of anything
I'd get more kick out of than knowing what you're going
to do. Honest Injun ! "

" Well," she said, " I want to be a newspaper woman.
Not just an ordinary one, going here, there, and everywhere, and being paid by the column as though a few
inches of newsprint were just the same as so many yards

of rayon. I want to be an international specialist, like Dorothy Thompson and Anne O'Hare McCormick. Have you ever heard of them ? "

" I've heard of Dorothy. I'm not quite sure about the other lady."

" She's really the better of the two, I think. Solider and more experienced, though Dorothy's got the brilliance. I want to put the experience and the brilliance together, but I'd like to do even more than that. I want to make Americans see things that aren't just under their noses. And make them *think*."

" But don't they already ? There seem to be far more books and newspapers in this country than there are at home."

" Maybe. An awful lot of Americans write plenty without thinking. And they run away from unpleasant things, like illness and death and wounds and poverty and starvation. That's why they go so savage and crazy when they're made to fight. They've not been prepared for the things they have to do and see — not in their minds, I mean. If they didn't go half-mad, they'd never get through."

Adrian was silent for a moment, caught up by a half-forgotten impression.

" It's funny you saying that," he said at last. " It somehow reminds me of my father. He's a V.C., you know. He got the V.C. in the last War."

" Oh, Adrian," she cried, really stirred, " how grand ! I've never envied anyone their father before — but a V.C. ! How proud you must be of him ! "

Adrian wriggled uncomfortably in his chair.

" I suppose I really ought to be — even though he's a parson, and I haven't much use for parsons. But, you know, he doesn't really seem to be a specially brave man. He gets awfully worried by the raids ; you can tell from his letters. I think he must have got the V.C. the way you said — letting himself go crazy for fear he'd break down."

" Well, even the people who do that don't all win V.C.'s, do they ? I expect you're a bit hard on him. . . ." She meditated, looking at the sun descending upon the topmost peaks across the great valley, while Adrian waited. " I don't know if I could ever be really brave like that, but I want to try. I want to go on battlefields, and other places where death is, and sorrow, and hunger. I've always been too comfortable and safe, like America itself. I haven't even been in danger, like you have. I want to make myself face things at their very worst, and then, in my articles, tell people here what it's really like. *Make* them read it. Make them *see*."

" But what about your father ? Does he want you to go into danger and all that ? "

She smiled, justifiably confident.

" Daddy's my best friend. He understands everything. . . . You know, I've often thought the Indian strain in us both gives us a sort of fellow-feeling with oppressed and subject peoples all over the world. And then, of course, I'm European through my mother."

" Wasn't she American, then ? "

" She was an American citizen. But she came from New Orleans, and the people there are different from the rest of America. I once went to see my relatives, after they'd forgiven Daddy for running away with her. It's like a bit of old Europe that's floated across the Atlantic, and lots of the people were originally Spanish or French. My mother's family had something of both, but they were mostly Spanish. She was called Juanita Ramados, and my second name's Juanita too — even if it does get cut down to Jane."

" She died when you were a baby, didn't she ? "

" Yes. I never knew her. But because of her I shan't be happy till I know Europe even better than America — tragedies and all."

Adrian paused, thinking. He watched the highest peak on the horizon eclipse the sinking sun before he spoke : " You know, Carol, what you said about going to Europe and getting to know its tragedies is rather the kind of thing I felt when I heard Damon Sullivan was missing."

" Damon Sullivan ! Why ? Do you know him ? "

" Yes, a little. He met us at Montreal when we came over here. And the Christmas before last he sent me a complete set of his plays, all autographed. He said I could sell them for the autographs if I liked — as if I should ! "

To his satisfaction Adrian realised that he had again managed to command Carol's interest.

" You *are* lucky ! " she exclaimed. " I've always wanted to meet him. I love his plays. After I saw *Bantry Bay* I nearly wrote him a fan letter, but I thought better of it. It seems queer his meeting you, though — especially two years ago. You must have been quite a little boy."

Adrian winced.

" I wasn't so very little. I was nearly fifteen. But why shouldn't he meet us, anyway ? "

" Well, people as famous as that don't usually have much spare time. I never guessed he'd take any interest in children. It's women he's supposed to go after."

" Oh, is it ? " Adrian looked startled. " He was a friend of my mother's. She's an actress."

" Was he really ? A great friend ? "

" No, I don't think so. Mummy hardly ever talked about him."

" That wouldn't necessarily mean he wasn't a great friend. Now would it ? "

" I really don't think he was. Mummy isn't that sort. At least " — he paused, the dawn of adult insight slowly illuminating his mind — " so far as I know her, she isn't. I don't suppose we actually know much more about our parents than they know about us. You and your father seem to be different. But then he's so much younger than most fathers."

" Is your mother beautiful? " asked Carol, still pursuing the intriguing topic of Damon Sullivan. " That might account for him being interested."

Adrian meditated, honestly seeking impartiality.

" People say she is," he said at length. " And I suppose she is, really. We thought her just lovely when we were kids." He added diffidently : " You know, as soon as I saw you, you reminded me of her, somehow. I don't mean your appearance — you're so dark, and my mother's got red hair like me. It's something about the way you move. Sort of finished, and somehow . . . kind of perfect."

It had, of course, to be just at that moment, when they were deep in a really grown-up conversation and Carol had temporarily forgotten that he was a child evacuee dependent on American charity and compassion, that the telephone rang and Warren Converse asked her to go to that damned dance at the Country Club. Adrian was moodily contemplating the darkening panorama which still failed to divert his attention from his own sense of angry frustration, when Clarence Brinton came on to the verandah.

" Hallo ! " he said. " All alone ? I thought you were with Carol. Has she gone out ? "

" Yes, to a dance. I heard Mr. Converse come for her in his car." Glumly he added, wishing he were at least two years older, " I ought to learn dancing, I suppose."

" Time enough ! It's more to the point that the moon's full tonight. You hadn't forgotten, had you ? "

" No — of course I didn't forget. But Carol was talking about what she wants to do — writing for the papers and all that. I got so interested, I didn't remember exactly what day it was."

" If she writes as well as she talks she won't do too badly," said her devoted father. " Let's have a Coca-Cola out here, and then we'll go in and look at the moon."

Two hours later, while they waited for the full moon rising above the mountain peaks to reach a favourable position, Clarence Brinton allowed Adrian to turn the telescope on to some of his favourite stars. He examined the Pleiades, where Alcyone shone midway between Atlas and Merope ; he inspected the cluster Auriga, with its star population of five hundred, and the great nebula of Andromeda, the orange-tinted double star which he had hitherto seen only with his naked eye. Then Clarence showed him how the light from Algol, the Demon Star in the constellation of Perseus, varied in brightness within a nine-hour period, its changes caused by the darker satellite which revolved round it three million miles away.

" That's a good illustration of the simple principle that governs the universe," said Clarence Brinton. " I mean the law that all effects have their causes and all causes their effects."

A vague memory stirred in Adrian's mind.

" My father once said something like that. But he was talking about Hitler."

" Well, Hitler's a good example too. He's an effect as well as a cause. Now what about the moon ? We shan't get a better angle than this. And don't forget, after the dizzy distances we've been talking about, that it's a mere 232,000 miles away."

Adrian put his eye to the telescope, and saw with

startling clearness the hills and mountains, plains and valleys, of the huge shining globe. Hard, clear-cut, and sharp, they appeared in such distinct relief that he felt he could touch them. The moon's face was inverted in the telescope, so that its " eyes " appeared in the lower part of his field of vision as a series of dusky plains, hundreds of miles in diameter, stretching right across the disk. These plains were packed with ring-craters, probably caused, as he knew, by violent volcanic changes in the past. No clouds or mist obscured the harsh outlines, and no half-tones softened them; this grotesque world appeared to be all silver high lights and dead black shadows. It made him think of a great glittering jewel without beauty or tenderness, sinister and frightening in all that it suggested yet left untold.

" I wonder if men ever lived there and got wiped out ? " Adrian speculated, reflecting uneasily that some of the hugely destructive bombs now being invented were capable of transforming his own planet into another such lava-land of black-and-white desolation.

" We can't tell," said Clarence Brinton. " Those craters you see must have been formed aeons ago. During the last three hundred years of telescopic observation, there haven't been any changes in the moon at all. But whether men ever lived on it or not, it seems likely they'll be able to go there relatively soon. Perhaps in your time, and possibly even in mine."

" You really think so, Sir ? How marvellous ! I'd love to go on the first expedition."

" Nothing can prevent it," Clarence Brinton told him, " but the limits to human adaptability and endurance. From the mechanical point of view, it lies in the logic of current developments."

" You mean some of the present war weapons might be adapted for travel through space ? "

" Yes. All sorts of things that will make it possible are being invented now — jet-propulsion planes, and giant rockets, and other secret devices even worse than those. Or better, according to the use men make of them. I only hope," he added, remembering that the boy was British, and London the most vulnerable city on the earth's surface, " that some of them won't be fully developed till the War's well over. Otherwise, the relation between cause and effect may end by blowing up half mankind."

*

That night, and for many nights afterwards, Adrian's dreams were confused but glorious. He dreamed that he and Carol went alone together on a trip to the moon, walking hand-in-hand amid those black plains and silver mountains until the harsh scintillating orb began to glow with the tenderness of their perfect companionship. On another night they rowed through the limitless ocean of the sky in a magic boat called Alcyone, visiting the nearer stars and even the great revolving planets as they followed their immemorial track through space. As the days of his visit lengthened into weeks, all disturbing recollections —England, the War, his father, the air raids, even Damon Sullivan — vanished below the horizon of his mind. He had never known or imagined such happiness. And then, just as the wonderful summer vacation had reached its highest level of enchantment, it ended like a meteor crashing to earth and burning itself out for ever.

One evening after supper the telephone bell rang, and Clarence Brinton answered it. He returned to the living-room with a rueful expression, reluctant to cut short a holiday for a guest who was so obviously enjoying it.

" I'm awfully sorry, Adrian," he said, " but I'm afraid you won't be able to finish your visit. That was Kathleen Downing on the phone. It seems your father has managed to get berths for you and your sister on a South American ship sailing to Portugal. It goes at the end of the week, and Kathleen says I must get you back to Acropolis as early as possible tomorrow."

He had been prepared for disappointment, but the sudden dumb whiteness of Adrian's face was more than he had expected. It seemed altogether disproportionate to the news he had brought. The boy looked as if someone had dealt him a mortal blow.

" It's a pity," he continued, trying to soften it. " Carol and I have liked having you here. But it's just one of those things that can't be helped."

Struggling, Adrian at last found words.

" Oh, Mr. Brinton, can't it? Must I go now? Couldn't I wait till the end of the vacation? "

" I don't see how you could. Passages on neutral ships aren't easily come by nowadays."

" I wonder how Daddy got them if it's so difficult," Adrian speculated miserably.

" Well, your father's a prominent sort of man, isn't he? I daresay he knows ways and means that aren't open to everybody. And then maybe you're wanted at home. After all, you're not a kid any more. There are probably plenty of jobs to be done in England by boys of sixteen."

" But couldn't he just stay another day or two if the ship doesn't go till Saturday? " pleaded Carol, sympathising with a misery more evident to her than its cause. " It seems kind of a rush, sending him away tomorrow morning."

" I know it does," said her father; " but Kathleen hasn't fixed all his papers yet. She's got to have him in New York the day after tomorrow to get his passport and sailing permit." He turned to Adrian. " If I were you I'd put my things together now. Then we'll ask Melanie to bring us an ice-cream soda, and maybe look in at the observatory round midnight."

Too deflated to protest any more, Adrian went up to his room as slowly and heavily as though the shallow stairs had each been a foot high. In deep dejection he gathered his few belongings together, but he did pack them quickly, hoping for that last talk over the log fire which Clarence Brinton lighted on chilly evenings in the great stone fireplace that would hold a young tree.

Coming downstairs more quickly than he had gone up, he was stopped by a burst of laughter from the living-room. Quietly going up to the half-open door, he saw Carol, her father, and Warren Converse standing round the fireplace whence came the fragrant scent of kindling logs. They had obviously forgotten all about him. He meant nothing to any of them; he was just an alien boy from another hemisphere whom Professor Brinton and Carol had taken in to oblige the Downings.

He knew now that he had always hated Warren Converse, a fair, hefty, open-air young man whom he thought dreadfully ordinary-looking, and quite unworthy of Carol. And tomorrow he had to go away and leave the field to this complacent mediocrity — if indeed he, Adrian, could be said ever to have had a foot on it. Surely, all the same, Carol couldn't really care about a man who spent his time analysing the American Constitution, and other Constitutions, all equally dull. Surely it was more likely that she'd get interested in someone who, like her father, pursued the marvellous worlds of the universe through the trackless regions of space — if only, only, that someone could have time!

Then Adrian saw Converse put his hand unchecked on Carol's bare arm with a familiar, proprietory air, and something snapped in his brain.

Passionately turning his back on the living-room, he rushed out of the front door and ran violently down the hill. Beyond the village where the road turned he left it and plunged straight on, instinctively rather than consciously following a woodland trail which he and Carol had sometimes taken on their afternoon walks. Driven by an overwhelming primitive emotion which took no account of time or space, he struggled downwards through the pitch-black forest, stubbing his toes, scratching his face, sometimes tumbling headlong, but barely conscious, in his mingled rage and grief, of pain or weariness. He had been running for over an hour when the thin invisible trail that he was following began to climb. His mad rush stopped only when the ascent grew so steep that he stood still in the darkness, his heart thumping in his chest till it seemed to suffocate him and a roaring like a waterfall pounding in his ears. Overcome by loneliness and fatigue, he flung himself down in the undergrowth beside the trail. Suddenly losing all control, he pressed his face into the sharp dry leaves and began sobbing as though his heart and brain would burst. He sobbed dry-eyed for a few moments, and then the tears poured down his cheeks on to the hard earth.

" Carol ! " he cried aloud to the black silence of the indifferent forest. " Carol, darling ! . . . Darling Carol ! . . . Oh, I do so love you. . . ."

At last, he didn't know quite when, he stopped sobbing and calling and lay exhausted, face downwards in the prickly leaves. He must have fallen asleep for a while, for when he became conscious of himself again he felt very cold ; and time seemed to have passed though the forest was still dark.

As sanity gradually returned, he realised that he had not the slightest idea where he was, nor how far from Neontora. At first it seemed that nothing better could happen to him than to die there in the forest, and never have to go home to think about Carol and realise that he could neither see nor speak to her for years and years; perhaps never again. Then, as the last vestiges of sleep fell away and reaction against the mad passion of the night took hold of him, he remembered that, whatever his unwanted emotional responses to Carol and her father might be, he had social obligations to them as well. They were, after all, responsible for his safety to the Downings, and beyond them to his own parents. He could not just die in the forest like an irresponsible child or a lunatic, leaving them to face the consequences.

He scrambled shakily to his feet and began to look about him, but he had lost all sense of direction except for the feeling of being on a height. He shivered in his thin summer jacket, but realised that it was useless to look for the way home without some light to guide him. When he had sat with his head on his arms for what seemed interminable hours, the black tree-trunks began gradually to grow grey and their outlines to become definite. At last seeing a gap in the trees, he went to it hoping to get his bearings, and then realised that, instinctively but providentially, he had run in a straight line from Neontora through the valley and was nearly at the top of the opposite peak. Across the deep bowl he could see the little domed roof of Clarence Brinton's observatory against the slowly reddening sky.

Now knowing his direction, he began to hurry downhill along the trail he had taken during the night, hoping to get back to Alcyone before anyone was awake. But this time the journey down to the valley and up again seemed endless; he became aware that he must have run four or five miles through the forest, virgin except for the trails that crossed it, which he now had to retrace. By the time that he climbed, tired almost to the point of unconsciousness, through Neontora village, he realised from the position of the ascending sun that breakfast must be about due at Alcyone and he could hardly hope to enter the house unobserved.

Avoiding the front door he crept into the thicket below the living room, hoping to climb unnoticed up to his bedroom window. But Clarence Brinton was on the verandah waiting for him.

" Come here ! " he called as soon as he saw Adrian, and Adrian went to him without a word. He knew that he must look a woe-begone, bedraggled object, with the grimy marks of tears on his face and his eyes red-rimmed from weeping and lack of sleep. But there was nothing to be done about it.

" What in God's name happened to you ? " asked Clarence Brinton sternly. " Do you realise you've been out all night ? "

" I'm sorry," Adrian murmured. " I didn't mean to stay out so late. I lost my way."

" But you went out after dark, in country you hardly know. You might have been lost for days. I missed you round midnight. I've got half-a-dozen men from the village searching the woods. Are you crazy ? "

" No," said Adrian. He was too tired to tell anything but the truth, so he only added wearily : " I don't want to go home, that's all."

" Don't want to go home ! " For once Clarence Brinton's boyish face looked angry and severe. " Well, I didn't think *you* were the sort to funk the War ! I never dreamed you were a quitter."

" I'm not," said Adrian stonily. " I didn't mean I was afraid to go home. I know I ought to go. I just don't want to leave America."

Words that he realised he must never utter jostled each other on his lips, but he fought them back. How could he say to his host : " Mr. Brinton, I'm in love with Carol ; I want to marry her ; I'll work myself black and blue if

213

she'll only wait for me " — he, an evacuated child, a
schoolboy who depended on the Downings for every cent
in his pocket, a Britisher who had to go back to England
to finish his education and then be called up for military
service? Why, long before his life was his own again,
Carol would be married to that beast Warren Converse
or some other foul guy. If the Professor knew what he
felt he'd think him as ridiculous as the boy in that play
his mother had once acted in, who got a crush on his
house-master's wife.

Clarence Brinton, widowed and a father before he was
of age, the one man in America who might have understood a premature passion of frustration and grief, looked
with growing perturbation at the storm of emotions that
struggled visibly in Adrian's pale, mutinous face. Like
his daughter he had thought of this English boy, quiet
and shy by American standards, as young and unde-
veloped, and Adrian's long-established habit of hiding his
feelings had given the impression that as yet he possessed
none which could be called adult. Now Clarence Brinton
felt less certain of his immaturity, though the explanation
of this sudden tumult eluded him just because it was so
obvious. It had not occurred to him that, among all the
stars above the Catskills which they examined together,
Adrian had found one that would never be discovered
on any sky-atlas.

He would have liked the boy, who had hitherto seemed
so sensible and self-contained, to leave his home happy
and contented after the enjoyable month that he had
spent there and those night-hours of eager exploration in
the observatory. But whatever Adrian's trouble might
be, it appeared too difficult and complicated to track
down in the time available. Sighing a little, he gave up
the attempt.

" Well," he said, " I suppose you'd better go and get

clean. We've got to start directly after breakfast."

" As soon as that ? " Adrian asked miserably.

" I'm afraid so. I promised to get you to Acropolis by
lunch-time if possible ; you're off to New York tomorrow.
I'm sorry there's no time to rest, but perhaps you can sleep
in the car. Carol's got some coffee for you in the dining-
room. She was up early too."

Adrian went upstairs, washed his hands and face,
brushed his hair, changed his shirt, and came down into
the dining-room where Carol was sitting behind the
coffee-pot. In her white sharkskin dress with its trim
scarlet belt she did not look as though she had been up
half the night. But Adrian felt ready to shrivel like a
pricked balloon with humiliation.

" I'm awfully sorry, Carol," he said. " I didn't mean
to worry you. . . . I never realised I'd gone such a
long way."

She did not speak, and desperately he went on.

" Your father thinks I funk going home — back to the
War. It isn't that at all. Oh, *please* make him see it isn't !
Carol — it's because of you I don't want to go. I just —
can't bear to leave you."

" Poor old Adrian ! " she said gently, for once nonplussed by a situation. Whatever she did, she mustn't
encourage the poor silly kid. Yet she didn't want to hurt
his feelings either, especially as he seemed so old-fashioned
and serious for his age, which was probably because he
was British. He was a nice boy, honest and sincere, if a
bit complicated compared with most of the boys she knew.
And her father had told her he was clever, and keen.

" Look here," she said, " you're not going away for
ever, you know ! I'm sure we shall all meet again after
the War. And you can write to me, can't you ? I promise
I'll answer."

She poured out his coffee and put some cereal into a

plate, though he shook his head.

"You must eat it," she insisted. "You'll feel better when you have. . . . I tell you what, there's a picture of me somewhere I had taken for Daddy's last birthday. I believe there's one left. Would you like it to remember me by? I can look for it while you finish your breakfast."

"You know I would," he said, brightening a little though his voice still shook. "It's most awfully kind of you. . . ."

Half an hour later, Clarence Brinton drove him away. At the bottom of the hill he looked back and saw Carol waving to him in her white dress, like a pale flower outlined against the dark wooden door.

CHAPTER XII

Father and Son

THE small Spanish-American ship drifted idly across the midsummer Atlantic. Unlike the *Lavinia* she was painted white, and each evening at dusk her lights were turned full on to illuminate the impeccable fact of her neutrality. Being in no special danger from submarines, she seemed to have no urgent reason for reaching Lisbon.

So far only a trickle of the 1940 evacuees, drawn homewards by patriotism or sentiment in spite of the transport famine, had begun to flow back to England. Apart from three very small girls with their mother, Adrian and Josephine were the only British children among the Spanish-speaking passengers. Their consequent dependence on each other's company, in addition to other reasons more complex and obscure, gave an unwonted sharpness to their mutual relationship.

The day had been oppressively hot, but sunset brought relief with a light, cool wind. Across the narrow grimy deck, Adrian lay on a battered lounge-chair with his eyes half closed. Ever since they left Acropolis, he had appeared to be tired. Josephine, irritated by his constant refusal to join in her activities, could not understand why. To her there had been nothing particularly exhausting in the final series of rushes between their travel agency and the various United States Government offices which seemed to exist in order to make sure that departing aliens did not lack occupation.

It was sad saying goodbye to the Downings, of course, especially as Kay seemed to mind so much. If Adrian had been deeply devoted to Kay or Dean D., Josephine would have understood his moody lethargy. But though his relationship with his foster-parents had been friendly, he had never grown specially intimate with either of them. Certainly not intimate enough to explain why he stayed in his stuffy little indoor cabin for the first twenty-four hours, lying on his bunk throughout a beautiful day with the sea as smooth as molten silver.

Unable to endure his expression of surly preoccupation any longer, she gave him a poke.

" Come for a walk round the deck, Wasp! It's cooler now."

" I wish you wouldn't push me like that! " he protested peevishly. " I'm not coming for a walk. I don't feel like it."

" You never seem to feel like anything."

" Well, I don't, if you really want to know."

" You are funny, Ady," she said for at least the tenth time. " When we came to America, you didn't want to leave home. Now we're going home, you don't want to leave America. I believe you *do* funk the bombs! "

" Hell! " he cried explosively, sitting up at this. " If you say that again, I shall throw you overboard! "

Why, he thought, almost at the end of his endurance, must people attribute to him a feeling that he really didn't possess — especially now, when at times the possibility of death seemed to offer a welcome relief from the conflict of his thoughts? Professor Brinton had suggested it, and now Josephine — as though fear were the only emotion in the world! People who talked like that must either have forgotten or else have never known the dark rages of love and grief.

" Look here," he continued, " if you can't sit still, why don't you go for a walk by yourself? "

" You know I don't like going by myself. It's so dull."

" Well, if you must fidget, go and fidget in your cabin. It's got a port-hole. It isn't hot like mine."

" I don't want to go to my cabin. It's too soon to go to bed."

" Stay up all night if you want to. I don't care, so long as you clear out."

This uncharacteristic repudiation of responsibility for her hours of rising and retiring inspired Josephine with an immediate impulse to go to bed early.

" Ady," she said, " if I do go down, will you come in and say good-night to me? I don't feel like going to sleep yet, but I can sit up and read *For Whom the Bell Tolls.*"

" It'll toll for you if you don't go away and leave me alone."

" But will you come in and say good-night? "

" All right. Only buzz off! "

When she picked up her book and clattered noisily towards the gangway, he sighed with relief. Then, forgetting all about her, he watched the smooth black water gliding past the ship as though it held some mesmeric fascination. " Carol ", he thought, " Carol ", and did not realise that his lips were repeating the name. " It's no good," he decided, as he had decided over and over again since Clarence Brinton had deposited him, jaded and half-asleep, at the Downings' home. " I've got to forget her. What's the good of writing, when I shall never see her again? And even if I do, she'll be married. I won't write. If I write, she'll answer. I just couldn't stand feeling like this every time I got a letter from her."

Only that morning, nerved to desperate resolution, he had gone to his cabin determined to tear up her photograph. But somehow he had been unable to carry out that final act of repudiation. The picture, taken with superb artistry by a first-class photographer for once presented with a nearly perfect model, looked so beautiful, so alive. It had caught her with just that light in her eyes which seemed to illuminate rather than conceal her deep concern for the woes of the world.

" I can't destroy it," he said to himself. " It would be a sort of — sacrilege. But when I get home, I'll put it away in a drawer. I'll hide it right at the bottom of some drawer I never have to open."

Down in her cabin, Josephine was thinking about Adrian. Ever since the vac. ended and they'd left Acropolis, he had been so cross. This voyage on a neutral ship, which she had been assured that submarines wouldn't attack, might have been such fun. And, instead of that, Ady's bad temper was making it perfectly mouldy. Perhaps, if she asked him very nicely when he came to say good-night, he would tell her what was the matter. She didn't really believe he was worried about the air raids.

Seeking some consolation for her mingled perturbation and boredom, she opened her largest suitcase, which was as usual in a state of colourful chaos. Almost on the top, half concealed by an uninspiring collection of school pants and stockings, she saw the pale pink satin pyjamas which Kay had given her as a parting gift just before she sailed. Dragging them out of the case, she flung off her shirt and shorts, and pulled them on. There was no mirror in the cabin except for the tiny square above the wash-basin, but even a glance at her head and shoulders filled her with satisfaction. Dressed like that, she could almost compete with Maria in *For Whom the Bell Tolls*. Giving her face a rapid sponge-over, and patting her hair once or twice with her new nylon brush, she flung herself down on her bunk and plunged into the passionate exchanges of Hemingway's lovers.

She had lost all sense of time when a sound made her look up, and she saw the handle of the cabin door being slowly, surreptitiously, turned.

" Ady's come earlier than I expected," she told herself. But the individual who entered her cabin was not Adrian. With a sick pang of terror she saw a Lascar sailor, black-haired and swarthy, whom she now remembered having noticed on the boat deck, watching her. Evidently he had waited for her to get undressed, knowing that the rest of the corridor would probably be empty because most of the adult passengers were attending a dance in the lounge. He turned the key in the lock behind him and stood with his back to the door, brown hands quivering and black eyes glittering with an avid stare as they rested on the tall immature girl in her low-necked, short-sleeved, pink satin pyjamas.

Josephine belonged to a sophisticated generation. At thirteen she would have scorned the vague terrors of her mother's contemporaries, who at a much later age only knew that they were liable to become, at the hands of men, victims of some undefined horror commonly reputed to be " worse than death ". She realised exactly why the Lascar was there, but she possessed much more useful information than that. In a week at sea she had learned all the idiosyncrasies of the grubby little cabin, and knew that the lock was broken. The turning of the key would have had, therefore, precisely no effect. She had only to play for time, and Adrian, who always kept his promises however disgruntled he might feel, would arrive to rescue her.

Summoning all her self-control, she resisted her first impulse to scream. Even if the occupants of the other cabins could hear and were able to understand her, the chance of their being there while that distant dance music was going on seemed extremely remote. And if she showed any signs of panic she might excite the sailor more. Perhaps he had a dagger concealed in his hand, and would kill her if she gave him away.

" Get out of my room," she said firmly, but as this was incomprehensible to him, it made no impression. While minutes seemed to pass he crept slowly closer to the bunk, his eyes never leaving her face. As she shrank back, now tense with fear, into the corner against the wall, she felt his hot, garlic-scented breath on her face. When one rough hand was laid on her bare arm and the other began to fumble with the glass buttons on her pyjama-jacket, her vanishing control left her. Resisting the sailor with all her considerable muscular strength, she shrieked aloud again and again.

It was just at that moment that Adrian, bored but loyal, turned into the corridor from the main gangway. He heard the screams ; he thought he recognised Josephine's voice. Forgetting his own heavy preoccupations, he rushed to the cabin. He opened the door just as the Lascar had pulled the bedclothes off the bunk and pushed Josephine on to her back.

" Ady ! " she screamed again, but her summons was unnecessary.

With all the strength latent in his own immature body, Adrian flung himself on to the sailor and pulled him away from Josephine.

" You damned lecher," he shouted. " You bloody, blasted swine ! " And a stream of imprecations poured from his lips which shocked Josephine even in her abyss of panic and relief. She had never dreamed that, even from the least civilised of the immigrant population whose offspring attended Acropolis High School with the Faculty children, he could learn such language.

But the Lascar, a tough, wiry man in his early thirties, was more than a match for sixteen-year-old Adrian. Foiled and furious, he determined at least to have his revenge, before escaping, on the English boy who had intercepted him. Clenching his fists, he pummelled Adrian's face and head with all the strength of his sinewy arms. Against these heavy odds Adrian fought back desperately, and the pair scuffled and struggled towards the door, knocking everything movable off the chair and basin as they went. Then, with a final outburst of abuse, the Lascar flung Adrian on to the floor, and banged out of the cabin.

When the fight started, Josephine began to cry in mingled thankfulness for herself and anxiety for Adrian. But now, as she contemplated him with dismay sprawling prostrate amid brushes, sponges, and broken glass, she scolded herself severely for this unwonted weakness.

" Dry up, you fool ! You're not a mid-Victorian ! There's nothing for you to yelp about. It was Ady got it in the neck, not you. Gosh, poor old Wasp ! "

She helped him, half-stunned, on to his feet. Regardless of the blood that splashed from his nose and broken lip on to her new pyjamas, she mopped his face with her sponge and towel. Then, half lifting, half pulling him on to her bunk, she went on bathing his forehead until they had both partly recovered.

"God, Jo — if I hadn't come just then!" he said. But she urged him to be quiet and rest. At last, with throbbing head and swollen nose and lips, he staggered off the bed and looked at his face.

"Hell, what an object! I seem as if I can't help being in the wars lately!"

"Why — when were you before?" asked Josephine, her curiosity aroused in spite of the fact that her heart seemed as if it wouldn't go back and beat at the normal rate.

"Oh, it doesn't matter. . . . Look here, Jo, you'd better go to my cabin for tonight; it's got a proper lock. I don't think he'll come back, but I'll put your suitcases against this door. Tomorrow I'll see the Purser and get the lock mended."

"Are you sure you'll be all right?"

"Yes, my nose has stopped bleeding. I'd rather be alone. Run along, and don't forget to lock the door. My God!"

As he lay in the warm darkness, nursing his wounded face, he thought of Josephine with a sudden fierce tenderness. What an escape it had been, poor kid! After all, he cared for her more than anyone in the world, except . . . Well, except. Not for anything would he have admitted this brotherly affection to Josephine or anyone else; but, as he lay there with his head aching till the pain seemed to envelop his whole body, the mere knowledge of his love for her comforted him. He'd taught himself to be " tough ", to hide his feelings; and sometimes he secretly suspected he had overdone it. Otherwise why was he so hard and often so rude to grown-ups, without really meaning what he said or knowing why he

said it? They often deserved it, of course, but still . . .
Anyway, he was glad to know for certain that he really
cared about Jo — as she, he thought, cared for him.

The next day his face, bruised, cut, and swollen, was
so unsightly that he stayed in his cabin and let her wait
on him, gratefully and, for once, conscientiously. For the
rest of the voyage, she was almost as subdued as he. Like
himself in the Catskills, she had been through an adult
experience.

*

So long as they remained on the boat, it was relatively
easy to keep out of the way of the other passengers — who
were not interested in them anyhow — and avoid awkward questions about Adrian's damaged appearance.
Even in Lisbon, a boy who looked as though he had come
off badly in a prolonged boxing contest was not a very
remarkable sight, though one would not, perhaps, have
expected to find it at the Avenida Palace Hotel.

Rumours had reached them that travellers were often
held up for weeks in Lisbon, which would have given time
for Adrian's face to regain its normal shape and colour.
They were disappointed when they learnt that they would
have less than a week of unsupervised freedom in the
exciting spy-ridden city, which was then the most crowded
and prosperous of European capitals. To the surprised
agent from Thomas Cook & Son who met them at the
boat and later escorted them to the night aeroplane for
their flight to England, Josephine earnestly explained that
Adrian's appearance was due to an innocent if unfortunate
accident.

" I know he looks funny! He fell downstairs on the
ship. Somebody pushed him by mistake."

But in the plane flying through perilous darkness over
the sea, their imminent meeting with their parents made
a plausible and consistently maintained explanation seem

more important than ever. Josephine was not sorry **to**
give her mind to this problem as she travelled, sleepless,
through the long night. Flying, she decided, was not
really very thrilling with blackened windows and the
noisy engine roaring in your ears. It was even a bit
frightening when you remembered the long-range German
fighters hovering over the Atlantic, waiting to shoot down
the aircraft of their enemies. Adrian's apparent indifference to this prospect, combined with the unhesitating
vigour with which he had rescued her from a physically
superior foe, had finally convinced her that, whatever
the real reason for his reluctance to go home, it was
not fear.

" What do you think we'd better tell Mummy and
Daddy about your face ? " she inquired.

" I don't mean to call them Mummy and Daddy any
more. It's babyish at my age."

" I don't think I could get used to anything else. But
then I'm younger than you. Ady — you wouldn't tell
them about the sailor, would you ? "

" Of course not. We'd better say I fell down a gangway, like you told the Cook's man."

" Do you think they'll believe it ? It didn't matter
about him ; he didn't really care."

" If they don't believe it, it'll be just too tough."

" What, for you ? "

" No, for them. . . . Jo, I wonder how damaged
England really is ? "

" It must be pretty bad. The American papers said
it was in ruins."

" We shall just have to get used to it. But let's shut
up for a bit. I want to lie back and get some sleep."

" Poor Ady ! I bet he still feels rather mouldy,"
speculated Josephine, newly obedient. She thought **it**
would be impossible to sleep in that noise ; but she **must**

have dozed, for it seemed only a few minutes before the steward was beside her, fastening her safety strap and telling her that they were coming down at Bristol.

On the way from the airport to the station they looked, with some curiosity, for the damage that they had read about, but England, apart from London and the South Coast, was then enjoying a period of respite from raids. Except for the shell of one large church, and a rubble-choked road which a fellow-passenger told them was called Wine Street, Bristol looked untroubled and peaceful. Their journey to London took them through some of the least disturbed country in Britain, and their hopes rose steadily that even in London they would find a sound roof over their heads. When they reached Paddington, their apprehensions were not to be compared with those of their waiting parents.

Josephine saw them first. Running excitedly down the long platform, she enveloped each of them in a capacious hug while managing with some skill to avoid being kissed.

" Hullo, Daddy! Hullo, Mummy! We're back! " she cried, as though they had just been away for the night. She hardly noticed that her parents' reactions were less spontaneous. Even Sylvia, looking at the tall thin girl who had left as a leggy little eleven-year-old, found it for the moment difficult to speak.

Adrian followed more slowly, half-consciously postponing the embarrassment of this family reunion, and examining the big terminus as he went. It looked normal enough except that the glass was missing from the roof; he was too far away to see the shattered waiting-rooms on Platform 1, and beyond them the row of demolished houses in Bishop's Road. As unobtrusively as he could he joined his parents and, to avoid any demonstrations of affection, firmly held out his hand.

" Hallo, Mother! How are you, Dad? "

For a moment neither of them recognised the boy who had grown into the near semblance of a young man ; his hair was the only indubitable reminder of the son whom they had known. Then Robert gave an exclamation strangely compounded of joy and distress.

" Adrian ! My dear boy ! I hardly knew you ! But — what in Heaven's name has happened to your face ? "

" It's all right, Daddy," said Josephine, sensing his sudden alarm that Adrian's appearance had permanently changed for the worse. " He had an accident. He'll tell you about it later. He generally looks more like he used to than he does just now."

When they had collected the luggage into a taxi after the usual delay in finding one, children and parents surveyed each other with the shyness of strangers who have once been intimate. His mother hadn't changed, Adrian decided. Her face was a bit thinner, perhaps, but then she had always been slender and was as lovely as ever ; he had been right to tell Carol she was beautiful. The one who really seemed different was his father. Dad always was rather grave and anxious-looking, but now and again there had been a sparkle about him, a kind of transient gaiety, that appeared to be gone. There were surely more lines on his face, too. What had drawn them there — grief, worry, endurance, responsibility ? Adrian began to realise, as he had been too young to realise at fourteen, that Robert's influence would not be easy to resist nor his authority to disregard. His father was, in fact, endeavouring to exercise it already.

" But, my dear son, when did you have this fall ? "

" Well — let me see — I guess it was a few days before we got to Lisbon."

" Ten days ago ! And you're still disfigured ! You must have been pretty badly hurt. Wasn't there a doctor on board ? "

" Yes, of course. But it didn't seem worth bothering him. I wasn't as bad as all that."

" It doesn't improve your beauty," interposed Sylvia, " but it'll get all right in time." Leave him alone, her expression telegraphed to Robert; and, realising that he would get no further information by pressing for it, he gave up the attempt. But later that evening, when Adrian was unpacking in his room at the Vicarage which seemed to be so incredibly the same, with Maria and Augusta Martelhammer still there like part of its permanent fittings and the usual string of suppliants and their worthy bene-factors coming in and out, Robert endeavoured once more to obtain the truth from his more amenable daughter.

" Jo, my dear — those bruises on Adrian's face. Did he really get them falling downstairs ? "

" Yes, Daddy. He fell down the gangway." She added conversationally : " It was at night. I expect he was going up to see the stars."

" I don't doubt he saw them all right ! He looks to me as if he'd been in a good scrap."

Josephine gazed at her father with wide-open, inno-cent eyes.

" Oh, *no*, Daddy ! Ady doesn't fight ! Lots of the kids used to fight at his school ; but Ady never did. He's not that sort."

Robert sighed. " Oh, well, I suppose it doesn't matter ! He'll be all right in a few days." Give me a forger, or a hardened housebreaker from Wormwood Scrubs, he thought, remembering how often he had elicited con-fessions from convicts during his prison visits. Evidently anything is easier than getting the truth out of one's own children when they reach adolescence.

At that moment the air-raid siren went. Dropping the subject for good Robert hurried Adrian and Josephine down into the Crypt, which had been reinforced with bricks and concrete, and turned, with his usual forethought for his parishioners, into a really efficient shelter. The raids had now ceased to be heavy, but the guns came into action more speedily and effectively than the inadequate London defences of 1940. A passer-by, caught in the street, ran almost as much risk from descending anti-aircraft shells as from falling bombs.

Sylvia, as usual, was at the theatre; her characteristic absence gave her children, more than ever, the strange sense of having never been away. Robert had grown accustomed to their separation during raids, though never to the anxiety that he always felt until she was safely back in the Vicarage. But that anxiety was a small price to pay for her companionship; for her calm, confidence-imparting presence of which he had been deprived during the heavy raids of 1940, when the various London theatrical companies went temporarily on tour in the provinces. Since their return in 1941 despite the risks that they still ran, he had never again been alone.

By the time that Adrian and Josephine had descended the steep stone stairway which led from the Church to the Crypt, the habitual shelter population was already there. Robert appeared to know them all; he moved through the various groups with the air of cheerful, encouraging confidence which his family, when he was alone with them, so seldom saw. Among the evening occupants of the Crypt were the usual " casuals " who had been passing by — soldiers, prostitutes, and the uproarious inhabitants of adjacent public-houses. They looked as i. they would require a good deal of controlling, but they never caused trouble within the precincts of St. Saviour's. Robert welcomed them too as warmly as though they had been close personal friends.

Unlike many incumbents he had never accepted the status nor worn the uniform of a Senior Air-Raid Warden for this in his opinion would have been a tacit endorsement of the values and assumptions which had created Britain's military machine. But the Warden's work which he actually performed in addition to his responsibilities as a priest was heavier than that of a normal member of the Civil Defence Force, for its duties were undefined and its hours unlimited.

Within a moment of the children's arrival they heard the guns, starting far away towards the coast like a roll of distant thunder, and gradually coming nearer until the clamour overhead approached that of a major bombardment. Seeing that the shelter population, who were accustomed to it, showed no sign of panic, Adrian determined to disregard the claw-like fingers which seemed to be clutching the pit of his stomach. His bruised face, set and expressionless, gave no hint of the instinctive reaction of his nerves to the ear-splitting explosions. This time it was Josephine, always at home in a crowd, who experienced the agreeable consciousness of freedom from fear.

" Oh, Ady ! " she cried. " Isn't it exciting ! We're really back in the War ! "

★

When Adrian had been at home for a week, Robert decided that the time had come to discuss his future plans. He did not want to hurry the process of readaptation for this uncommunicative boy who seemed almost a stranger, sometimes still a child and sometimes on the verge of manhood, with his deep unfamiliar voice yet further changed by its American intonations. But though it was only the beginning of the summer holidays in England, final arrangements for the Michaelmas term would not wait. Adrian's house-master at Eton, unwilling to refuse a father with so long an Etonian family tradition as Robert Carbury, had reluctantly agreed to take Adrian back. But it was, he emphasised, a major concession ; after two

years of American high-school education, Adrian would
be far below the normal English standards for his age.
He hoped it would be possible to confirm this arrangement, and perhaps obtain some holiday coaching in classics,
as soon as Adrian returned.

Adrian's reticence about his own reactions did not
make Robert's task any easier. Tentative endeavours to
ascertain his son's state of mind had elicited from Adrian
only the comment that he had been quite happy in America, but did not object to coming back. Finally Robert
resolved that, whether Adrian was ready or not, the
immediate decisions must be faced. He chose one early
evening when Sylvia had gone to the theatre but the
interrupting night raids were not yet due.

" Look here, son," he said, with a hampering sense of
awkwardness, " we've got to have a talk about your
education."

Adrian sighed, and put down his book. He had not
been reading it, but it was a useful screen for his thoughts,
which had escaped to the Catskills.

" What about it ? " he inquired, in a voice half extin-
guished with boredom.

" I've arranged for you to go back to Eton next term,"
said Robert. " It was rather difficult, but Mr. Kidderminster has agreed. I promised to confirm it as soon as
you arrived. He wants you to go down there and talk
to him."

Adrian reopened his book and turned a few pages
before he answered.

" I'm sorry you've had all that trouble, Father, because I'm not going back."

" Not going back ! " Robert kept his voice subdued
and reasonable, as he had learned to do in conversation
with the recalcitrant half of humanity. " What do you
mean ? "

" Just exactly what I say, Father. I wouldn't go back to that dump if you gave me a million bucks."

" Surely it's a matter for discussion between us, isn't it? Decisions about your education don't rest entirely with you."

Adrian stood up, and faced his father.

" Well, if they don't, they damn well ought to! I travelled three thousand miles all through the submarines when I was a kid of fourteen, and I've just been about four thousand more on my own again." (*And* fallen in love — *and* saved Jo from being raped, added his raw memories.) " If that doesn't entitle me to choose my own education, I don't know what does."

" But what's your objection to Eton? "

" Well, to begin with, they'd want me to stay there two or three years. I don't mean to go to school that long; I'm not a kid any more. And to go on with, I object to doing my work in a dark so-called study looking out on ash-cans. There wasn't a Polish or Italian boy in my school at Acropolis who didn't have a better place to live in than that."

Robert sighed.

" You must remember America's a country of wide-open spaces. We're not; we're an old country with traditions."

" Well, the sooner we get rid of them the better. I always loathed the place anyway."

" I'm sorry, Adrian. I didn't realise. But you've still to get through at least one exam in the next two years before you can go to Oxford."

" Who says I'm going to Oxford? "

" Nobody, yet. But I've always assumed you'd follow your grandfather and me at Christ Church."

" Well, I shan't. I've decided to go to Cambridge and study Astronomy under Eddington."

" And have you decided to pay the bills too ? " inquired the voice of Robert's growing exasperation. This beloved only son, to whose return he had looked forward with such eager anticipation, was certainly giving him some practice in keeping his temper. He compared Adrian's unmannerly statement of intention with his own considerate yielding to his father's distress when he had wanted to make a similar choice. Truly, he thought, my generation gets all the rue and none of the rosemary ! Not only has it been involved in two Great Wars ; it has been perpetually ground between its dominating parents and its arrogant children. But he did control his impatience, remembering his own sharp disappointment when he had sacrificed his preference to his father's wishes. Adrian's scientific urge, at least, was something that he could understand.

" Of course you shall go to Cambridge if you prefer it to Oxford," he said quietly. " I once nearly went there myself — as a Mathematics tutor after I'd finished at the House."

A small stir of interest shifted the dead weight of Adrian's sullen resistance.

" Did you, Dad ? I knew you were awfully good at Maths, but I never realised you'd thought of being a don."

" I only thought about it. The last War happened instead."

During this momentary release from tension, Adrian's mind had worked quickly.

" Look here, Dad, if I've only to get through an exam or two, why can't I go to a London day-school and take them there ? "

" You could, of course. But I don't know where there is for you to go. St. Paul's and Westminster are both evacuated."

Adrian made another movement of impatience

233

" Oh, Father, why do you always talk as if I couldn't go anywhere but a public school! There aren't any public schools in America. At least " — he corrected himself — " there are a few, but they're called ' private ' schools over there, and only the snobs go to them. Wouldn't any place do that takes exams ? "

" That's rather a utilitarian attitude to education, isn't it ? "

" It *is* my attitude — anyway at this stage. I wouldn't go to school again at all if it wasn't a means to an end. Isn't there any high school around here, where I could just go and mug up the exam ? "

Regretfully, Robert considered.

" There's a boys' college at Camden Town. That would be about the nearest. It's just an ordinary second-ary school and quite new. I don't know much about it."

" Wouldn't it do all right ? I could go on the subway."

" I suppose you could," Robert agreed, ruefully con-trasting the rich mellowness of Eton with the probable crudities of Camden Boys' College.

" Couldn't you telephone, Father, and make an appointment for us to see the headmaster ? " With characteristic impatience he added : " Why don't you ring up now ? "

" I'd rather have time to think it over, Adrian. Any-how, the headmaster is probably away for the holidays."

" He mightn't be gone yet. If you think it over for a week, I shan't change my mind. Can't you just *try* ? "

" Oh, very well," said Robert, feeling that it would be best for this uncomfortable discussion to end at all costs. " But remember," he added, as he went upstairs to tele-phone from his study, " the choice is yours."

The headmaster was still at his private house, and agreed to meet Robert and Adrian the next day in his office at the school. As soon as he saw Camden Boys'

College, Adrian felt comfortably at home. This raw red-brick building, which neither had nor pretended to have any traditions to live up to, reminded him of the high school at Acropolis which he had liked so much better than Eton.

The young headmaster, Joseph Merrion, was equally well satisfied with his prospective pupil. The boys at the College were mostly the sons of local shopkeepers or men in minor professions, and the idea of teaching Robert Carbury's son inspired him with an enthusiasm which he hardly troubled to conceal. Though a Methodist himself, he had listened eagerly to Robert's broadcast sermons before the War. As an admirer also of Sylvia's stage performances, he was prepared to be as cooperative as even Adrian could wish. In the circumstances, he thought, it would be better for Adrian to try to matriculate by getting a sufficient number of Distinctions in the School Certificate papers, rather than to attempt a more advanced examination in the short period that he had suggested. It would mean working mostly with boys a year or more his junior, but he could probably arrange for Adrian to take extra Mathematics in a higher form. The school had even a small specialist group studying Astronomy, which he would be delighted for Adrian to join.

Returning home with his father on the Underground, Adrian felt well satisfied with the results of his firm stand. Prompted by the future Astronomy class his thoughts, well concealed by the blank, withdrawn expression that Robert now interpreted as sulkiness, leapt the Atlantic Ocean and raced back to Professor Brinton's observatory. From there it was all too easy a step to new speculations about Carol. He wondered what she was doing at that moment, and mentally reaffirmed his resolution never to write to her, lest a reply should shake the resignation to her loss which he had imposed so stoically upon himself.

His preoccupations became so absorbing and painful that he did not even hear the remarks which his father addressed to him when the train stopped at the stations between Camden Town and Armada Square. He was, therefore, quite unprepared when at tea-time Robert uttered a definite though tolerant rebuke.

" What upset you at the College, son ? "

" Upset me ? " exclaimed Adrian, genuinely surprised. " Why, nothing upset me ! I liked it a lot. I don't know what you mean."

" Well, you were rather like a bear with a sore head all the way home, weren't you ? "

Adrian's expression of aggrieved surprise deepened.

" I wasn't, Dad. I was thinking. I just didn't want to talk."

Hell, he reflected. Why does the fussy old thing always expect me to say what's in my mind ? My thoughts are mine. I'm damned if I'm going to share them with him — or anyone else from the past ! They're all fuss and worry. They've never learnt to take things as they come.

" Then your choice of school satisfied you ? " Robert continued.

" It certainly did. If it gets me through that School Cert, it'll do all I need. And I can live at home, instead of being ordered around by some moron of a house-master."

" The one disadvantage of that is the raids. They may get worse again," Robert reminded him. But the reminder only moved Adrian to fresh impatience.

" I do wish you'd wouldn't keep on about the raids, Father. You're as bad about them as you are over public schools. I shall only be at this College about a year. Then I'll be drafted, and have to go and fight in Burma, or Egypt, or wherever the War's got to by then. What's the use of worrying about raids ! "

Robert paused a moment and then said deliberately :
" There are alternatives to joining up, you know."

" What alternatives ? I didn't come home to dodge
the draft by staying at school and pretending to work for
a scholarship."

" I wasn't thinking about scholarships, Adrian, and I
certainly don't want you to shirk anything you regard
as your duty. It was a question of principle that was on
my mind."

" Well, it isn't a principle that interests me."

Clearly and uncomfortably in the near future, Robert
foresaw yet another conflict looming ahead between himself and his son. He thought sadly of the many young
men and women from his Builders of Jerusalem who were
serving terms of imprisonment because they refused to
fight in any war but the one limited to spiritual weapons.
Ted Rogers, for instance, though nearing forty, was now
in Wormwood Scrubs Prison, at last fully expiating his
involuntary share in the death of Erica Varley.

Robert missed, more than even he could have expressed, Ted's good-humoured common sense at the
Committee meetings of the B.O.J. Owing to causes arising
from the War, the Executive had lost several of its weightier
members. Beatrice Trevelyan was in India with the
Young Women's Christian Association ; Cyril Benjafield
had gone to China as a driver for the Friends' Ambulance
Unit ; Jonathan Wiltshire, temporarily without a curate,
had been obliged to resign owing to pressure of work ;
one or two of the others were in prison. The nerves of
the remainder, rasped by raids and the interminable War,
seemed to become more exhaustingly on edge as the months
went by. They were worse now, thought Robert, than
they had been in 1940, when the shadow of imprisonment
and the excitement of potential martyrdom sustained them
all. Today the disapproving authorities were no longer

afraid of them. The danger of invasion had passed, and the B.O.J., like Robert himself, could best be countered by official neglect.

In spite of this ingenious and inexpensive method of wearing down rebel resistance, the B.O.J. had continued throughout the War to agitate for a negotiated peace. As it could no longer prevent the tragedy that brought excruciating death to an ever-growing number of innocent victims, it concentrated its energies on seeking to limit the tortures imposed by barbaric ingenuity upon the vulnerable human body. Its members could not reach the men and women dying horribly in Nazi concentration camps and gas chambers. But they kept a reluctant British public constantly reminded of the children in occupied countries starved into disease and death by the Allied blockade, and the helpless German and Italian families slaughtered or dispossessed by Allied bombs. They insisted, with unpopular if unsuppressed assiduity, that a policy of retaliation was inconsistent with the Christian professions which church- and chapel-going Britons had never officially repudiated.

Though Plymouth Hoe Avenue, unlike Armada Square, had suffered intermittent damage in the raids of 1940–41, the committee meetings where these periodic campaigns were discussed took place in the original office. Plasterboarding had replaced glass in most of the windows, and the roof leaked continually through gaps left by missing tiles, but the much-shaken structure still stood. Outside, the roar of traffic from Queen Elizabeth Street echoed down the dilapidated roadway.

In the crowded committee room, filled with the individualistic and increasingly articulate members of the Executive, the atmosphere frequently grew heavy with smoke and argument. On hot summer afternoons, the sunlight straggling into the dingy room through the few remaining panes of smeared glass revealed the bookcases dustily crammed with files, pamphlets, and much-thumbed volumes on international relations and social reform. Always tired now from increasing parish duties and decreasing clerical help, Robert struggled against insidious, pervasive sleep to fulfil his obligations as Chairman. His task was not made easier by the fact that many committee-members were now practised speakers, who had developed the habit of explaining their points of view in long controversial orations.

As the War rumbled portentously on through raids, ship-sinkings, the Nazi invasion of Russia, the Japanese invasion of Malaya, the surrender of the Philippines and the fall of Singapore, the windows and shelves of the office became dirtier and the individual expressions of opinion more vehement. Occasionally the series of undertakings which had become known as the " Basis of Membership " were called in question by inside critics who wanted to start everything all over again. In the tiny entrance hall the clock above the door, which had invariably been ten minutes fast or ten minutes slow, received a final shock to its nerves during the air raid of May 10th, 1941, and like many other London clocks stopped altogether.

Throughout these phases of spiritual conflict and physical disintegration, Robert never mistook the argumentative wrestlings of his followers for a failure of courage or a slackening of purpose. Though they might occasionally become as disputatious as the early Christians, he knew that a minority fired by an idea for which the time is ripe has power to move the world. His hundred thousand Builders, though embryonic in administration and young in experience, were none the less an organic group. Their work, he believed, would long outlast his life and example, and he had once hoped that Adrian, when he grew up, would take his place and carry on the B.O.J. after its founder had become too old and tired to direct its vehement crusades.

It would have been comforting to know that a younger embodiment of himself was ready to assume these responsibilities in a few years' time. But Adrian, it seemed all too clear, neither was nor wished to be his embodiment. His son's opinion of the B.O.J., expressed in one or two subsequent conversations during those summer holidays, showed that the hope of enlisting Adrian's support for his now widely extended organisation had been one of the many vain dreams which the boy's return revealed as the chimeras that they were.

One late summer morning the Vicarage bell rang shortly before lunch, and Adrian, who happened to be in the hall, answered it. A young man stood on the doorstep — an under-sized young man with horn-rimmed spectacles, mouse-coloured hair, green corduroy trousers, and brown canvas shoes.

" Is M-M-Mr. C-Carbury in ? " he inquired, struggling with a stammer.

Adrian gave him a blank look of utter contempt, turned round without answering, went upstairs, and, hardly troubling to knock, entered his father's study.

" There's a man at the door. He wants to see you," he said.

" Did he say what he wanted ? "

" No. But I guess you'll see him. He's one of your disciples, Dad."

Robert looked searchingly at him, but Adrian's face was empty of expression. It appeared to be equally free from mockery and cynicism.

" All right." Robert sighed as he laid down his pen. " Take him into the dining-room, and tell him I'll be there in a moment."

But when the visitor had gone, and father and son

were alone together for lunch because Sylvia had taken
Josephine on a school-shopping expedition, Adrian returned to the subject of the B.O.J.

" Father, why did you give your society a stuffy name
like ' Builders of Jerusalem ' ? "

" The name is based on Blake's poem. I don't think
it's a stuffy poem. Do you ? "

" I don't know. I've heard it sung badly so often I
don't remember a line of it. What's the idea ? "

" Well, the idea is that the real enemies of humanity
are injustice, and cruelty, and poverty, and hunger, and
disease — and war. Especially war, which causes all the
others. They're far more real and permanent enemies
than the Germans or the Japs."

Adrian was silent for a moment. Then he asked
casually : " I suppose you've never thought of changing
the letters ' B.O.J.' into ' B.O.S.H.' ? "

" No," said Robert, with determined serenity.
" They wouldn't represent what we stand for."

" Some people might think they did."

" If that's what they think, there's no need for them
to join. The B.O.J. is a voluntary organisation. It's one
of the few things left in this free country that aren't
compulsory."

He rose quietly from his chair and went out of the room,
leaving Adrian sitting alone at the table.

" So what ? " commented Adrian *sotto voce* as the door
closed. Shrugging his shoulders, he began his solitary
meal.

CHAPTER XIII

The Adolescent

As 1942 moved heavily on into 1943, Robert Carbury became increasingly conscious of a weariness so deep that it seemed more like an illness.

Christmas, it was true, had been peaceful; it had brought them all a brief respite of colour and gaiety which even Adrian seemed to enjoy. For a few days the Crypt was transformed into an underground parish room, with a small illuminated Christmas tree in the corner, and coloured paper streamers, saved from previous years, trailing their crisp patterns of blue, green, and scarlet across the low roof. Wooden chairs were arranged in rows so that the parishioners could watch St. Saviour's Nativity Pageant, in which Sylvia played her usual part of the Madonna on the small temporary stage. To the enthusiastic audience she appeared hardly older than the young mother of a baby son who had come to the parish with Robert nearly sixteen years ago. Between perform-ances four tiny Christmas trees stood on the stage against the green backcloth curtain. In the centre a miniature Santa Claus, made of painted cardboard, held a snow-powdered toy fir in his hands.

But when the last echoes of " Nowell, Nowell ! " and " Adeste Fideles " had died away and the gaudy decora-tions had been removed, the shelter and the winter seemed darker than before. The War had petrified into stalemate on all fronts; there appeared to be no particular reason why it should go on, and still less why it should ever stop. Yet in many countries of Europe and Asia, ill-clad half-frozen mothers were desperately asking, " How long ? " and wondering whether the ever-postponed victory would come before death had claimed their under-nourished children.

In his dreams every night Robert saw their pale faces, and seemed to hear their pitiful voices. Their sorrows, like the griefs and frustrations of his parishioners, made the burden of war too heavy to carry ; yet it could not be thrown off. Although he had inconspicuously celebrated his fiftieth birthday while the children were away and according to the age-perspectives of the older parish workers was still a relatively young man, he had not been able for two years to run up the Vicarage stairs to his study with the boyish energy of the previous decade. If ever he did so, a sharp vice seemed to close in his chest and leave him feeling choked and breathless.

Repeatedly Sylvia told him that he needed a holiday, and begged him to take one. He longed, indeed, to follow her advice ; to lose himself in nights of unbroken sleep in some quiet village on the Welsh coast. There was Borth, for instance, where he and his father had spent a summer vacation half a lifetime ago. But how, even for a few weeks, could he quit his job, when his poorer parishioners, who were as tired as he, had neither the money nor the time to indulge their fatigue ?

He did begin to wonder, though, whether the decision to bring home his beloved children — those critical, resistant, independent adolescents — had really been wise after all. At first he pushed the thought away from him, for in his determination to restore the treasured family life which was his emotional mainspring, he had — in the Civil Service phraseology which he sometimes bitterly repeated to himself — explored so many avenues, unturned so many stones, pulled such a variety of promising strings. And having at last achieved the result which his friends had said was impossible, he found it recoiling upon his head. To begin with he had believed that Josephine, apparently so affirmative and responsive, would be the easier child to control; but now he wondered whether her amiable opposition, combined with occasional excursions into thoughtless candour, was really more bearable than Adrian's sullen negativity. Perhaps, after so long an interval, it would have been better to wait and let them return as adults, endowed with the considerate reasonableness of normal adulthood. Deeply as he loved them both, his profound weariness seemed now to be his dominant sensation, and he began to dread their critical attacks as deeply as he dreaded the air-raid siren.

After Christmas, for the time being, the criticisms ceased. Adrian, now seventeen, proved unexpectedly cooperative in his insistence upon taking his turn in Robert's fire-watching rota of curates and parishioners at the Church and Vicarage. This responsibility seemed to his wounded mind to offer at least some answer to Clarence Brinton's hint that there were jobs waiting for boys of his age in England, though of course the Professor would never hear of it and thus revise his opinion of the boy he had known. In the Easter term, too, after a wearisome process of equipment which seemed to absorb all the family clothing coupons, Josephine went away to school.

For once Sylvia had opposed Robert in an educational decision. When Josephine was on the way home he had begun to talk about Cheltenham and Roedean, but Sylvia told him firmly that if their daughter seriously intended to follow her on the stage, she could afford to spend no more time in orthodox schools. Josephine's ambitions, it appeared when they questioned her, had remained as consistent as all her emotions. She wasn't quite sure yet whether she wanted to be an actress or a dancer, but she was serious enough to be sent to the Central London School of Drama and Dancing which was evacuated to Malvern.

During her absence, Adrian spent less time at the Vicarage. He was not only working conscientiously for his School Certificate despite the superior attractions of the Astronomy class, but at the Camden Boys' College, unlike Eton, he had found a friend.

Tony Terracini, born two days before Adrian, was the son of a naturalised second-generation Italian who ran a small but prosperous restaurant called " Antonio's " near Camden Town Station. The older Antonio, safely distant from his father's native Amalfi, had long been even more vehemently anti-Fascist than his British neighbours, and Tony was indistinguishable from any other English boy except for his warm Southern colouring and courteous manners. He was, nevertheless, neglected by his contemporaries at the College. They did not tease, molest, or persecute him, but they left him alone.

After the landings of the Allies in North Africa, and their subsequent attack on " the soft under-belly of the Axis " which was later to prove its resistant backbone, Tony was politely ostracised more firmly than ever. Inspired at first by pure contra-suggestiveness but soon by genuine liking, Adrian sought him out. Shyly one morning Tony invited him to come home to lunch at his father's restaurant, instead of eating at the school canteen.

Adrian was relatively indifferent to food ; he had been much less impressed than Josephine by the contrast between the lavish American meals provided by Kathleen Downing's coloured cook, and Maria's single-handed experiments with the rations. But even he found the canteen meals nauseating at times, and he accepted Tony's invitation gratefully. He was the more pleased with his perspicacity when he discovered the miracles that Antonio and his wife had learned to perform with dried egg and margarine.

Before long he spent every lunch-hour with Tony and

his voluble family, where his own volubility would have surprised his father. Tony's parents, profoundly grateful for the prestige newly conferred on their son by the most conspicuous boy at the College, would gladly have fed Adrian for nothing. But here Robert, though he approved of this friendship which Eton could not have provided, became adamant; Adrian, he said, must give at least as much for each meal taken at Antonio's as he would have paid at the College canteen. On this basis the agreeable arrangement continued; but Tony had other advantages besides the ability to provide palatable food. Not only did he possess the native sensitiveness of his ancestors to music and art; he was a specialist in these subjects from whom, Adrian soon discovered, he had much to learn. Nearly every week-end he accompanied Tony to a Promenade Concert or under his guidance explored London art museums, which varied from the National Gallery to the obscure home of some unexpected treasure in a distant suburb.

*

This instructive routine, peaceful for both Adrian and his father, helped Robert through that spring which saw the beginning of obliteration raids on Germany. In May came the breaking of the Eder and Möhne dams, which flooded the Ruhr valleys with a torrent of swirling water and annihilated scores of helpless families. To Robert's constant imaginative participation in the agonies of children burned and drowned was added the fear of retaliation on the equally helpless families in his parish. The barrage balloons, hanging low over London beneath the evening clouds, seemed to symbolise the perpetual dread which depressed his spirit.

His relations with his family lost their placidity when Josephine returned for the Easter holidays. Robert sometimes thought that his son and daughter took a perverse delight in stimulating each other's recalcitrance. One Sunday evening, during the late supper which habitually followed Evensong, Adrian passed on an invitation from Tony to Josephine to accompany him to a performance of Parry's *The Pied Piper of Hamelin* at the Cavendish Hall and have supper at Antonio's afterwards. Robert's inquiry whether Adrian would be there as well immediately provoked a characteristic tirade.

" It's got nothing to do with you, Father. Tony invited Jo."

" I didn't say she couldn't go, son. I was only asking for information."

" I suppose you think it would be improper for Jo to go by herself with Tony ! "

" Have I said so, Adrian ? "

" No. But you think so. After all, you're a Victorian, Father. You can't be expected to understand the point of view of our generation. We stand for just about the opposite of all that."

Of all what ? Robert's memories inquired, though he did not speak. He only recalled the many past occasions on which he had fought so hard against complacent curates, elderly church-wardens, and conservative parishioners to remove from St. Saviour's the dead weight of that Victorian tradition which the War of 1939 had finally thrown on the scrap-heap with other traditions which could less easily be spared. What had he, revolutionary to his father and reactionary to his children, really achieved by those sixteen years of effort ? Black-listed by his Government and an object of cautious if friendly vigilance to his Bishop, he seemed sometimes to have done no more than retain the affection of simple, bewildered people who still followed him in their thousands because, like himself, they felt lost, friendless, and forlorn.

Sylvia always refrained from interfering during

Robert's altercations with the children, and the four of them finished their supper in silence. When it was over Adrian strolled nonchalantly upstairs to his bedroom, and Sylvia, now compelled by the growing shortage of household help to be domesticated on Sunday evenings, cleared away the supper plates and carried them into the kitchen. Josephine, in whom domestic cooperation was not yet an acquired characteristic, continued the attack on her father.

" You really *are* a Victorian, you know, Daddy! You belong to the older generation. Even that suit gives you away."

Robert looked down ruefully at the ageing clerical suit which cassock and surplice satisfactorily concealed.

" It's seen better days, I admit. I haven't a cupboard full of American clothes like you, Jo. But it's still a very useful suit. What's wrong with it? "

Josephine examined him critically.

" It's really your figure that's changed. You had that suit made about ten years ago, when you were quite a young man. Now you're getting a bony old man, and it just hangs on you." She added, as though seeking to soften the blow: " Mummy's the same. She looks quite young at a distance, but when she takes her paint off she's got crowds of little wrinkles round her eyes."

" I hadn't noticed them. . . . I expect she sometimes gets tired, as we all do nowadays. You don't mind being candid, do you, Jo? "

" Well, Daddy," she said, suddenly confidential, " the fact is, kids between twelve and, say, eighteen don't like their parents to behave as if they cared about them. You know — soppily."

At least I'm beginning to get the truth now, thought Robert.

" How ought they to behave then? " he inquired.

" Just ordinarily. The way Mummy treats us is quite all right."

" I see," said Robert reflectively. How ironical it seemed that Sylvia's benevolent detachment towards her children should be more congenial to them than his own deep devotion! " You know, Jo," he continued, " love is not a quality so freely given among human beings that anyone, of any age, can afford to repudiate it. Not even," he added, " when it comes from one's parents."

" Oh, I don't mind being liked by my contemporaries," said Josephine serenely. " It's only older people who make me curl up! I'm always afraid they're going to kiss me."

Robert sighed.

" Well, I won't offend again." He took out his watch. " It's time for community singing. Are you coming? "

" Not tonight, Daddy. I want to read."

" Well, you might give your mother a hand with the supper things first. And if the siren goes, don't play about upstairs as you did last night. The planes come over so fast in these tip-and-run raids, you've only just got time to get into the shelter."

Belatedly conscience-stricken, Josephine went downstairs to the basement kitchen. Sylvia, always rapidly efficient over tasks that she disliked, had almost finished the washing-up, but she did not protest about Josephine's delay. She only said quietly : " I suppose you and your father have been arguing again? "

" Not exactly arguing, Mummy. I just told him he was a Victorian — and getting old."

" He's not really old, Jo. He's very tired and over-burdened, and dreadfully hard-worked. I wish you and Adrian wouldn't be so unkind to him."

" We don't mean to be unkind. But he's so old-fashioned! "

249

Sylvia polished the tumblers and put them methodically into the kitchen cupboard. Then she said : " I suppose I am, too, from your point of view. But you're not unkind to me."

" You wouldn't mind if we were. You don't like us as much as Daddy does."

If this downright judgment penetrated Sylvia's emotional armour, she gave no sign of it.

" But surely," she said, " that's not a reason for being unkind to *him* ! "

" It is really, Mummy. The one thing that's true about all kids is that they don't like their parents to show they like them."

" I think I understand. But explain a little more."

" Well . . . parents do such soppy, sentimental things when they like you. It's sort of embarrassing. It makes you want not to be alone with them."

There was a brief silence as they put the plates and cutlery away. Then Sylvia spoke with emphasis.

" You mustn't expect us to do all the understanding, you know. You must try to understand your father. His life has been hard — and in some ways disappointing. He's always given more love than he's received. . . . Perhaps you'll see this for yourself, one day. Till then, don't hurt him more than you can help. Where's Adrian ? "

" Upstairs in his room. . . . Are you going to talk to him about Daddy too ? "

" Don't you think it's time I did ? "

" I daresay you're right, Mummy. But I don't believe it'll do any good."

" Perhaps not. But I'm going to try."

But she did not try after all that evening, for when she knocked and went in, Adrian was standing in front of his dressing-table gazing at a photograph that she had never seen there before. It was the likeness of a black-haired, vivacious-looking girl, with large dark eyes that held a depth of melancholy which betrayed her smiling features. He made a sudden movement as though to conceal the portrait, but when he saw that the interruption came from his mother and not from his father, he stood silently regarding her. In her dark blue dress, with her bronze hair untouched with grey and the contours of her pale face still exquisite, she appeared to him just as he had always known her. It was impossible to think of her as a middle-aged woman nearing fifty — as impossible as it had been to think of Carol as a child only just seventeen. Perhaps it was really that ageless quality, rather than the grace of their movements, which had made him see a likeness between Carol and his mother. They both seemed completely detached from time.

Sylvia glanced away from the portrait as though she were indifferent, and made no comment. If she had asked whom it represented Adrian would not have told her, but her air of regarding it as unimportant piqued him into an explanation.

" That's a girl I met in America," he said. He added awkwardly : " Her name's Carol Brinton. She's the daughter of the Professor I stayed with in the Catskills."

" Oh, is she ? " said Sylvia, appearing as unimpressed as though Carol Brinton had been a pin-up girl from the pages of the *Ladies' Home Journal*. " Was she nice ? " she inquired, deliberately choosing the least emotional and most colourless words she could think of. " Did you like her ? "

" Nice ! What a word to use about Carol ! " cried Adrian, explosively defensive, and thereby confirming all Sylvia's suppositions. " She was an absolute knock-out ! At least, I mean," he added, his diminuendo reflecting his realisation that he was giving himself away to his mother, of all people, " she wasn't half bad — not for an American girl, that is . . ."

" She looks older than you," observed Sylvia nonchalantly; and again Adrian hastened to explain.

" She was — but not so much as you'd think. She was only about six months older. That's the worst of American girls. They seem to grow up when they're about thirteen, and get interested in men nearly old enough to be their father, instead of taking up with guys of their own age. . . ."

His sore need of consolation suddenly overcame him. He would have seen himself dead rather than ask advice of his father, but his mother didn't fuss. She never cared all that much about anything, and he'd probably given himself away anyhow.

" Mummy," he began, completely forgetting his severe resolution to address his parents more formally, " supposing, when you're still quite young — not absolutely grown up, I mean, but nearly — supposing something happens that upsets you a lot . . . how long does it take before you forget about it ? . . . I mean, not so much forget, but stop really minding any more ? "

Sylvia stood still, thinking. She knew that she had discovered, without asking, one reason for Adrian's insufferable behaviour. At that moment, she realised, her son was closer to her than he had ever been — or perhaps ever would be again. He was calling upon her experience for a philosophy of life : one that she might be able to give him because she, as much as anyone, knew its bitter cost.

" Well," she said, her voice still resolutely unemotional, " most people do get over things in time. . . . Most people. But you know, Adrian, I'm not sure that getting over them too well is really a good idea." In spite of herself, she sighed deeply. " You see, what really matters is to be alive. Many people in the world are half dead : some because they've never lived, and others because they've lost — something or somebody that made life worth while. But if you can lose, and still stay alive — that's a real victory. And you can't really live unless you know what it means to suffer. Suffering . . . like loving . . . is part of living. It's better to know, even if knowing hurts, than to be half dead."

" I see," he said very slowly. " I believe — I see." An urgent desire to be alone and think right through the implications of her words suddenly overcame him. " Look here, Mummy, I'll come downstairs in a little while."

" All right, Adrian. You'll find me in the drawing-room if you want me."

She opened the door very quietly. As she turned to close it, she saw him take the photograph off the dressing-table and put it away in a drawer.

*

During the summer term Adrian was much preoccupied with plans for spending most of the holidays away from the Vicarage. In this scheme Tony Terracini willingly abetted him. His mother, an Englishwoman, had a brother who owned a fruit farm in the Vale of Evesham, in Worcestershire. Like all farmers in war-time, he was short of labour. Nothing would suit him better than to have Adrian, Tony, and Josephine as additional " hands " during August and September.

By the time that Adrian announced this arrangement to his parents, Robert had ceased to protest at his son's cool assumption that he would consent to plans about which he had never been consulted. He merely reminded Adrian that, ever since his return home, a visit to Hodder-shall Ash had been proposed for that summer. Robert had practical reasons for the expedition. Although he had offered the manor house to the Government for child evacuees during the War, its upkeep was a growing liability, and he was anxious to know what use Adrian proposed to make of it.

" I can't think why you want me to go," Adrian said ungraciously. " But, if I must go, I don't mind going at the end of July. My exam will be over by then, and Tony's uncle doesn't expect us till the first week in August."

In spite of this characteristic lack of cooperation, Robert travelled with Adrian to Staffordshire invigorated by a substantial dose of wishful thinking. Owing to the War and its preceding alarms it was ten years since Adrian had gone to Hoddershall; in his mind's eye his father could still picture the slim little boy of seven running excitedly up and down the terraced lawns. With his bronze hair and green sweater, Adrian might have been one of the orange-hued ancestral dahlias which had jumped from its root and started to race round the garden. He had loved the old place then; his enjoyment seemed to lend substance to those dreams of family continuity which had given Robert so much happiness before his birth. Surely, when he saw the house and garden again, that pleasure would be renewed, those hopes reinforced !

It was true that the twenty evacuees from Manchester, who now lived there under the control of his caretaker and a school teacher, had not improved the appearance of Hoddershall Ash. The house, littered with their books and toys, looked dilapidated and shabby. They had turned the lawn below the terraces into a cricket-field, and had carved their names on the trees in the ash-grove. But the small west wing of the house where Robert had slept and worked as a boy had been kept private for his own occasional use, and the terraces — the only part of the garden still carefully cultivated — were closed to the evacuated children. The famous dahlias were now in flower, the same glory of purple and yellow, orange and scarlet, as they had been in his boyhood. Their unchanged beauty filled him with a sharp nostalgia, bringing back forty-year-old memories of his father and his youth.

He and Adrian went over the house and round the garden almost in silence. When the boy had seen the drawing-room, and the billiard-room, and the study where his grandfather had prepared his speeches, Robert showed him the portraits in the dining-room of James Carbury, M.P., as Lord Privy Seal, and of James's father, another Robert, the social reformer who had been Mayor of Hoddershall and a Justice of the Peace. When the old house had been thoroughly explored they went for a walk down the terraces, and round the lawn on which the evacuees were noisily playing rounders, and then through the quiet solitude of the ash grove where the top branches of the tall trees mingled to shut out the sky. That night Adrian slept in the small room which Robert had occupied as a boy; but it was not until they were half-way back to Euston in the train next day that he made any substantial comment.

" I can't think why you don't get rid of that old-fashioned place, Dad," he said. " The grounds are swell, I admit. But the house is an awful old mausoleum."

Wounded in his fondest memories, Robert also recalled the drain on his pocket which Hoddershall Ash had involved over many years. But, as always, he was determined to keep his temper.

" It's been waiting for you, my son. I've always hoped that one day you and your children would live there. Apart from whatever you decide to do in the world, you should have sufficient means to keep it up."

His hands deep in his pockets, Adrian looked at the

mild Northamptonshire countryside which seemed to amble past the windows of the dilatory wartime train. A sudden recollection of his journey to Liverpool three years earlier increased his inexplicable feeling of resentment.

" It's a pity you didn't consult me," he said, as though he himself made a practice of consultation. " Maybe it's just too tough, but I should never want to live in a ramshackle old place like that. I'd rather have the money to build myself something modern and compact."

" Doesn't family tradition mean anything at all to you, then ? " asked Robert gravely.

" God, no! Why should it ? I'm interested in the future. I've no use for people who live in the past."

That evening Robert went alone, as he had gone so often during the painful and lonely years of war, to kneel in the Chancel of his Church and ask for the guidance of his friend Jesus in his relationship with his son. He did not pray now for strength to resign himself to Adrian's bitter departure, but for the power to control his own reciprocal impulses towards anger and resentment, and to exercise unlimited patience. He pleaded too for the grace which would enable him to accept, as part of his perpetual burden, the end of that family continuance which had always meant so much to him.

Sylvia, he knew, would never live at Hoddershall Ash even if she eventually retired from her profession, and a house so far from London would be of no use to Josephine once she went on the stage. He was reluctantly convinced that Adrian would not change his mind ; he realised that the dream of seeing his son, and his son's children, in his old home had been nothing but a wishful figment ot his imagination. All Adrian's traits, his inclinations, his contra-suggestive individualism, made it seem obvious that to him pieties and precedents were merely so much dead wood of which one rid one's self as quickly as possible.

To show that he did not indeed cherish any grievance towards his son, Robert decided to sacrifice a morning's work and see Adrian and Josephine off to the farm where Tony had gone two days earlier to prepare for them. Sylvia could not go to the station; a rehearsal of Stafford Vaughan's new drama, *Turn Again Home*, was timed for the same hour as their departure. But though Josephine's conversation rattled amiably on against the roar of the Underground train to Paddington, Adrian did not appear to appreciate Robert's paternal gesture of reconciliation. Throughout the journey he was, as usual, silent, and when they had taken their tickets to Evesham and found two seats in the front of the crowded train, Robert's mild request for a postcard announcing their arrival encountered the customary resistance.

" Whatever do you want a postcard for ? "

" Well — your mother will be glad to know you're there all right. It'll be a weight off her mind."

" That's nuts, Father. You know when Mummy's doing a new play she never thinks about anything else."

" He means a weight off *his* mind," prompted Josephine from inside the carriage. She merely wanted her father to go, so that she could squeeze into her middle seat and read *After Many a Summer*. " Don't be a nuisance, Wasp ! Tell him you'll send it."

But for once Adrian disregarded her. He looked resentfully at Robert, who seemed so constantly to forget that he had travelled to America and back, and was over seventeen. His eyes, normally clear but now opaque and expressionless, suggested that his father was nothing but a second-rate compendium of fussy triviality.

" Anyway, supposing we weren't met," he said. " Supposing we never did arrive. What could you do about it ? "

" I'm only asking you," said Robert patiently, " to do what I always do for your mother when I leave home for more than a night or two."

At that moment the whistle blew, and the train, with Adrian standing at the window, moved out of the station. As it reached the end of the platform, Robert raised his arm in a final salutation. But no response came from Adrian. He remained staring out of the window as though his father did not exist until the coach disappeared from view.

A sudden ache gripped Robert's throat, and a mist swam before his eyes as he walked back to the station entrance. How much more of this calculated insolence would he be able to endure? Everyone confided in him; he was the listener to innumerable heartbroken monologues, the daily reader of illegible epistolary biographies. Yet to no one had he confided his own secret grief: the dislike and contempt which his son appeared to feel for him. It was even more bitter than Sylvia's long-accepted detachment from his interests and Josephine's casual, cheerful indifference to his hunger for affection. Their attitude, however galling it might be to his vanity, was neutral, but Adrian had an infallible aptitude for mocking his love, wounding his pride, and stabbing his susceptibilities where they hurt him most.

He needed, he felt, the support of some disinterested advice. When he reached home he telephoned Frederick Westerly, and asked him to dinner. Lord Westerly knew that Robert would never send for him at short notice without sufficient reason. He cancelled a previous engagement, and went.

*

By the time that Maria put the coffee on the table, Robert had talked only about the progress of the War, the business of the parish, the shortage of curates, and the

Government's attitude towards the B.O.J. He looked inordinately tired, thought sixty-five-year-old Lord Westerly, and for a man barely fifty-two seemed unduly to have lost confidence in the handling of problems which, burdensome though they were, had long been part of his normal routine.

" Look here, Bob," he said at last, " you didn't ask me here to discuss the parish, or even the B.O.J. Has something special gone wrong? "

" No, not exactly. But I *am* very troubled. I thought perhaps you could help me."

" I'll always do my best. You know that, I'm sure."

Robert sat back in his chair away from the light, which made his head ache on that heavy August evening.

" I want to talk to you about Adrian," he said. " The plain truth is, Fred, since he came back from America I can neither get near him, get on with him, nor understand him. This afternoon he went off to Evesham with a scowl on his face and not even a ' Goodbye ' — simply because I asked him to send us a postcard to say he'd arrived."

Lord Westerly was not altogether surprised by this information. Since it was on his advice that Robert had sent his children away in 1940, Frederick had helped him to get them back in 1942. He had approached useful " contacts " at the Foreign Office, the Ministry of Transport, and the Children's Overseas Reception Board, explaining that Robert had parted with his son and daughter against his will and, being an exceptionally devoted father, was actually hampered by their absence in his great mission at St. Saviour's.

England, he subsequently reflected, was a unique country in its peculiar way. Just because there were aspects of Robert's mission which these Government officials earnestly deplored, they seemed to have been only the more ready to assist — in order, he supposed, to display their democratic impartiality towards a minoritarian. But when the children actually came back and he learned that Adrian had refused to return to Eton and insisted upon going to Camden Boys' College, he wondered whether Robert had not brought on himself a family problem of unexpected dimensions.

" I'm sorry to hear that," he said. " But do you think a childless bachelor has any advice to give worth hearing ? "

" Certainly he has. At least you'll be able to see things more clearly than I do. I'm much too emotionally involved to be detached."

" Well," admitted Frederick Westerly, putting down his coffee-cup. " I've a number of nephews, if that's any help. And chairing the B.O.J. Campaign for Refugee Children has taught me a good deal."

It certainly had. Only that afternoon the conscientious committee had spent three hours analysing the idiosyncrasies of the children already in its care, and trying to anticipate the temperamental reactions of those whom it was still hoping to bring from the Continent.

" How old is your boy now ? " he inquired.

" Seventeen. It seems to me he ought to have outgrown some of the things he says and does."

" It's an awkward age, all the same—especially for his generation. They're so busy protecting themselves against this, that, and the other, they don't get time to develop an adult equilibrium. After all, to achieve that sort of balance a young person does require a measure of tranquillity."

Robert paused while Maria came in to remove the coffee-tray. Then, handing Lord Westerly a pre-war cigar, he went on.

" But surely his age oughtn't to make all that difference ? It doesn't seem to at school. Merrion gives him consistently good reports, and apparently he really has worked hard for his School Certificate. Why should he be so difficult at home?"

"In what special way is he difficult, Bob?"

"It would be easier to enumerate the times he behaves reasonably — they happen seldom enough. He's perpetually rude, particularly to me — though so far, with God's help, I've managed to keep my temper. He takes what he can get out of us, and is persistently ungrateful for it. He never consults us about anything, but always expects us to consult him."

Lord Westerly sat silent for some moments, quietly smoking his cigar. Then he said: "I know it's unwelcome advice for a Christian confronted with un-Christian behaviour — especially when you're always so successful with young people who don't belong to you. But if I were you, I'd let him severely alone."

"Honestly, Fred, I've tried that. He seems to seek me out and attack me."

"That's because he feels you're judging him. It's his peculiar way of testing your affection. How does he get on with his mother?"

"I wouldn't say they're exactly boon companions. But neither he nor Josephine is as aggressive with her as they both are with me."

They know she's more interested in the stage than in them, thought Frederick Westerly. They realise they can't hurt her much, so they don't try. Aloud he said: "Well, her profession takes her away from the house a good deal of the day. Yours doesn't. At their age it's better to see too little of them than too much."

Robert smiled ruefully.

"I'm sure you're right. But when Adrian goes out of his way to behave badly, I can't stop using my judgment, can I?"

Lord Westerly meditated.

" Don't think me impertinent, Bob, but it seems to me that's exactly what you must try to do — suspend judgment not only in word but in fact." He paused again, considering. " I'm the outsider who sees most of the game," he continued. " My guess would be that your boy has had some sort of emotional experience which is affecting his conduct. He won't tell you what it was — not yet. Until you know, you can't see his behaviour in its proper perspective."

Robert looked startled.

" Do you mean he's had a premature love affair, or something of that sort ? "

" He might have had, but it doesn't follow. His conflict may merely arise from the contrast between two civilisations — the freedom from actual war in the one, and the perpetual wartime frustrations of the other."

Robert remained silent, and Lord Westerly developed his theme.

" The trouble with us is that we happened to be born at the end of one of the calmest periods in the world's history. I saw more of it than you did, because I'm older. In consequence we made the mistake of regarding it as normal, and anything worse as a deviation. Look at the literature of the last War. Most of it is one long cry of indignation for this very reason. Its poets and novelists couldn't get used to the terror, uncertainty, violence, and brutality that Adrian's generation takes for granted."

This reminder took Robert back into his own past.

" It's a strange irony, Fred," he commented. " I remember, before Adrian was born, thanking God he'd be coming into a more peaceful world than mine. And now . . . look at it ! "

" I daresay most parents of your generation have been struck by the same contrast between hope and reality.

And the trouble is, children don't benefit by regarding chaos and uncertainty as normal."

" We really are more fortunate, I suppose," said Robert. " At least we have the memory of a stable civilisation."

" Yes. We know that happiness and tranquillity once existed, and are therefore possible. Your boy and girl don't even know that. Consequently they tend to believe in nothing."

" How can one give them faith, Fred — the Christian faith that all things work together for good to them that love God ? "

" *You* can't do it, I'm afraid, Bob. Not all your prayers will achieve it for them, because you happen to be their father. Eventually stability will come to them through some human experience — a philosophic discovery, or a personal relationship. But it's hardly likely to happen yet. Have you ever tried to draw up a catalogue of Adrian's memories ? "

" He hasn't favoured me with much self-analysis. Carry on, and tell me what influences *you* think have moulded the boys of his age."

Lord Westerly stood up and leaned against the mantel-piece, puffing at his cigar.

" It's hard," he said, " to realise that even the seventeen-year-olds, like Adrian, were barely eight when Hitler came to power. Remember that, from the time of their earliest consciousness, they've heard their parents discussing crisis in Germany, crisis in Austria, crisis in Czechoslovakia, crisis in Poland. They've eaten crisis with their breakfast and drunk it with their tea. They've read posters and newspapers prophesying war. And when it came, their nightmares turned into reality — for millions."

For millions indeed, echoed Robert. He thought of the children for whom the new B.O.J. campaign had been

launched : children who had been left to wander, parent-
less and homeless, amid incredible hardships in which only
the fittest could survive ; children who had been reduced
to a level of starvation which changed once-cherished
boys and girls into living skeletons ; children for whom
no hope of restoration to normal health and intelligence
could be anticipated even after the long-delayed coming
of peace.

" At least Adrian and Jo haven't known the worst,"
he said. " They haven't been left friendless and starving,
with parents put to death in concentration camps or gas
chambers."

Lord Westerly threw the stub of his cigar away and
lighted a cigarette.

" Have you forgotten 1940 already ? The gas chambers and concentration camps weren't so far from you
then. That's why you were right to send the children to
America. If ever a list comes to light of the people the
Nazis meant to shoot when they landed here, I'll bet you
a fiver your name's somewhere near the top ! "

" But they didn't land, and I wasn't arrested. The
children can't have been disturbed by possibilities they
didn't even suspect."

" You can't be sure how much they may have suspected. And you mustn't underrate what they've actually
experienced. After all, they've been pushed from school
to school and country to country ; we were obliged to
deprive them of family security much too soon. They've
been certain of nothing — except that each new event
was bound to involve them in danger and upheaval. Is
it surprising they lack the capacity for wonder, which is
the basis of reverence ? Why, our own peaceful childhood
was paradise, compared with theirs ! "

" I wonder," mused Robert uncomfortably, " how
long it's going to take them to get over it."

" Get over it ! My dear Bob, they're still in it — the same as you and I are ! Air raids, broken nights, interrupted lessons. What with all these tip-and-run raids, Adrian must have sat for his examination with one eye on the paper and the other on the clouds ! You can't look for placid stability in children who never know what to expect from one day to the next ! "

Robert rose from his chair and began half consciously to pace the room. Frederick Westerly's analysis had both comforted and disturbed him. He now thought with love and pity of his son ; of the tragic premature philosophy which seemed to criticise everything, believe in little, and hope for nothing. But he wondered whether any basis for confidence in Adrian's future remained.

" Are you warning me, Fred, that the consequences ot this early insecurity will continue for life ? "

" Good Heavens, no ! " exclaimed Lord Westerly. " I merely meant that adjustment is more difficult for young people today, and therefore slower. Your boy is in process of providing himself with an armoury against Fate. He's developing a faculty for confronting catastrophes such as you and I have longed for in vain. These boys and girls are faced with a world of tragedy and death. It's only natural they should learn to survive in their own way rather than ours."

He took out his watch.

" It's getting late, and I must go. But don't let your faith, of all people's, be shaken now — and least of all in your own children. They've suffered prematurely, it's true. But premature suffering can be a formative process, provided it's not excessive. It can end by creating a fellowship — the sort we aim at in the B.O.J. A world-wide fellowship of men and women, whose hope and faith are based on common experience."

Picking up his hat from the hall, he took Robert's arm

as they went down the Vicarage steps and out into the dark summer warmth of Armada Square.

" Good-night, my dear Bob, and don't worry ! Your Adrian opposes you now because you represent a mixture of authority and conscience — always an intolerable combination to a boy of his age. He's more like you than you realise. Just because his values are instinctively your own, he tries to make them different. But in the end you'll probably find him walking along the same road to the selfsame goal."

CHAPTER XIV

Roads to Manhood

WHEN Adrian came back from Evesham, he told Robert that he had passed his School Certificate examination. After only a year's work on an unfamiliar syllabus he had in fact done very well, having achieved Distinctions in Mathematics, Science, History, Geography, and English Composition, and Credits in English Literature, Latin, and French. This achievement easily reached Matriculation standard, and exempted him from any further public examination before he went to Cambridge. He had known his results for some days, but it had not apparently occurred to him to communicate them to his father.

Robert, deeply gratified by Adrian's success, ignored the discourtesy. But it was less easy to disregard the further challenge which his son presented to his renewed determination to understand and forgive. While they were at Evesham, said Adrian, he and Tony had registered for military service. In the hope of having some opportunity to practise his Mathematics he had put in an application to join the Royal Engineers, and Tony, on the chance that this might at least enable them to start their training together, had done the same.

Overburdened as usual with work, Robert had forgotten that the registration date, which preceded by three months the call-up at eighteen, would occur while Adrian was on holiday. Though he knew that Adrian's action was irrevocable, his own principles would not permit him to let it pass without pointing out the issues involved.

" It was rather a fundamental decision to make on your own," he said. " Don't you think we might have discussed it first ? "

" I didn't see any point in it, Father. I know your opinions. I'm not such a child that I can't understand them. I just don't happen to agree with them, that's all."

" What exactly don't you agree with, my son ? "

" Oh, Father ! " exclaimed Adrian impatiently. " Must we go into it all over again ? I tell you, I accept war as a fact. It's always been the final way of settling disputes, and it always will be. Any other idea is just romantic nonsense ! "

In spite of his deep disappointment Robert resolved that, as Frederick Westerly had advised, he would suspend judgment.

" Doesn't it seem just as nonsensical to train yourself to kill other boys who had as little to do with causing the War as you had ? Like your friend Tony, for instance ? If his grandfather hadn't happened to settle in England you might be going out to Italy to shoot him, instead of joining up with him."

Adrian shifted uncomfortably from one foot to the other.

" I know it seems a bit tough when you put it like that. But what's the alternative ? "

" One can always refuse to be trained."

" But what *good* would that do ! " cried Adrian, as anxious to persuade himself as to convince his father. " It only puts a spoke in the wheel when the machine's already started. Of course," he added, " if people take the Gospels literally, as you seem to, I suppose they've got to go on turning the other cheek, and so forth. But you can't expect statesmen to behave like that."

" Then you don't think the Gospel of Christ was addressed to statesmen ? "

Adrian shifted back to the original foot.

" Oh, as an *ideal*, of course ! But we aren't living in an ideal world. They've got to face things as they are."

" Supposing, Adrian," said his father, " a statesman appeared who really did try to practise the Gospel of Christ. Supposing he attempted to live by those revolutionary principles, even in war-time. Wouldn't it be bound to have an effect on all the others ? Mightn't it even play a direct part in bringing war to an end ? "

Adrian tossed his head arrogantly.

" I don't see why. Look at Gandhi ! He gets great publicity for himself, of course, but what have his ideas actually done to alter things, even in India ? He just spends his time in and out of prison, doing spectacular fasts and being treated as a saint — but making no real difference to anyone. And that's in the East, where people are far more used to cranks and fanatics than the West. If a statesman here started preaching such tripe in war-time, I guess he'd just get lynched or something. It would be too bad, of course, but that's what would happen."

" If it did, he'd be sharing the fate of Christ Himself. Isn't it possible that for that very reason he might have an influence on the world comparable to Christ's ? And wouldn't his suffering and death be more than worth while ? "

" Oh, you might think so, I suppose, but I shouldn't.
All this craze for martyrdom is just sentimental tosh ! "

He strode irritably across the room and banged the
door. But in his room, with his head between his hands,
he faced the problem which he had refused to confront
in Robert's presence. What his father had said was not
nonsense, he knew. But how could he and Tony take
their stand on principles which they had not yet worked
out and accepted for themselves ?

" Why do I say the things I do ? " he groaned, miserably repentant, yet still too much exasperated by his
inward turmoil to feel able to offer his father an apology.
" I don't really believe in war, of course, because I only
partly know what it is. How can I know what it is till
I've tried it for myself ? I can't assume things are true
just because Father says so."

Throughout that autumn at Camden Boys' College,
his conflict accompanied him. Because his examination
was successfully over and he could hardly hope for a
whole term to elapse before he was called up, he spent as
much time as he could steal from other classes studying
Astronomy in the new but well-equipped school library.
Joseph Merrion, reluctantly aware that Adrian's schooldays were now numbered, did not interfere even when
he cut Latin or Scripture. At the end of November, a
fortnight after his eighteenth birthday, the summons came.
He and Tony were both ordered to report the following
day at a training camp inaccessibly situated between
Newark and Nottingham.

Next morning the family at the Vicarage all rose early,
though Adrian insisted that he wanted no one to accompany him to St. Pancras where he was meeting Tony.
While Maria cooked his entire bacon ration and Sylvia
made the tea he sat in the kitchen, his father's ancient
service mackintosh covering a worn-out striped American

football sweater and an old pair of slacks. In his determination to take only what could be stolen without loss to himself and to avoid looking " posh ", he managed merely to appear the more remarkable. He ate his breakfast with equanimity, slung a khaki haversack containing a few personal possessions over his shoulder, and shook hands with Maria, who unashamedly dried her eyes.

Robert opened the door of the Vicarage to see the dawn light flooding Armada Square like a cascade of grey water. Everything looked cold and unreal; the roofs of the houses against the gradually lightening sky appeared sharp-edged as though carved out of tin. The one warm colour was that of Adrian's hair, severely brushed back above his strongly marked eyebrows. His face expressed only the philosophical resignation taught by their life of successive upheavals to the youth of a violent generation.

He held out his hand to his parents with a gesture of unconcealed impatience, which made clear that he would have preferred to cross this Rubicon alone.

" Well — goodbye, Mother! So long, Dad! " he said awkwardly. Then he walked equably down the steps and out into the cheerless empty Square.

" Queer unemotional kid," commented Robert, his own heart wrung by a mixture of exasperation, compunction, and frustrated love.

" He's not really unemotional," said Sylvia, a stab of reluctant comprehension piercing her habitual armour of indifference. " The sensitiveness that used to worry us is still there. He merely imagines he conceals it now."

They stood together for a moment on the top of the steps, listening to the unnaturally loud reverberations oı Adrian's footsteps in the dawn stillness. Then the echo died, and a hostile silence dominated the Square.

★

In after-years Adrian could never clearly recollect those desolate weeks as a " rookie " in the bleak December Midlands.   He seemed to have plunged into a lampless abyss, circumscribed by innumerable petty and irrational restrictions.   Had it not been for Tony, that period of training would have meant unmitigated hell.

Everything made it obvious that he was now far re-moved from the civilised surroundings and reasonable human beings that he, however unreasonable himself, had known at home.   Looking back after an interval, he could only remember a dark confusion of unpleasant experiences in which some were more definitely painful than others.

He recalled especially the endless waiting about which was never adequately explained ; the consistent incivility of superiors ; the long hours of " square-bashing " in a bitter wind which pierced through a uniform perpetually damp, and turned cold feet into lumps of ice ; the rough unpalatable food and the fight to obtain it.   In the long stuffy hut where he fell on to his iron bed each night completely exhausted, neither warmth nor privacy was attainable by the occupants.   When after a fortnight he was moved into billets to make way for a yet newer group of trainees, his tiny cold room in the cottage of a farmer with a large noisy family that kept the radio on all day gave him little more of the one or the other.   Added to these discomforts were the babble of gross conversation which he described in his letters to Josephine as " smut ", and the perpetual imprecations that seemed appalling even by the lenient standards of Acropolis High School.

Perhaps it was the interminable fatigue that oppressed him most.   Before he joined up his mental activity had been incessant ; but the training given in those first few weeks was entirely physical, and he found the change dis-concerting.   In the Army, it seemed, few recruits attempted more serious reading than the daily newspaper.   Like the rest of his contemporary trainees, he spent more and more of his off-duty time in making up the sleep that he had missed. Although he had never cared much for smoking, he also found himself using more cigarettes than ever before. Now that each day was punctuated by breaks of five and ten minutes for " lighting-up ", it became automatic. So, on half-days, did " going to the pictures " — not to see a film that attracted him, but merely to get two hours of rest and warmth.

But even amid this exhausting and meretricious routine, his thoughts, as usual, mattered more to him than his external surroundings. Before long, his mind was compelled to accept some unpromising discoveries about scheming and scrounging, which seemed to pay bigger dividends in the Army than honesty and truth.

The new recruits were invariably taken for their evening parade along a main road which passed within a few yards of Adrian's billet. During the parade they were permitted a short break for smoking, in which he and Tony were accustomed to climb over the gate of the nearest field and talk behind the hedge out of sight of the others. One evening a method of shortening the tedious exercise occurred to Adrian.

" Why don't we just stay here when the parade forms up again ? " he suggested. " After it's gone, we can go back to the billet and cut the march to the Depôt. I bet they'll never miss us."

" O.K.," agreed Tony. " I'll risk it if you will."

As Adrian had expected, they put this scheme into operation without discovery. It was only when they had successfully practised it for a week that he realised with a shock how quickly he had acquired the Army's universal habit of deliberate evasion.

At last the short but violent nightmare of their training period ended. In small groups the recruits wandered up and down, wondering what would become of them, and listening to the rumours that always spread like forest fires through the camp. Eventually the newly qualified trainees were split up into batches, which were distributed between various units. Adrian had hoped for a move nearer London, but he and Tony were sent with thirty-eight others to a Royal Engineers' Field Company only a few miles away.

Here the training was more intensive and specialised. Adrian found that his scientific mind quickly mastered the technical mysteries of Bren guns, Sten guns, mortars and rifles; but to Tony their construction remained an insoluble jig-saw puzzle. He was constantly in trouble, being unable to understand for what purpose the numerous pieces of equipment issued to him were designed, or how they fitted together. Even with Adrian's help he could never do more than master, parrot-wise, a few mechanical details.

Manœuvres, sometimes lasting only for a day and sometimes protracted to a week, now became a regular procedure. To the officers in charge of them, Adrian supposed that there was some purpose behind these schemes; to the recruits involved, they merely represented a concentrated attempt to create maximum discomfort. But as the mild opening weeks of 1944 advanced towards early spring, he began to find occasional compensations for damp clothes and aching limbs. Even in that unexciting rural area near the River Trent the birds sang in the early morning; and at night, lifting the flap of his tent, he could see his old friends the stars, and watch what he now knew to be their movements millions of miles away until he fell asleep.

In February, with pulverising unexpectedness, came the " Little Blitz " on London. Bombs crashed down on Chelsea, Hammersmith, and Chiswick. One of the heaviest fell in the West End near St. James's Square, destroying a wing of the London Library. Adrian read of the battered city being ringed, night after night, with fires caused by phosphorus incendiaries. This time he did not feel indifferent to the fate of the Vicarage and his parents. He thought of them constantly, with an anxiety that surprised himself.

A week after the new attacks started, Adrian saw a notice in their Mess asking for ten volunteers for bomb-disposal in London. Within half an hour of reading it, he and Tony had obtained an interview with the Commanding Officer. A pleasant-looking, bespectacled surveyor of forty, the C.O. regarded these eighteen-year-old recruits with some perturbation.

" Aren't you both rather young? " he commented. " Why do you want to do this dangerous work? "

" Our homes are in London, Sir, and we'd like to help defend them," said Tony with characteristic eloquence. " My father," he added, " has a restaurant."

" And mine," put in Adrian, " has a church."

One of the two unusual names which had been given to him suddenly aroused the C.O.'s interest.

" Where is your father's church? " he asked Adrian.

" In Armada Square, Sir."

" Then — are you the son of Robert Carbury? "

" Yes, Sir."

" Your father's a V.C., isn't he, Carbury? "

" Yes, Sir.   He won it in the last War."

The C.O. smiled.   " I'll think it over," he said. " You'll find the list of names in your Mess this evening."

When the list went up, both their names were on it. By the following evening they were back in London amid the fires and the bombs.

*

During the heavy raids of 1940-41, the Sappers engaged in bomb-disposal had learned their work as they performed it, and often paid for their lessons with their lives. By 1944, recruits had begun to attend special " New Intakes " courses at the Duke of York's Headquarters in Chelsea. To the barracks on this much-bombed London battlefield, Adrian and Tony went for a week. Here, under officers who had done the work of bomb-disposal since the first year of the War, they studied the size and purposes of various Nazi bombs.

Among the smaller high-explosives employed in the air raids on Britain was one which weighed, they learned, 50 kilograms or about 110 pounds. This modest bomb was capable of doing much damage; one had crashed with disastrous effect into the crowded Café de Paris in 1941. But the sizes used had now risen to 500, 1000, 1400, and even 1800 kilograms, the last being appropriately known as " Satan ". The most usual weight appeared to be 250 kilograms, which could demolish an old-fashioned building of moderate size. Besides learning how to recognise and de-fuse these bombs, the recruits at Chelsea studied parachute mines, which they had previously but incorrectly known as " land-mines ", and the various types of incendiary bomb then in force. During the spring of 1944 the use of fire-raising phosphorus bombs, interspersed with high-explosives, appeared to be the latest device for destroying civilisation.

While he mastered these technical details, Adrian also listened to the innumerable bomb-stories which were related with gusto by some of his veteran instructors. These too formed part of his education, for they left him in no doubt about the risks that he had volunteered to run.

" It was in the City, back in '40," said the sergeant who was teaching him how to remove time-fuses. " It fell right between two Government buildin's. That made it a priority bomb."

" Priority ? "

" Yus. Unexploded bombs fallin' on war plant or vital thoroughfares went into Category A, and work started regardless. We allus asked for volunteers for these big risks, and the Squad stepped forward to a man. That time we started work soon after midnight, and the bomb detonated in the morning, before we reached it."

" Were there any casualties ? "

" You bet yer life. Three o' the Squad went west outright. They was there one minute, and the next in Kingdom Come. What? No, nothin' except a few trouser buttons. But the officer and N.C.O. stardin' on the edge of the excavation was worse off. Not 'arf knocked about, they was. The Sergeant's never been right in his 'ead since, pore chap. Saw 'im a week or two ago, and 'e looked as vacant as a cock wi' the jitters."

Why was it, Adrian wondered, that the slightly sick, slightly cold sensation that this story gave him seemed reminiscent? Then he remembered. Long ago, when he was a small boy, he had looked at the moon and expected it to emit a trump which would reduce the earth to chaos. Just the same cold, sick feeling had gripped his vitals as he waited for the terrible sound.

That night, as though to remind him that there were sources of chaos much nearer and more threatening than the now familiar moon, a heavy bomb fell in a residential thoroughfare a hundred yards away. Obviously intended for the barracks, it wiped out a dozen small modern houses and broke three hundred windows in the nearest block of flats.

It was the closest escape that Adrian had so far experienced in his life of potential perils, and it reinforced the conviction that he would die in the War which had subconsciously been his as long as he could remember. When did it start? he wondered. Was it at the time that Josephine was ill and Hitler invaded Prague — the time that he saw the poster " War Imminent ", and pictured the evacuation of London which had since partially occurred? Or did it begin with a still earlier placard saying that the Italians had entered Addis Ababa, or even further back in those half-forgotten childhood days when he saw a German helmet on his father's desk and identified it with a scalp?

He did not know. He only knew that the feeling, for all the dread of non-fulfilment that it gave him, had a positive as well as a negative aspect. It was responsible for the sense that his stomach was turning over which came every time that the siren sounded or, later, when he was called out to an unexploded bomb; but it also caused the wild exhilaration that he felt when he survived a heavy raid or helped his Squad to master a bomb before it blew them up. To live dangerously, even though briefly, was preferable to the illusion that he was dissolving, out of sheer boredom, into the mud of the Midlands. His mother had been right, that evening he talked to her about Carol; it was better to be alive and suffer than to be half-dead.

Their short training concluded with several visits to the Royal Hospital bombed site, where they learned the art of timbering excavations, and a final journey to the bomb-disposal museum in Exhibition Road. Passing South Kensington Underground on his way back to Chelsea late that afternoon, Adrian was struck by the pathos of the local families from the poorer streets, trudging to the station with babies and bundles in their arms to spend the night in the shelter of the deep Piccadilly Tube.

" That's civilisation, 1944 ! " remarked Tony, intuitively responsive to his friend's preoccupation.

"Just what I was thinking too," Adrian said. "I suppose one's got to go through this experience, if only to realise the meaning of our age. But I wish some of the comfortable families I knew at Acropolis could change places with these Londoners for a week! It would be a real contribution towards stopping a third World War."

Those Americans, he thought, would never endorse a conflict that lowered the level of their own civilisation, so efficiently and expertly created in the teeth of handicaps almost as great as war itself. Even more than the terror and horror, they would detest this return towards the level of the beasts; this compulsory lack of clean beds, soap, hot water, and freshly laundered clothing.

When their training had ended, Adrian and Tony were sent to work under instruction on an old bomb-disposal assignment, in which, before the "Little Blitz", a number of men had spent several weeks looking for a heavy 1940 bomb which was buried deep in the back garden of an abandoned house in West Kensington. Finally they were posted to the bomb-disposal headquarters at Chiswick, in a pleasant suburban avenue half a mile from the Chiswick High Road.

This peaceful byway, shaded by trees already budding in the mild spring air, stretched at right angles to the Thames where the tow-path led to Strand-on-Green and Kew Bridge. But for nearly a month Adrian had no time to explore the river; there was not even sufficient leisure for thought or fear. The irksome monotony of Home Service had vanished as it vanishes in a hard-fought campaign. London was again a battlefield, and his work, like that of his companions, had the desperate urgency of battle.

Bombs were still falling heavily each night on Southwest London; they appeared to be aimed at the various

Headquarters of the 21st Army in Victoria, Kensington, Earl's Court, Hammersmith, and Fulham. The unexploded bombs now tended to outnumber the men trained to tackle them; as soon as one raid ended, a race began to complete the work that it had created before the next occurred. The Nazis seemed to be copying some of the more malignant devices used by the Royal Air Force on Hamburg and the Ruhr cities during 1943; they were bombing with the aid of marker flares and using phosphorus incendiaries. In soft soil these bombs would sometimes penetrate to a depth of seven or eight feet. Adrian's days were spent in digging down to them, removing the phosphorus filling, and taking it to the main dumping ground in Richmond Park where his mother, though he did not know it, had so often met his father's predecessor. Here the phosphorus was set on fire and left to steam harmlessly away.

Sometimes Adrian and his companions managed to deal with two or three of these bombs in a day. As he became accustomed to the routine he seldom felt afraid; the work of digging down to the bomb was too hard, the excitement as it was gradually uncovered too absorbing. Occasional incidents led to casualties; one afternoon he saw a venturesome police constable killed by a bomb which went off when the Disposal Squad had gone to a nearby canteen for a cup of tea. The bomb was a small one, and though the man had died from the shock of the blast he was not blown to pieces. Adrian regarded his crumpled body and shocked expression with curiosity rather than horror. In spite of his own vague but persistent anticipation of early death, he could not imagine himself in the constable's place.

By the end of March the incendiary raids were over, and few unexploded bombs remained. When work-services and the study of new-type missiles replaced the adventurous days and fiery nights, ordinary off-duty times were resumed. Adrian was at last able to visit Armada Square for longer than an occasional half-hour between the end of the working day and the wail of the nightly siren.

*

For the first half of the Easter holidays, Josephine remained at Malvern; Robert refused to allow her to return to London until it seemed certain that the " Little Blitz " was over. But in the middle of April she came home, and Adrian, feeling very mature after the perilous experiences which seemed to him to have added years to his age, took her over the bomb-disposal headquarters and then gave her tea at a Chiswick café. As always she was indignant over her exclusion from the scene of action.

" I don't know why I had to be kept away. I'm nearly fifteen. And the Square isn't even damaged ! "

" No, it's escaped again. The London Library bomb was the nearest it had. But plenty of other places caught it all right."

" I always seem to miss everything. It *is* a shame ! "

" Don't you be too sure it's a shame, my girl ! If you'd seen people knocked dead by blast, or rushing about the street with their faces burned and their clothes all bloody, you might be thankful you were safely at Malvern."

" I shouldn't really, Wasp. I don't like being safe ! "

She consumed the remnants of a large bun filled with synthetic cream, and then remarked with her customary candour : " You know, I can't understand how Daddy ever got the V.C. He's much more frightened of the bombs than Mummy."

Adrian meditated as he finished his cup of tea.

" I think you're a bit hard on him, Jo," he said slowly. " I mean, we both are. I know he's looked terrible since the raids, and Theodore says even his sermons aren't up

280

to the mark. But I don't believe what he feels is fear, as one usually understands it."

During the past four months, it had almost seemed as though he and his father were beginning to understand each other. When he was in the Field Company in Nottinghamshire Robert had written him some first-rate letters, never once referring to the topics of their previous disputes. And in those weeks at Chiswick Adrian had come across men, older than himself and indubitably brave, who shuddered with apprehension when the siren sounded but turned out to do their dangerous disposal job without flinching or hesitation.

"It's queer," he went on, "but I haven't found him nearly so hard to get on with since I joined up. And I shouldn't wonder if what looks like fear isn't just the fear of being afraid. The other day, when we were talking about the raids, he told me that ever since the War began he'd been haunted by the thought that if he were involved in an incident he'd fail. Really involved, I mean — damaged, or buried. He was afraid he'd lose his nerve and be no use to anyone."

"And don't you think he would, Ady?"

"I don't really believe so. I think it's just the thought of it. There are chaps in my Squad who get scared stiff when they start out to kill a bomb, and yet when they're on the job they never turn a hair. The only unreliable kind are the ones who make out they're never afraid."

"Oh, well, I daresay you're right," she said reasonably. "I suppose none of us really know how we'll behave till the moment comes. I wasn't so awfully brave over the Lascar. . . . But even if Daddy's not scared, he works much too hard. I never seem to see him these hols — or Mummy either, for that matter."

"I knew she was busy. She's got a Shakespeare season when *Turn Again Home* finishes its run. I reckon she's awfully tired of that play. She hoped it would come off when the audiences went down during the raids; but now it's as crowded as ever."

"And when she's not playing in it she seems to be studying all the women's parts Shakespeare ever invented," said Josephine. She stood up, shaking the crumbs from her skirt. "There's hardly a soul to talk to at home. I'm glad I've got you."

And I'm glad I've got her, thought Adrian, when he was back at his headquarters. Now that the raids were over and time often moved heavily, it was depressing to find that the conversation in the Squad so closely re-sembled the aimless discussions in the Nottingham Field Company. How bored he would be by sex, smoking, and cinemas, if it wasn't for Tony and the smudgy, volatile letters from Josephine! It was strange, he thought, when he sat down in May to write to her for her fifteenth birth-day, how much more, when once you had been near to death, you began to value the living.

DEAR EARWIG,

I am supposed to be on duty, but there is not much doing in London now, and I might as well write your birthday letter while the other inhabitants of the barrack-room are talking shop and smut. It doesn't shock me, but I find it dreadfully boring. Luckily they can't subdue my thoughts. When I am thinking, outside interruptions and discomforts never seem to touch me.

It's funny how brothers and sisters take each other for granted till they are nearly grown up. Perhaps they go on doing it unless they live in a period like this, when everybody's life is threatened to some extent, and therefore one is conscious of people in a way that doesn't seem to be the case in what are called "normal times". You are so much a part of me and my background that there is no one in the world whose non-existence I find it more difficult to imagine.

I have never thought of you as being any particular age, and I don't really think of you now as fifteen, simply because you have always been there. And yet, oddly enough, I can remember the day you were born; in fact it is the first thing I remember clearly. Nannie Higginbotham had promised me a " surprise ", and while I was waiting for it, very bored at being alone for so long and looking out of the window at the Square, a wonderful thing happened. The Square was suddenly full of people, and some of them carried banners and posters in orange and scarlet which they proceeded to prop up against Drake's statue or hang from the bushes.

I can still see those vivid colours amid the bright green o. the spring trees; it seemed to me like a fairy tale, the most marvellous thing I had ever seen. Actually it was only some kind of Labour demonstration, but I thought it was the surprise itself until Nannie came in and took me to Mother. The fact of having two big surprises in one day meant that I have never forgotten either of them. Yet I don't think of the baby I saw that afternoon exactly as you, but just as a baby who had been brought for me to play with, and very naturally had hair just like my golliwog.

If we keep clear of raids perhaps you can come up to London for half-term, and I'll take you to a show as a birthday present. Meantime, many many happy returns of the day from

Your loving   W<small>ASP</small>

*

But the War was not of a kind which left its participants alone for long. In June came D-Day, and almost immediately afterwards began the new attacks by robot missiles which were first known to the people of London as pilotless planes, then as flying bombs, and finally, with the amused contempt of shaken but determined bravado, as " doodlebugs ".

In spite of this derisive nickname, Adrian's fellow conscripts in the Bomb Disposal Squad soon agreed that the new bombs were wearing down their potential victims as the noisy H.E.s and incendiaries of the " Little Blitz " had never done. Somehow, in their mechanised invulnerability, they seemed so much more diabolical. The ordinary bomber, however malevolent its mission, was manned and piloted by human beings, susceptible to the fears and weaknesses of mortal flesh. In previous raids man had been pitted against man ; but now he was at the mercy of machines, mindless and soulless Juggernaut gods without that element of pity which lurks in even the most primitive consciousness.

Like the rest of his comrades he came to detest even more than the actual robots the now incessant, blood-chilling sirens. Each one seemed to him a clear warning that even this World War, with such weapons at its disposal, might be capable of obliterating the human race. Apart from these individual speculations the entire bomb-disposal personnel, still tired from the concentrated strain of February and March, seemed to be reduced by the perpetual listening and anxiety to a nervous condition which with one or two bordered upon hysteria. Some members of the Company found strange places to sleep, varying from deep cellars to the middle of the Polytechnic Sports Ground. No attempt was made to interfere with these spontaneous experiments in self-defence.

Adrian himself remained in his small attic at the top of the old red-brick house, which seemed to shake even before a flying bomb had fallen. He knew that, if he once admitted to himself that he was afraid to sleep there, his own nerve might go. Before the new attacks began he had come to have quite an affection for this little room, with its sloping roof and narrow window looking over the tree-tops towards the river. The Southern Railway passed along the bottom of the back garden, and each time a train went up or down the line he could feel the whole building vibrate. He was accustomed to set his watch by the midnight train as he lay reading. So he stayed there even after one robot seemed to lift his hair from his head and pull the trees out of the road before it crashed in a small inlet adjoining the Thames. There it wrecked several house-boats and killed two of their occupants. With the rest of the Squad Adrian ran to the scene of pitiful mud-spattered ruin, helping the Civil Defence Services to remove casualties, clear rubble, and salvage personal belongings.

For the first few days the bomb-disposal personnel were not required to give such assistance in the many incidents that occurred in London ; the officers in charge expected that a number of unexploded flying bombs would require demolition. But when these proved to be few, and mainly confined to the Balloon Barrage Sector on the outskirts, help was demanded in digging graves and salvaging furniture from badly damaged houses. Adrian's chief duty now was to rescue from the rubble whatever could be saved. In buildings where the structure had been impaired this task was dangerous ; it was also pathetic. Long after he had forgotten the ever-imminent peril, he remembered the requests made to him by patient, long-suffering, grateful householders to search for objects of value to themselves in the heaps of debris which had been their world.

" If you come across the wife's photo, chum, I'll take it kindly."

" Look here, old chap, somewhere in that pile there's likely to be a gun-metal watch my kid used to play with. Yes — he was killed at El Alamein. It's only a small one ; you might overlook it. . . ."

Perhaps, he reflected again and again, it does need suffering to make us understand the meaning of toleration, and pity, and tenderness. Perhaps we must plumb the depths of hell before we can wear the crown of life.

He knew now, and had known before the end of the " Little Blitz ", that his conviction of early death was shared by all his comrades — and probably, he thought, by every civilian in London. And since death seemed inevitable, it was natural that one should want to live as fully as possible first. But if the question " What is death ? " was unanswered, the inquiry " What is life ? " seemed equally baffling. It was obvious that, to most of his fellow Sappers in the Squad, life meant meals, girls, pubs, the radio, the pictures. These things were not " life " to him, but what was ? The problem troubled him after each escape from death.

Throughout the ten weeks of the V-1 raids he went as often as possible to St. Saviour's Vicarage, even when he could only manage an hour or two and both his parents were out. He now recognised that his home, with all its turmoil and suppliants and congestion, represented the most solid and stable element in his ever-changing, transitory existence. It began to appear, too, that through the frequent interchanges in which they described similar experiences, he could even help his father.

As always in a period of heavy raids, Robert looked pale and haggard ; it was evident that he suffered agonies of apprehension with each flying bomb that zoomed towards Armada Square. So many seemed either to fall just short of it, or else to fly over and then immediately explode, that Adrian began to wonder whether Robert's prayers for his Church and parishioners really had conferred on the Square its apparently charmed life. But he realised more clearly than ever that neither his father's fears nor his prayers were directed towards his own safety ; it was the dread of failing those for whom he was responsible that drew those lines of anxiety on his face.

Whenever an incident occurred within reach of his parish, Robert seemed to be on the spot immediately, helping and comforting the victims.

A phrase from a poem by Amelia Earhart — " the livid loneliness of fear " — once flashed into Adrian's mind. Perhaps, after all, his father's response to that loneliness was not so different from his own. One night he took from his bedroom drawer at the Vicarage the letters that Robert had written to him when he was in the United States. He had not valued them then, but he had kept them ; it was his habit to keep, file, and methodically arrange all his possessions. Perhaps, if he re-read those letters, they would have something to teach him now.

His mother, it seemed, was as usual in no need of moral support. When the flying bombs roared, as they roared so frequently, over the roof of the Pall Mall Theatre where *Turn Again Home* was still obstinately holding its own, she appeared not to hear them. When the crash came, she never moved a muscle or missed a line. The rest of the cast was less impervious. When the raids had racked the players' nerves for nearly a month, a young actor, Terence Codmer, came to her in her dressing-room after a particularly harrowing performance.

" Miss Salvesen," he said desperately, " this play's had a long run in London. D-don't you think it's time we took it on tour ? "

" And where shall we start, Mr. Codmer ? " asked Sylvia mildly. " Folkstone ? "

She remained in London, and so did the play. But her refusal to leave preceded by only two or three days a shock, involuntarily administered by Adrian, which affected her more profoundly than any bomb that had just missed the Pall Mall Theatre.

Whenever it was possible he now came, with hundreds of other boys and girls in uniform, to the Sunday evening service at St. Saviour's. Usually he stayed to supper, for it was the one night on which both his parents were at the Vicarage. On the third Sunday in July, he brought with him a letter from Kathleen Downing. It contained a clipping from the Acropolis *Daily News* which he had read in his attic beneath the sloping roof.

DEATH OF DAMON SULLIVAN

Information has at last been received through the Protecting Power about the fate of Damon Sullivan, the playwright. Mr. Sullivan had been reported missing ever since the occupation of the Philippines. It is now known that early in January, 1942, he was arrested and interned with other American civilians in Santa Tomás, a former college which was used by the Japanese as an internment center for enemy aliens. At the time of his arrest he was nearly sixty, and under internment conditions his health failed rapidly. He died from malnutrition, aggravated by malaria, at the end of last year.

Mr. Sullivan went to the Philippines in 1941 to write a play with the struggle for Philippine independence as background. It is stated that he completed this manuscript after his internment, and that it is being carefully preserved by his fellow internees. We understand that it is entitled *The Evening Star*, and is dedicated to the British actress, Miss Sylvia Salvesen.

By permission of the occupying authorities, Mr. Sullivan was buried in the American Cemetery at Manila. His grave has been numbered, and the position is known.

When supper at the Vicarage was over and Robert had gone to conduct community singing, which was now held in the Crypt, Adrian handed the press-clipping to his mother.

" This came yesterday," he said. " It was in a letter from Kay."

He sat silently at the table while Sylvia read the paragraph, also in silence. When she had finished, she put the clipping down beside her plate. She recalled the words, which she knew almost by heart, of the strange emotional letter that Damon had written her after meeting the children:

"I love you, Sylvia. I really mean that. The day I spent with your boy and girl has somehow made it clear. Whatever I may have meant to you, you were not a passing fancy to me. You have grown upon me with the years. The very next play I write will prove it to you. I have always loved you, and I shall love you till I die. At the hour of my death you will be with me, dearer than life, better than God."

Was I? she wondered. This manuscript play that he dedicated to me — will that tell me what I really meant to him?

The silence became so long that at last Adrian broke it. "Do you mind if I have the clipping back, Mummy? I'd like to fix it in one of the books he gave me. He was awfully decent to us."

"Of course, dear," she said quietly. "Put it in your book by all means."

When he had gone she cleared away the supper, and arranged the plates and glasses methodically in the cupboard. Then she went upstairs to the drawing-room, and gazed without seeing them at the stone galleons in the yellow evening light. A flying bomb roared from the south, boomed over the Square, stopped suddenly, and exploded in the neighbourhood of Tottenham Court Road. From the hall Robert called to her to come down to the Crypt, but she heard neither him nor the bomb. She remained sitting in the window until the summer twilight, its illusionary peace punctuated by distant crashes, deepened into night over the Square.

CHAPTER XV

Incident in Armada Square

In the middle of August, the flying bombs at last began to diminish. An increasing number were shot down over the coast, and the Allied armies, racing through France, captured many of the sites from which they were released. A sense of relaxation pervaded London, which believed that its long ordeal was over. For the first time since he came to Chiswick, Adrian had sufficient leisure to walk and talk beside the river with Tony, or to sit by himself and think.

The members of the Squad worked in eight-hour shifts, and Adrian was usually free after 5 P.M. Whenever he and Tony were off duty together they strolled along the towing-path past Strand-on-Green, where the small painted houses fringing the river suggested to him the probable appearance of Chelsea Embankment a century ago. In the still August air, a warm smell of mud, tar, and rope rose from the anchored barges. Little tugs, incongruously self-important, bustled up and down stream past a green island stacked with wood.

Close to the towing-path stood a small inn; at the back its wild, overgrown garden still bore traces of the havoc caused by a bomb which had fallen near it in 1940. Here Adrian and Tony sat on coloured chairs at an iron table, drinking beer and talking politics with members of the Non-Combatant Corps temporarily attached to their headquarters. Occasionally these mild civilian troops, mostly conscientious objectors, were varied by small groups of American soldiers whose attitude to the War, and to England, was more disturbing. They had found the British cold, they said, and unappreciative of their presence.

These misunderstandings are going to colour Anglo-American relations in the post-war period, Adrian reflected uneasily. He tried to explain, without much consciousness of success, that the spontaneous warmth shown by Americans to strangers was just not part of the British character.

We're dogged, steadfast, kindly, he thought, with a detachment born of his American experience. And we're much more tolerant than they ever are. But we haven't their gift for generous hospitality. We don't know how to welcome strangers and put them at their ease.

As August advanced and the Anglo-Americans pressed forward in France, there was an excitement in the air which reminded his father of the weeks preceding the Armistice of November, 1918. Adrian, like Tony, began to feel that to discuss their future no longer involved an undue temptation of Providence.

" I wish you were coming to Cambridge with me," he said as they walked past Kew Bridge, and along the asphalt path which led through crowded Richmond towards peaceful Teddington.

" So do I, in a way," agreed Tony. " But it'll be two years or more before we're demobbed, and Cambridge would mean another three at least. That's a bit too late to start learning the restaurant business. You have to go into it early."

" You really do mean to go into it, then ? "

" Oh, yes. It's in my blood. But I shan't be satisfied with just a little eating-house. I want to have a small gallery attached, with a few really good pictures, and perhaps occasional concerts."

" Then shall you move to the West End ? " Adrian inquired.

" Oh, no ! " said Tony firmly. " I shall make the

West End go out to Camden Town. When the War's over, Father and I mean to get hold of the bombed site next door. That's where I shall build my gallery. I want it to have a ceiling that symbolises the sky. Perhaps you can give me a few hints when you're an astronomer — if you still intend to be one, that is."

" Certainly I intend to," said Adrian. " I've always been keen, but now I'm keener than ever. After all the disorder we've seen, I want to understand a system where everything is subject to law. Perhaps if more of us understood it, we'd be able to create a period of order for our own children. More like it than we've seen while we've been growing up, anyway."

When Tony was on duty and Adrian sat alone in the garden of the riverside inn, he often thought over the years that he remembered, and realised with growing clarity that the phase of history which had coincided with his brief existence made everyone, and especially his own generation, live too intensely. They tried, it seemed to him, to seize all experience, instead of selecting what was of positive value and rejecting the rest. In the pages of newspapers they were often blamed for this by the " old men " of earlier generations, who denounced their promiscuous relationships and their habit of living for the moment. But how, meditated Adrian, could he and his contemporaries, whose tale of years had ended suddenly for so many, live for anything else? Those who decried them had been, with rare exceptions, members of that large apathetic crowd who by sheer inactivity had permitted war to dominate the world instead of peace and justice — achievements that people had to *work* for. And far from trying to make amends, they condemned their young successors for encountering more experience than they could assimilate and responsibly use.

Adrian knew now that his father was not one of those

who condemned, or should be judged as he had previously judged him. He had begun to understand that the conflict which involved Robert and himself was part of an inevitable clash between two generations, intensified by the fact that events and circumstances which would always seem abnormal to his father appeared quite normal to him. Looking back on his short life he realised that he had grown up expecting war, so that the declaration on September 3rd, 1939, which had made his father look so pale and ill, was for him only one more incident in a succession of similar occurrences lasting as long as he could remember.

From the time of his earliest conscious recollection, the adults surrounding him had talked about Hitler and war. What war would mean when it came, and how it would differ from the unrest and apprehension which to him was everyday life, he had then no idea. And indeed, when it did come, nothing changed much for several months. He went to the same school, wore the same clothes, ate the same food, and did the same things, all confirming his impression that the war and pre-war periods had been one continuous series of events. His world had not drastically altered until the German breakthrough on the Western front and the fall of France.

Then indeed, with his journey to America, had come the uprooting that he had so long dreaded. But, emotionally disruptive though it was, he had not found that journey and its cause so monstrous and appalling as it had appeared to his father. It was simply a dramatic extension of the disturbed scene in which he had grown from babyhood to boyhood; an event more decisive than other events, but essentially of the same general quality.

And, in consequence, reflected Adrian, watching without seeing a laden coal-barge lumbering heavily upstream, he had not developed that conviction of having a right to live his life through which seemed to have been characteristic of his parents' generation and, he supposed, of all men and women who passed their formative years in a peaceful age. Instinctively he pictured all human existence as surrounded by enormous dangers, which only the exceptionally fortunate survived. Had anyone asked him, when he returned at sixteen from the United States, whether he expected to be alive at the end of the War, he would probably have replied that he did not see why he, any more than anyone else, should have the luck to live on into old age. He had sympathised with his mother's refusal to shelter when the flying bombs began ; he understood the philosophy which prompted her to say : " I'd rather be killed comfortably in bed ! "

So many of his elders, he thought, when he had paid for the beer that he had hardly touched and was walking slowly towards his headquarters, seemed to be perpetually looking back to some halcyon era in the Victorian or Edwardian age ; they confronted with half-averted eyes the perilous and comfortless epoch in which they now had to live whether they liked it or not. Well, this was his epoch. Sometimes it inspired him with a feeling of disillusionment to which his meeting with Carol and her father had contributed ; such contacts brought a vision of satisfactions which were presumably possible yet never seemed to be realised. But at other times he felt glad that he had not experienced anything better, since to have known happier and more tranquil days seemed so often to involve such a nostalgia of longing, a futility of resentment.

Why, he wondered, couldn't his seniors realise that just because their period of history was their fate, it was also their responsibility ? The engulfing frustration which now encompassed his own best years and those of his contemporaries was their doing. At any rate they hadn't saved their successors from it, however good their intentions might have been. That " better world " which for some unknown reason was identified with the post-war years still appeared to him to be very far away. He sometimes wondered how much youthful energy he would have left when he became part of it, and whether, when those years arrived, they would offer anything other than further varieties of disturbance and fear.

Well, he thought, entering the door of the old house and going up the stairs to his attic, he would make them different in so far as he had any power. He would turn his attention from the works of men to study the stars, and perhaps learn from them some major truth which could be applied to the undisciplined human race. I. the law which those heavenly bodies obeyed had any personal sponsor it was God — the God whom Robert Carbury also worshipped and sought to obey. Perhaps, in their mutual study of that law and its Maker, he and his father would some day forge another link in the family chain that bound them together.

*

The first week-end of September found a holiday atmosphere in London. The sirens had ceased, Londoners had been officially informed that their battle was over, and the West End, deserted by visitors two months ago, was crowded and gay. Adrian, off duty on Saturday, and Josephine, who had reluctantly spent the first half of the summer holidays with her aged grandmother in Newcastle, watched the jubilant holiday-makers who overflowed from Armada Square into Queen Elizabeth Street and stretched like a phalanx to Piccadilly Circus. The relief on their faces was so visible that you almost felt you could pick it up and handle it.

And then, veritable bolts from the blue, came the rockets.

For the majority of London's millions, these mechanical monsters remained " noises off ". The unlucky minority who were killed, injured, or dispossessed, never saw their diabolical assailant. Nearly two months passed before the " V-2s " were mentioned in the Press or officially recognised by the National Government. Yet when Robert, early in October, preached a sermon on the text, " Thou shalt not be afraid for the terror by night ; Nor for the arrow that flieth by day ", every member of his dejected congregation understood the reference. Nothing could have suggested more appropriately than those words of the Psalmist the huge flying cylinders, faster than sound, which crashed unannounced out of the stratosphere, leaving the long rumbling roar of their flight as an aftermath of the explosion.

At least as weary and despondent as his disillusioned listeners, Robert meant his words to be as much a challenge to his own courage as to theirs. For the happy-go-lucky who took life as it came, the rockets were preferable to high-explosives and flying bombs ; no warning siren was possible, and if you weren't dead when the crash came it meant you had escaped. But for the imaginative or anxious who possessed Robert's native streak of apprehension, a peril which could neither be foreseen nor resisted was ever-present. There was no guarantee, each time a member of the family left the house, that he or she would ever return. From the time that the rockets began to fall, Robert died a hundred deaths a day for his Church, his parish, Sylvia, Adrian, and last of all for himself. Only Josephine, once the new term began, was mercifully removed from his mind. Her school, which had been making plans to return to London that autumn, heard of the new menace just in time and decided to stay at Malvern for another year.

One of the first two rockets, fired almost simultaneously on September 8th, landed noisily in Chiswick. Adrian, reading on his bed before supper and quite unprepared for any incident, was lying close to the edge and suddenly found himself on the floor. At first he thought that the house had collapsed or the roof fallen in; then he saw that his surroundings looked normal, and imagined that the violent upheaval of his bed had been due to an earthquake. He soon learnt the truth — unlike the rest of London, which was temporarily soothed by the explanation that a damaged gas-main had blown up, and subsequently christened the V-2s "flying gas-mains". That evening he and his comrades found themselves back on the familiar job of tunnelling under ruins and salvaging personal possessions from an annihilated road of small houses some distance from their centre.

In spite of this episode, the bomb-disposal headquarters at Chiswick were closed at the end of September, and the few remaining personnel distributed between No. 2 B.D. Company at Balham, and No. 21 B.D. Company at Wanstead. For the first time since their call-up at the end of 1943, Adrian and Tony were separated. Adrian went to Balham, where the Company was responsible for all incidents south of the river, and Tony to Wanstead, which assumed responsibility for the northern half of the city.

For a variety of reasons, that autumn and winter seemed to Adrian the longest period of the interminable War which had begun when he was a grubby, homesick schoolboy not yet fourteen, and now, after he had turned nineteen, was still going on. He did not make friends easily, and acutely missed Tony's gentle, unexacting companionship. His work made few demands on him, for though the rockets laid waste even larger areas than the flying bombs they were less frequent, and the Civil Defence Services could usually cope with incidents unaided. Inevitably he shared in the frustrated depression of a nation which had believed its War over, and found it prolonged, first by the V-2s and then, towards the end of the year, by the von Rundstedt offensive against the Allies in Luxembourg. Finally, his immediate surroundings compared unfavourably with the pleasant riverside area where he had spent the past few months.

Balham was not an attractive suburb like Chiswick, though the district which contained the 2nd B.D. Company's headquarters had obviously been prosperous, and even pretentious. He guessed that those great spacious houses, with their large gardens shaded by thick shrubs and heavy old trees, had been built by commercial magnates of the late nineteenth century who had passed them on to their less wealthy but still substantially endowed successors. Designed before the age of steel and concrete, the capacious old-fashioned structures offered sitting targets to bombs, and fate had not spared them.

When Adrian first reported for duty, the once complacent suburb resembled a battlefield. At the nearby crossroads, where the wide street in which he was to live joined a main thoroughfare, two formerly ornate mansions facing each other at opposite corners had been blasted almost out of existence by a flying bomb. Their grim, silent remnants, protruding through derelict trees, stood open to the weather, showing the jagged brickwork and down-slung floors which were typical, he soon discovered, of the South London borough which had received the maximum number of " doodlebugs ". Across the road from his headquarters, a row of lightly-built modern villas with once-trim miniature front gardens displayed roofs without tiles and windows without glass.

In one of these, he found, he was to sleep, sharing with

some half-dozen others a small ground-floor room filled with bunks as soon as the Army had " fixed " it.   The change was disconcerting after his solitary attic at Chiswick ; dejectedly he explored the Company's headquarters in a vain search for privacy.   This large four-storey house, structurally very strong and designed with a view to utility rather than charm, had originally been built in the 1930's as a headquarters for the Territorial Army.   Yellowish-grey brick composed its exterior, and an imposing white-painted front door at the top of twelve stone steps suggested that the architect had intended to impress the suburban householders with the importance of their national defenders.

At least, thought Adrian, as he went in and examined the concrete staircase and passages, it looks as if it'll stand up to anything but a direct hit.

These passages, he discovered, were haunted continually by staff personnel, who appeared to be engaged in every type of occupation but work.   The dimly-lighted Mess Room at the back of the house seemed to offer, between meals, the only hope of solitude.

*

In this room Adrian sat alone on a late evening in February when the long dreary winter was almost over.   Moved by a sudden impulse, he had been re-reading a batch of his father's letters which he had brought from the Vicarage.   He was officially on duty, but no one appeared to object to this harmless occupation or to his strange preference for being alone.   Though he was hardly ready even yet consciously to admit it, Robert's words conveyed to him a message from a world of saner values ; they were an assurance that everything was not lost to chaos and evil, a guarantee that this unsatisfying life of trivial conversations and companionships, so inappropriate to the death he had once faced daily, was only an interval — or rather, a testing prelude — to the work that was really his.

The letters spread before him on the table bore dates of over a year ago, when he had been in Nottinghamshire. One that he now examined had contained two enclosures from German refugees which he had returned to his father.

" It is always hard ", Robert had written, " for different generations to understand each other, even at the same intellectual level. If the parents are well-known and relatively well-endowed it becomes harder still, for the more conspicuous the parent the more individualistic the child, and the more determined not to let his family run him !

" That is why, on an impulse (perhaps a mistaken one, but I hope not), I am sending you two letters from unknown readers which reached me yesterday. No, they do not come into the category of the anonymous and scurrilous ! There is no hurry about returning them, but I should like them back eventually, because letters of this kind are a good defence against the self-disgust that we all endure at times. They help to persuade me that my existence is justified."

Adrian could not remember the enclosures, but they had evidently been friendly and reassuring. He went on reading.

" In the past seventeen years I have had hundreds oɪ letters like these from all over the world, as well as plenty of the other kind. Before the War they were even more numerous, since they were mostly inspired by my broadcast services which I have never been permitted to resume. But the point about the enclosed two is that they are both from German refugees. A good many letters used to reach me from Germany itself, but naturally I have not had many German correspondents since the War began.

If it does not bore you to read these, I think they will explain my concern to find an alternative to war better than any argument I could use. In fact the strongest of all arguments is the one that emerges from them — the basic unity of mankind, the oneness of human joys and sorrows, whatever the national label or skin pigmentation.

"I am quite sure that no 'unconditional surrender', no foreign occupation or compulsory disarmament of Germany, will prevent a Third World War any more than the aftermath of the First prevented the Second. No one can hurt another without being at least as much hurt himself. I agree with the writer of the longer letter that one main hope of peace lies in carrying into Germany, when the War is over, the knowledge that there are groups of people both here and in America who neither hate nor condemn the Germans for everything that has passed, but prefer to start by finding out where they themselves were at fault. Christ's injunction to us, in the Sermon on the Mount, to cast the beam out of our own eye before looking for the mote in our brother's is not merely a noble ideal, but sound common sense. After all, the school code of 'owning up' is based on the same idea. If only the statesmen so largely educated at Eton and Harrow had carried this code into their adult lives, 'the old school tie' would have been an influence making for the end of war, instead of leading, as so often, to its perpetuation. . . ."

Cr-aa-ck! R-rrrr-rrr. . .!

For a second, outside the now uncurtained windows of the Mess Room, a vivid green flash lit the cold dark sky.

That's the ninth since tea, and it's right on London, thought Adrian uneasily. He looked at his watch. Twenty-five minutes past nine. After long practice he could now locate almost to a mile the district struck by a descending rocket. When it appeared to have fallen on the West End, he could never go peacefully to bed.

Sometimes, though it seemed silly, he rang up the Vicarage. Again abstractedly glancing through Robert's letters, he wondered whether to do so now. He was still thinking about it twenty minutes later, when he heard a voice calling his name.

"Carbury! You there? You're wanted on the phone."

He ran to the switchboard, his heart suddenly pounding.

"Hallo!" he cried breathlessly, and at the other end he heard Tony's voice.

"That you, Adrian? It's Tony. We've — just had news of an incident in our area — I thought you ought to know about it."

"Where is it?" asked Adrian, though he knew the answer.

"Armada Square. I'm afraid it's — rather a big incident."

Adrian waited a moment, getting back his breath. Then he asked quietly: "Did the chap who phoned give any details?"

"Yes, a few. As a matter of fact, I spoke to him myself."

"Did he say anything about my parents?"

"He didn't mention your mother."

"But did he say anything about my father?"

There was silence at the other end of the wire. Adrian shook the telephone in the urgency of his suspense.

"Tony — for God's sake tell me! I'd rather know."

Tony's reluctant voice replied.

"He said: 'I hear the Vicar's copped it.' But it mayn't mean a thing, old man, really it mayn't. You know how these rumours spread. . . ."

Adrian hardly listened.

"Thanks for ringing, Tony," he said mechanically.

" I'll see the N.D.O. and get leave to go over."

Pale-faced and suddenly so cold that he could hardly prevent his teeth from chattering, he hung up the receiver and went in search of the Night Duty Officer. Permission to go to Armada Square was readily forthcoming; a father's possible death was an adequate reason, especially when that father was Robert Carbury. If any demand arose during the remainder of Adrian's period of duty, any one of the stray personnel loitering about the building could take his place.

Like an automaton fulfilling a scheduled task, Adrian went back to the Mess Room and gathered up his father's letters. He walked across to his billet, put on his overcoat, and hurried through the dark roads to Balham High Street. Hitherto he had not been anxious about his mother, assuming that she would still be at the Temple Theatre where she was again playing the part of Queen Katharine in *Henry the Eighth*. Adrian had recently re-read the drama, which interested him because he knew that this was the rôle that Sylvia had played just before his birth. The theatres still began at their wartime hour of six-thirty, and he now recalled that once or twice, when he had been off duty and at the Vicarage, she had come home soon after half-past nine.

The thought that she might have been caught in the street and demolished by the rocket was more horrible than he could bear. He began to run up Balham Hill as though the Furies were pursuing him, until panting and trembling he stumbled into Clapham South Underground Station, and fell into a train that was just about to move. The noisy swaying coach made him feel so sick that he hardly knew how to control himself. When the train stopped at the stations on the line, the delay seemed unbearable. He alighted at Charing Cross, fearing that the entrance to Armada Square Station might be blocked, and ran the half-mile north from the Embankment. By the time that he came near to the Square, his heart was beating till he thought it would choke him.

As he approached, he perceived that the darkness which he had left by the river was growing appreciably lighter. Since the coming of mechanical weapons the black-out had been partially lifted, but the half-drawn blinds of the windows in the streets were not sufficient to account for this white, ghostly glare. Then he realised that the Civil Defence Services must be conducting their rescue work by searchlight. He hurried into its range and then stood still, trying to take in what he saw.

The rocket had fallen immediately north-east of the Square, laying waste indefinite acres of the shops, offices, cinemas, and flats that stretched behind St. Saviour's towards the City. To some extent the department stores in Queen Elizabeth Street had protected the Church, but in the white ray of the searchlight Adrian saw that most of its roof, like its windows, had disappeared. The Vicarage, itself sheltered by the Church, appeared relatively undamaged from where he stood, but its front door and all its glass were gone. He learned later that every ceiling on the two top floors had come down, and part of the roof above his father's study.

In the old graveyard the moss-grown tombstones, whose original owners had doubtless expected them to remain there till the Day of Judgment, were nearly all laid flat, but two had been hurled across the Square into the privet hedge behind a Spanish galleon. Sir Francis Drake and the galleons themselves appeared to have survived intact, but by some trick of blast the Armada Book Company on the side of the Square opposite the Church had been completely demolished.

Adrian gazed at the unbelievable ruin as though he had just gone down into hell and was trying to learn its geography. This was not merely damage as such; it was the grotesque transformation of the familiar. He could not regard it, as he had regarded so much previous havoc, with impersonal detachment. Instinctively, and with a sense of growing horror, he compared each macabre example of destruction with the orderly scene known to him before.

One of the cinemas had been crowded, and here most of the many casualties had occurred. Adrian watched their covered bodies being carried away on stretchers by light rescue workers, wearing the usual laconic expression. Most of them, living and dead, were being taken into Queen Elizabeth's Hospital, which seemed providentially to have escaped with minor damage. A long line of dejected-looking strangers being shepherded by a policeman into the Drake Hotel suggested that this fashionable rendezvous had been commandeered as a rest centre for the homeless.

As Adrian picked his way, slowly and with dread, through piles of jagged bricks and broken glass towards St. Saviour's, he saw that heavy rescue workers were strenuously endeavouring to clear away the masonry which had fallen from the roof of the Church across the entrance to the Crypt. From his previous experience of raids, he guessed that they intended to use the Crypt for light casualties in order to relieve the crowded hospital. A First Aid Post, half sheltered by the battered but upright vestry, had been established beside the Church close to the still blocked steps. And there, amid a group of Red Cross workers, he saw his parents. . . .

He learned afterwards that at twenty-five minutes past nine, Sylvia had still been in her dressing room at the Temple Theatre, talking to the dramatic critic of the *London Review* while she waited for the final curtain. From the stage she had just heard Haydon Slater, who played

305

the part of Cranmer, declaim some lines from the closing scene which depicts the christening of the infant Elizabeth,

" She shall be loved and feared : her own shall bless her ;
    Her foes shake like a field of beaten corn,
    And hang their heads with sorrow . . ."

when the rocket fell. The crash seemed to uproot the theatre, though it was nearly a mile from the incident. Startled into momentary panic, the audience sprang from their chairs ; a few pushed and jostled towards the doors. Raising his celebrated stentorian voice, Haydon Slater reassured them.

"Keep your seats! The bomb hasn't hit us! If it had, you wouldn't be here!"

Within seconds came the information that Armada Square had " caught it ", and a few minutes later followed the news about Robert that Adrian had received. Without waiting to change her dress, Sylvia had taken the taxi summoned for her by the dramatic critic and with him had driven as close as possible to the Square. He had helped her to make her way through the rubble despite her flowing draperies, and she reached the Vicarage just when the rescue workers had succeeded in digging Robert out of the piled-up beams and tiles which had descended upon him from his study roof. His head and face were hardly recognisable through the blood that covered them, but he insisted that his injuries were not serious. After brief first-aid treatment by a Red Cross orderly, he had headed the group of volunteers who were now attending the lighter casualties.

Sylvia, in the incongruous Tudor robes of Katharine of Aragon, stood beside him giving such help as she could. Her dress, Adrian perceived, was stained with blood from Robert's wounds and those of other victims, but she did not appear to be injured herself. With expressionless eyes she was handing bandages and safety pins to Robert amid the dirt and debris. Only when she saw Adrian did a sudden flicker of emotion pass over her face.

His own revulsion of relief at finding them both alive told him more about his relationship to them than he had yet known. Afraid in the first intensity of his thankfulness that he might give himself away, he went up to Sylvia almost casually.

" Hallo, Mummy! " he said, and then turned to his father.

Robert's face was the colour of old parchment, and his lips had a bluish tinge which Adrian had never seen there before. Round his head was twisted a hastily adjusted bandage; on the front of it a large bloodstain had spread and dried. The sleeves of his clerical suit were torn to rags, and the front was spattered with dirt and plaster. But his expression was serene with a serenity completely new to his son. He looked strangely like a conqueror — as indeed he was, for he knew now that the triumph over fear which had earned him his Victoria Cross a generation ago had been no unreliable flash or momentary recklessness. It represented a latent capacity for constructive valour which would always serve him when occasion demanded. His courage, which seemed so often to have failed his calls upon it at surface level, was deeply rooted in the spiritual power that gave him his influence over his fellow men.

" Why, Dad — you're hurt! " exclaimed Adrian awkwardly. Now that the tension of suspense was over he felt tongue-tied and embarrassed, for never before had his father appeared to him as an object of concern. He did not know whether to congratulate Robert on still being alive, or try to express the shock given to him by the sight of a blood-stained bandage on that familiar face. And the odd tingling which began behind his eyes when he first realised that his parents were not dead left him more nonplussed than ever.

" Oh, that's nothing ! " said Robert, with a cheerful confidence in his voice which was almost as strange to Adrian as the damaged appearance that seemed to give him the very attributes of sainthood so long regarded with derision by his son. " A brick or something made a hole in my forehead. But it's only skin-deep. I don't even feel it ! "

Throughout that night he remained there in the shadow of his bombed Church, bandaging, consoling, giving absolution to the dying, saying prayers for the dead. Adrian, digging, tunnelling, removing debris, carrying stretchers, worked beside him till dawn.

CHAPTER XVI

Day of Salvation

THE morning after the rocket fell, Robert consented to rest for a few hours at Lord Westerly's flat while part of the army of builders and carpenters summoned to Armada Square from all over London replastered his bedroom ceiling and put glass back in the windows. But though large bruises came out on his face and head, and the long gash above his left eyebrow proved to be deeper than he thought and had to be stitched, he refused to take any more time off. He would not occupy, if only for a day or two, a bed in Queen Elizabeth's congested hospital ; and to go to another outside his parish was unthinkable when the incident had left so much work behind it.

Even a short period of quiet in his own patched-up bedroom seemed impossible when the Crypt had been turned into a temporary annex to the hospital, and the funerals to be conducted among his own parishioners were so grievously many. In the Crypt he had to give no more than occasional supervision, for half the women of the parish had called at the Vicarage to offer their services as volunteer nurses. But even though Theodore Martel-hammer and the junior curate were ready to take the funerals, the men and women who had lost parents, children, brothers, or sisters begged the Vicar to usher them to their graves himself. He must, he thought, have appeared a peculiar object as he presided at these services in the roofless Church, with his black-and-blue face and bandaged head. But the mourners seemed to find it appropriate that their massacred relatives should be buried by a priest who looked as if he had been interred himself and dug up again after several days.

By the time that he knew the Burial Service by heart, the bandage had been replaced by a long strip of plaster. When the plaster was eventually removed a red jagged scar stretched half across his forehead, suggesting to the more imaginative parishioners that it might have been made by a crown of thorns. Long after the rockets had ceased to fall the scar remained conspicuous, livid against his pale skin when the bruises had disappeared.

For the rest of February and throughout March the V-2s had been frequent, frantically delivered by a beaten enemy before his conquerors captured the sites. But Robert no longer feared or even remembered them. In spite of the death and damage all round him and the headaches from which he suffered daily, he seemed to be uplifted by a deep contentment.

" When the thing you dreaded has happened," he told Adrian, " you get an extraordinary sense of freedom. I can't explain it. It's like nothing else I've known."

" I guess I understand, Dad," Adrian said abruptly. He felt ruefully, remorsefully proud of his father, but he was still tongue-tied. Even when the dead had been buried, the injured were recovering, and the less-damaged houses round the Square had been made habitable by first-aid repairs, Robert refused to take any rest.

" The end's so near now. I'll knock off a bit when it's all over."

It was indeed evident that the War in the West was ending. The Americans, racing forward from the Rhine bridgeheads though President Roosevelt lay dead, met the Russians pressing on from the east. In the north the British, who had advanced into Germany from Holland, made preparations for the signing of peace. On the Italian front, the fight was already over. Mussolini was summarily and savagely executed, and Hitler's death was reported from captured Berlin. In England shells were still falling heavily on Dover, Folkestone, and Deal, but they represented the last kick of the expiring Nazi dragon. The scar on Robert's forehead was still red, and St. Saviour's was still roofless and windowless, when VE-Day came. Twenty-four hours earlier he had been invited, to his incredulous astonishment, to broadcast a Thanksgiving Service from his Church on the evening of victory.

Theodore Martelhammer, who accepted the invitation on Robert's behalf, suggested to his Vicar that the National Government, which had geared a reluctant nation to war and had now to manœuvre it back again to peace, wanted to strike the appropriate note at once, but even in the Church could find hardly one public character in whom the transition, on the very day of celebration, would not have seemed specious. After serving for nearly twenty years a man who really tried to be a Christian, Theodore had become cynical about the motives of all political administrations.

But Robert was seldom capable of cynicism, and never of recrimination. He did not know, and never learned, what secret admirer in high places had been responsible for the invitation. He only knew that it was an obvious prelude to the resumption of his monthly broadcast services, which would carry his message outside the confines of his parish to the people of England and beyond them to the world. What mattered to him was the opportunity, and he seized it gladly.

*

On VE-Day Robert's morning started with three Celebrations of the Holy Communion, all crowded. He followed them by a short Matins in which he emphasized the need for penitence and thanksgiving rather than jubilation. Throughout the warm, thundery day of May 8th, 1945, bells were ringing and flags flying. British bombers, no longer dedicated to the work of death, circled low over London. In the afternoon, when the Prime Minister announced the end of the war in Europe from Parliament Square, his audience stretched from Westminster to the battered tower of St. Saviour's. But though it was good-tempered and enormously relieved, that crowd did not appear triumphant and excited like the London crowds which Robert remembered on Armistice Day, 1918. Too many of its members were still dazed by their years of anxiety and peril, and by their sense during the past few weeks of being perpetually bludgeoned by events. And they had all emerged too recently from the shadow of death.

Many of them that evening sought relief from their conflicting emotions at Robert's broadcast service. Never had he seen his Church so closely packed, and those who could not secure a place stood waiting for his voice to be relayed to them in Armada Square. None of his own family could attend that service. Sylvia was taking part in a Victory Pageant at the Temple Theatre; Adrian had been chosen by lot to join a Victory Parade round the south-western suburbs; and Josephine, though she had been promised the following week-end at home for her sixteenth birthday, was expected to join in her school's celebrations at Malvern. But those who obtained seats in the Church remembered afterwards that, though Robert still looked ill and frail, he had worn a strange appearance of transfiguration.

Once again the challenge of St. Saviour's great bell, protected from damage by the tower that enclosed it, echoed over England. It sounded across desolate Europe, bringing a note of hope and reassurance to littered battle-fields, flooded streets, and dying cities. Listening in the Mess Room at Balham after his parade was over, Adrian heard the hymn which had comforted him long ago during his first terrified investigation of the moon and stars:

" Holy, holy, holy! though the darkness hide Thee,
Though the eye of sinful man Thy glory may not see,
Only Thou art holy, there is none beside Thee
Perfect in power, in love and purity."

For the first time since his pre-war childhood, he listened to his father's voice coming over the radio.

" And now, because we are all unworthy of the great mercy which has been vouchsafed to us and desire to bear witness to our knowledge of our unworthiness, let us repeat the Confession from the Communion Service."

He heard the stir of the congregation kneeling as Robert led them in their expression of penitence.

" Almighty God, Father of our Lord Jesus Christ, Maker of all things, Judge of all men; We acknowledge and bewail our manifold sins and wickedness, Which we, from time to time, most grievously have committed. . . . We do earnestly repent, and are heartily sorry for these our misdoings; The remembrance of them is grievous unto us, The burden of them is intolerable . . ."

Why, wondered Adrian with a million other listeners, did the preacher pause at this point? Why did his voice almost fail? Neither he nor they shared Robert's memory, which for a moment threatened to overwhelm him, of his hour of conversion thirty years ago on the great rock at Symond's Yat. He recovered himself immediately, and went on.

" Have mercy upon us, most merciful Father; For thy Son our Lord Jesus Christ's sake, forgive us all that is past; And grant that we may ever hereafter Serve and please thee In newness of life, To the honour and glory of thy Name; Through Jesus Christ our Lord."

The congregation stood up as the choir of St. Saviour's began to sing the Ninetieth Psalm.

" Lord, thou hast been our refuge: from one generation to another.

" Before the mountains were brought forth, or ever the earth and the world were made: thou art God from everlasting, and world without end.

" Thou turnest man to destruction: again thou sayest, Come again, ye children of men. . . .

" Comfort us again now after the time that thou hast plagued us: and for the years wherein we have suffered adversity.

" Shew thy servants thy work: and their children thy glory. . . ."

Then Theodore Martelhammer read the first eleven verses of the eighteenth chapter of St. Matthew, in which Jesus called a little child, and set him in the midst of His disciples. The Lesson was followed by Robert's voice, " Let us pray," and again Adrian heard the congregation kneel.

" Let us pray," said his father, " that the War in the Far East may be swiftly concluded, and that once again we may live at peace with our brothers and sisters of Japan.

" Let us remember the men and women still engaged on those distant battlefields, to whom this day of thanksgiving can mean very little ; and let us ask our Father to bring a speedy end to their bitter experience.

" Let us pray for the men, women, and children of that great nation which we and our Allies have again beaten to its knees. Let us ask God to restore it through suffering to order and prosperity, and by His Mercy make it a noble influence, worthy of its culture and history, in the family of nations. And let us plead with Him to grant us the vision and magnanimity which will enable us to help Him in that mighty task.

" Let us pray for all on both sides who have died in prisons and concentration camps at the hands of their enemies ; and for those who have been bereaved and can find no cause for personal rejoicing in the coming of peace to the West.

" Let us pray for wisdom and insight to be given to our rulers, and especially to that new Government which the people of this country will elect in the coming months.

" And finally let us pray for ourselves and our Allies, that we may become conscious of our sins and, realising our unworthiness, may make ourselves better members of God's Kingdom on earth, and prepare ourselves more faithfully for citizenship in His Kingdom of Heaven.

" We beseech Thee to hear us, O Lord."

He announced the second hymn ; again it was no cry of triumph, but a confession of wrong-doing, and a prayer for forgiveness and grace.

" Weary of earth and laden with my sin,
I look at Heaven and long to enter in;
But there no evil thing may find a home,
And yet I hear a voice that bids me, ' Come '.

" So vile I am, how dare I hope to stand
In the pure glory of that holy land ?
Before the whiteness of that Throne appear ?
Yet there are hands stretched out to draw me near . . ."

When the hymn ended, Robert's voice came strongly
and confidently through the loudspeaker.

" In the name of the Father, and the Son, and the
Holy Ghost, Amen. My text is taken from the Lesson
that you have just heard : ' Verily I say unto you, Except
ye repent, and become as little children, ye shall not enter
into the Kingdom of Heaven.'

" My friends in St. Saviour's and wherever our broadcast service reaches, we are celebrating today an occasion
so rich in possibilities for good, that all hatred, all bitterness, all desire for recrimination, should be banished from
our minds.

" Nearly six years ago, on the day that war was declared, I asked the Londoners then assembled at this
Church to believe that the powers of death and hell
could not prevail against it. I reminded them that one
day the struggle would end, and that some of us would
then be left to resume the building of God's Jerusalem
on earth."

Into Adrian's mind, as Robert spoke, flashed the
memory of that declaration of war ; the bewildered crowds
in the Square ; their sudden scattering as the siren sounded,
and his own mingled emotions of excitement and fear.
His father went on.

" That time has now come. The Church of Christ is
not unimpaired ; grievous damage has been done, by both

sides, to its values and standards. But it has not perished; it has survived the onslaughts of its spiritual foes. And many of us, by God's mercy, are still here, after six years, to take up the task of restoring it in the name of Jesus, our Master.

"During those years, we in this ancient land have endured a long ordeal. The evidence of that suffering is around us, here in this bombed and roofless Church. Our young men and women have gone forth to die in many theatres of war, and sixty thousand of our fellow-countrymen have met death in this island. Some of us in this Church tonight came close to it only three months ago. That incident, which left its mark on our homes, has taken from us many friends who used to worship here. Their bodies lie in the grave, but their souls have passed into the keeping of their Heavenly Father. Let us remember them in faith and hope. It may be that those of us who survived have learned from our experience to value more humbly the gift of life, and the months or years given back to us to prepare ourselves better for the Life Everlasting.

"But though we have suffered, our suffering does not compare with the anguish of our neighbours in Europe. Perhaps it has taught us enough to enable us to enter imaginatively into their tribulations, whether they be friends or foes, and to remember that we have all sinned, friends and foes alike. But we have been spared the agony of invasion; we have not actually been called upon to resist our opponents on our fields and hills, which are still beautiful and unspoiled. Our cities have been battered but not obliterated, and our children have never known starvation. Because of these mercies, my friends, we have now a second chance."

He made a long pause, but no sound or movement came from the congregation.

"Twenty-six years ago," he continued, " we had the

opportunity after another Great War to remake the world and build the temple of peace. We missed that opportunity, because not only our statesmen, but we, the people of Britain, were unready for it. We were a mighty nation, and we feared the sacrifices of power, pride, and privilege which true peace must always involve. The implications of Christ's exhortation to love our enemies were plain to us, but we were afraid to take the risk.

" Today, in a manner that would be incredible if we did not know that God's compassion is beyond our understanding, that chance has come again. Do not think it will be any easier to accept than it was in the years after 1918. This time we cannot hope to recover from the War so quickly as we recovered then. Though our physical perils are over, we have a long period still before us of minor hardships and inconveniences which will test the faith and patience of us all. But, by offering us this second opportunity, God has shown His trust in us, His erring, disobedient children. We are His creatures; and because of the potential divinity with which He has endowed every one of us, we have the power, if we will, to build Jerusalem — not only here, but throughout the world."

Adrian could picture his father as he leaned over the high pulpit and stretched out his hands in a familiar gesture which seemed to gather the whole congregation into an intimate circle of friends and colleagues.

" If we, His children, pray to him with humble and contrite hearts, He can strengthen our wills and bring them closer to His own. He can inspire us with vision to perceive the magnanimity and courage which the future demands, and the difficult choices, involving conflict and sacrifice, that we must make in order to put His Glory before the satisfactions and rewards of this world. Let us ask Him to give us, through His Grace, that will, that vision, and that courage in the days to come.

317

" And now, because the future matters more than the past, and we must learn how to create a better society in our own land before we can teach the lesson to others, let us end our service by singing Blake's *Jerusalem*."

The chords of Sir Hubert Parry's music crashed out over Balham and the rest of England, and across Europe and the dividing oceans. Each listener pictured some friend or relative far away who might be hearing them too.

I wonder, thought Adrian, whether Carol is listening? I wonder if she remembers? Would she understand why he had not answered the two charming letters — so much too kind and thought-provoking — that she had sent him with Christmas cards the December after he left America and again the following year? Last Christmas neither card nor letter had come, and he had only himself to thank. Perhaps a long, long time hence, when they were both middle-aged and he had forgotten how sore he still felt, he would seek her out and explain . . .

Then, for the last time, he heard his father's voice.

" Wherever you may be, my friends, I bid you good-night and Godspeed. Let each one of us at his own bed side thank our Heavenly Father for the great mercy that He has shown us, and ask Him to grant us the humility, understanding, and love which will make us worthy of it. The Lord bless you and keep you, the Lord make His face to shine upon you and be gracious unto you, the Lord lift up the light of His countenance upon you and give you peace, now and forever more. Amen."

*

It was only natural, after such a long day of prayer and preaching, that Robert should feel more tired than even he had felt during the recent exhausting weeks of pain, endurance, and triumph.

Before she left for the Victory Pageant, Sylvia had

urged him to go to bed immediately after his broadcast. She had long formed the habit of sleeping in the spare room when she was kept late at the theatre, and she promised that she would not disturb him. Adrian, he knew, was not coming that night; he had been given leave for the next day, and would arrive at the Vicarage in time for breakfast.

But though he was so exhausted and his head ached intolerably, Robert did not feel like sleep. Instead he climbed, step by slow step, to his study, where the roof had been temporarily repaired and the scattered books restored to their places. He looked with weary distaste at the pile of unopened letters on his blotting pad, but at least he need not read them now. Like other problems on his loaded desk, they would keep till the morning. Tonight he did not want to work, but to think; or perhaps not even think, but let the wayward images of memory take their own path through his mind. . . .

For minutes which lengthened into hours, those images displayed themselves before his inward eye. He saw his father again, and their old home at Hoddershall Ash; the spacious green of Tom Quad at Christ Church; the interminable lines of trenches on the Western front in the First World War, and the slag heaps at Loos where he won his Victoria Cross. He recalled Symond's Yat, and those moments of vision in the Forest of Dean which the solemn congregational Confession at his recent service had so poignantly revived for him; he pictured as in a kaleidoscope the varying scenes of his work at Battersea till it led with a directness that seemed predestined to his meeting with Sylvia.

Remembering the sad beauty of her young face uplifted at the Communion rails and the rich glow of her copper hair beneath the gold-hued East window, he relived the early months of his passion for her and the long years of their marriage. She would never know how much she had given him. Her kindness and faithful companionship had been his throughout their life together, even though she had not everything to bestow that his love, in spite of itself, had desired.

The unfolding pictures brought back to him the birth of their children, so long hoped for and so dearly beloved; the challenging years of his ministry at St. Saviour's; the founding and swift extension of the B.O.J. His work had been hampered and limited by the Second World War, but now, like his children, it was restored to him in the fullness of time. There had been a period in which those children, and especially Adrian after their return from America, had caused him perplexity and even pain. But that, as Fred Westerly had shown him, was an inevitable feature of their growth in such an epoch as this. How could he have expected Adrian, during his few short years, to adapt himself to a revolutionary era in which God's world had been torn asunder by the hands of men; an apocalyptic age that was witnessing, like the Renaissance and the Reformation, one of the great turning-points in human history?

Yet recently Adrian had shown that, when really called upon for strength and service, he could respond creditably to the demands of his time. Robert had hoped that he would bear witness against the evil wrought in war by refusing to obey his call-up, but he was nevertheless proud of Adrian's work in the Bomb-Disposal Squad. It was work, after all, which did not increase the havoc of war, but had helped to heal its wounds. It required great courage, and Adrian had shown that he possessed it. He had overcome — at what cost Robert could readily guess — the sensitive reactions to danger and fear which he had inherited from his father. He had offered his life to the city where he was born and the people amongst whom he had grown up. The men and women of London would never know how much they owed to the boys who demolished the bombs which would otherwise have cost thousands of lives. But Robert, who had seen so much damage and been present at the aftermath of so many incidents, understood and was thankful.

Surely God had abundantly blessed him! And He would bless him again in the new opportunities for service that peace would bring; and in the growth of understanding, and perhaps even love, which maturity would give to his son and daughter . . .

Robert sat up suddenly as he realised that St. Saviour's bell was sounding midnight. Too tired to stand, he dragged his chair across the room and sat by the window looking down into the Square. On the opposite side, beyond Drake's statue, a small crowd of boys and girls were dancing jubilantly round a bonfire which crackled on the bombed site of the Armada Book Company. Above his head, subdued by the low clouds, a display of searchlights began to illuminate the arch of sky over London.

They were not the harsh, dramatic spears of light which had caught and imprisoned the enemy bombers, but a tender flickering glow reflected from the clouds. Robert pulled his chair closer to the window to watch them, though the movement meant an enormous effort and weights seemed to be tied to his feet. No longer the cruel illuminations of man's wrath, he thought, but gentle, like the mercy of a forgiving God. He leaned back in his chair, finding the subdued beams appearing and reappearing in the misty sky strangely comforting to his illimitable fatigue.

Lights, he said to himself. Faint lights, but real. As real as the infinite pity felt by a loving Father for his erring children. All disobedient, but all His children. *All* . . .

Robert's eyes closed, but opened again for a second to see the soft elusive lights still playing will-o'-the-wisp amid the clouds. Then a darkness spread over the sky, and the lights faded away.

CHAPTER XVII

Beyond Victory

THREE days later, Adrian stood alone in the drawing-room of St. Saviour's Vicarage, waiting for his father's funeral to begin, and watching the crowd gathering in the Square. It was strange how many of his life's outstanding events had taken place with that crowd as their background. Like a Greek chorus perpetually assembling, it seemed to be always there.

Today a large proportion of it was composed of soldiers and airmen in uniform, and half the Civil Defence Services from Central London were apparently present as well. Adrian supposed that, like Robert himself, they had seen war at close quarters, and were grateful to the man who had been willing to sacrifice prestige and preferment to his quest for new values and revolutionary loyalties.

He thought of the conversation that he had overheard, coming from Balham on the Underground early that morning, between two middle-aged men with newspapers who looked like bank clerks.

" I see Bob Carbury's being buried today."

" Yes. I suppose there'll be a big crowd there."

" I expect there will. You know, George, I never could quite understand the hold that man had on the life of London — and England too, for that matter. He was a good preacher, I grant you — but we've had others. He identified himself with the people, but he never pretended to be one of them; he was always an aristocrat at heart. And he hadn't any overwhelming charm of manner."

" George " had paused before he answered. " I suppose what really got people was his absolute sincerity. He'd his own conception of Christianity, and he stuck to it through thick and thin. He was ready to give up anything for it, including his career."

" It seems to me he did pretty well as it was."

" Not from the professional angle, I think. He'd have been a Bishop by now if he hadn't taken the line he did about the War. Superficially he mayn't have been a specially attractive personality, but I bet you church life in London will be a good deal poorer and duller without him."

In the three days since the ending of the War in Europe Adrian felt that he had grown at least five years older, for it was he, reaching the Vicarage early in the morning, who had found his father dead in his study. Even in that moment of overwhelming shock he had been impressed, beyond his power to put the emotion into words, by the benevolent serenity of Robert's face. The scar on the cold forehead had stood out sharply, like the stigmata on the brow of a saint, and still faintly visible on his cheek was the mark from the bullet which had pierced it at Loos. But the lines of anxiety and fatigue which had been part of Robert's expression as long as Adrian could remember had totally disappeared. On that last affirmative evidence of his father's faith in fallible humanity, the coffin had now closed for ever.

When he arrived at the Vicarage for the funeral, his mother had called him to her room and shown him a copy of Robert's Will. It had been drawn up in August, 1943, just after he had taken Adrian to Hoddershall Ash. It made his executors responsible for selling his ancestral home, and directed that, since his wife and children were already well provided for, the sum realised when all expenses had been deducted should be divided between the Parish Fund at St. Saviour's and the Builders of Jerusalem. After the detailed disposition of his other effects, the Will had ended with a personal clause which echoed, a persistent challenge, through Adrian's mind.

" As the burial ground at St. Saviour's is no longer in use, I desire to be buried in the churchyard of All Souls, Battersea, where I was married to my beloved wife and where my dear son was christened."

Too late for him to respond or show that he understood, the words conveyed to Adrian the boundlessness of his father's love and the depth of his capacity for forgiveness.

The door opened, and Anselm Ensor came in. The Bishop of South-west London was now a statesmanlike prelate nearing seventy, with an impressive coronet of white hair and a strong resemblance to the portraits of Cardinal Wolsey. He had asked to be allowed to conduct Robert's funeral service, with the assistance of Jonathan Wiltshire, the Vicar of All Souls, and Theodore Martelhammer, whose years of loyal service to Robert would probably make him the next incumbent of St. Saviour's. As Robert had expressed a wish to be buried at Battersea, it was obvious that the concluding part of the service must be held there. But because no one could accept the idea of the Vicar leaving the scene of his long labours without a public tribute, the beginning was to be conducted in St. Saviour's Church.

As the Bishop entered, Adrian greeted him gravely; he had seen him twice since his father's death. Glancing at the Square, he said to Anselm : " There's a bigger crowd than ever there today. I suppose they're waiting to hear Daddy's funeral service. You know, Sir, until quite recently I used to think he was very unpopular. People wrote him such terrible letters, and put awful things about him in the papers. And yet, now he's dead, they seem as if they can't say anything good enough."

The Bishop, his back turned to the boy, stood by the window looking at the silently increasing multitude before he replied.

" That's typical of the public, my son. It has a bad habit of withholding till after death the admiration that would make all the difference to a man or woman in life." He paused, and added : " And not only the public. It happens in families, too. If only, all the time, we showed our parents, or our children, something of what we feel an hour after we've lost them, family life would become the haven of love and security that it sometimes is and always ought to be."

Adrian said nothing. Whatever memories reproached him, he kept them to himself. At last he spoke.

" But surely people wouldn't express admiration after death if they hadn't felt it at all in life ? I knew Daddy had lots of followers, of course, but I thought they were mostly cranks. I've let them in — depressed-looking women in homespun tweeds, and young men with long hair and coloured trousers. But all that crowd can't just be cranks. There seems to be thousands of them. A lot of ordinary people must have admired him after all."

" Of course they did," said Anselm Ensor. " In his life and teaching he accepted the full implications of Christianity, and people respect a man for that, however much it inconveniences and upsets them. They attack him savagely because they hate their own uncomfortable suspicion that he may be right. I counted your dear father as one of my best friends, yet he often upset and inconvenienced me, and I daresay he regarded me as one of his persecutors. But if he hadn't upset me I should have loved him less."

" I don't think I quite understand that."

" Perhaps not yet. It's something that is easier to understand about one's juniors than one's seniors. But you will understand it, some day."

The strokes of Big Ben sounded eleven, and the Bishop walked with Adrian across the old graveyard to the Church. Robert's flower-covered coffin was already there ; for two days his body had lain in state while an unending line of his parishioners filed past it. The coffin stood just below the Chancel steps, where in the crises of his life he had so often prayed. Above it stretched the boundless blue of the calm May sky. To the congregation which packed every corner of the roofless Church, that recent evidence of catastrophe gave a special poignancy to the hymns and prayers which commemorated the life of the man who had tried in deed and in truth to be their shepherd. At the end Theodore Martelhammer spoke simply and briefly of Robert's work at St. Saviour's, and of all that they had laboured to achieve together since his mission began there in 1927. The hymn " Abide with Me " concluded the short service, and then the Bishop briefly directed the congregation.

" Our brother's last journey will now begin. All those who wish to follow his mortal remains to their resting-place are welcome to come with us."

Everyone in the Church did wish to follow, it appeared, and the throng waiting in the Square as well. After the bearers had carried the coffin down the aisle preceded by the choir and clergy singing " Lord, now lettest Thou Thy servant depart in peace ", the congregation lined up behind the long row of carriages standing outside. When the Psalm ended and the procession assembled, a military band struck the solemn opening chords of Beethoven's *Marcia Funebre, sulla morte d' un Eroe* from the Twelfth Sonata.

The band was composed of volunteers from the London City Artillery Company. This regiment, headed by its Commanding Officer, had been accustomed to attend the services at St. Saviour's. The C.O. was well aware that Robert had opposed the War ; but he also knew that he was a V.C., and that was sufficient for him. When he offered the Company's band for the funeral procession, Theodore Martelhammer had hesitated. But after consulting Sylvia, he had accepted the Colonel's suggestion. From one point of view, perhaps, it seemed incongruous for Robert to be accompanied to his grave by a military band. But from another the arrangement was wholly appropriate ; he had meant more to the thousands of young conscripts passing through London than any clergyman in the British Isles.

The band of the Artillery Company now led the long procession to Battersea, followed by the clergy and choir walking in front of the hearse. On either side of it marched the pall - bearers, headed by Frederick Westerly, who looked pale and stricken. In spite of his sixty-seven years he had insisted, like Anselm Ensor, upon making the considerable journey from St. Saviour's to All Souls on foot as a tribute to Robert's memory. Behind the hearse Adrian and Josephine walked solemnly together, preceding the succession of carriages.

In the first of these, Sylvia sat alone. On her lap lay a small bunch of early roses which Augusta Martelhammer, her eyes red from the tears that she had been unable to restrain while her husband was speaking of Robert's work, had thrust into her hands as she came out of St. Saviour's. It was a shock superimposed upon other shocks to realise that the once jealous Augusta had developed through the years into her devoted admirer. The delicate scent of the roses filled the carriage like a benediction.

She was alone because Josephine had pleaded to be allowed to go on foot with Adrian.

" Oh, Mummy, I don't want to ride! Can't I walk with Ady ? " she had entreated, and Sylvia, as usual, had told her to do as she wished. Does she want to pay respect to her father, or only to get out of driving with me ? she had asked herself realistically. Then, looking at her daughter's innocent face, she had realised that Josephine was merely excited by the prospect of walking in a procession.

I tend, she told herself as the cortège passed along Victoria Embankment, to look for explanations that are too complicated. Jo isn't like Adrian ; she's not subtle. She means exactly what she says, neither more nor less. I suppose she takes after Robert's mother — or perhaps my father. Even her oddly censorious moral values seem a bit Victorian in someone who so palpably belongs to the twentieth century.

She thought of the unusually intimate conversation between Josephine and herself early that morning.

" Mummy . . . do you think there's really an after-life ? "

She had hesitated, and then answered truthfully. " I used to think so — or rather, I tried to believe it. But after I played *Mary Rose* I wasn't sure I wanted to believe it any more. That play makes you realise there's no room for people who come back. Somehow, life closes over them . . . or ought to. . . ."

She was silent for a moment, and then went on.

" Death is like a stone thrown into a pond. At first the circles it makes are sharp and narrow. Then they get wider and wider, and finally disappear. People remember the stone, but they can't see where it went in any longer."

"But," Josephine had said, "I wasn't so much thinking of people coming back. What I meant was, do we go to them? Is there really another world where we shall meet Daddy after we're dead?"

"It's possible. You can't deny a thing unless you positively know it to be untrue. But if there is another world, it must be of a kind inconceivable to our imagination. It would be an awkward sort of place if it were like this one. There'd be such a conflict of loyalties, to begin with."

"It would be specially awkward for people like you, who've been married twice. Wouldn't it, Mummy?"

"Yes, Jo, it would indeed," Sylvia had said. Now, as the procession passed the Royal Hospital Gardens, she remembered the question which has troubled millions of women all down the centuries: "And whose shall she be at the Resurrection?"

They're all gone, she thought, the three men whose love I have known — and all, in their different ways, victims of war. First Lawrence — my only beloved. Then Damon, so incongruously dead of malaria and starvation in a Japanese prison camp. And now Robert. I knew him best — and yet I seem to be thinking of him least. . . .

Riding behind the coffin which she could not realise as his, she noticed the considerate turning aside of the spectators lining the route as they caught sight of her still lovely, familiar face, and observed how quietly she sat there in her mourning. She was getting their sympathy, she felt, on false pretences. . . . Leaning forward, she looked at the river dancing in the noonday sunlight, as it had danced on that early morning when Robert asked her to be his wife. Although she had lived with him for a quarter of a century, her widow's garments were less conspicuous than those she had worn for Lawrence, her husband of three weeks.

I ought to be grieving for Robert, she thought. I ought to be discreetly wiping away the tears that these onlookers expect. I've so often imitated tears on the stage, yet I can't even pretend to cry now. Why not? Don't I care at all? Surely I shall miss him, and the tender unfailing love he always gave me? He was so sensitive that he must have known very soon that he didn't mean to me what I meant to him. I must have disappointed him deeply, but he never showed it. We all disappointed him — Adrian, perhaps, most of all. . . .

Is it because of Adrian that I have to live on, though my three men are all dead? Will he be the fourth man who matters to me some day? At present he and Josephine are indifferent to me, and like all their generation they don't try to conceal it. I've irritated them less than Robert did because they have meant less to me than to him, and therefore I have never demanded much from them. . . . Will their indifference to me pass, as mine to them is passing? Adrian is my own son; I could talk to him if he'd ever let me. He understands everything he chooses to understand. We could be great friends if I hadn't the misfortune to be his mother. . . .

The funeral procession was now moving slowly along Chelsea Embankment. It passed the Green Parrakeet, and the sombre ruins of Chelsea Old Church. At that moment the military band, playing Chopin's Funeral March, reached the high transcendent notes of the final passage. The echo of the chords soared triumphantly above the ruins, an undaunted challenge to the authority of death over man and all his works. Sylvia noticed that many of the spectators beside the road were weeping. In the May sunshine the river looked like smooth grey silk, with spangles on its surface. As the hearse turned to cross Battersea Bridge the trams stopped, and the men on the Thames barges stood silently to attention, lifting their caps.

This is just like another Armistice Day, Sylvia reflected. She remembered how, in seven successive Novembers of the 1920's, she had passed the Two Minutes' Silence on that bridge, looking towards Charing Cross where she had last seen Lawrence. Four days before Adrian's birth she had stood there, remembering her young lover, and completely forgetting the supreme reward won by Adrian's father in battle. And now Adrian was nearly twenty, and Robert was dead.

The procession stopped at All Souls Church, where another large crowd awaited it. As Sylvia walked down the sloping path through the churchyard, she saw the heaped mound of earth above the open grave where Robert's body was to lie. Its rawness was disguised by the bank of spring flowers piled up beside it, wreaths, crosses, and chaplets flinging their scent into the air. No doubt, she thought, suddenly unable to bear the sight, it was not by chance that the grave had been made on the identical spot where Robert had asked her to marry him, twenty-five years ago. If he had lived a few months longer, they would have celebrated their silver wedding

The Church had already been thronged with workers from Battersea before the procession from St. Saviour's arrived. Sylvia moved quietly into the front pew beside Adrian and Josephine, and heard the Bishop intoning the Prayers which begin the Burial Service.

" I am the resurrection and the life, saith the Lord : he that believeth in me, though he were dead, yet shall he live: and whosoever liveth and believeth in me shall never die."

Then the congregation, moved by one thought and

acclaiming their lost leader with one voice, broke into
the opening hymn :

> " For all the Saints who from their labours rest,
>   Who Thee by faith before the world confess'd,
>   Thy Name, O Jesu, be for ever blest ! Alleluia ! "

More prayers followed, and the singing of the Twenty-
third Psalm. When it was over, Sylvia listened to
Jonathan Wiltshire reading the Lesson that she had
chosen. Frederick Westerly had suggested the time-
honoured passage from the Book of Wisdom : " For the
souls of the righteous are in the hand of God ", but she
had asked for the Beatitudes to be given instead. Robert,
she said, had never believed in his own claim to righteousness ; it would be more appropriate to repeat the principles
by which he had tried to live. She heard them again now,
knowing that these words, at least, would bring her
husband back to her till the end of her life.

" Blessed are the poor in spirit : for theirs is the kingdom of
heaven.

" Blessed are they that mourn : for they shall be comforted.

" Blessed are the meek : for they shall inherit the earth.

" Blessed are they which do hunger and thirst after righteousness : for they shall be filled.

" Blessed are the merciful : for they shall obtain mercy.

" Blessed are the pure in heart : for they shall see God.

" Blessed are the peacemakers : for they shall be called the
children of God.

" Blessed are they which are persecuted for righteousness'
sake : for theirs is the kingdom of heaven.

" Blessed are ye, when men shall revile you, and persecute
you, and shall say all manner of evil against you falsely, for
my sake.

" Rejoice, and be exceeding glad : for great is your reward
in heaven."

When St. Saviour's choir had sung the anthem, " Comfort ye, my people ", from Handel's *Messiah*, Anselm Ensor went up into the pulpit. He spoke of the thirty years in which he had known Robert ; of the young man who had won the Victoria Cross in France and was badly wounded ; of the convalescent who, while recovering in hospital, had been called to dedicate himself to the service of Christ. Those who were present, said the Bishop, had seen for themselves the inspiration with which Robert Carbury had fulfilled that service, both here at All Souls and during the long period of his ministry at St. Saviour's.

He mentioned Robert's failings, which he did not attempt to disguise.

" Our dear brother was deeply sensitive, and for this reason often lacked confidence in himself. He had none of that imperviousness to the feelings of others which it is now fashionable to describe as ' toughness '. In spite of the great courage which his country rewarded, and which you, my friends, have seen manifested in a high degree during the past three months, he was often racked by anxieties and apprehensions which never appeared to leave him until the final triumphant weeks of his life. But nothing ever shook his loyalty to his convictions and his conception of his mission. For that he sacrified the plaudits of the world, official approval, ecclesiastical preferment, perhaps life itself."

The Bishop then referred, less guardedly than usual, to Robert's struggle against war.

" Those convictions caused him also to believe that, if events compel us, we must sacrifice even our love of our country to literal obedience to Christ's teaching. And who, in this costly day of victory, dare say that he was wrong ? Sometimes, to the saints and rebels of mankind, a vision is vouchsafed beyond that of the appointed leaders who appear to possess more wisdom. It is men like Robert

333

Carbury who carry the whole human race to new levels of accomplishment in the realm of the spirit. There are few to whom we can feel with more confidence that our Master will say : ' Well done, thou good and faithful servant ; enter thou into the joy of thy Lord.' Let us remember him always, with humility and gratitude, believing that in God's good time we shall see him again."

For a moment Anselm Ensor remained in the pulpit, his head bowed in prayer as he looked upon the coffin which contained the physical semblance of the man whom he had known.

" And now," he said, " before we escort his body to the grave, let us sing the song that to him was both a national anthem and the practical expression of his creed — that song which at his broadcast service three days ago went out to our own countrymen and the stricken peoples of Europe."

As the thundering chords that Adrian had heard so recently filled the Church and echoed through the open door across the river, he noticed, mingled with the workers from Battersea, a large contingent of the B.O.J., led by Ted Rogers. Wearing their badges, they stood devoutly to attention as Blake's song reverberated from the organ. Among them the solemn young men in corduroy trousers and the middle-aged women with horn-rimmed spectacles were no more attractive than they had been before ; but they seemed to Adrian much less ridiculous. In fact, he no longer found them ridiculous at all. Behind their odd manners and eccentric costumes they were seeking an elusive but genuine Good — a Good that he, perhaps, would never find, but that some men and women must discover if suicidal humanity was not to dig its own grave and then tumble into it. Their determination to over-come death by life was symbolised by the ardour of their ringing voices :

" I will not cease from mental fight,
Nor shall my sword sleep in my hand,
Till — we — have — built — Je-ru-sa-lem . . ."

They were not ridiculous to Sylvia either. Far from despising them, she was envying them bitterly. She knew that in effect they would canonise Robert, carrying on his work and giving life to his ideals, while for her, though his children were hers, he would be no more than the fading memory of a second husband.

Dear Robert, she thought. I lived with you all those years and you were always so good to me — and yet I feel nothing, nothing! Why can't I care? Oh, Lawrence, Lawrence!

And suddenly, to the embarrassment of Adrian and Josephine, she fell on her knees and remained there, her head bowed on her folded arms and her shoulders shaking with heavy noiseless sobs. Concerned and uncomfortable, they drew closer together and away from their mother.

They knew, of course, that her first husband had been killed in 1918; but because that distant war was now a mere history-book episode for them, it never occurred to them that it could still be a source of emotion for her. Their experience had been too short to teach them that she was weeping, not for their father, but for the death of love, and its obstinate refusal to rise again.

Epilogue

I

On the first Saturday of August, 1947, Adrian Carbury, Lieutenant, Royal Engineers, took his Volkswagen from its garage at Cologne and prepared to drive to Hamburg. A fragment of news, heard the previous evening from an unexpected source, had induced him to make this long journey instead of spending the Bank Holiday week-end at Bad Godesberg with Tony Terracini.

Two years ago, when the conclusion of the War with Japan had put an end to further opportunities for bomb-disposal, Adrian and Tony, still liable for a long period of service, had applied for commissions in the Engineers. When their training was finished they had both been sent to Germany, to become part of the British Occupation Force in place of officers with longer service due for demobilisation. Though separated they were not far apart; Tony had gone to Düsseldorf, and Adrian was stationed at Cologne.

Here he had begun by supervising the rebuilding of the shattered Rhine bridges until the German authorities could make themselves responsible for this work. He was now one of the few remaining subalterns in charge of the British troops repairing the railway. This job too would soon come to an end, for the Germans were taking it over as well. In mid-August the group of Engineer officers to which he belonged was going home. Already their Mess in Marienburg, the least-damaged suburb south of the Alte Stadt where they occupied the pleasant house of a former Nazi who had been numbered with the transgressors at the local denazification trials, was a confusion of kit-bags, haversacks, and wooden packing-cases.

Soon after his return, Adrian himself would be due for demobilisation. He hoped it would come in time to enable him to sit for a Scholarship at Trinity College, Cambridge. If he won the Scholarship he might be given a place there in the Hilary Term, 1948. But even though he had to wait till the following Michaelmas, he would still be better off than his older contemporaries whom the War had caught at the end of their schooldays.

He could no longer fulfil his intention of studying Astronomy under Eddington, for Sir Arthur was dead; but he had left successors who would equip Adrian for the work that he still desired. From earliest childhood his choice of a profession had been consistent and determined, but if ever he had entertained doubts, they would have been removed by his constant comparison of the chaos that was post-war Germany with the exquisite order in the skies above. Again and again he resolved, as he had first resolved at Chiswick, to learn how to relate to human society the obedience of the stars to the divine laws which determined their movements.

When he came to Cologne fourteen months ago, Adrian's first impression had been one of weeds — huge sordid growths springing up amid acres of ruin, and turning the still half-cleared side-streets into semblances of ill-kept country lanes. His next impression was that of dust, which filled his eyes, mouth, and shoes from the piles of debris lying everywhere. Finally he had noticed the macabre shapes of the ruins themselves. Most of these remained exactly as the bombs had left them; the problems of a city which was 95 per cent destroyed were too overwhelming for any noticeable reconstruction to have been done in a year. Shattered halves of once noble houses, long looted of their contents, stood gaping above the cleared main thoroughfares. Fragments of buildings, now as narrow as the width of a window, pointed like accusing fingers at the sky. In and out of them grew the dusty untrimmed trees and shrubs which had once been part of their well-kept gardens.

In his letters to Sylvia and Josephine, Adrian found it impossible to choose words which would convey the impression made by acres upon acres of these grotesque survivals. If the world were to end, he thought, and Earth, grown dead like the Moon, were to be rediscovered after several centuries by men from another planet, the remaining evidences of our forgotten culture might well resemble the ruins of Cologne.

Until he became accustomed to the sight of them, it seemed strange to see men and women queueing, cycling, and making love amid these spectral counterfeits of normal living. Yet somehow, somewhere, nearly half a million human beings had already returned to the city, living in cellars beneath the debris or in patched-up rooms which represented the only habitable parts of buildings that looked totally demolished. It was a strange sensation, coming into Cologne after dark, to see light gleaming through a glassless window-frame at the apparently inaccessible summit of a burned and twisted column of stone.

With their spare bodies and yellow faces lined through hunger, the Germans who lived in these fantastic homes certainly suggested survivors from a former existence. Adrian did not know whether he was glad or sorry that he had not seen Cologne before the War, but he sometimes tried to picture what that former existence had been. In the house of his acquaintance Professor Werner Gehnich, a retired scientist from Berlin University who had come to Cologne in 1938, he once found a guide-book which told him something of what he and humanity had lost.

" From the days of Constantine to our own time ", he read, " every century, every style and transition period have left their mark, as in a giant record, with buildings as its documents and memorials. Cologne is an historical compendium in stone and gold of the history of nearly two thousand years."

Some of the pictures in the guide-book showed him those historic memorials which had disappeared into heaps of rubble, and still covered thousands of corpses whose flesh had long been devoured by rats from the Rhine. The great Rathaus, with its Hansa-Saal and Muschel-Saal; St. Martin's Church, a small rival to the Cathedral overlooking the river; the round Church of St. Gereon with its pointed roof; the Wallraf-Richartz Museum which had contained a priceless collection of glass and mosaic; the ancient Dance Hall of the Gürzenich — what would posterity think of the insane generation which had so irresponsibly, so almost jubilantly, destroyed its own heritage from the past?

Dad was right about the raids, he concluded reluctantly, for his fundamental sanity told him that his preoccupation with his father's memory was becoming an obsession. He wondered how, in his own necessary concentration upon the Nazi bombs which battered London, he had failed to realise what British bombs were doing to Germany. Robert had been accustomed to say that the treasures of the ages did not belong to England or America any more than they belonged to Hitler, and that nobody had the right to cheat mankind out of its inheritance.

During his fourteen months in Germany, Adrian had visited many other cities. His work had taken him to Hamburg, and Hanover, and several devastated towns in the Ruhr, and once he had spent a week-end with Tony in the formal desert of tall ruins which was still recognisable as Berlin. But nothing he had seen had yet convinced him that his father was wrong. He understood as it had never been possible to understand in England, where the habits of the people retained their continuity though the social fabric had been gravely impaired, how fragile was the way of life called civilisation. Sometimes, walking back to his Mess from the derelict home of a German friend through the moonlit caricature of the city, he wondered whether Europe could survive the magnitude of its disaster. Then he would look up at the stars and silently thank their Creator for the example of ordered perfection that He had given to the perverse and disorderly children of men.

One morning, as he watched the Sappers in his charge draw the wreckage of the once impressive Hohenzollern Bridge from the deep green waters of the Rhine, he remembered Kepler's words recorded after the discovery of his Third Law : " The book is written to be read now or by posterity — I care not which ; it may well wait a century for a reader, as God has waited six thousand years for an observer."

At Cambridge he would learn to see time in relation to eternity. He would realise how small and ephemeral were the hot ambitions of power-seeking men, who created violent but temporary chaos, in contrast to the slow working out of God's gigantic intention. Through the study of Astronomy, which recorded the infinite patience of the Creator as revealed by His Universe, he would find a cure for his own destructive impatience and that of others. Like his predecessors who had spent their lives in learning the lessons of the stars, he would work for ends he would never see and rewards he would never know.

*

The Officers' Mess, with its sun-porch, swimming-pool, large armchairs, and private bar, was extremely comfortable by German standards. Adrian knew that the

subalterns who shared it with him thought him rather
an outsider for spending so many evenings in the draughty,
crowded rooms of the Germans whose acquaintance, in
spite of his habitual reserve, he seemed to make so easily.
But he did not care. His regard for public opinion had
never been excessive, and now it concerned him even less
than before. Not one of his fellow Engineers interested
him half as much as Professor Gehnich, whose top-floor
attic was also in Marienburg, or Musik-Direktor Felix
Schiller, who performed so superbly on his Bechstein piano
when he was not feeling too hungry.

But even more frequently he took a strictly forbidden
gift of sugar or coffee to the Countess von Redelstädt,
who had been educated in England, and now lived on the
reconstructed second floor of an otherwise totally damaged
house in the Oberländer Ufer facing the Rhine. She belonged to the Deutsche Versöhnungsbund, or Fellowship
of Reconciliation, and while they drank the coffee she
would talk earnestly of the guilt of Germany in permitting
Hitler to monopolise power.

" We should have opposed him at whatever sacrifice
of safety and possessions," she insisted. " What is life,
compared with integrity ? Now we have to find a way of
atonement. So long as we live, my generation must strive
to atone for the suffering inflicted on the innocent peoples
of Europe ! "

The Countess's conversation always reminded Adrian
of his father ; she had the same impulse to accept crucifixion on account of national sins for which she, like
Robert, had been one of the least to blame. Adrian had
grown up with a detached knowledge of his father's conversion ; the fact that Robert had entered the Ministry
out of penitence for killing some Germans in the First
World War had been part of his background of family
history ever since he saw the German helmet on his father's

desk. But now he was no longer a child, and Germany as he knew it after the Second World War gave life and reality to the decision which a young winner of the Victoria Cross had made so long ago. Sometimes he wondered whether his own concern for the defeated enemy of two generations had been actually inherited from Robert. But whether this was possible or not, he felt that his talks with the Countess helped him to understand his father — and to understand Robert had become one of the subsidiary passions of his life.

It began, he thought, even before his father's death and burial, which had affected him so profoundly. But he consciously realised it just after coming to Cologne, when he was driving back to the Alte Stadt through the wrecked suburb of Mülheim after a visit to Düsseldorf, and saw a weather-beaten cross of grey wood, with a black-lettered name printed upon it, stuck into an anonymous heap of rubble. Before leaving for Germany he had visited, for the first time since Robert's burial, St. Saviour's Church and his father's grave at Battersea. The wooden cross at Cologne suddenly appeared to him as a symbol, not only of that modest grave, but of Robert himself.

Immediately after the funeral, his mother had found a flat in Kensington and moved there. In that flat she had shown him the short letter which had been given to her by Robert's solicitors a week after she had read his Will. It told her that, as she had suspected, he had asked Jonathan Wiltshire to bury him, when his time came, on the spot in the churchyard where he had asked her to marry him. He then made one final request:

I do not wish my grave to be marked by any elaborate memorial. I should like it to resemble as closely as possible the simple wartime graves of the men whom I killed in 1915. I deprived them of their chances of fulfilment. I am therefore less worthy of remembrance than they.

Robert's parishioners at St. Saviour's had found this idea impossible to accept. The bombing of their Church gave them the opportunity to commemorate his ministry in a new East window, superbly carried out by the refugee stained-glass artist, Delius Müller. It represented the Last Supper, and Robert's likeness was shown, with exquisite discretion, in the face of the Disciple whom Jesus loved. On a scroll which surrounded the design were inscribed the last four lines of Blake's *Jerusalem*.

But Sylvia had carried out Robert's wishes in both letter and spirit. By the time that Adrian visited his father's grave a grey stone cross stood there, so simple and slender that from a distance it seemed identical with the temporary wooden crosses which had marked the graves of the men on both sides who fell in battle during the First World War. Fastened to the centre, a black-lettered plaque carried an unadorned inscription :

ROBERT CARBURY, V.C.

Born September 9th, 1891
Died May 8th, 1945

All Souls, Battersea, 1919–27
St. Saviour's, Armada Square, 1927–45

At the foot of the cross, after an earnest request by a deputation from the B.O.J., Sylvia had authorised the addition, in very small letters, of the words :

And I saw the Holy City, the New Jerusalem.

From the time that he noticed the pathetic home-made memorial in Mülheim, his father had seldom been far from Adrian's thoughts. He had always realised that the larger share of his inherited qualities came from his mother ; Sylvia had given him not only her appearance but her detachment, her self-sufficiency, and the peculiar emotional dichotomy which enabled her to exist on one plane while living in another. Yet he was not, as he had formerly supposed, completely devoid of his father's characteristics. He recognised as Robert's the overwhelming sense of responsibility which induced him to assume unpleasant duties when every instinct was against them. Robert's too was the deep conscientiousness which impelled him to do a job as carefully as he could, even when he most wanted to scamp it.

As he came to realise how many and vast were the problems which the defeated enemy and their conquerors must solve or perish, he wished that he could call his father back and consult him about the task of rebuilding Germany. Life moved so swiftly that the world of 1947 already contained some overwhelming facts which were unknown to Robert on VE-Day. There was the atomic bomb, for instance, and the Labour Government, and the suicidal behaviour of the Allies after Potsdam. But Adrian felt convinced that his father's message would not have altered. Robert would have said that God had power, through men, to use the harnessing of atomic energy for the good of His children, and to change the hearts of the political leaders in Russia — and in America and Britain — even though they denied His existence.

I wonder, meditated Adrian, walking back to his Mess from the Countess's room through the prolonged daylight of a June evening, why I never hit it off with him till almost the last. Was it because, in spite of our different appearances, we were more alike than I ever allowed for ?

It seemed as though both he and Robert had been cheated of something. They had never experienced the deep and close relationship which had been there waiting for them to enter into.

I wish I'd really *talked* to Dad, even once, he thought.

All those men raising their caps on the Thames barges — they wouldn't have done that if he hadn't been worth knowing — and worth loving. I always fought shy of talking to him, because I was so afraid he'd get emotional, as he sometimes did in his sermons. . . . Would it have mattered if he had? Aren't people of my generation perhaps rather too scared of emotion?

At the corner where he turned from the river into Marienburg he paused, looking with an absorbed expression at the Rhine, and unconsciously voicing his reflections.

"It would have been easier to talk to Mummy if she hadn't always been too busy with plays and things. One doesn't have to be afraid of emotion with her — except, of course, at Dad's funeral. I suppose that was only natural, but it certainly surprised me. I never thought she cared all that much for him, but perhaps I was wrong. We don't really know our parents any better than they know us. . . . If Mummy wasn't my mother, I believe I should like to talk to her. I'd like to see if I couldn't get behind the queer sort of barrier, so gentle and yet so impervious, that she puts up between herself and the world. . . . Perhaps I *will* try. I'm not a kid any longer. If she really knew me, I don't believe I should bore her. She must be awfully lonely now Jo's gone to South Africa."

He had spent his last long leave with Tony in Naples, and had not been at the flat in Kensington since he left England for Germany. After he was demobilised, he and Sylvia would be alone there together. It was difficult to think of Josephine, his tomboy sister, as a pretty eighteen-year-old actress playing her first parts in the Connoisseurs' Repertory Company which was now touring the Dominions.

I'll try talking to Mummy when I'm demobilised, he resolved, opening the gate into the garden of his Mess.

I'll get her to tell me about her early life, and so on. And I'll ask her what *she* really thought of Dad.

*

But on the road to Hamburg, Adrian did not think about Sylvia and Josephine — or even, for once, of his father. His mind was dominated by the information which he had obtained the previous night at the Linden Club from the representative of the New York *Public Ledger*.

He did not often go to the Club; its four-course meals and crowded bar so close to the homes of his half-starved acquaintances gave him a feeling of conscience-stricken discomfort. But the evening was the hottest yet in a week of brilliant exhausting sunshine, and the flower-boxes foaming with petunias and convolvulus on either side of the white stone steps looked inviting and cool. He crossed the courtyard massed with parked cars, entered the grey stone building with its green-shuttered windows, and went into the long shady lounge.

At a table in a corner one of his fellow subalterns, Vincent Newman, was sitting with a stranger who wore a short-sleeved khaki shirt. As soon as he saw Adrian, Newman beckoned to him to join them.

" This is Wade McKinley of the New York *Public Ledger*," he explained. " He's doing some articles for his newspaper on the British Zone." Turning to the American, he added with a touch of malice : " You'll like to meet Adrian Carbury. He can tell you more about the Germans than anyone in our Unit."

Wade McKinley put down his seventh glass of iced whisky, and regarded Adrian as though he were some peculiar zoological specimen.

" Say, you're one of these fraternisers, are you? Maybe you can tell me some stories about the native population? But not tonight. I've just had a helluva drive, and I'm taking an evening off. Got mixed up with a lorry outside Bielefeld."

Adrian looked up and discovered that Newman had unobtrusively vanished, leaving him alone with the American journalist. In a few moments he understood why. Whether it was due to the accident, or the whiskies, or merely to natural exuberance, Wade McKinley was the most talkative newspaper man he had ever met. He told Adrian, in elaborate and unflattering detail, what he thought of the British Army of Occupation and the Control Commission. He described his experiences in Schleswig, Kiel, Lübeck, Hamburg, Hanover, and Bad Pyrmont. Only when his glass was empty did he break off.

" You're not drinking anything," he said to Adrian. " You'd better let me buy you a whisky."

" Thanks," said Adrian, " but I don't care for it when the weather's so hot. A pint of bitters is more in my line. Can I bring you one too ? " he asked, standing up.

" Nothing doing, old boy. Your British beer's a soft drink to me. I don't mind if I have another highball."

Adrian crossed the dining-room to the bar, which was encircled by the usual assemblage of officers and civil servants. He came back with the two glasses.

" Here's your drink," he said, and added for the sake of conversation : " It's odd — you're the first American journalist I've seen in this Club. I didn't know your papers took much interest in the British Zone."

" Most of them didn't till lately. But now they've got to. You know — bipartite arrangements and the Marshall Plan. The great American nation must be told what it's letting itself in for. Well, here's how ! " He took a long drink of the whisky, and went on. " We've quite a lot of newspaper men going round your Zone at the moment. One of them's a girl, and a young one too. If you boys want something easy on the eyes, you should fetch her down to this old burg."

" What's her name? " asked Adrian indifferently, hoping that Wade McKinley would soon begin to feel tired and go away.

" She's a kid called Carol Jane Brinton. Only about twenty-one or -two, and already doing an assignment for the Brooklyn *Times-Herald*. It's one of the Briggs-Pillby chain of newspapers. Always ready to give a chance to the young and lovely, and make a few useful contacts on the side. . . ."

But Adrian was not interested in the calculating virtues of the Briggs-Pillby syndicate. The big lounge seemed to be spinning round ; he felt as if he, and not Wade McKinley, had drunk seven highballs.

" Carol Brinton ! You mean she's over here ! Here in Germany ? "

Adrian's sudden agitation impressed itself even on the journalist's befuddled consciousness.

" Sure she's here, and some girl," he said, looking at Adrian with a new curiosity. " Why, do you know her ? "

" I did once. . . . Where did you see her? "

Wade McKinley meditated, looking at the melting ice in his glass.

" Well, now, let me think . . . The first time was a year ago, in Holland. She was still at Bryn Mawr then — going back for a final year to get a Ph.D. The Brooklyn paper was trying her out on a vacation assignment. I met her at the Red Cross Headquarters in Nijmegen ; she was doing a story about Arnhem. You know — ruin, recovery, the heroic Dutch . . ."

Adrian broke impatiently into the spate of reminiscences.

" I don't want to know where she was a year ago.

Where is she now? Where? Doing what?"

Wade McKinley emptied his glass and refilled it from a flask he carried.

"Now where was it I saw her?" he asked himself with a solemn effort at concentration. "Where the hell could it have been? Lübeck? No — wait a mo. I've got it. It was last Sunday, at the Officers' Club in Travemünde. You know — that place where they give you Danish cheese, and you sit on the terrace and look bang across the Baltic into the Russian Zone——"

Adrian broke in once more to put the question he could no longer restrain.

"Is she married?"

"Not she. I guess she's a careerist. She won't even let a guy book her for a week-end. You know — all scruples and scholarship. It's just too bad when a good-looker like that goes in for cultivating the pleasures of chastity."

"Did she say where she was going from there?" Adrian interrupted.

"Let's see . . . I don't recall . . . Yes, I do, though. She was going to spend a week in Hamburg, writing up the bombed suburbs. You know — rubble, miles of it. Thousands of bodies still buried under the ruins of their homes. Granny's grave, planted in the debris, tended and watered by heart-broken family. I heard a saying up there that I put down somewhere: 'The Russians have the food, the Americans have the scenery, the French have the wine, and the British have the rubble'. It's certainly true of your lousy old Zone."

"Are you sure she was going to Hamburg?"

"Sure enough, old boy. It's the right place for stories about the British."

"Where was she staying?"

"How should I know? I'm not her keeper, worse

349

luck! Say, now I come to think of it, why do you
want——"

But Adrian was on his feet again.

" I'm awfully sorry, but I have to go. I've a long
journey to make tomorrow, and it means an early start.
Can I show you where you're staying or anything ? "

" Thanks a lot, but there's no need. I've got a room
in this lousy old Club. Not bad — looks over the garden.
I guess I can climb the stairs by myself if I use the hand-
rail."

Adrian suddenly remembered that sleeping accommo-
dation at the Club was difficult to obtain. Making his tone
as casual as he could, he inquired : " Are you staying here
long ? "

" Only over Sunday," said Wade, yawning. " Have
to keep on the move. On Monday I've got to start doing
the Ruhr. I reckon that's going to be a helluva job. . . ."

On his way out of the Club, Adrian asked the German
manager to reserve Wade McKinley's room for him after
the loquacious representative of the New York *Public
Ledger* had departed.

" I may want it," he explained, " for another American
journalist. . . ."

II

Only when he was well-advanced on the eight-hour drive
to Hamburg did Adrian begin to feel misgivings about
the craziness of his mission. He'd spoiled Tony's Bank
Holiday week-end, and it was too bad that he couldn't
give him a convincing explanation. As he raced along
the Autobahn which divided the country between Cologne
and Hanover like a colossal scythe, the shimmering midday heat turned his small Volkswagen into an oven.
To try to find Carol in Hamburg would not exactly be
looking for a needle in a haystack, since the number of

places where members of the Occupation Forces could stay was limited. But the chances that she had left, or that it was not Hamburg where she had gone at all, began to seem overwhelming. Wade McKinley's fuddled recollections were not exactly a basis for confidence. Adrian had stopped only once for a drink and a sandwich, and as he drove through Lüneburg into the outskirts of Hamburg, the colossal excitement which had sped him on his way began to ooze out into fatigue.

Reaching the centre of the town, he parked his car and walked into the Atlantic Hotel on the Binnen-Alster, the small lake surrounded by buildings which had suffered little damage and still maintained the appearance of a city. It was the best Club in Hamburg, and the place where the few Americans who came there usually stayed ; but when he inquired for Carol at the reception desk, he learned that they had no knowledge of her.

Dejectedly sitting over a late cup of tea in the open-air courtyard, he wondered what to do next. As he struggled with his disappointment, he began mentally to reconstruct the month that he had spent with the Brintons in the Catskills, and remembered as clearly as if it had been last week his conversation with Carol about her plans for the future. Americans, she had said, were too comfortable ; they ran away from unpleasant things. . . . Perhaps, after all, the fact that she had not come to the Atlantic didn't mean that she was not in Hamburg. Now he came to think of it she'd be more likely to go to a transit hotel, or some such workaday place which gave her facilities for her job without emphasising in every detail the contrast between Allied comfort and German misery.

He determined to go systematically through all the hotels and hostels used by Allied personnel, from the Reichshof opposite the Central Station to the Y.W.C.A. If he failed to find her he could doubtless track her down through the American authorities in Frankfort; but this might take time, and in a fortnight he would be on his way back to England. In any case he was on duty again on Tuesday; the Bank Holiday week-end gave him only two more days.

Impelled by a sense of urgency, he started forth. It seemed hardly probable that he would find Carol in a stuffy hotel lounge or bedroom on that sweltering afternoon, or that she would be alone. He was suddenly possessed with a jealous rage against the unknown American journalist or British officer who had doubtless taken her out again to Travemünde, or else to the over-luxurious Country Club in the suburb of Blankenese. But if she had come to Hamburg at all, he could at least find out where she had registered. The Reichshof just up the street was the nearest of the many possible places to be investigated, and he determined to begin his inquiries there.

He hurried in the direction of the Central Station, passing a large heap of debris where the remains of a doorway were marked with a black cross. Local rumour said that these crosses indicated a building beneath which the dead still lay unburied, though an official who had talked to Adrian on his first visit insisted that, in the four years since the heavy raids, the miles upon miles of fantastic rubble had been systematically searched for corpses. It didn't seem likely to Adrian, and as he walked up the burning pavement a hot effluvia which suggested stale putrefaction seemed to indicate that the gruesome industry of which he had been assured came nearer to wishful thinking than fact.

He crossed the broad main thoroughfare and went into the Reichshof. It was a dark, crowded, business-like hotel, which before the War had probably been frequented by the most impressive type of commercial traveller, and had escaped destruction when its more ornate cosmopolitan neighbours went down under the bombs. In spite of his certainty that he was due for another disappointment, his breath came in jerks as he approached the blonde German girl clerk at the reception desk.

" Have you a young American lady called Miss Carol Brinton staying here ? "

The girl consulted the list of guests.

" Yes, Sir," she said politely. " Do you wish to speak with her ? "

Again, as at the Linden Club, the crowded hall seemed to sway. Adrian hoped that he still looked and sounded normal as he found his voice.

" Is she in the hotel ? "

Uncertain, the girl glanced at the male clerk writing in a ledger beside her.

" Yes, Sir. She came in about half-an-hour ago."

" Will it be all right if I go up to her room ? "

" I think so, Sir. Are you a friend of the lady ? "

" Yes — an old friend. What's her number ? "

" It is Number 47, on the first floor. You can take the lift."

But to wait till the lift came down was more than Adrian could endure. His heart was pounding now, and at the top of the short staircase he had to wait to get his breath. Then, compelling himself to deliberation, he walked past the room numbers from the twenties to the forties, and knocked on a door at the end of the passage.

" Come in ! " said the voice that he had heard so often in his memory and his dreams. He opened the door and stood in the entrance, looking into the room.

Carol was sitting at the table in front of her typewriter. It was a dark room, its only window opening upon the stone floor of the well which forms the centre of continental hotels, and she had switched on the electric lamp which seemed actually to possess a tolerable bulb. Its light threw into sharp relief the black hair and delicate features that he had so long remembered.

" Carol ! " he said.

She stood up ; for a moment her eyes looked puzzled and uncertain. Then she cried, with an unmistakable note of gladness in her voice which turned him first hot and then cold again, " Why — it's Adrian Carbury ! "

She appeared no older than the girl who had entertained him at Neontora, but she had grown even more elegant. She was wearing a flowered silk dress in soft shades of blue and green which looked cool and attractive in that airless bedroom, but he wondered for a moment why she seemed smaller than the Carol of his recollection. Then he remembered that he had grown at least three inches since his visit to the Catskills, whereas her height had remained unchanged. He was now over six feet tall, as his father had been, but broader than Robert. In the electric light his copper hair shone like a flame. She regarded him keenly as she spoke again.

" But, Adrian — I never realised you were in Germany ! Are you stationed in Hamburg ? How did you know I was here ? "

" I'm not usually in Hamburg," he replied. " My job is to supervise railway repairs at Cologne. But last night a fellow called Wade McKinley came into the Officers' Club there. He said he'd met you at Travemünde."

" That's true. I saw him there last Sunday. But I don't know him very well ; he talks too much. How did he happen to mention me ? "

" You came up quite by chance. He was talking about American journalists going round the British Zone. I asked him where you were, and he said you'd gone to Hamburg. He was pretty tight by then, and I didn't know whether to believe him or not. But we all had the week-end off for the British Bank Holiday, so I thought I'd drive up here and try to find you."

A slight flush gave new warmth to her pale olive skin. " You came all this way — on the chance of finding me ! " She paused a moment. " Then . . . why didn't you answer the three letters I wrote you ? "

He did not reply but looked at her in silence, incredulously trying to take in the remembered features and dark inexplicable eyes, so brilliant in their clear vitality yet so melancholy in their brooding depths.

She went on. " I sent you a letter and a Christmas card two Christmasses running."

" I know," he said. He remembered how passionately he had destroyed those friendly letters ; and felt, as he now felt so often, amazed at what had indubitably been his behaviour.

" And then I wrote after your father died . . . I did think you'd answer that."

" I ought to have, of course. I behaved unforgivably. Some day I'll try to explain . . ." He plunged on with a desperate eagerness. " But, Carol — why did you go on writing when I didn't answer ? "

She contemplated him thoughtfully. " That's what I don't quite understand myself. . . . I felt so sorry for you that last morning, after you'd been up all night in the forest. Do you remember ? "

" Do I ! It isn't exactly the kind of experience one forgets."

" Daddy and I were more anxious about you than we let on," she continued. " You see, one or two people have disappeared into that forest and never been found. . . . He was all set to give you a real thrashing when you turned up — a thing he'd never done in his life ! And then, somehow, when you did come back we couldn't even be angry. You looked so all-in, as if something had finished you. I just couldn't get over it afterwards."

" I behaved disgracefully. But did you ever guess why I ran away that night?"

" No, not exactly. You said you didn't want to go back to England, but Daddy and I never felt you really meant it. It wasn't somehow like you."

" It was true I didn't want to go back. But it wasn't because I was afraid of the bombs, as your father seemed to think. Later on I volunteered for bomb-disposal, just to prove it wasn't."

" Oh, Adrian," she exclaimed, " was that really why? Kathleen Downing told us you were doing it, and I often wondered if you'd get through. . . ." She paused again before she continued. " When you were with us you looked so young — just a schoolboy, and rather pathetic. But after you went in for that dangerous job, you seemed to grow up in my thoughts."

" You were always grown up in mine. . . . But now you don't look a day older than you did at Neontora."

" Don't I really? I was twenty-two in May."

" I know . . . And I shall be twenty-two in November. We were born in the same year — 1925."

" But you look at least twenty-four. . . . I wonder if that's what always happens to boys and girls?"

They regarded each other in silence. There was so much to say that it seemed impossible to utter another word. At last Adrian spoke.

" Look here — are you doing anything special tonight? Won't you come and have dinner with me at the Atlantic?"

" There's nothing I'd like better," she answered truthfully. " But " — she glanced at the sheets of typescript on the desk — " I've this story to finish about the Wandsbek and Barmbek suburbs. One of your Public Relations

Officers drove me round them this morning. Oh, Adrian, they're terrible! . . . And then to think there are people at home who oppose the Marshall Plan! I've got to make them *see* those acres and acres of rubble which were once houses . . . and lives . . ."

" I've seen them too," he said. " But in the Hamburg suburbs at least the ruins are flat. The ones in Cologne make me feel worse. They're like fingers pointing at you all over the city. I always imagine they're calling down vengeance on the people who destroyed it — which means us."

" I must see Cologne," she said thoughtfully, " but it really is important I write about Hamburg."

" Of course it is. But couldn't you write about it tomorrow? It's only Saturday night, and with the Bank Holiday there won't be any postal arrangements worth mentioning till Tuesday."

She smiled. " That's true! I'd forgotten how seriously the British take their holidays! All right. For once I'll do what I want to do. Wait in the lounge till I get clean, and then I'll come with you."

At dinner she told him about her years at Bryn Mawr, and the assignment at Arnhem where the burned-out tanks had been cleared from the broken bridge, and the nightmare semblances of houses and churches were being restored so systematically that the town which had seen so many battles was getting back its former silhouette. He listened eagerly while she described Clarence Brinton's latest experimental researches into the celestial journeys of the comets, but he did not mention his own family. Instead he told her about his bomb-disposal work during the War, and the concern that he now felt for the future of Germany.

The time had nearly come to take her back to the Reichshof when he said abruptly : " I didn't tell you why

357

I ran away that night. . . . It was because I was jealous of your friend Warren Converse."

Carol laughed, and her laughter sounded in his ears like a hallelujah chorus.

" You mean you were actually jealous of poor old Warren ! Heavens, how flattered he'd have been ! Why, I always looked on him as Daddy's contemporary. He was about as thrilling as a maiden aunt."

" That's just how he struck me. But I thought you'd marry him and I'd never see you again. That's really why I didn't answer your letters. . . ."

The orchestra had stopped playing, and the room was almost empty of diners. Carol stood up, and spoke with a catch in her breath as though she had been running.

" It's been grand seeing you, but now I ought to get back. I've a heap to do, and you must be awfully tired after such a long day."

" I never felt less tired in my life ! But I'll let you go if you'll promise to come out with me again tomorrow."

A sudden unexpected emotion flickered over her face. If it had been less fleeting he might, astonishingly, have described it as panic.

" I don't see how I can, Adrian. I've got that story to write about the Wandsbek suburb. And I really ought to look around Hamburg a bit more. There's so much to see in the city itself, I never even got outside of it till today."

What was it that fellow McKinley had said ? " I guess she's a careerist." He suddenly thought of his mother, and the quiet determination with which she had always eliminated every personal and domestic handicap to her work on the stage. Perhaps, after all, he had a more formidable obstacle than Warren Converse to fight ; to fight with the understanding that was his because he was Sylvia's son.

As they left the Atlantic and walked slowly up the bombed street towards the Reichshof, he took Carol's arm with an urgency that communicated itself to her like an electric current.

" Look here, Carol. . . . Couldn't you do that article about Wandsbek in the morning and come out with me in the afternoon? We needn't go right away from Hamburg. I could take you to a late lunch at the Country Club in Blankenese, and then we could drive along the Elbe. There's lots to see there."

She remained silent. In the darkness he could not interpret the expression on her face. He continued still more urgently as they crossed the road to the Reichshof.

" This is my last free week-end in Germany. On Tuesday I'm on duty again in Cologne, so on Monday night at latest I'll have to drive back. And ten days after that I'm going home. I didn't tell you before, but I'm going to be demobilised. I just must see what I can of you, after all these years. . . ."

Her desire for his society overcame her, and her self-protective vigilance relaxed.

" That's different, Adrian. I hadn't realised you were going away so soon. If I get up early, I could finish the story before lunch."

" Then you'll come with me to the Country Club, and let me drive you along the Elbe? "

" Yes. I'll come. You'll find me here by the reception desk at one o'clock."

*

After lunch they parked the car and sat down on a dry bank overlooking a bend of the river. Across the Elbe a crumpled mass of useless concrete marked the much-bombed but irremovable submarine pens. In the distance, nearer the centre of Hamburg, a grotesque colossal

skeleton, stark against the sky, showed where the Blohm &
Voss shipbuilding yard had stood.

But in the wooded suburb little damage was visible.
The lurid nights when the S.S. guards had gone round
shooting the worst-injured air-raid casualties and throwing
their bodies into the Elbe and the Alster seemed very far
away. Adrian felt, all the same, that he could not have
brought himself to bathe in those waters; but the local
juveniles did not appear to share his antipathy. Fifty
yards away some boys were swimming; they were very
thin, but the deep tan of their naked bodies disguised their
emaciation. The bombing of Hamburg was already part
of history. Its population suffered a different agony now
— the agony of slow death instead of mass annihilation.

For a time they sat in silence, gazing at the sparkle of
the water in the perpetual sunlight. Surely, thought
Adrian, this golden year must be a record, both for
England and for Europe! At last he spoke.

" That was a wonderful letter you wrote me after my
father died. It comforted me in spite of myself, as it
were."

" Poor Adrian! Were you so much in need of comfort?"

" I suppose I was. His death upset me more than I
ever thought possible."

" Is that why you never mention him? I wondered
why it was. You used to talk about him quite often at
Neontora. I've always been interested in him since you
told me how he won the V.C."

A sudden realisation that relief from tension was being
offered him if he wanted it penetrated Adrian's consciousness.

" I haven't discussed his death with a living soul —
not even my mother. Would it bore you if I talk
about it?"

" Of course not. I'd like to hear whatever you want to tell me."

He stared at the Elbe for a long time before he spoke again.

" I'd have given anything if I could have seen him just once on VE-Day, instead of only hearing him. It was the last day of his life, and he had a lot of work — services and things — to do in his Church. There seems to have been something about him that day that no one who saw him ever forgot."

" Why weren't you there? Were you on duty? "

" Yes. I was given leave the day after instead. On VE-Day we had a Victory Parade in the suburb where I was stationed. Balham was its name, and Balham its nature." She looked up inquiringly, and he added : " I can't explain any better. Some day when you're in London I'll show you the place, and you'll see what I mean."

The rattle of a lorry passing along the road brought back the roar of the Underground train which had taken him to Armada Square the following morning.

" Next day," he said, " I went to the Vicarage. Our Squad was always up very early, and I got there long before breakfast-time. When I let myself in, the house felt very quiet. That wasn't surprising since nobody was down, and yet there seemed something strange and oppressive about it. At once I instinctively connected it with my father. I don't know why, because only the night before in our Mess I'd listened-in to him conducting a broadcast service, the first he'd held since before the War. While the War was on they stopped him doing it ; I guess his sermons were too full of peace and good-will to go down with the Government. But that night his voice came over the radio as clear and strong as I'd ever heard it."

" I know," she said quietly. " I heard it too."

Adrian started. " Why, Carol, how queer ! I thought about you when I was listening to him ! I wondered whether by some remote chance you were listening too, though I hardly believed you could be."

" Daddy and I were in New York," she said. " We'd gone there for the Victory celebrations. In the afternoon at our hotel there was a broadcast programme giving a first-hand picture of the scenes in London. We're five hours behind you, remember. The programme ended with your father's service. Somehow or other it moved us both tremendously, and I wondered if you were there in the Church."

They lapsed into silence, each trying to recall the emotions with which they had listened to the broadcast and thought of one another. Then Adrian continued.

" I don't usually dream much, but all that night I dreamt about Dad — and you. When I went into the Vicarage, though, the oppressive feeling that came over me was entirely connected with him. It was so strong, I felt I had to speak to him at once. I knew my mother would be sleeping in the spare room ; she always did when she was late at the theatre. So I knocked at his bedroom door. There was no answer, so I peeped in. When I saw the bed was empty and obviously hadn't been used, I knew I was right in my feeling that something had happened. I started to look for him."

He paused. She was listening attentively, and he went on.

" There were two places where you could be pretty sure of finding Dad. One was the Chancel of his Church ; he always used to go and pray there when he was upset about something. The other was his study on the top floor. I decided to go to the study first, and then look in the Church. As soon as I opened the study door I got

a bit of a shock, because he wasn't at his desk as I'd
expected. He was sitting in an armchair by the window,
with his back to the door. Then it occurred to me that
he'd been watching the searchlight display we'd had the
night before, and fallen asleep. He was always pale, and
when I went up to him and saw him looking so calm and
peaceful I thought for the moment he was just sleeping.
Then I was struck by something queer about his face. It
looked . . . sort of sculptured. I touched his forehead
and found it was cold."

This time the pause was still longer, and again Carol
did not speak.

" The doctors said it was heart-failure caused by
shock," Adrian went on. " They told us he must have
died about midnight — either just before or just after.
Anyway, we put VE-Day down as the day of his death in
the records. It was kind of symbolical, because the War
really killed him."

" That's what I thought. Our papers said it was due
to a raid."

" It was — but the raid happened some weeks before.
In February the Church and Vicarage were badly damaged
by a V-2 rocket. It wrecked the whole of Armada Square,
and Dad was injured. Not exactly seriously, but the roof
of his study fell in on him and buried him, and his head was
pretty well knocked about. According to the doctors his
heart had probably been strained by years of overwork,
and the bomb finished it off. He might have been all
right if he'd taken it easy straight away ; but he wouldn't
rest because the incident made so much work in the parish.
It must have meant more courage than winning the V.C.,
keeping up the way he did."

He waited while another lorry thundered down the
road, and then resumed.

" I went all through the inquest and funeral in a kind

of dream. There were big crowds, and a long procession. I felt stunned, and I went on feeling it for about a year. My mother left the Vicarage immediately after the funeral and took a flat in Kensington. They were still quite easy to get in those days; the people who ran away from the bombs hadn't come back. Whenever I was on leave I used to stay with her, and somehow I couldn't bring myself to go to St. Saviour's till just before I came here, over a year ago. Then, when I went, I wondered why I hadn't been before; it seemed to bring Dad back so clearly I could hardly believe he was dead. His chief curate is the Vicar there now — a man called Theodore Martel-hammer."

" What an odd name! " commented Carol.

" Is it? I suppose it is. It never struck me as odd because I grew up with it. He came to St. Saviour's from Australia, years and years ago. Somehow he was so much part of the place it seemed impossible Dad wasn't there too. And ever since then I can't quit thinking about him."

" It must have been a terrible shock for you, finding him like that," said Carol sympathetically. She could not imagine what she would feel if she suddenly came in and found Clarence Brinton dead.

" It was," said Adrian, " but there was more to it than that. You see, when I came back from America I treated him worse than anyone. I can't think why I behaved the way I did." His glance rested on her for a moment. " Or perhaps — I can." He went on. " I suppose Dad was a sort of embodiment of my conscience, and I didn't want to give in to it. In his particular way he was a saint, and I resented that too. One doesn't fight saints, and I wanted to fight him."

Her own intimate relationship with her father gave Carol an intuitive understanding of this unusual pre-occupation with a parent.

" Since he was the kind of man he obviously was, from his broadcast service," she said gently, " I'm sure he understood . . . Not at first, perhaps, when you hurt his feelings in a way he hadn't expected. But afterwards, when he'd thought it all out, I'm certain he did."

" I daresay you're right. He was never impatient with me. I don't remember him losing his temper, even once. But that doesn't alter the fact that somehow or other I've got to make up for the way I treated him." He continued thoughtfully : " I've made a German friend in Cologne ; she's a Countess, and about my mother's age." In his ears echoed Frieda von Redelstädt's words : " We have to find a way of atonement." He went on : " She's always saying her generation must try to atone to the peoples of Europe for letting Hitler do what he did. Well, I feel just the same way — about atonement, I mean. But the person I have to atone to is Dad. I can't do it directly because he's dead, so I have to find a way of doing it in my work, or my life."

" I expect that often happens," said Carol. " It so seldom seems possible to make up for the things we do to people. We have to be kind to somebody else instead, and hope it all adds up in the end."

They lay on the bank and stared at the river, pre-occupied with their thoughts. Then Adrian sat up and looked at his watch.

" Heavens, it's half-past six ! The sun's still so hot I didn't realise. You must be getting hungry again. What about going back to the Country Club and having dinner there ? "

" I couldn't eat another large meal," she said. " I don't know whether it's the heat or my conscience, but I haven't felt like eating since I came to this country."

" It gets me down that way too. . . . But we could have a drink and a sandwich at the Club and stay in the garden till it turns cooler. And tomorrow . . ."

He looked at her sitting passively on the grass, a half-smile on her face.

" Carol," he said, with a new determination in his voice, " I'm sure you've found enough stories about Hamburg. It's time you wrote up the Rhineland and the Ruhr. So tomorrow — I'm going to drive you to Cologne ! "

*

The Volkswagen with its straight-backed utilitarian seats sped austerely but rapidly south through the Lüneburger Heide in the Land-Kreis of Soltau. Sitting in the front beside Adrian, Carol looked out at the pines dotted over the wild heath and the roadside banks yellow with ragwort. The boughs of the mountain ash, she observed, were already heavy with scarlet berries. Across the blue-grey surface of the sunny road, the shadows of the trees lay like dark delicate lace. On the heath grew magenta clumps of the same rosebay that half-concealed the ruins of Hamburg.

" The country's not very interesting here," said Adrian as they drove through Soltau, a small undamaged town of red-brick houses with brilliant gabled roofs of vermilion tiles. " There's more to see beyond Hanover, when we get on to the Autobahn again."

Throughout that morning they drove mostly in silence ; they had said so much to each other during the past thirty-six hours that a period of contemplation had become essential. Adrian suddenly remembered that the day was the 4th of August ; that Bank Holiday marked the thirty-third anniversary of the War in which his father had won the Victoria Cross. Yet somehow, after his talk with Carol on Sunday afternoon, his preoccupation with Robert seemed to have vanished like a burden sliding off his mind. Henceforth, he felt, he and his father could be friends.

366

Although Robert was dead, this fact seemed to make no difference to that spiritual relationship. Perhaps, after all, there was no death. . . .

Along the road they passed a broken ribbon of traffic — small military cars, big Army lorries carrying machinery or stores, messengers on motor bicycles wearing steel helmets, and sometimes German farm carts with the driver sitting on a high seat behind two horses. They drove through Bergen and Celle, a pleasant country town with wide tree-shaded roads and a Rathaus distempered pink, like strawberry ice-cream. The flat country and width of sky made Adrian think of Essex. Continually they passed between fields of reaped and stacked corn, the first-fruits of the scanty harvest which would mean so much to Germany's population.

At least, reflected Carol, though these people lost their cities, they have kept their clean and orderly countryside. The villages are not depopulated, as they were after the Thirty Years War. They haven't lost everything; they've maintained a continuity with their own past. That, at least, is something to build on.

When they reached Hanover they stopped for an hour, and lunched at the Transit Hotel close to the half-destroyed station.

" This place isn't flattened, like the suburbs of Hamburg," Adrian told her. " In the centre the damage is more of the kind we had in London, on a larger scale — huge incidents which sometimes demolished several streets at a time. But it still looks like a city, and you can see what kind of city it was."

" I'll have to come back here," said Carol. " You can't see much from this hotel."

Adrian smiled gaily.

" Come back by all means — after I've gone! Till then you're going to stay in Cologne."

"Am I really? Just exactly where?"

"I've reserved a room for you at the Linden Club. It's the one Wade McKinley had. I found out he was giving it up this morning."

"So you even booked a room for me on the chance! How did you guess I'd come if you found me?"

He smiled again.

"It was a good bet, wasn't it, Carol! You may find the Club a bit too luxurious, but it's the only place in Cologne you could stay except for the Belgian Transit Hotel."

"Belgian?"

"Yes. Our gallant Allies are part of the Army of Occupation in Cologne and Aachen, and one or two other Rhineland towns."

"I see. But what made you think I wouldn't care to stay somewhere luxurious?"

"Partly because I don't care for it myself — not in this country. But I guessed it because you didn't put up at the Atlantic in Hamburg."

"I meant to," she said. "It was the place Wade recommended. But when I saw it, I knew I couldn't bear to live there. All that eating and drinking, in a city with half-starved people around you — it just didn't work out."

Beyond Hanover Adrian turned the car into the great Autobahn, and they started on the three hundred kilometres to Cologne. It reminded Carol of an American state highway, but over there Adrian would not have been obliged constantly to slow down in order to cross the Bailey bridges which replaced the originals destroyed by the Germans in retreat. At first the fields were flat as in the agricultural area between Hamburg and Hanover, but after the car had travelled fifty kilometres it emerged into wide, rolling country, occasionally darkened by thickets and sprinkled with tiny red-roofed houses, like toys tossed on to the earth from a celestial playground. A patchwork-quilt of fields in every variety of green and gold covered the slopes of the nearer hills.

The Autobahn by-passed all the large towns; at intervals roadside signs directed travellers by subsidiary routes to Bad Oeynhausen, Bielefeld, and Hamm. When the afternoon shadows were beginning to lengthen the Volkswagen reached the Ruhr, running between slag-heaps and tall narrow chimneys like slate pencils dissolving into smoke. The outskirts of Dortmund crept close to the highway; damaged houses appeared beside the road overshadowed by the drunken spires of derelict churches. Yet the car still passed between sheaves of corn; small fields of wheat and cabbage stretched to the edges of mines and factories.

"The English Black Country is rather like this," Adrian told Carol. "In Staffordshire, where my father was born, you get potatoes and cabbage-patches all mixed up with potteries and coal-heaps."

Within the Ruhr the broken bridges and bomb-craters along the Autobahn became more frequent; big signs marked "Umleitung" involved long diversions. One beyond Gelsenkirchen took them four kilometres out of their way through the shattered streets of Duisburg; the bridge which had spanned the Dortmund Canal trailed in the water like the skeleton of a huge mammal with a broken back. Thick woods of beech, birch, and pine began to appear between the chimneys, which now flanked the sky-line on both sides of the road. Their smoke, acrid and yellow, drifted over cornfields and thickets, dimming the August sunshine like winter fog. Towards Elberfeld the road rejoined the Autobahn; close to a pile of rusting girders and formless lumps of broken steel, a sign showed that they were by-passing Düsseldorf. A few minutes later the dark silhouette of Cologne Cathedral appeared in the distance against the sultry sky.

The Autobahn had now grown very broad. On either side, patches of tussocky grass concealed the traces of two-year-old battles. Away to the east, flat fields stretched sullenly to the edge of low hills. The suburbs of Cologne, skeleton buildings rising from sordid weeds, encroached like the ruins of a lost world upon the car. Driving at sunset through the Mülheim suburb, Adrian crossed the Rhine from Deutz by the only available bridge, and pushed his way through traffic and debris to the Dom-Platz in the Alte Stadt.

At Carol's request he stopped the car, and they walked through dust and littered stones to the Cathedral standing like a battered giant above the desolate Square. The main entrance was blocked by a towering mound of rubble, but a side door stood open where builders were at work beneath the worst-damaged part of the roof near the railway station, and Adrian drew Carol inside.

She looked up through a maze of steel scaffolding to the wide gap which showed the open sky. From a pinnacle far above her head a falcon, startled, flapped his wings, swung into the air through the large bomb hole, hovered, and disappeared. In the growing interior darkness she stumbled over an obstacle which appeared to be a pile of worn-out tarpaulins, but felt hard to the touch. Adrian explained that these heaps of melted lead from the roof lay all over the floor and had not yet been cleared.

"What a story this will make!" she exclaimed. "Everyone at home wants to know what happened to Cologne Cathedral. We were always told the bombing was so smart it didn't suffer, but I don't think anyone really believed it."

Adrian took her arm and guided her back to the entrance through scaffolding, wheelbarrows, and heaps of debris. On a wall which was part of the surviving fragments of a once fashionable hotel in the Dom-Platz, a fair-haired boy and a dark slim girl sat locked in each other's arms, indifferent to casual observers. The idea of love-making amid the rubble no longer seemed quite so incongruous to Adrian. Though he spoke with a resolute cheerful detachment, his voice trembled a little.

" I can give you plenty of material for your story. ' The Cathedral received fourteen direct hits. The scaffolding supporting the damaged roof amounts to thirty tons of steel. One of the twin spires is still sound, and by mounting the four hundred and ninety-eight steps, the visitor can look down on a fine panorama of broken bridges and dusty ruins. . . .' "

He started the car.

" There's lots more, but I won't tell it you now. It's getting late, and you must want a rest. But as soon as I can organise an afternoon off, I'll take you over the place. I've never known a queerer feeling than you get when you climb the spire and look down on the wreckage from above."

He manœuvred the Volkswagen back to the river, and drove south along the Embankment. In the gathering twilight the disembowelled dwellings and spectral fragments of chimneys seemed part of a forgotten civilisation peopled by ghosts. As they turned into Marienburg from the Oberländer Ufer, Carol looked back and saw the red afterglow of the sunset, like spilled blood, still reflected in the waters of the Rhine.

*

The terrace of the Linden Club looked over a wide, closely-trimmed lawn, surrounded on three sides by yews and miniature firs. Round the lawn ran a footpath beneath a formal row of small clipped limes, backed at one end by a high clump of weeping willows which separated the Club from the outer darkness of destroyed Cologne.

371

But usually Adrian could not forget that, according to local gossip, the dispossessed owner had committed suicide.

Tonight his private preoccupations had displaced that uncomfortable memory. Sitting over their coffee on the lighted terrace, he and Carol watched a couple of water-wagtails mincing in and out of the shadows. They bowed, tilted their tails, and set to partners as though performing an elaborate quadrille.

She finished her coffee and turned to Adrian.

" Shall we walk about the garden a bit? I still feel rather stiff from the drive."

" I was afraid you would. A Volkswagen isn't exactly a Rolls-Royce. They seem to be made for people about five feet tall."

The evening was close and windless. Now and then a mutter of thunder echoed from the distance, and a hint of rain trembled in the air. The moon, only two days past the full, gave a subdued light which filtered through heavy masses of cloud. Under the clipped limes the sheltered pathway was very dark. From the clustered trees rose an intoxicating scent of sun-drenched firs moistened by dew. Carol's voice came quietly out of the shadows.

" You're right about Cologne. It's the worst place I've seen yet. It makes you realise how much there is to do."

" They say it'll take thirty years to rebuild," he said. " In Germany you do see violence carried to its logical conclusion. . . . Sometimes, since I've been here, I've just loathed the age I belong to, with all its hatred and hideousness and unrest. But at others . . ."

" At others," she took him up, " you're glad to have been born into it, as I am. It does give us a real job."

" Yes," he said, " that's just it."

Suddenly he felt breathless. Something whirled round

in his brain and, stopping abruptly, brought him to a decision. Had he but known, it was exactly the same sensation that his father had experienced in a Battersea churchyard twenty-seven years earlier.

" Carol," he said desperately, " with all this chaos to build up, and a real job to do — couldn't we try to do it together ? . . . I mean . . . will you . . ."

There was a long silence.

At last she said, very slowly : " I can't tell you right away, but I think . . . some day I might. You see, although I consciously thought of you as just a kid, I believe I went on writing to you because I was . . . somehow disturbed about you. You were different from anyone else I'd known. You were part of Europe, and you made me realise I was too. I've met lots of American boys in the past five years, and some of them have wanted to marry me. But instinctively I always compared them with you, and they seemed — well, just light-weights."

In the glimmer that came across the garden from the lamps on the terrace, she saw a radiance of hope stealing over his face. She went on with an effort.

" Now you're not a boy any more. You're really older than I am. You've gone in danger of your life, and that always makes people grow up. But there's one difficulty for me about — getting married."

A chill seemed to settle on his blood.

" What is it ? " he asked urgently, finding the suspense unbearable. " You mean — your father ? "

" Oh, no ; not Daddy. He always understands. He'd never stop me marrying the person I wanted."

" Then . . . what ? "

" It's my work. I just couldn't give it up. As long as I can remember, I've wanted to write. I suppose I'm ambitious, but that really isn't all."

She paused for a moment, trying to find words in which

to convey exactly what she meant.

" You know that bit in the Bible, about the people who don't see with their eyes, or hear with their ears, or understand with their hearts ? Well, we've got lots of people like that in the United States, and I want to become their hearts and ears and eyes. There's so terribly much to see and understand. . . . I suppose if I were religious, I'd say I had a kind of mission."

" You are religious," he said. " That's just what you are. It's one reason why I love you. . . . Of course you've got to write. I do know that a woman's work means as much to her as a man's to him. I couldn't possibly be such an egoist as to expect you to give it up and look after me."

She did not speak. In her glance, visible even through the darkness, he saw the hint of a questioning scepticism.

" I know what you feel," he continued. " You're thinking any man would say that to get the girl he wanted. He would, of course — and then he'd probably go back on it. But I won't. You see, I've seen it all happen in the previous generation, and I know what it means."

A profound thankfulness for his mother surged into his heart, an overwhelming gratitude to her for being what she was. Because of that, she would help him to win the joy that she herself had glimpsed and tasted but never really experienced.

" My mother's still on the stage," he said. " She was married twice, but she never stopped acting."

" I know that, of course. I've often wished she'd come to America."

" I believe she's going to, soon. At present she's playing in a Vaughan comedy called *Summer's End*. She's taken star parts ever since she was nineteen, and she'll probably go on taking them for another twenty years. She's only about fifty now, and she still doesn't look forty."

He turned to Carol eagerly. " I wish you could meet her.
She wouldn't be a bit like — a mother-in-law."

" She certainly wouldn't. I'd love to know her."

" When Jo and I were children we adored her," Adrian
went on. " We didn't see much of her, but we thought she
was beautiful — as she was. And then when we were
adolescents, frightfully independent and secretive and
insufferable, we liked her because she never tried to
interfere. She had too many interests of her own to
bother if we didn't tell her things, and of course that made
us want to . . . She's the only person I ever told about
you."

Again Carol looked at him questioningly, and he
continued.

" It was one evening when I'd been back from Acropolis a few months. She happened to come into my
bedroom when I was looking at your photograph."

" So you didn't tear that up too ? "

He laughed. Yes, it had almost become a laughing
matter.

" I meant to — but when it came to it I just couldn't.
So she saw it. I was awfully grateful to her for taking
everything for granted — as if it was a matter of course
that I should be head-over-heels in love when I was barely
seventeen. . . ."

" But your father ? Didn't he mind about her working ? "

" No, never. He encouraged it. She told me once
she did leave the stage for a short time after her first
husband was killed, and it was Dad who made her go
back. That was when he first got to know her, but he
never altered. He was tremendously proud of her looks
and her success. The only time I ever saw him angry
was when people tried to criticise her for not doing more
in the parish." He meditated. " It must have been

375

awfully hard for him, with such an exacting job — and for her too, fitting in with it. But I never knew them to quarrel. I don't think she loved him as much as he loved her, but that was because of her first husband. It wasn't anything to do with her work."

His heart began beating fast again as he turned to her imploringly.

" So, you see, I'm very well trained ! "

" I realise that, Adrian. It helps a lot."

" Anyhow," he went on, urgently persuasive, " it'll be years before I can be anything like settled. I'm miles behind you, remember. Directly I'm demobilised I've got a Scholarship exam before me, and all the years at Cambridge, and then perhaps a period of research before I can really begin my job. I wouldn't bother you all that time. But —" His suppressed longing came out in another rush of words.

" Oh, Carol, if only we could be married first, it would give everything security — a kind of peace ! I know you've had that in your life with your father. But I'm British, and I never have. As long as I can remember, one crisis after another has uprooted me. Often I've thought, If there was only one thing in my life I could really be sure of, I'd ask for nothing more. I'd be content."

" I do understand. I'd like to give you that security. I think I could, just because I've had it. But I've got to take a little more time to think. Only twenty-four hours. After all, we've only known each other this time for two days——"

" Yes. But I've thought about you for five years."

" Well, I didn't exactly forget you either. . . . I'll tell you for certain tomorrow evening."

" All right, Carol. I've waited so long, I guess I can wait that much longer. I know you're tired. If you like,

I'll take you up to your room."

He escorted her across the clipped lawn and through the lounge, and then up a shallow isolated staircase to a bedroom secluded from the rest of the Club. It was a long low room with five small casement windows looking over the garden, and on that sultry night it felt very hot; but she assured him that she was tired enough to sleep equally well at the Equator or the North Pole. A subdued buzz of voices drifted up from the terrace; on the lounge piano the German pianist who performed at the Club was playing a Liszt Rhapsody. In the little passage outside her open door they were quite alone.

" Good-night, Carol," he said. Taking her hand, he kissed it with a gentle restraint that seemed to require the most stupendous effort he had ever made.

Suddenly, putting her hands on his shoulders, she stood on tiptoe and kissed his lips. Unable to restrain himself any longer, he folded her in his arms and held her tight. His body quivered and grew taut as he kissed her mouth, her forehead, her eyes, stroking back her hair with a hand that shook. Those deep sombre eyes, he saw, were brilliant with tears — tears of relief, of surrender.

" Good-night, Adrian," she said gently.

He closed her door and walked unsteadily down the stairs. His knees trembled; the impulse to possess her had been so strong that he felt as though he had just emerged from an illness. Hardly realising where he was going, he went through the lounge again and out into the garden. From the near distance came a roll of thunder. Summer lightning flickered like an elusive searchlight between the trees, but he did not see it. A strange freedom from anxiety possessed him; in the tender beauty of Carol's face as she kissed him good-night, he had seen that his long period of frustration was over. But, like her, he needed time to take in the tumultuous emotions which had racked his mind and body during the past forty-eight hours.

Pacing in the darkness beneath the willows on the farther side of the lawn, he went over and over their conversations in Hamburg and on the long drive to Cologne. Carol and he would be luckier than his parents, who had occupied so much of his thoughts during the past twelve months. They would be able to put together Robert's love for Sylvia and Sylvia's passion for her first husband, young Lawrence Mayfield. And there was a real chance that their love would endure.

It didn't seem possible that a time could ever come when Carol would lose, as a wife, the enchantment that she possessed for him today. Yet with his native tendency, intensified by the shocks of his era, to calculate potential future sources of disillusionment, he wondered whether this would happen, or whether he had indeed inherited his father's capacity for perpetual devotion. No doubt the idealistic twenty-one-year-olds of Robert's generation would have called him cynical; but he didn't think that he really was. He was merely schooled, through temperament reinforced by experience, to a philosophic acceptance of the contrast between dream and reality.

" I suppose," he reflected, with mature insight, " I shall expect an awful lot from our children, just as Dad did from me. And then they'll grow up and disappoint me, exactly as I disappointed him. But perhaps not in the end. Not if I live a bit longer than he did. . . ."

Heavy raindrops thudded into the trees, but he did not hear them. Intuitively he perceived that in every lifetime a period comes when the friction between two generations is outgrown; that the clash between the older and the younger is a permanent conflict which with time and tolerance is always capable of reconciliation. And, with this new knowledge, he realised that he had at last found an answer to the question which had troubled him at Chiswick during the air raids, when he first meditated on the problems of life and death.

To go on because the process of time would bring adult understanding; to know that transcendent joy might turn to sorrow. disappointment, disillusion, and yet be ready to accept these things because they were the price of experience — this was life.

THE END

OTHER BOOKS BY VERA BRITTAIN

TESTAMENT OF FRIENDSHIP

In *Testament of Youth,* Vera Brittain passionately recorded the agonising years of the First World War, lamenting the destruction of a generation which included those she most dearly loved – her lover, her brother, her closest friends. In *Testament of Friendship* she tells the story of the woman who helped her survive – the writer Winifred Holtby. They met at Oxford immediately after the war and their friendship continued through Vera's marriage and their separate but parallel writing careers, until Winifred's untimely death at the age of 37.

Winifred Holtby was a remarkable woman. In her short life her generous, loving, talented nature shed a special light on all who knew her, on the many causes and campaigns for which she worked. When she died her fame as a writer was about to reach its peak with the publication of her greatest novel, *South Riding.*

Vera Brittain's life was marked by the tragic loss of those she loved, but in this portrait of her friend a spirit of love and confidence shines through. *Testament of Friendship* records a perfect friendship between two women of courage and determination, a friendship which transformed their own lives and illuminated the world in which they lived.

'An intense account of the love between two women writers . . . vivid glimpses of literary journalism of the period' – *Sunday Times*

Already published

TESTAMENT OF EXPERIENCE

In this her third testament Vera Brittain continues the story of those who survived the devastation of the First World War. Once again Vera Brittain interlaces private experience with the wide sweep of public events. Personal happiness in marriage and the birth of children, pride in her work as writer and campaigner are set against the fears, frustrations and achievements of the years 1925-50, one of the most crucial and stirring periods the world has known. The depression, the growth of Nazism, the peace movements of the 'thirties, the Abdication, the Spanish Civil War, the full horror and heroism of the Second World War come alive again through the eyes of this remarkable woman, who was herself a testament to all that is best in the times she lived through.

'A remarkable record' – *The Times*

'Lucid, intelligent, eye-witness account of events whose repercussions are as loud today, as ever' – *Time Out*

'Her record is honest and moving' – *Evening Standard*

Already published

OTHER BOOKS OF INTEREST

ANDERBY WOLD
Winifred Holtby

Mary Robson is a young Yorkshire woman, married to her solid unromantic cousin, John. Together they battle to preserve Mary's neglected inheritance, her beloved farm, Anderby Wold. This labour of love – and the benevolent tyranny of traditional Yorkshire ways – have made Mary old before her time. Then into her purposeful life erupts David Rossitur, red-haired, charming, eloquent: how can she help but love him? But David is a young man from a different England, radical, committed to social change. As their confrontation and its consequences inevitably unfold, Mary's life and that of the calm village of Anderby are changed forever. In this, her first novel, Winifred Holtby exhilaratingly rehearses the themes which come to fruition in her last and greatest work, *South Riding*.

'It is in the vividly affectionate detail with which she describes the routine of petty squabbles, small-town pride and the rhythm of the farming year that the book finds its life' – *Event*

Already published

THE CROWDED STREET
Winifred Holtby

This is the story of Muriel Hammond, at twenty living within the suffocating confines of Edwardian middle-class society in Marshington, a Yorkshire village. A career is forbidden her. Pretty, but not pretty enough, she fails to achieve the one thing required of her – to find a suitable husband. Then comes the First World War, a watershed which tragically revolutionises the lives of her generation. But for Muriel it offers work, friendship, freedom, and one last chance to find a special kind of happiness...

With the exception of *South Riding*, this is Winifred Holtby's most successful novel; powerfully tracing one woman's search for independence and love, it echoes in fictional form the years autobiographically recorded by her close friend Vera Brittain in *Testament of Youth*.

'Rather as if Jane Austen had thrown her cooling shadow a hundred years on – the same quiet humour and observation of the set stages in the social dance – but then there are bursts of Brontëesque passions stirring in an isolated Yorkshire farmhouse...it is painfully vivid' – ALEX HAMILTON, *Guardian*

Already published

If write to us
at 4 atalogue.

2002

Cl

OCT 1 1 1994